ANGELS OF DEATH

ROBERT PEART, a former Fleet Street journalist, has reported major news stories at home and abroad. Now a full time writer, he lives with his wife and two son in Glamorgan.

Angels of Death is his first novel.

D1434140

ROBERT PEART

Angels of Death

FONTANA PAPERBACKS

First published by Fontana Paperbacks 1982

Copyright © Robert Peart 1982

Made and printed in Great Britain by
William Collins Sons & Co. Ltd, Glasgow

TO TRISH WITH LOVE
FOR
ALED AND GERAINT

PROLOGUE

'Nat. It's time.'

The old miner brushed back the torn sack which was draped over the entrance to the shelter they had built when the rains had begun. Peering inside, the Welshman saw his young countryman still asleep in a sitting position, his back propped against the rusty tin wall with his head slumped onto his chest. Even in sleep, he looked exhausted.

'Nat,' repeated George Williams, leaning forward to shake his comrade by the shoulder. 'Nat, wake up. It's time, boy.'

Morgan slowly opened one eye, then the other, and smiling at the thin grey face above him, stretched forward to rub the life back into his numb legs.

'Has it stopped raining?' Nat Morgan asked warily, fearing the reply would be yes.

'Just now,' said Williams. 'It's time to be going.'

Morgan threw back the moth-eaten greatcoat he'd used as a blanket, gathered up his rifle from the dirt floor and crawled stiffly from the shelter to join Williams.

In the light of the pale Spanish afternoon, he noticed the constant deluge of the last few days had washed away most of the thin red earth from the side of the abandoned valley which wound in coils through the foothills towards the plains of Barcelona. The withered orange trees, whose roots once bound the soil together, had gone the way of the men who'd tended them, and died long ago.

Now the only sign of life in the valley was the small group of men clustered around the two ancient, open-backed trucks parked in the rock-strewn clearing.

They turned and watched the two figures shuffle towards them. Although this ramshackle band could not have known it, this, the third day of November, 1938, was for all but one of them, to be the last day of their lives.

As Morgan and Williams approached, the men split into two groups and climbed into the waiting trucks. The young Welshman got into the second vehicle then turned and held out his hand to Williams. The miner clasped it firmly but Morgan felt the bony grip slacken as the old man's slight frame bent double in a sudden bout of vicious coughing.

'It's all this bloody rain and damp, buttie boy,' explained Williams thumping his chest. 'I'll be all right. Just give me a minute.'

Morgan knew otherwise. As a child, a cough like that had been his bedtime lullaby. His own father's lungs had also borne the ravages of a lifetime hewing coal from the dark earth beneath the valleys of South Wales.

He dropped back to the ground, took off his greatcoat and wrapped it around the miner's shoulders. Then, with one movement, he lifted Williams onto the truck and, after securing the tailboard, sat beside him protectively with his knees drawn up under his chin.

One of the men banged on the roof of the cab with his fist and the truck rattled along the road that led to the small town of Arajo. It had been under heavy siege by the rebel forces of General Franco and stood defiantly between them and the gates of Barcelona. There were reports that a crack unit of SS troops on loan from Hitler was also present.

'Sweet Jesus,' thought Morgan, as he scanned the faces of the men around him, 'these are the reinforcements to save Arajo.'

Two years of waging a foreign war they now knew was lost, showed in their strained expressions, yet their sunken eyes still refused to accept the hopeless evidence of an inevitable end. Morgan felt proud to be in the same truck.

When he had first met them, he had been a reporter for the *Daily Express*. Readers in England had become bored with the cold daily accounts of Spain disembowelling herself in civil war. They needed something more colourful than plain facts to digest along with the breakfast toast and marmalade.

'Live the news for them,' Morgan had suggested. 'Give them a first-hand report of what it's like to fight with an International Brigade unit.'

He had done. Then just one week after meeting George Williams and the others, Nat Morgan had put down his pen and picked up a gun. There was, he had decided, more to justice than writing about it in newspapers. It was the right of people like George Williams – his own kind of people – to live without fear. That was the reason they had come to Spain. And for that, like them, Morgan had been still willing to die.

Now three months later and three hundred yards from the red

tiled roofs of the whitewashed suburbs of Arajo, the two trucks came to a halt in a cloud of hissing steam.

The men remained in the first truck. The others, rifles dangling in hand, ran crouching towards the deserted town. Fifty yards from the boundary they stopped and gathered on their haunches in a small circle.

The torrential rain and constant shelling had transformed the countryside into treeless craters. Morgan saw that the town had not died without a fight. The grotesque corpses bore silent testimony. Soldiers, old men, women and children were all frozen forever in their last defiant gestures. Morgan gripped his rifle until his knuckles turned white and fought back the vomit he felt rising in his throat.

One of the Spaniards went first. Bent double, he sprinted through the stench until he reached a stone drinking fountain in the middle of a small square. As he ran, Morgan noticed his boots were tied together with string.

'It's OK. All clear. Come on,' called the man urging them forward with his waving hand.

One by one the others followed, with Morgan and Williams bringing up the rear. Only the frantic pounding of their shabby boots echoing on the cobbles filled the air.

Nothing else.

Nothing but a silent cemetery of unburied dead.

Then, as they entered the square, they heard a faint high-pitched whistle. Then another. In seconds the whole sky seemed to be whining.

Morgan looked back and saw a shower of bare brown earth and stones cascading into the air alongside the truck of waiting men.

The second shell was a direct hit. A billowing ball of red and black smoke mushroomed into the grey sky. When it cleared, there was nothing except the empty, smouldering hole. A murderous blast of automatic fire reverberated through the streets of Arajo. From the blown-out windows of the broken buildings, scything bullets ripped through the figures standing in the square.

Silver flashes of steel bounced off the cobbles, hurling the ragged band off their feet until they hung momentarily in the air like dangling marionettes before crashing to the ground.

In that split second George Williams, or more precisely, his frail body, saved Nat Morgan's life.

The ferocity of the fusillade threw him back a full ten feet smack into Morgan. The momentum carried them both through a jagged gap into the ruins of a butcher's shop.

Unhurt, Morgan eased himself from under the old man's body. Alongside, the corpse of what had been the butcher, still clung to the fly-infested carcass he must have been carrying when the shop was first hit.

Then, as if Morgan needed any reassurance it would take more than that to kill an Abercynon miner, the old man said, 'What a bloody cock-up! We was had, my buttie boy. Fucking well had.'

Outside another burst of automatic fire rang out. Now none of the crumpled heaps lying the gutter twitched.

'Bastards,' hissed Morgan through clenched teeth and reached for his revolver. Williams took his arm and shook his head. His lips parted to speak but as they did so a thin dark red trickle seeped from the corner of his mouth.

Morgan dragged him to the other side of the butcher's counter. He ignored Williams's plea that he would stand a better chance on his own. He would wait for night and then try to make for the open country and the long overland haul to the safety of the Pyrénées.

They waited in silence for the Spanish night. At last it fell with a rapidity that ignored the courtesy of the dusk. For that Morgan was grateful. It saved time.

With the old man wheezing on his shoulder, Morgan picked his way through the rubble-strewn streets until the town was behind them. Then came the fields. Swaying through the liquid earth, he sank up to his knees with each step he took. With every stride he felt his strength ebbing from his aching muscles.

Then halfway across the second field came the sound of gunfire.

Slithering, gripping the old man tightly to his shoulders, he slid into the safety of a crater left by a Howitzer shell. The jolt made Williams wince with pain as he fought to draw the damp air into his ruptured lung.

Morgan cradled the old head in his arms and listened to the sporadic bursts of fire that continued until the bleak dawn. He guessed that the Fascists were mopping up the last pockets of Republican resistance.

From the east, the ghostly thin yellow sun drifted above a hunchback hill and lit the carnage with the pale rays of first light. The old man's coughing had got worse and although he did not know how, or where, or even what, Morgan realised he must get help. George Williams would live, or, he swore, they would both die.

Each man still had his revolver. Morgan took and emptied them both. They contained a total of seven bullets. He reloaded his gun and left a single bullet in the other.

'Just in case,' he said handing it to the old man. 'Don't let them take you alive. I'll be back.'

Williams never doubted it. 'Take care, my boy,' he said as Morgan vanished over the rim of the crater.

Morgan crawled for what seemed like hours through the slime until his outstretched hand felt the damp, bloated flesh of a dead mule. Strapped to its swollen belly was a Red Cross medical kit. Unbuckling it hurriedly, he followed his trail back through the mud.

He had almost reached the crater when he heard the sound of a single shot. He redoubled his efforts until he saw the dead man's bulging eyes. A tongue jutted from his twisted mouth and in the centre of his forehead there was one round hole. The man's head and shoulders were draped over the edge of the crater. His lapels bore the insignia of the Nazi SS.

Morgan inched closer and gaped into the hole. The vision was to stay with him to the grave.

The three remaining Germans had their backs to him. One, a private, was urinating. The second man's bayonet had ripped open the miner's stomach and he was carefully wiping the blood off on the old man's coat.

The third was an officer. He stood silhouetted against the skyline on the far rim of the crater. The collar of his full-length coat was turned up to protect his neck from the rain. Hands behind his back, he tapped his silver-tipped baton against his black-gloved palm. He hovered over the macabre cameo like an angel of death.

Morgan squinted as he took aim. His first bullet ripped into the skull of the soldier with the bayonet and, for a moment, the man tip-toed, arms outstretched in a profane gesture of crucifixion, then fell face down into the mud.

The private, flies still undone, turned in horror. One shot hit him in the shoulder, the other in the groin and he sank screaming to the ground.

The officer remained motionless, except for the tapping of his baton.

Morgan raised the gun and pointed it at the nape of the Nazi's neck. Still he did not move.

9

'Face me, you bastard,' yelled Morgan. 'Face me!'

The officer calmly turned towards him. He wore a look of cold disdain. He noticed the tears running down the mud-caked face of his executioner and his thin lips parted in a contemptuous sneer.

Morgan fired.

The officer dropped his baton and slapped his right hand hard against his temple, his fingers clawing at the side of his head. Still bolt upright, he lowered his arm and toppled backwards over the edge of the crater. As he fell, Morgan saw the shot had almost severed the ear from the side of his face.

Morgan leapt into the hole, and clasped the miner's body to his chest and wept like a child. He looked at the thin, dead face lined with blue scars of the pit, the close-cropped hair, grey before its time, the gnarled, rough hands. There was a son at university in Aberystwyth, saved, like Morgan, from a life in the pit. At home in a terraced house in Cardiff Road, Abercynon, there was a warm daughter and a plump wife. In a sea of Spanish mud, there was a cold, dead collier.

Eyes black with anger, Morgan picked up the bayonet and turned to the wounded private still writhing on the ground. Morgan stood over him, lifted the bayonet and plunged it into the throat of the dying member of Hitler's elite corps.

Then he sank to his knees in the mire and raised his arms towards the sky. He lifted his face to the falling rain, and, although his lips moved, no sound came. Then, at last the pent-up air burst from his lungs and carried the words from deep inside him into his throat and out from his trembling mouth.

'He only wanted . . . justice.'

His scream echoed over the desolation, then died in the foreign mud.

CHAPTER ONE

As the dusty old locomotive stuttered to a halt, the large black limousine waiting on the station concourse slipped into gear. The crowd hovering to greet arrivals around the raised passenger barrier grudgingly parted to make way, as the car glided onto the platform and drove slowly towards the sleeping car section at the tail of the train.

The white circle in the centre of the scarlet flag fluttering from the gleaming bonnet of the Mercedes, contained a black swastika.

The car stopped alongside the last coach and the driver got out to open the rear near-side door. He came stiffly to attention as the two Abwehr officers, their eyes still tired and red with sleep, stepped down from the train. The senior officer, a colonel, carried a black leather briefcase attached to his wrist by a thin silver chain.

Four uniformed motorcycle outriders waited at the gates of Gare St-Lazare. As soon as the limousine approached, they gunned their powerful BMWs into life and took up escort positions to shepherd the car carrying Colonel Ernst Ulrich and Major Rudi Helm through the Paris rush hour.

Twice during the drive the Mercedes incurred the wrath of outraged French motorists when the driver was ordered to make unsignalled turns into the tangled side streets before rejoining the main road further along the route. After twenty minutes the convoy swung into the neglected drive of a drab, detached house set well back from a quiet residential avenue that had been used to grander times. Although not dilapidated, the house lacked the cosmetics of regular occupation. Paintwork had started to peel from the window frames and small tufts of grass sprouted from the rusty metal gutterings.

As the car pulled up, the front door was opened from within. As soon as the two officers stepped inside, it closed behind them.

'They are all ready and waiting for you, Herr Colonel,' said a man in an ill-fitting grey suit.

Ulrich nodded, and with Helm at his heels, followed the man through the large double doors at the far end of the room.

11

Waiting beyond, under the high ornate ceiling, were twelve men. They wore no uniform, although by their bearing and manner Helm guessed that they were military men. Unlike Ulrich, he did not know they were members of the ruthless but efficient Sicherheitsdienst – the SD security force.

'You may be seated,' said Ulrich. The SD officers arranged themselves on two rows of chairs set out neatly below the table. Ulrich and Helm remained standing.

Before he began, Ulrich took a key from his pocket and unlocked the chain holding the briefcase to his wrist. He placed the case carefully on the table in front of him, but made no attempt to open it.

The officers waited in silence. Helm shifted his weight from one foot to the other. He was as baffled as the rest.

'Gentlemen, I will be brief and come straight to the point,' Ulrich announced in the clipped, guttural accent of southern Bavaria.

'At 20.00 hours tonight we shall begin the first of a series of raids. The targets may strike you as a little unusual, but that is not your concern. We shall raid a number of specially selected bordellos, high-class bars and the apartments of well-established courtesans – whores!

'This operation is to be carried out with the maximum security. None of you will ever know, or question, the reason for these raids. The whole exercise will look like a routine vice round-up.'

Ulrich banged his fist down on the desk to hammer home the point.

'Routine,' he repeated. 'That is why no one must ever learn who you are. Each of you will lead a raiding party containing six soldiers. These men have been hand-picked; all are dedicated. Party members. They, like you, can be trusted to keep their mouths shut.'

He turned and pointed to a red pin placed in a large-scale map of Paris hanging on the wall behind him.

'The girls will all be taken here. It is a former girls' boarding school. There your responsibility for them will end and then you will wipe the events of these next few days from your minds completely. It never happened. Understood?'

The SD officers nodded in unison, trying hard to conceal their total bewilderment. It was insane. That feeling was shared by Major Helm, still standing at Ulrich's shoulder.

Like the security men facing him, he had not been told the

12

reason for his summons by Ulrich to this anonymous house in this nondescript suburb. It certainly was not one of the regular Abwehr premises dotted in similar areas of the city.

All the colonel had said during the long train journey from their base in Lisieux, where they worked on intelligence matters for the Western Command, was that it was a top-security matter. He had been completely in the dark – until now. And now he could not believe his ears. He was a soldier, not a pimp, and as the whores of Paris could not all be Mata Haris, he could see no reason to abduct them.

Ulrich seemed pleased with the effect of his briefing and posed theatrically, resting the side of his face on his gloved hand.

'And now,' he continued, 'the girls. I want the best in Paris. Only the best will do. God help any of you that wastes my time bringing in some poxed-up, syphilitic slut. The girls I want, as a general rule, will all be under thirty. They will also be very beautiful.'

He repeated his last words, rolling his tongue over the phrase to savour the syllables. His manner embarrassed Helm who felt his colour rising.

'It goes without saying they will all be European,' said Ulrich, grinning, 'none of those Algerian or Moroccan half-breeds which the French have allowed to pollute their bloodlines. If they struggle when you pick them up, use only enough force to keep them quiet. I do not want them marked – on their faces or their bodies.

'The raids will continue until I am satisfied I have in my grasp the most desirable girls in Paris,' he said. 'The best.'

As the bemused officers filed from the room, their mutterings no more than whispers, Ulrich turned to Helm with a smile: 'I think it's time I put you fully in the picture. They have prepared an office for us here for the duration of the raids.'

The office was a small, converted bedroom, patterns of damp running beneath the plaster and lifting it from the wall in bubbles of cracking paint. Coffee had already been placed on a table covered with a grubby off-white tablecloth. There were two wooden chairs. Ulrich took one and gestured to Helm to do the same.

Seated, Helm watched his superior officer as he heaped spoonfuls of sugar into the steaming black liquid. He detested the man. Fanatical Nazis like Ulrich would certainly cost Germany the war. Even a straight, uncomplicated soldier like

Helm knew that Ulrich's appointment as Intelligence Chief for the Western Defences must have been a political one. Ulrich, after all, had been a Nazi since the early Munich days.

Ulrich sipped his coffee. Helm found the noise off-putting.

'Rudi,' began Ulrich, 'I think we both agree that the general morale of our forces in the West is low. The whole war effort seems to have lost its momentum. Our officers are under increasing strain daily – and that could spell disaster.'

Helm could only nod in agreement. Ulrich's assessment was an understatement. He knew the officer corps was totally disillusioned and in danger of splitting into two distinct factions.

His kind of army from the traditional Germanic school of warriors, weaned on discipline and duelling scars, were up against men like Ulrich. Political gangsters. Daily military good sense was being overridden for purely ideological and political motives. Officers, like him, supported Field Marshal Rommel's conviction that the Allied landings would come in Normandy. But their voices were unheard in the military wilderness created by those like Ulrich.

'Well?' said Ulrich.

'You are right,' agreed Helm, 'and this constant threat of Allied landings . . .'

'Threat,' interrupted Ulrich, his voice rising to the Messianic tones of a Lutheran preacher. 'Threat. We should not be thinking in terms of a threat – but as an opportunity to establish our supremacy for all time.

'That is the state of mind we must have to build our new world – and to motivate this, we must have the right quality of leadership. We must have officers who can inspire. It must come from the top.'

He placed the briefcase on the table, unlocked it and removed a fat folder, which he placed on the table between them.

'This,' explained Ulrich, 'contains a plan to improve morale. It is the sweet pill to take away the bitter rivalry that is gnawing away at our unity like a cancer. As you can see by the seals, it has been approved at the highest level. Its nature, I am sure you will agree, necessitates the highest discretion. In the wrong hands this could be very damaging propaganda. Hence the security.'

As ordered, the major began to read the contents of the folder. The more he read, the harder he found it to conceal the disgust

14

he felt for his superior officer – whose idea he was convinced it was.

'A brothel?' he asked incredulously. 'A military-run brothel?'

Ulrich smiled and handed Helm a batch of photographs.

'Right there. In that château,' he said. 'This will give the senior staff something more than festering discontent to occupy their minds.' He paused, then added, 'But to describe it as a brothel is an injustice. It will be a gentlemen's club staffed with sophisticated and beautiful women who will satisfy every whim, without question. A place where an officer can safely unwind and relax. A place where he can shed the frustrations of waiting for the fight ahead.'

'I see,' said Helm, his mind racing.

Ulrich eyed him carefully. 'Within months, the whole morale of the men will have changed for the better. This will be because the attitude of their leaders, their superior officers, will be relaxed and confident. Confidence is contagious. Rommel will have a united army.

'The château is called Beaupré. It is near Lisieux and will be used by only key officers. That is all, Rudi.'

Helm got slowly to his feet. As he closed the door behind him, he was more sure than ever Ulrich was insane.

As Helm's footsteps echoed along the dusty passage towards the stairs, Ulrich thumbed through the folders on the table, pausing over the photographs of the girls already shortlisted for possible selection. He stopped when he came to the file of the one raid he would lead himself. It would be the last of all.

On the plain brown paper cover, under the emblazoned crest of the Third Reich, were typed two names:

Clair La Croix
Colette Claval
17, rue de l'Eglise.

CHAPTER TWO

For Colette Claval, the road to Paris began on a small farm near the village of St-Aubin, in north-eastern France.

The family holding was run by a father in the frugal and puritanical traditions of generations of French peasants before him. A smile had not passed under the thin line of hair on his top lip since his deaf-mute of a wife after giving birth to five daughters had, finally, produced a son. Like his mother, the boy was denied the gifts of speech and hearing. From that day onwards, Paul Claval decided that the women with whom he had been condemned to spend the rest of his life, were a punishment sent from heaven for some unpardonable, but unremembered sin. When he spoke to his daughters, it was only to give them the commands necessary for them to carry out their duties on the farm.

One night, in the summer of 1942, the sum of his conversation with his daughter Colette was the word 'Eggs'. It was a word that was to change her life.

It meant that next morning she was up at dawn and, after tending the family cow, collected the eggs from the hens that grubbed their existence from the bare earth and sparse shrub around the ramshackle house.

Then, with a basket of eggs to sell on each arm, she set off for the village sixteen kilometres away. Although it was still mid-morning, the August sun had already sent the temperature soaring into the seventies. As she walked, whistling to herself, along the winding dirt road, her loose sandals sent tiny clouds of white dust puffing into the air.

At the brow of a hill, she heard the faint drone of a truck's engine and, peering through the heat haze, she picked out its vague outline shimmering in the distance. Then the sound ceased, and the blurred image was gone. Only the rhythmic trilling of an unseen lark and the constant buzzing of a bee filled the air. Colette Claval felt it was good to be alive.

At the foot of the hill lay a tree-shaded clearing where she always stopped and bathed her feet in the cool waters of the stream. It was there she dreamt her dreams of Paris.

But when she reached the clearing, she saw the truck. Sitting in the shade of its shadow were three German soldiers. Long loaves of fresh bread and cheese were spread around them on the grass. They had placed several bottles of white wine to cool in the stream's fast-running waters.

One soldier, a red-faced man in his thirties, got unsteadily to his feet. His grey tunic was unbuttoned to reveal a sagging beer paunch. He clutched a half-finished bottle of wine.

'Who the hell are you?' he gestured, waving the bottle in front of his face.

Colette froze. Her first thought was to run, but fear seemed to root her to the grass.

'Well,' said the soldier, taking a lurching step towards her, dipping his shoulder as he almost lost his balance, 'what do you want?'

The girl lowered her head. She did not dare reply. Talking to Germans, the priest had said, was a mortal sin.

'Gunther, come and sit down. You are frightening the poor kid to death.'

Colette looked up. The owner of the voice was a young fair-haired private. His tone was reassuring.

Colette committed her first mortal sin. She blurted: 'This is my place. I always stop here to cool my feet.'

No thunderbolt came. Instead the third soldier said: 'Oh, your place is it? Then,' he added laughing, 'please forgive us for trespassing.'

He sounded just like her uncle George. Colette was sure she had been granted instant absolution, and felt better.

'Well, well,' said the young blond private noticing the girl relax. 'Why don't you cool your feet, and in return for allowing us to rest at your private oasis, perhaps m'mselle would do us the honour of having lunch.'

They watched, washing down the chunks of bread with wine, as the girl removed her sandals and hitched her floral skirt above her knees. She sat on the bank and splashed her legs into the bubbling waters.

'How old would you say she is?' asked Gunther, undoing his top trouser button to release a few more inches of his girth with a loud burp.

'It's hard to say. Probably she's older than she looks,' said the private.

'Fifteen? Sixteen? I guess not more,' added the corporal, the one who sounded like the girl's uncle.

'If that,' said Gunther, 'but then . . . I like them young.'

'You'd split her in half,' replied the blond, uncorking another bottle of wine. They laughed, and changed their position to get a better view of the girl.

Although she did not look it, Colette was just seventeen, the eldest of her father's six children. Her jet-black hair was cut short to a fringe which bobbed when she walked, giving her a pretty, almost waif-like appearance. As usual she was wearing a loose-cut smock because, for reasons only adolescents themselves can explain, she was self-conscious about her breasts. Alone, she massaged them, watching herself in the mirror of the bedroom she shared with her younger sister. She prayed that they would get larger, like those of her friend Claudette, who knew boys because of it. How she envied Claudette.

Her feet were cool now, and she unhitched her skirt and got to her feet. As she did so, she saw the young private take off his tunic and lay it out on the grass, spreading it smooth.

'Come and sit in the shade,' he called, 'and join us.'

Colette shook her head.

'My father does not permit me to talk to Germans.' She paused, taking a breath before adding, 'Or . . . men.'

'We won't tell him and besides, it would be ungracious of such a lovely lady to refuse an offer of lunch,' he said.

Then, for reasons she would never be able to recall, Colette blurted out, 'One day I am going to run away to Paris and be famous.'

'Ah, Paris,' said the young private.

'Have you been to Paris?' The girl was open-mouthed. She bubbled with excitement. She smiled as the thought of her sister Bernadette's face when, that night, she would tell her she had been wined and dined by someone – a German even – who had actually been to Paris. She sat down on the outstretched tunic. Paris.

Gunther wiped the wine from his mouth and handed her the bottle.

The private took the wine from Gunther, poured it into a mug and handed it to Colette.

'To a lovely lady,' toasted the private.

'To a lovely lady,' echoed the others raising their bottles. Colette blushed and lowered her eyes. She sat, bewitched, as the young soldier in his perfect French told of the wonders of Paris. The theatre, the restaurants, the cafés, the clothes, the sophisticated women. The bricks upon which Colette Claval had built her childhood dreams materialised in elegant palaces of wonder before her very eyes. As they spoke, they drank, and the courteous Germans made sure that the girl's mug did not want for cold white wine. For the first time in her life she was being courted and Colette stole secret glances at the young soldier.

Glances she would never forget. He was handsome. The square jaw, the fair hair was so different from the village boys. Those piercing blue eyes. Just wait until she told her sister.

She graciously accepted his offer for a stroll in the sun. As they walked, she felt a strange mixture of pleasure and guilt at the touch of his fingers around her waist.

Then the feeling turned to sheer terror. Her feet left the ground as his hands, tearing her bra in two, cupped her breasts and lifted her, kicking, into the air. He spun her towards him, ignoring the look of abject terror on her face.

She smelt the stale smell of wine on his breath as he bit her lips to part them, then forced his tongue into her mouth.

He threw her face down onto the grass and placed his jackboot into the small of her back to hold her in position while he unbuckled his belt. His fingers tore at his flies and he swung his hips to rid them of his trousers. He pulled them down to his knees and lifted his boot from her back to stand astride Colette. It was the second she needed.

Free from the force of the leather heel, she wriggled through his legs and, kicking off her sandals, rolled onto her feet and ran for the cover of the trees.

Colette plunged blindly through the bristling undergrowth, her head bowed and arms swinging wildly from side to side. She knew she must reach the road. But which way? Where?

'Please, sweet Jesus, please, which way?'

Then she tripped over a curling root and fell exhausted to the ground. She willed herself onto her knees but lacking the strength to stand, knelt, resting on the palms of her hands. Suddenly there was silence except for the panting panic of her breathing. She was safe.

Colette lowered her head and felt the tears running down her face. But she must reach the road, she had to.

The girl had to make one final effort to get up. She lifted her head and saw in front of her the hideous grin extending between the beads of sweat glistening on Gunther's face.

He swung his arms around her waist and carried his prize in triumph – like a spoil of war – back to the clearing. He claimed the victor's right to be first.

Colette's mumbled pleas for mercy were silenced with a punch. The corporal and the blond private pinned her arms to the ground above her head. Gunther hoisted her skirt around her waist, ripped the pants from her struggling legs and spread her legs. Unbuckling his belt, he knelt between her thighs.

Colette's scream of terror turned to an agonising screech as the soldier's frantic thrusts finally ruptured the hymen with searing pain.

His watching comrades tossed a coin to decide who would be the next. The corporal won.

'I want you naked,' he said, hauling Colette to her feet. But the bruised girl just stood there trembling, stunned into incomprehension, with hands held defensively over her breasts.

'Strip,' he shouted.

Colette just stared in terror. Then there was a loud crack, and the earth and grass exploded around her feet. She looked towards the truck. The blond soldier was holding a smoking revolver.

'Don't kill me,' screamed Colette.

He fired again, over her head this time.

'Dance,' he ordered, 'and take off your clothes.' The others started a slow handclap in accompaniment to Colette's pathetic twirling movements, as, bit by bit, she removed her clothing until she stood naked on the grass.

She offered no resistance and he left her kneeling on the turf, mud ingrained beneath her fingernails where she had clutched the earth.

The corporal stood up and glanced at the private. He smiled.

'It's not his style,' said Gunther. 'She is not the right sex.'

'You just hold her in that position,' the private said pointing to the kneeling girl. Then he stood astride her and parted her buttocks. Colette lapsed into unconsciousness at his brutal penetration.

They flung her into the back of the truck, like a broken rag doll, and rested.

The next morning they dumped her out on the dirt road a mile from the farm.

Half-stumbling, half-walking, the bruised and dishevelled little figure finally reached home. Her father stared in horror, his mouth open but speechless as he listened to his daughter's near-hysterical account of her ordeal. He turned away, then he

20

lunged at the girl, who sank to her knees from the blow of his open palm.

'Slut,' he hissed, and spat on the cowering figure in front of him. 'You filthy, defiled little Jezebel.'

'Please, Papa, please,' she sobbed. 'They raped me.'

'Get out of my house. You have shamed us,' he bellowed. 'Disgraced us, you vile little whore.' He pushed her through the door into the yard. 'You can sleep in the barn until I decide what to do with you – with the other animals.'

Colette threw herself on to a pile of hay and wept. Her confusion was complete. She had done nothing.

When her father returned, he was holding a pair of scissors.

'What are you going to do?' asked Colette backing away, her hands held out defensively.

'Do?' he shouted. 'I am going to crop your hair. Then we will see who will touch a little cow who fornicates with the Boche.'

'They raped me,' screamed Colette. 'Please understand, they raped me.'

'You enticed them. You took their wine and paid for it with your body.'

He moved towards her to complete his punishment. It was then Colette saw the pitchfork. She grabbed at it and swung wildly. It caught her father across the temple and he slumped to the floor. She ran past his crumpled form and into the house. Her mother, standing before the stone sink, opened her mouth but as usual the sounds were unintelligible and Colette ignored them. She grabbed the painted biscuit tin from the kitchen dresser. It contained the family savings. Colette stuffed handfuls of notes into a bag and fled the farm, never to return.

In Paris, a country girl and her money are soon parted. There was the food, the fares, the fruitless, tramping search for work in a city where jobs were scarce. And there was the hotel.

Hotel? A seedy, broken-down back-street pension, heavy with the permanent stench of stale cabbage and fresh disinfectant.

At night Colette found it almost impossible to sleep. When she did doze off, she would wake, screaming, as the recurring images of soldiers driving into her bleeding loins and her father's twisted face of hate danced through her mind. The very presence of men made her flesh crawl.

That was unfortunate for the clean-cut young Panzer officer ogling her through the window of the bar.

'May I join you, m'mselle?' he asked politely.

Colette raised her eyes. Her stomach churned and she retched as if she was about to vomit.

'Are you ill?' he asked. 'You look as if you are going to be sick.' He turned to a passing waiter. 'You, garçon, fetch some brandy for the young lady. Quickly.'

He reached out and placed his hands on Colette's shoulder to steady her. She recoiled in revulsion and retreated, slowly, inch by inch along the seat until her back rested against the plate-glass window.

The white-coated waiter scurried to the table and placed the glass in front of her.

The German's face began to fade and lose its shape. The blurred spectres of her nightmare floated in front of her eyes.

'You filthy bastards,' she screamed and leapt to her feet. She hurled the contents of the brandy glass into the German's face. As he reeled back, she grabbed a bottle of mineral water by its long neck and aimed a wild blow at the man's head. It missed.

As Colette drew back her arm for a second blow, she felt firm fingers tighten around her wrist. She turned to face her new attacker, and saw to her total surprise the face of a beautiful woman, her long blonde hair piled high into a mass of curls.

The woman caught Colette by the wrist, and pulled her quickly past the astonished customers sitting at the tables out into the boulevard. By the time that the German had wiped the sting from his eyes and looked up, the pair had melted into the passing Parisian promenade.

Dragging Colette behind her, the woman, still without speaking, turned into the nearby rue de l'Eglise. It was deserted, save for a uniformed nanny preoccupied with pushing a large pram. The girls slipped past her and through a black-painted door.

Behind it lay a carpeted foyer, heavy with the scent of freshly cut flowers. They were arranged carefully in vases set on marble pedestals along the walls which were hung with mirrors. Colette caught her reflection as she was pulled towards the waiting lift. Her surroundings made her feel dowdy.

A heavily made-up woman with double chins eyed them frostily and snatched up her poodle as the girls rushed past her. She entered the lift, tutting her disapproval, as the blonde woman dived into her handbag for the key to the penthouse. Colette was bundled inside.

The peasant's daughter from St-Aubin had never seen such

luxury. This was how she had always thought Paris would be. Her rescuer bolted the door behind them and carelessly tossed her fur wrap over an antique gold chair. Until now Colette had thought only film stars and royalty wore ermine.

This lady was dressed in an expensive, tight-fitting, blue satin halter-neck dress that plunged in a deep V at the back to the base of her spine. From every angle the dress highlighted the exquisite body that had paid for it.

Colette marvelled at her perfect poise. Her face had a classic, aristocratic shape with chiselled, high cheekbones. Her eyes were deepest blue and when she spoke for the first time, her voice was deep and her accent impeccable.

Her hostess walked to the well-stocked bar at the end of the room, kicking off her elegant shoes as she did so. As she scanned the labels of the rows of bottles on the shelves above her, she rubbed her stockinged toes into the deep pile of the carpet.

'Something special I think,' she said and took down a flask of Napoleon brandy from the top shelf. She filled a glass and handed it to Colette. Then she poured her own, swishing it in her hand to take in the aroma. 'Run away from home?' she asked suddenly.

Colette made no reply.

'It is nothing to be ashamed of. I did when I was about your age,' she laughed, revealing perfect white teeth. 'It was all rather funny really, but it seemed like the end of the world at the time. Dear Papa came home early from riding one day and caught me in bed with the chauffeur.'

She caught the expression on Colette's face.

'Shocked? Don't be. It could just as easily have been the maid. Sweet little thing – a poppet. She looked rather like you in some ways, the same big round eyes.'

She moved across the room to a deep velvet sofa. She sat, carefully crossing her legs and puckering her lips before lighting a cigarette and exhaling a smoke ring. She stretched her fingers and patted the cushion beside her.

'Come and sit,' she said, 'and please stop staring at me like that. I am not going to devour you.'

Colette sat beside her, clasping her hands together in her lap.

'Are you pregnant?'

'I don't know,' shrugged Colette, biting her lip.

'I think you had better tell me about it.'

Between the sobs that she could no longer keep at bay, Colette

23

relived her nightmare. She spoke quickly, without interruption.

'So you have no money, nowhere to go. No one.'

Colette held her head in her hands, saying nothing. Her hostess stood up, walked back to the bar and refilled her glass. She carried the flask back towards the sofa and stood in front of Colette.

'I should introduce myself. My name is Clair La Croix and this is my apartment. Would you like to stay here for a while? You can help me around the apartment by running errands and things.'

Colette leapt to her feet and flung her arms around Clair's neck and wept with joy.

As the weeks turned into months, Colette became totally captivated by the sisterly kindness and reassuring presence of Clair.

The initial bewilderment of the steady procession of paying lovers, turned to the fascinated admiration of the haughty dominance which Clair held over them.

In the beginning Colette was horrified by Clair's lifestyle. She would lock herself in the bathroom and not come out until she heard the lovers leave. Once she ruined a dress when she decided to stay out in a rainstorm rather than go back to the apartment while Clair was entertaining.

It was after this that Clair insisted Colette should be present to receive her guests, fetch them drinks and pander to them. Observing the fools first-hand, only increased Colette's contempt for the male of the species. They were fools, but generous fools.

She noted that each of Clair's sessions was by strict appointment only. They lasted no more than an hour. Her clients were all established regulars, sophisticated, rich and even famous. They all lavished on her expensive gifts.

'I have total power over them,' explained Clair. 'And it pleases me.'

She would never receive anyone later than seven in the evening and each visit always followed the pattern set down and insisted upon by Clair. Each paying lover had his, or in the case of a famous coloured jazz singer, her, own key.

'I really do believe you are just a tiny bit jealous,' said Clair after a day Colette had devoted to conducting a non-stop verbal assault on the attributes of the singer.

That night Clair gave her the silk nightdress. She lay back in the bed they had shared for the last two months, like sisters, and watched Colette dance around the bedroom with delight as she held the soft garment to her olive skin, revelling in its smooth sensual touch.

'I feel so safe,' said Colette, as she slipped into the satin sheets. 'And happy.'

Clair leant over and kissed her gently on the forehead. Colette closed her eyes. Slowly the blonde unlaced the flowing nightdress and hesitantly began to fondle the little dark nipples. Carefully avoiding the lips, Clair began to cover her with slow kisses. She ran her tongue slowly around the small, pert breasts, then caressed the flat belly with open lips.

Colette lay motionless, her body unresisting but refusing to respond to the soothing words and long searching fingers that stretched over the soft, tufted triangle. Gently, softly, Clair's fingers felt little pearls of moisture between the girl's slender loins. The deft finger movements brought the first murmured gasp of delight from Colette. Her body began to throb, making spasmodic circular movements and her thighs jerked impetuously as the intensity of the long slow finger movements increased.

Clair watched as the whole of the slender body began to writhe under her hand. The fingers moved faster. Faster. Colette arched her back, thrusting against them as she melted into a sea of sensations.

Then Clair gently parted the yielding legs and knelt before her new love as if in worship.

'My sweet love,' she whispered, 'my sweet little love.' She began to kiss her with slow revolving movements of her head. As the movements increased so did Colette's frantic writhing until she screamed out in an uncontrollable moment of sublime ecstasy.

In the silence of their joy, they lay gazing at each other. Colette wiped a single tear from the corner of her eye and nervously reached out until her hand enveloped the milk white breast of her blonde goddess and said quietly, 'I love you.'

It was the thin-lipped baron de Lazare who had first made the suggestion that would make the girls the highest paid in all Paris.

'My darling Clair, you know I just exist for my moments with you – but if that sweet child could join us it would just be too divine.'

At first, Colette had resisted the idea, but a determined argument put up by her lover, eager to explore sensuality to its limits, changed her mind.

From that time on the list of adoring visitors who fell under the spell of 17, rue de l'Eglise, became more exclusive than ever. And the gifts they showered on the long-legged bi-sexual blonde and her petite svelte lover became legend. The girls were the toast of Paris, a Paris beyond Colette Claval's wildest childhood dreams.

CHAPTER THREE

From the early afternoon a steady succession of unmarked black police vans drove past the Gare du Nord, and turned into a shabby side street, known then as the rue Vieux. They bounced over the cracked cobbles between the boarded-up and long abandoned buildings towards the studded oak gates in the high brick wall. The grim building beyond housed the police barracks of the Paris gendarmerie.

As each van approached at regular intervals, the gates opened and the civilian drivers swung their vehicles across the flagstone courtyard and parked in a neat row outside the main building on the far side. The drivers did not leave their cabs.

The last of the dozen police vans was followed by the first of the canvas-roofed Citroën trucks. The rear flaps were tied tight to conceal the uniformed German troops sitting in the back. Each of these trucks contained six men and an NCO who also remained in their vehicles until the number of trucks equalled the police vans.

Then, group by group, the soldiers disembarked and, in double time, marched into the main building. Apart from the German soldiers it was completely empty. The signs of a hurried and unexpected evacuation were everywhere. Half-finished reports littered the desks next to undrunk cups of cold coffee. A radio receiver crackled police messages which echoed in the stillness.

The soldiers followed their NCOs through the silent corridors to the deserted locker rooms. There, laid out in neat bundles on the rows of changing benches were seventy-two police uniforms. Each was numbered. Each soldier went to his allotted number and hurriedly swapped the grey flannel of Hitler's Reich for the dark blue of the French gendarme.

Then as the clock from the Gare du Nord chimed the hour, the heavy gates of the barracks swung open and the convoy of black police vans slipped unnoticed from the side street and joined the heavy traffic heading along the boulevard Rochechouart towards the lights and smells of Montmartre.

At eight-thirty the police van pulled up at the kerbside on the boulevard Clichy. The Club Lapin was a haunt of visiting businessmen from the provinces. No Parisian man-about-town would have been seen dead there.

Inside was a small dance floor. The bar ran the whole length of one wall. A back staircase led to the bedrooms above where – subject to successful negotiation – customers could hire the exclusive services of their hostesses for the night.

The club was only half full. On the dance floor a middle-aged businessman shuffled awkwardly with a buxom redhead to the tired strains of the bored band. Sitting alone at the table near the door, Elaine Bisset lit another cigarette and glanced nervously around the room. The ashtray in front of her was already full of her lipstick-stained butts.

She bit the back of her clenched fingers as she saw Madame Gilot, the club's owner, waddling through the tables towards her. She was a fat woman in her late forties with a face and figure ravaged by the excesses of her chosen profession. Her painted face fell in circles of fat that hung from the neck.

'My dear, you look a mess,' she leered at the demure girl. 'Just look at yourself. Who taught you to make up – a circus clown?' Her eyes scanned the dejected face.

'What did you put your lipstick on with – a broom? And the mascara – terrible. A bloody mess. Go and wash it off and make up properly,' she snapped. 'Otherwise, dear, you will starve on what you earn.'

Elaine bit her lip and, clutching her handbag, rushed to the powder room.

She stared at the mirror and realised the old whore was right. She did look a mess. The rouge apples on her cheeks looked ridiculous and the lashings of ill-applied crimson lipstick and heavy green eye make-up gave her a bizarre appearance. Tearfully, she began to wipe it off and try again.

Alain, her husband and so far sole lover, had hated make-up. But he wouldn't see her on her first night as a hostess at the Club Lapin. Not from the unmarked grave where his unrecognisable body, mutilated by the blast of a panzer shell on the outskirts of Reims, had been dumped almost three years ago.

The idea of working at the club had tormented and revolted her for months. But not as much as the torment and revulsion she felt when she heard the nightly cries of her child with an empty belly – a child born the day Alain died and now tucked up for the night in his grandmother's house in St-Denis.

As she wiped the last trace of make-up from her pale oval face, she heard the shrill piercing blast of a police whistle. Panic-stricken, she made for the door.

Girls and their would-be clients were crashing into each other in a screaming stampede of confusion as they tried in vain to elude the baton-carrying gendarmes.

Only Madame Gilot kept her head. Experience of countless raids had taught her that the police could only catch what they could see. Coolly she made her way to the fuse box on the wall at the end of the bar. She was stretching out a puffy hand to pull the switch that would plunge the room into darkness, when the heavy white-painted riot stick swung down with a dull thud and crushed the bones in the fat fingers. A second blow cracked three ribs and sent her floundering onto the broken glass that littered the dance floor.

The frightened men were checked for identity papers and then allowed to leave. The girls were lined up in a row in front of the bar for inspection by the plain-clothes officer.

Slowly he strutted down the line and back again, mentally undressing his charges. In turn he held each of their faces, turning them to inspect from various angles. At last he made his choice. Four girls were finally selected, among them was Elaine Bisset.

During the raid none of the police had spoken a single word which would have revealed their true nationality.

Also among those taken on the first night was a statuesque Danish blonde called Eva Nielson. She had left her native sea-side village of Saeby just before the outbreak of war to pursue her greatest ambition in life – to become a whore. She was witty, well-read and intelligent. She was also stunningly beautiful and pursued by almost all the men in her home village – most of whom were married. It occurred to the good-natured Eva that her body was her fortune, but sleepy little Saeby was not the best place in the world to set up her business. She left for Paris. Money was not the main consideration in choosing her profession. She had an insatiable appetite for sex. Becoming a whore was by far the most sensible way of satisfying the hunger. In truth, Eva Nielson was never happier than when she was working.

That night her client had been a great disappointment. He was a small, pink-faced, paunchy civil servant who was unceremoniously dragged squealing from the blonde's bed by the gendarme who had kicked the door off its hinges.

Eva watched with undisguised amusement as the civil servant, red-faced and eyes popping, hopped from one leg to the other and began to stammer and splutter excuses. As he danced he kept both hands cupped protectively over his genitals.

Eva was now sitting up in bed, leaning back on her arms. Her large breasts heaved with uncontrollable laughter at the little man's now hysterical performance.

The SD man nodded to one of the gendarmes, who grabbed the Frenchman by the scruff of the neck, and, with a well-aimed punch, sent him headlong into the corridor outside. As his clothes gently floated from the window into the street below, he fled wailing into the night.

The officer motioned Eva to get up and she obliged with a smile. She slipped from the silk sheets and stood before him, arms outstretched. The long, straight blonde hair cascaded past her shoulders. His eyes moved from the large pink nipples and soft breasts to the ample curves of her lightly-tanned body. Her long legs seemed to flow forever from the broad, smooth thighs. He swallowed hard at the vision before him.

'Am I being arrested?' said Eva.

The officer just pointed to her clothes. One of the gendarmes picked them up and handed them to the Dane.

'So very friendly,' said Eva, adding in Danish, 'Miserable French pigs.' She discarded the underwear and stockings and pulled the almost transparent white tight-fitting dress over her head. She moved to the full-length mirror at the foot of the bed and smoothed out the creases, running her hands sensually over her body. She noticed the look in the man's eyes.

She turned and twirled before him.

'Like it? It cost a fortune. More than they pay the police I'll bet,' she said.

Again the man said nothing but indicated the empty door frame with his head.

Eva shrugged, grinned, and followed him to the street. As they walked to the waiting van, she slipped her arms through his.

'You should have come a little later. That little fat worm left without paying. It would have taken care of the fine.'

The man just stared ahead.

Eva tore her arm from his and stamped her foot on the ground.

'What the hell is the matter with you? Have you not got a tongue in that head of yours?'

Silently he bundled her into the van and closed the doors.

Although he did not know it, Eva Nielson was going to bring a lot of pleasure to some of the most famous names in the German army.

At the end of the raids Ulrich's report would note in cold print that one civilian had been shot. It would add that the man was a Sicilian pimp, Benito Sicluna.

Sicluna was a swarthy, thin, hook-nosed man with the features of a sparrow hawk and a head of greasy, tight black curls. He was the most detested whoremaster in France. His silver-tongued duplicity had become a by-word for treachery. Never caring whom he exploited, Sicluna catered for every social class and taste, from newspaper editors to the porters at les Halles market.

The night he died, he was pondering over the accounts in the luxury of his office suite above the bedrooms he provided for big-spending clients at his casino in rue de Rivoli.

His brother burst into the room. Ricardo, his voice high with anger, yelled in disbelief: 'It's a police raid. The shits are actually raiding us.'

Sicluna leapt to his feet and dashed downstairs. In the third-floor salon above the gaming room, he saw the police had emptied the bedrooms and lined up his girls – all in various states of undress – against one wall.

Among them was Maria Luardi, an Italian with a lion's mane of black hair. She, for the price of escape from Mussolini and a forged entry permit to France, had become Sicluna's personal plaything. Naked from the waist up, she was struggling with two uniformed gendarmes. The rest of the girls were standing quietly, hands on head.

Sicluna leapt across the floor and spun the plain-clothes man inspecting them towards him.

It needed only a slight movement of the head and one of the gendarmes stepped forward. Sicluna was hurled sideways by the force of a trained fist to the temple. In a second he was back on his feet – an open flick-knife in his hand. Crouching, he moved towards the officer, who remained motionless, his hands still buried in his raincoat pocket. He calmly drew out his right hand and watched with disinterest as a look of wide-eyed amazement crossed the Siclian pimp's face. A German army-issue Mauser was pointing at his head.

From that distance, the bullet left a perfect, neat, round hole in Sicluna's forehead. With his eyes still transfixed in a deathly stare of unbelieving terror, he crashed face down onto the carpet. The SD man turned and continued his inspection. He pocketed the pistol and noted with interest that, on leaving the pimp's head, the bullet had taken half of his skull with it.

'The quality is far above average,' he noted and selected eight girls, which was a record. They included Maria Luardi, who kicked and screamed all the way to the waiting van.

Also taken were two girls who claimed to be actresses. They were Annette Duval and Benedite Philippe.

CHAPTER FOUR

No one had lived there for years, except the caretaker. The count, the only son and a bachelor, had been killed the last time German armies rolled over the soil of his homeland. The count's widowed mother had left for the more manageable comforts of a Paris apartment, where she had died the year before. Or, more precisely, she just stopped living, because there didn't seem much point anymore. Because there was no one left to leave anything to, she hadn't made a will. A team of lawyers now managed the estates for a trust and none of them had ever thought to ask the caretaker to leave, which was why old Albert Boniface still lived on alone in the Château Beaupré.

It was a building which rose up on the Normandy landscape, a constant reminder to anyone who cared to remember of a bygone age of grace. It had been built with pride by the Beaupré family in the seventeenth-century style of the châteaux of the Loire valley, with fairy-tale round towers crowned with pointed domes that had turned green with age. It was set in an elevated position in its own walled grounds. Two wings, extending at right angles from the main body of the building, faced each other over a paved courtyard, where the great carved stone fountain no longer worked. Each year the winter frosts were followed by the damp Atlantic winds, and both bit further into the soft sandstone masonry. The age of grace had truly passed and the old place had been haunted by an air of neglect. The terraced lawns which rolled from the front of the château to the distant birch woods were cut only when Albert could be bothered, which wasn't very often. The rest of the grounds behind the padlocked, wrought-iron gates were rambling and overgrown, the flower beds and landscaped walks swamped by unchecked weeds and briars. The château had fallen on hard times.

It had become a sad forgotten place. The nearest village, Ste-Yvette, lay three miles away at the end of a winding country lane off route Nationale 13, the main road between Caen and Lisieux. No one ever used that turn-off because, unless they lived in Ste-Yvette, there was simply no reason ever to do so. That, and the fact the old countess had been the last of the

Beaupré line, was why Colonel Ernst Ulrich had requisitioned the château in the name of Hitler's Reich.

That was a month ago.

Now even old Albert had difficulty in recognising the former family seat of the counts of Beaupré. Although the façade had been hardly affected, the interior had been transformed. A legion of painters and decorators had, with dozens of craftsmen, descended on the château from Paris. They'd toiled day and night under the shrill but tireless supervision of a thin-waisted designer with a passion for pastel cravats, narrow slacks and ballet pumps. He was able to add the special feminine touches.

Off came the dust covers, in came the sunlight and out went the fading furniture. The family portraits in their massive gilt frames were rescued from the cellars, where they had been stored, and were returned to hang in all their former glory. There were other masterpieces too, a Matisse, some Cézannes and a few early Renoirs. But there were also new, unfamiliar paintings. They had been looted from a private collection in Amsterdam. The former owner had, in turn, taken them from a palace in Persia where they'd hung for centuries. These pictures by Aziz depicted Eastern erotica at its most superb. The soft colours and gentle brush strokes served to accentuate the sheer sensuality of the scenes. These were hung in the guest bedrooms and in the drawing room where a large roulette wheel had been installed. Although the old caretaker had no complaints about the way the rest of the house had been restored, even the bathrooms with those double sunken baths, the drawing room was something else. For one thing, it did not look much like a drawing room anymore, not with all those buttoned, red velvet settees everywhere. And Albert thought that by hanging those saucy foreign paintings on the walls, the lisping designer with the ivory cigarette holder had made the room look like the salon of some high-class brothel. Which, of course, was just what the man had been ordered to do.

Nicole McGragh lay waiting for Colonel Ulrich's knock on the door. She was in the suite directly above the old drawing room and once occupied by the old countess. Ulrich had installed her there immediately after her arrival from Paris. Now, on this July evening, they were to go through the final selection details of the most exclusive whores in Paris.

Nicole was reclining full-length on a chaise-longue, admiring her newly varnished nails. She blended perfectly with the room's ambiance, which was no more than she expected. There were no Persian paintings on these walls. The Degas above the imported Adam fireplace was more in keeping with her taste.

Although she looked no older than thirty-five, Madame McGragh would, in fact, be forty-three next birthday. She was a true Capricorn, and her single-minded arrogance was coupled with an insufficient heart. With self-assured confidence in her ageless appearance, she had, for years, always insisted on being called Madame, despite never having married. It gave her a greater authority and respect, she thought. It was also ironically apt in view of the assignment she had accepted to undertake for Ulrich.

Unlike most Frenchwomen of her time, the sight of the distinctive uniform of the officers who had first put the proposal to her, did not send shivers down her spine. She had no more reason to hate the Germans than she hated the French, or for that matter, the English. For Nicole McGragh had a Breton for a mother and an Irish patriot for a father. Her flaming red hair and fiery temper were inherited from his side of the family. Liam McGragh had wed her mother in the tiny Breton fishing port of Concarneau. He fled there from the peat of his native County Mayo after killing a British soldier in an ambush. Years later he was foolish enough to return and join his fellow Republicans in their fight to shed the English yoke. The Black and Tans exacted their revenge and shot him dead in a Dublin street riot. He left behind him in Brittany the only things he'd ever possessed: his family bible, a fishing boat with no one to sail it, a young widow and a six-month-old daughter who was weaned on a deep, burning Celtic hatred. This was to be divided, without favour, between the English, who occupied an Ireland she'd never seen, and the French, whom she considered were committing cultural genocide on her Breton nation.

Breton was also her first language. When she spoke French, it was with the accentless authority of acquired fluency. Then at sixteen, strange, mystical rhythms began to stir deep inside her. Much to her mother's chagrin she became a dancer; Isadora Duncan was her heroine. By the time she was twenty-five, she had become an actress of note. Adoring threatre-goers had claimed to have sipped champagne from her slippers in Paris, Rome, Vienna and Berlin. She'd refused to grace the London stage.

In September 1939, she was playing Ibsen's *Hedda Gabler* to the captivated audiences who queued to catch her performances at Berlin's Festival Theatre. She regarded that month's declaration of war with calculated indifference, and in no way let it interfere with her nightly curtain calls of adulation. After all, no one had declared war on Brittany or Ireland.

But Nicole McGragh also had a secret. She had kept it, sometimes even from herself, for more than twenty years. Those who adored her timeless beauty did so from afar; she was the perfect fantasy, utterly desirable and totally unobtainable. This multiplied her mystique. So, even when Ulrich entered her suite that evening, it was with a respectful awe.

As always, he was struck by her poise. She wore a long, white, silk evening dress with a black velvet choker around her neck. The dress was cut in a classical Grecian style. He did not expect her to rise from the chaise-longue and was more than content with just a smile. The one she always used to tip minions.

His pink lips parted thinly in response. He too loved the theatrical and for a moment wondered why such a woman had agreed to stage-manage and cast the scenario he was about to create in the Château Beaupré. He knew it could not only have been for the money, although he knew every woman had her price, and it was certainly not from any ideological leaning to Hitler's brave new order. She must be one of the very few women in war-weary Europe who had not been seriously affected by the hostilities. She had even insisted on her Swiss chef being brought daily to the château to provide the meals. Ulrich admired that. It was typical of the way her lifestyle had progressed with a steady momentum untroubled by the scarcity of luxuries. He concluded she did not want that to change.

Just a few seconds in her company and he was more certain than ever before that his scheme would work. Her choice of bedmates to grace the château sheets would be, as always, perfect. Simply perfect.

He crossed the room to where she lay and looked down upon her. 'Do you have the final list of names?'

She smiled, her eyes wide, and said: 'I think I have found you the seven best whores in Paris, or for that matter, in the whole of Europe.'

Ulrich grunted. Sipping a brandy, he began to read eagerly the names before him. There were five, and each was followed by the girl's biographical details and photograph.

'These are the ones I have selected from the final shortlist of thirty. The ones most suitable for your purpose – the best,' said Nicole.

Ulrich read on; then he looked up and said: 'What about the twenty-five other girls?'

'They are still being held with this five.'

'And the other two? The pair you recommended personally?'

'This . . .' Nicole paused, savouring the bitterness of the name, 'Clair La Croix. And that friend of hers, Colette Claval. I want to be there when you take them. You can look on it as a special favour.'

'Well,' Ulrich asked Helm, 'now you have had a little more time to consider the Bordello Project, what do you think?'

'I think it might achieve your purposes; but I still have reservations.'

'Reservations, Major?'

'A scheme such as this could be highly embarrassing for the officers concerned if news of it got into the hands of the wrong people,' said Helm.

'That is why no one, except carefully selected officers who will have use of the place, will ever know of its existence. No one. But, you, my dear Major, will of course be included in the elite band.'

'Me?' Helm looked taken aback.

Ulrich patted him on the shoulder then reached into his inside pocket and took out a long brown envelope.

'Open it,' he ordered.

Helm did. It contained a woman's photograph. The name, Clair La Croix, had been scrawled across it in black ink.

'She's very beautiful. Who is she?' he asked.

'She's yours, if you want her,' said Ulrich. 'Yours for the taking.'

'Mine?'

'From Friday. That's when you come with me to pick her up,' Ulrich said.

Helm's reaction was a mixture of guilt and delight. Part of him cried out that he had no right to this woman in this way, but another part reasoned that if Ulrich was going to give her to someone, then it might as well be him. The hedonist in him won the day and when he left the tiny office, he noticed there was a fresh spring in his step that hadn't been there for a long time.

Left alone, Ulrich picked up the phone and his heavily-stained fingers dialled the unlisted Berlin number. The number was not known to any member of the Abwehr intelligence service, including its supremo, Admiral Canaris.

When the voice in Berlin answered, Ulrich said: 'It's all set. I have even arranged Helm's whore. We have provided Rommel's messenger boy with a concubine. I shall pick up the last two girls on the list on Friday, and bring them and the other five to Normandy.'

The voice said: 'You have done well, Ulrich. Well.' Then the phone went dead.

That, Ulrich knew, had again been praise indeed. He made another call. To Paris.

As a result, the twenty-five girls not on his final list were given a surprise champagne party in the abandoned convent, where they'd been held since their abduction. They were allowed to drink their fill and told they were free to go.

Each girl, happily tipsy, was escorted from the convent by two polite young men. These men, members of the Sicherheitsdienst – SD – security force, drove the laughing girls to a wood near Versailles.

The girls were never seen again.

Dinner, that July evening in the château when the seven whores came together for the first time, was a banquet. It was, Nicole McGragh explained from the head of the table, a mere taste of things to come. The girls feasted on Coquilles Saint-Jacques in vermouth, followed by Boeuf en croûte, grilled vermicelli and asparagus with Hollandaise sauce. The cheeses preceded the Nègre en chemise laced with kirsch. The wines, like the cognac, were vintage.

The girls looked exquisite in the evening dresses which they had found in the complete wardrobe waiting for each of them. Now they all sat side by side at the long baronial table, the silver gleaming on a cloth of Amiens lace.

But none of it fooled Colette Claval. That's why, sitting next to Clair at the end of the table, she had not touched her meal. The thought of what lay ahead sickened her. For despite all the promises that McGragh woman had made about unlimited material comforts and a substantial cash payment in the end, Colette knew she was a prisoner. Even with Clair at her side she felt totally alone – and afraid. She reached out under the table, found Clair's hand and squeezed it.

Clair, engrossed in conversation with one of the other girls, turned her head towards Colette and smiled. Colette squeezed more tightly the hand she held under the table and their fingers entwined.

Colette closed her eyes and shivered at the memory of their last night of freedom. It was just before midnight. She and Clair had gone to bed early, intending to make love. But as they lay naked between the sheets lulled by the comforting warmth of each other's bodies Colette had drifted into sleep.

At first she thought she'd dreamt the sound of Clair screaming, and when a German soldier holding a rifle appeared in the bedroom doorway, she was convinced that her sleeping mind had once again conjured up the nightmare of her rape. She willed herself awake, then to her complete terror she realised she already was. The soldier stepped aside and there, standing behind him, was the figure of a woman. She was wearing a long red dress and had a black stole around her shoulders.

Bewildered, Colette sat up and held her hands to her face as the silk sheets fell away from her breasts.

What had she done? What had they done?

A German soldier. Why was a German soldier standing in the bedroom door? What was he going to do?

Rape? Kill? Worse?

And that woman in red. She knew her face, her name. Frantically she tried to remember when and where they'd met. Then it came to her. Nicole McGragh. They'd met at some film director's party in St-Germain. That was it. The woman had gone out of her way to insult Clair.

Then she saw him for the first time. The thin man in the pin-stripe suit and trilby. Ulrich. He was dragging Clair by the satin sleeve of her Japanese dressing gown, which hung open around her. He flung her onto the settee where she sat, mumbling in a state of shock. More soldiers came into view. She smelt the polish on their jackboots. Colette's vision blurred and the soldiers' faces began to turn before her eyes. The nightmare which she'd thought had gone forever had returned.

The man, leering down at her from the foot of the bed, was real. She felt his eyes abuse her and she curled up into a foetal position as he tore the sheets from the bed.

'Get up.' The sound seemed to hiss from his lips. He reached down and grasped her shoulder and shook her. Colette bit him. She felt her teeth meet beneath the skin on the back of his hand. He released his grip with a scream.

Colette could taste the blood from the wound on his hand. She was not going to let anyone take her this time.

As he clasped his bleeding hand, Colette flung herself at him. She began to scratch, claw, bite and punch at any part of Ulrich's body she could reach. Clair had jumped onto Ulrich's back. Colette saw her twine around Ulrich's waist and his face distort in pain as the long red nails sank into his thin cheeks, pulling them in opposite directions. Colette was sent sprawling back onto the bed. She began to weep, but with tears of rage. She threw herself forward and lunged once again at Ulrich. But this time, free from Clair, he was ready.

Colette felt the reaction of a trained soldier as the short-armed blow ended with the clenched fist sinking into the pit of her stomach.

She heard Ulrich's voice bark: 'Get them out of here. Now,' and felt herself being lifted, still dazed, over a soldier's shoulder and carried from the room. She recalled, as she was hoisted over the threshold, looking up and seeing the icy stare of Nicole McGragh.

Now, under the table, Colette again squeezed Clair's hand. She looked along the table and, between the candelabra, again saw that flat, icy stare. But this time it was fixed on the smiling face of Clair La Croix.

Nicole McGragh's expression was, Colette noticed, in complete contrast to her diamond earrings, which sparkled in the light from the overhead chandeliers. Colette watched the woman rise and tap the enormous brandy glass with the tip of a silver spoon. The after-dinner small talk, flowing smooth with the wine, began to cease. A second tap on the rim of the glass brought silence.

The Breton actress had her stage. Her expression changed and she practised her curtain call smile.

'Ladies,' she announced, 'I would be pleased if you would all join me in the salon for a glass or two of champagne. Please follow me.'

She turned and, as she made her exit towards the large double doors, her dress rustled. When she reached the doors, the whores, giggling their approval, rose to follow.

But then one of them spoke.

'I hope it's real French champagne, not a cheap German imitation.'

The way the word German was pronounced made Colette prick up her ears. There was venom in that voice. She saw it belonged to Maria Luardi, the girl with a lion's mane of black hair. As Colette followed the others across the hall to the salon, she decided she would get to know this fiery Italian.

The champagne was waiting in buckets of crushed ice and arranged in rows along the newly installed, but now covered, roulette table. It was set at the far end of the room, under an erotic Oriental masterpiece.

Nicole McGragh popped the first cork. The wine ran in bubbles over gold-coloured foil around the neck of the bottle. It bore the Bollinger label.

'Please, ladies,' said Nicole, 'feel free to help yourselves. There are no shortages here. There is enough to bathe in.'

Annette Duval and Benedite Philippe needed no second bidding. They launched their new careers in a spray of foaming wine. Nicole McGragh filled her glass, moved back from the roulette table, and eyed her charges. The seven best whores in Europe. They would have to be.

She had watched them all at dinner and now, in the salon amid the endless flow of champagne, she felt the first twinge of doubt about her selection. She might have made a mistake – three mistakes.

They were all drinking champagne and were called Colette Claval, Maria Luardi and Elaine Bisset, the young widowed music-teacher. The statuesque blonde Dane, prostitute and proud of it, Eva Nielson, however, more than made up for it. Eva Nielson was a real find, and Annette and Benedite already promised to be as accomplished as Clair La Croix.

But the other three. That was another matter. She sensed, somehow, they were going to be a trilogy of problems. Her eyes sought out Colette Claval.

The girl was on the far side of the roulette table talking to Maria, each had a glass of champagne in her hand. Originally Colette had not been part of the plan. It was Clair La Croix whom Nicole had wanted to see taken. But when she had mentioned it to Ulrich and shown him the photograph of the girls, he had insisted on them both being taken. Nicole thought he had seemed obsessed with the girls' relationship. The idea disgusted her anyway, but then what could one expect from someone who bore the name La Croix.

Then there was Elaine Bisset. Although her fine features and graceful style could match those of any of the girls in the room, Elaine seemed different. It was, Nicole decided, the girl's air of gentle vulnerability. She wondered how Elaine would cope with what lay in store for her. For her sake, Nicole hoped it would be well.

Glass in hand, Nicole made towards the lone girl. Nicole noticed the way Elaine gripped the stem of her glass and nervously bit her lip as she approached. The weak smile, too, was apprehensive. Nicole tried to put her at ease.

She said: 'The piano was brought here especially for you.' Nicole gestured towards the baby grand in the far corner of the salon. 'I remembered how much you said you enjoyed playing,' she added.

Elaine lowered her eyes and mumbled, 'Thank you, Madame.'

'I am sure that when the gentlemen come, they will enjoy your playing too. You know how musical the Germans can be. I can't tell you how much they adore culture. Berliners were always my most appreciative audiences.'

'I hope I shall be up to standard,' Elaine said meekly.

Nicole studied the girl. She could see just how much men would be attracted to her. But how was she going to make a whore out of her? 'Of course you will be up to standard. In fact, you can play for us now.'

Nicole turned to face the other girls. As she did so, she felt Elaine's fingers grip her sleeve.

The girl's voice was urgent. She said: 'Please, Madame. Did you ask about the money? I am sick with worry about what will happen to Alain.'

Nicole removed the girl's hand from her sleeve. 'I will see to it you get your money,' she said kindly. 'More than you need. Now, please, play for us.'

Then the actress raised her arms and called for silence. She announced: 'Ladies. Elaine Bisset is now going to play for us. Please show your appreciation.'

She led the applause. One by one the other girls followed suit. When Elaine sat at the piano stool and ran her delicate fingers over the keyboard, Nicole noticed the girl was blushing. She knew now that as long as the girl had to feed her child, she had, no matter how reluctantly, the makings of a whore.

Then, to the pop of a champagne cork the sound of Chopin filled the room.

Three glasses of champagne later and Eva Nielson was bored. Chopin, Eva thought, was as dull as dishwater. And not even Nicole McGragh could suppress a smile when Eva told Elaine as much.

42

'Why don't you play something good,' boomed Eva in a heavy Danish accent. 'Something we can dance to.'

Nicole noticed Elaine looked aghast. Then she smiled when Annette Duval called out: 'Play "The Stripper"!'

Annette whipped the cloth from the top of the roulette wheel and flung it into the air. It drifted down towards Eva, who caught it and wrapped it around herself tightly. Eva pulled her long blonde hair over her face like a veil. Then, in what even Nicole thought was a passable imitation of Greta Garbo, croaked: 'Where are the men? I hate to be alone.'

The girls, flushed with champagne, began to clap in time with the tune Elaine pounded out on the piano. Eva, enveloped in the dust sheet, twirled around the room until Elaine, overwhelmed by laughter, could play no more. Then, as the music died, Eva fell into a chair and let the dust sheet drop to the floor.

When, like the music, the laughter also began to fade, Nicole McGragh became aware of a new sound and turned to face it. She saw the white ball bouncing around the spinning roulette wheel. Maria was standing on tip-toe with her hands pressed together as if in prayer. The Italian girl's eyes were also pressed tight and Nicole noticed her lips mimed the word 'seven'. Then the sound of the rolling ball ceased.

Maria opened her eyes.

'Seven,' she cried out joyfully. 'Seven. I told you so.'

'Let's hope your luck holds when you play with the gentlemen,' said Nicole, who secretly hoped Maria's love of gambling would do something to soften her fiery temper.

But she saw the dark eyes spark as Maria snapped: 'That depends if I can keep my winnings, no matter what the stakes are going to be.'

But it was Colette who answered. She just said flatly: 'Us.'

Nicole McGragh pricked up her ears. Behind her smile, her twinges of doubt began to grow.

The study smelt of the leather-bound old books which lined one wall from floor to ceiling. Some of the titles would have made the Vatican librarian frown. The room had more of the air of a progressive headmaster than that of a village priest. But then, Father Marcel Delon did not look much like a village priest.

He was a big man with broad shoulders and large unmarked hands. His hair was thick and black, flecked with silver lines which spread back from his greying temples. The bushy eyebrows set off a commanding face, faintly lined and distinguished. He looked as if he would be more at ease in a business suit than a cassock. He would, however, not have felt it.

For Father Delon could never have sold anything for profit. He would rather have given it away. This trait of unthinking generosity showed best in the way he cared daily for the spiritual, emotional and often material needs of the villagers of Ste-Yvette. It was a duty he carried out with unflagging devotion. No problem, great or small, merited anything except his undivided attention, and he was meticulous in all things. So, when the knocker thudded on his front door, he rose from his worn club chair and went to the door. He smiled at the old caretaker standing on the step, wringing his black beret.

'Albert Boniface,' the priest said warmly, and noticing the way the old man puffed for breath added: 'You look as if Satan himself has chased you here all the way from the château, or maybe it's too many cigarettes.'

'Please, Father, don't preach at me. This is important,' panted Albert.

The priest settled in his chair. 'Well, what is so important that brings you racing to your priest?'

'Whores. Seven of them.'

'Whores? I don't quite follow.'

'In the château. The countess would turn in her grave if she knew. The bloody Germans have put seven whores up there and are going to run it as some kind of brothel for Nazi high-ups.' Albert was beginning to get agitated.

Seeing this, the priest said: 'All right, Albert, calm down. So the Germans have hired the services of these ladies. Distasteful, but there it is. We are both men of the world and unless these ladies are in need of my services as their village priest, I cannot see what it has to do with me.'

Albert's excitement was getting the better of him. The way he kept repeating himself made the priest feel like a simpleton who had missed some obvious point.

He said: 'What, these days, is so dreadful about being a whore? After all, wasn't Mary Magdalen a whore?'

'Who?'

Father Delon tutted.

'Mary Magdalen. She became a saint.'

Albert heaved an audible sigh of relief. At last he had been understood. He said: 'That's what I was trying to explain. Saints are for helping people in need. The French are in need.'

Then suddenly Father Delon understood too. Slowly the lines on his face rearranged themselves into a soft smile.

'The whores of Nazi high-ups.' He began to chuckle. 'It's so obvious,' he said. His shoulders heaved and, as Albert joined in, the chuckles got louder.

For the first time in years, the empty house rang with the laughter of undisguised hope.

CHAPTER FIVE

The French House was correctly called the York Minster, after the Christian abbey, but no one used that name.

It was a pub in Dean Street, Soho, the red light district of London's West End. It became 'French' during the previous German war when a Monsieur Berlemont took it over from one of the Kaiser's subjects who was called Schmidt. During the early days of the Blitz, the late Herr Schmidt's countrymen showed their disapproval at the transaction by dropping a bomb on a nearby church. The blast also blew down one of the pub's inside walls on the ground floor. But all that did was to succeed in giving the French House an undivided bar and a more authentic Parisian atmosphere. That, and the fact it was one of the few places in London with a healthy stock of good wine, was why the Free French forces under Charles De Gaulle used it as their headquarters.

And that was the reason why, when she was working, Miss Debbie Forster used it too. If they had known what her work entailed, some grey-minded men, like friends of her father, the bishop, would have called Debbie Forster a slut. More reasonable men would have said she was a woman with a totally unselfish attitude to duty. But then, very few knew what Debbie Forster's work was.

And that July night in the French House, Debbie was working. She was looking for two things that evening; one was information, the other was a man. A man she had been told to seek out. A man from the past. A man she had once known and had to find again. The information she wanted, she knew, was going to be difficult to obtain. It was the easiest part of her task.

She lifted the fine net veil from her face and rested it on the brim of her hat, then crossed her legs to emphasise the curve of her thighs under the tight skirt of her matching two-piece navy-blue suit. She finished her wine and decided to start with the barman, young Claude. Barmen were always a good bet. They seemed to have a monopoly on gossip, especially in establishments like the French House, frequented by exiles – Free French exiles with contacts in Nazi-occupied France. Barmen are even better bets if they are infatuated with the customer. Debbie Forster thought young Claude was infatuated with her. She smiled at him, held out her glass and mouthed silently: 'Same again.'

Claude, Debbie decided as the barman reached for the wine bottle, had one of the neatest backsides she'd ever seen. One day, when she had nothing better to do, he might make an acceptable piece of fluff on the side.

'And have one yourself,' she said taking the French cigarette he offered. She eased forward on the high stool and allowed him to light it for her. 'What news of Paris? I do so miss the place.'

Normally that would have been Claude's cue to lean his elbows on the bar, rest his chin on his hand, undress her with his eyes, broaden his French accent, assume he was adorable – and talk. He should have begun by revealing who had become whose mistress, before changing to more serious stories of life under Occupation.

That night he didn't.

He just said: 'Nothing much.' If this unaccustomed reticence threw Debbie Forster, she did not show it. She was too good for that.

She said: 'Then you haven't heard?'

'Heard what?'

'About all those whores.'

'Whores?' From his feigned surprise, Debbie knew he had.

'Oh come on now, Claude,' she said. 'Everybody does. Some people are saying that you chaps in the Free French were behind it.'

Claude shrugged. 'Who needs whores?'

Damn him, he knows but he is not going to say anything, thought Debbie. Not yet anyway. Not here. Claude's stature as a bit of fluff on the side was beginning to grow.

She said: 'No. I don't suppose *you* need whores, do you, Claude?' But before Claude could answer, the door to the almost empty bar swung open. The man who came through it immediately relegated the Free French barman's knowledge of whores to a matter of secondary importance as far as Debbie Forster was concerned. At least for the time being.

For the dark-haired man who had just come in, now sitting on a bar stool just three places from where she sat, wearing the insignia of a captain in the British Commando, was him. The one she had been told to seek out. The man from the past she would have to test.

She watched Claude set a glass of Armagnac in front of him

47

and saw him push the coins over the bar without looking up. Debbie got off her stool, picked up the bag she'd had made to carry around her gas-mask and stood behind the commando.

She tapped him on the shoulder and waited as he slowly turned his head.

Debbie studied the face and said softly: 'Hello. It's been a long time.' She watched his dark eyes flash in recognition, and although he smiled, she was aware of the sadness about him. But then she'd been told to expect that.

The commando said: 'Debbie.' He sounded pleasantly surprised. As he swung himself off the stool, Debbie flung her arms around his neck and kissed him. She had begun her test.

Minutes later she was hanging on his arm in mock adoration as they walked through the streets of Soho towards Piccadilly Circus, its statue of Eros protected from air attack by sandbags, and the bus home to a warm bed.

It was when the commando captain and Debbie Forster left the French House, that the little man in the corner who had been watching them closely, stood up, picked up an old brown suitcase and walked towards the bar. On the suitcase, written in black crayon, was 'Archie Smith, Esq. Brush Salesman'.

Archie Smith laid his case against the brass rail running along the bottom of the bar and rested his foot on the rail. He spoke to Claude.

'She, the British, know about the disappearing whores,' Claude replied to his question. 'But how much they know is anybody's guess.'

'It can't be less than us,' said Archie bitterly. 'We are supposed to be British allies and they treat us like shit. Tell us nothing.'

'The bastards have never trusted us,' said Claude.

There was undisguised venom in Archie Smith's voice when he said: 'Trust us with what? France? It is France we are supposed to be fighting over – with them.'

'That's not the way the British and Americans see it. To them we are just a nuisance.'

'Well, this time it is going to be different,' Archie said. 'If the British intelligence service are concerned about a bunch of Parisian whores, then so are we.'

'But why?'

'Dammit. I don't know why. But they are, and that is good enough for me. I know how these English minds work. I know that if they send that Forster woman here to pump us, they don't know as much about it as they would like to.'

'A whore to catch a whore,' Claude sniggered.

'Fool,' thought Archie, his mind turning to the question of why and how the British were concerned about common prostitutes.

He asked Claude: 'Who was that commando officer Debbie Forster picked up?'

'Don't know his name. Speaks fluent French though and comes in a lot.'

Again Archie thought: 'Fool.' He said 'Debbie Forster just does not pick up anyone. Find out.'

Then the little brush salesman picked up his case and walked out into the July night just as an air-raid warning began to wail.

The wave broke, sending hissing tentacles of white foam across the beach. When it retreated reluctantly, it left a motionless figure lying face down in the sand.

A second breaker, much larger than the first, rolled in with the Atlantic tide and the figure was washed further inshore.

Then, as the waters ebbed, he rose cautiously onto one knee and listened. He scanned the beach but the thin crescent of new moon was blotted out by inky clouds, and he could barely distinguish the silhouette of the dark cliffs.

It was perfect. Just as they said it would be.

The lone British commando crouched on the sand, his eyes narrowed and he sniffed at the air, like a predatory cat. Then, sleek and black, he began to thread his way through the maze of twisted metal which ran the length of the shoreline, ready to rip the tracks off invading tanks. That, the commando noted, bore the mark of one man: Rommel.

Once through the maze the man dropped onto his belly, drew his dagger and began to crawl. He held the dagger at arm's length and scraped at the sand's surface, listening for the tell-tale scratch of metal upon metal which would have meant a landmine.

For almost an hour he worked carefully, tirelessly, filling the pouches he carried with sand. Then a voice inside him, without warning, said, danger. He obeyed his instincts and froze. Then, above the surf, he heard a sharp crack, amplified in the solitude by the wind. He tightened the grip on his dagger and moved his head in the direction from which the sound had come.

There he saw the shadowy face of a German sentry illuminated by the flickering orange flame of the match he cupped in his hands. The soldier's rifle was slung across his back.

I can kill him before he can unsling it, never mind pull the trigger, thought the commando. But hoped it wouldn't come to that. It was vital that he return undetected with the sand samples. The Nazis, it had been explained, must never know of the Allies' interest in this beach in Normandy. Never.

A sudden gust of wind parted the clouds blacking out the moon. Just for a fleeting moment the commando saw a bony finger of pale moonlight eerily light the beach. Without moving his head, his eyes followed the dim spotlight over the sand. The German was alone.

To his left, he heard the sentry cough and the commando turned to face him. He watched the glow from the tip of the German's cigarette bob up and down as the man set off aimlessly on his patrol.

He knew that meant just one thing. The beach was not mined.

Then the man turned suddenly. He tried to unsling his rifle. 'He saw me,' thought the commando. He flicked his dagger from his left to right hand. His killing hand. Then pressing the balls of his feet into the sand, launched himself at his victim. He threw himself so his left shoulder crashed into the German's back, then locked his left arm around the man's throat, hurling him face down into the sand. With his right arm he raised the dagger and aimed for the vulnerable mastoid bone behind the ear. There was always less blood if you knifed a man there – that tiny soft spot of flesh between the top of the lower jaw and the lobe of the ear. The dagger – not too wide – found its mark. With a mouthful of sand to choke back any scream, the young man died without uttering a sound.

The commando left the dagger jutting from the back of the dead man's head and moved back into the night.

Digging with both hands now, he moved freely over the sand, knowing the beach was not mined, and carefully filled the rest of his pouches.

When he had completed his task, he took some fishing line from his pocket. This he twined around the limp German, making it fast in a clove hitch around his neck. He pulled it tight and then emptied the man's pockets. Wallet, papers, letters, cigarettes – the lot. He put the contents into a waterproof bag and placed it in his right breast pocket.

Then he waded into the sea, towing the body behind him, and hauled himself back to the waiting sub.

He hammered on the steel hull. The hatch opened and a bearded naval officer, revolver in hand, emerged.

The commando pulled the dagger from the man's head. The blood flowing from the wound dissolved in the lapping waves.

'Pull him on board,' said the commando and climbed onto the deck. There both men stripped the soldier naked and tossed his clothes down the open hatch. Then the commando captain tied the length of line still around the German's neck to the submarine's safety rail and followed the sailor below deck.

Minutes later the submarine dived below the black waves. Towing the German behind her, she headed for the open ocean leaving a trail of underwater bubbles.

The submarine surfaced off the western approaches to the Isle of Wight. The commando opened the hatch and climbed onto the deck. There he took out his dagger and cut the line from the safety rail. He stood, expressionless, as he watched the unnamed body, white and bloated now, drift slowly towards the vast Atlantic on the ebbing Solent tide. As the commando looked down on the dead man's pale features, he felt a pang of remorse at such a waste of young life.

Then he felt the dawn wind whistle through his hair and he shivered. He turned and climbed back below decks.

Space below decks consisted of one long narrow passage, not wide enough for men to pass each other. The commando squeezed past the hatch ladder and made his way to the stern. There the sentry's possessions lay piled on a table which folded down from the wall.

The commando picked up the dead man's tunic. He stared at the winged swastika sewn onto the heavy serge. He shivered again, but the remorse he'd felt minutes before had left him. Driven out by the bent cross. Hitler's cross. The sight of it expelled any compassion he'd felt for the man he'd killed. For him there could be no hapless innocents in this war, his war, against Fascism and all it stood for. There were no blue-eyed Prussian farm boys fighting for the folks at home and not giving a toss for the politics of why. Not this war, this crusade. For that, in the end, was how he saw it. A crusade against evil. He had seen men in another war fight it. Another war and another place; but the enemy was the same. He had no truck for men, boys, who put their patriotic duty above right. Above justice. Those men he'd seen die in the other war, had done so for a cause, not for a geographical tribe called a country. Not like the man he'd just killed. If men like him wore Hitler's uniform, they, to him, were Hitler's children. The spawn of his madness. He would kill them. That was the price of justice.

He picked up the waterproof bag and emptied the contents on to the table and sifted through them.

An unfinished letter to a Fräulein Rosen in Würzburg complained the army planned to move the dead sentry again. Security, he'd written, forbade him to disclose where. The travel warrant told the commando it was from his base at Bayeux, Normandy, to St-Omer. That was fifty kilometres from the port of Calais. That fact would go in the report the commando captain was about to write on his solo excursion into Normandy.

He knew this snippet of information, along with all the dead man's possessions, would be passed on to intelligence officers in Whitehall. Yet he was aware that all this was just a bonus. The commando captain had been told the sand samples, so carefully collected, were what mattered most. The samples had been requested by General Omar Bradley, Commander of the US First Army. The general feared the sand had a high clay content, which might bog down tanks.

But now, standing on the Portsmouth dockyard, all Captain Nat Morgan, formerly a reporter with the *Daily Express*, was concerned about was to get on and file his report on the night's work. Then he was due for weekend leave. Leave to be spent with a girl called Debbie Forster.

The sonorous tick of the wall clock hanging above the unlit gas fire emphasised the boredom of Morgan's wait. He stood, hands buried deep in his pockets, facing the window and watched the death throes of the English summer.

The swirling drizzle, which had begun as the submarine berthed, now swept across Portsmouth dockyard and spread in spiderweb patterns on the glass. Their shapes changed with every gust of September wind driven inland from the grey sea beyond.

Morgan looked at his watch for the third time in five minutes and again checked with the clock on the wall. He hated being kept waiting. Two and a half hours. What in hell were they doing in the office along the corridor? Morgan tried to imagine how anyone could take so long to list the items he'd brought back from Normandy on a single receipt form, countersign his report and produce the pass he needed to get through the dockyard gates to get back to London and his leave with Debbie.

He looked at his watch, then took the last cigarette from the packet of Capstan Full Strength and lit it, dropping the match in the overflowing saucer he was using as an ashtray.

'Why does it always have to rain when I'm due for leave?' he mumbled to himself.

Then his thoughts turned to Debbie.

The office down the corridor was a featureless room, devoid of any furniture except a trestle table. The floorboards were bare, but swept, and two folding wooden chairs were placed each end of the table which stood in front of an empty fireplace. Two men faced each other across the table.

The taller took a box of Swan Vestas from his pocket and struck a match which he allowed to burn brightly before puffing thoughtfully on his briar pipe. This man was over six feet tall, erect and in his mid-forties. His hair, swept straight back from a low forehead, was greying. The moustache, also greying, was thick but cut close to the lip. The insignia on his uniform denoted he bore the rank of colonel in British military intelligence.

The other man was a civilian, overweight and bald, except for a sandy fringe which ran from ear to ear around the back of his head. He wore a heavy tweed suit and brown brogues, the kind favoured by country squires. His stubby little fingers leafed through the untidily written pages of Morgan's report.

'He's thorough,' said the civilian, 'I'll give him that. I like his observation on the anti-tank obstacles having the mark of Rommel. Damn thorough.'

'So he should be,' said the colonel coldly.

Godsell, the smaller man, ran his hand over his face and glanced up at the soldier. 'My dear Cameron,' he said softly with all the guile of an accomplished Whitehall predator, 'I'm afraid time is no longer on our side. I am convinced this is our man and I want him.'

'Really,' said Cameron flatly, re-lighting his pipe. His tone echoed the disdain he felt for civilians. He moved over to the table and took a thin folder from his attaché case. It bore a 'Top Secret' seal under its typed title 'Château Beaupré'.

He held out the folder towards Godsell. 'You civilians never cease to amaze me,' said Cameron contemptuously. 'You bury your heads in the sand when it comes to things that really matter, yet when something like this sordid little affair drops among your tea cups, you react as if the outcome of the war depended upon it.

Godsell fixed him with a stare and said: 'You never know. It just might.'

Cameron snorted. 'As far as I'm concerned the whole set-up merely consists of a few French sluts prepared to open their legs for a bunch of sex-starved Huns.'

Godsell knew it would be a waste of time arguing with Cameron. He, Godsell, had the authority and he was going to use it.

He said: 'The matter is not open to debate. Allied intelligence can not afford simply to ignore it. I want a man assigned to work full time on this château business – and the man our people want for the job, Colonel, is this Captain Morgan. I hope I'm making myself clear.'

'I wish it to go on record here and now that I'm opposed to any of my units at the Special Operations Executive wasting their time on such an assignment. This Morgan fellow is just not the kind of man I want on my staff, Mr. Godsell. From what I've heard, his record leaves everything to be desired.'

Godsell was beginning to lose his patience. 'My people never make mistakes. We have watched his every move for the last couple of months. We know whom he drinks with, how he thinks, who his friends are. In some ways I feel as if I know him better than I know my own son. There is no doubt he is the man we are after. He is the one.'

'You people are always so damn sure of yourselves,' snapped the colonel. 'Next you will be telling me whom the man sleeps with.'

Godsell smiled. 'Certainly, we arranged it. Nothing has been left to chance. Nothing at all.'

Cameron did not have to dig deep into the wells of his military experience, to realise he had been outmanoeuvred. By a bloody civilian. An amateur. It was obvious to him that someone up the line had, in a moment of madness, agreed with this wretched civil servant that the Château Beaupré was important. He disagreed, but as a true professional he would follow orders which he would, of course, interpret in the best interests of his section at SOE. But being saddled with this man Morgan. That was another matter.

'Now look here,' said the colonel. 'I'll be frank with you. In my opinion, the man is just not officer material at all. If it was not for this war, I doubt if he would have made lance-corporal

54

in the pay corps. He never went to a proper school as such; his father was a wretched coal miner and a pinko agitator in some union or other, and as far as I can see Morgan seems to be a chip off the old block. Everything he does seems to assume the proportions of a crusade against some imagined injustice or other. Why the man's a bloody idealist – and in my section there is no room for a half-educated idealist. I want trained men who will obey orders – to the letter.'

'Half-educated?' said Godsell. 'He speaks fluent French, German and Spanish. His Italian is more than passable. These linguistic talents and his insight made him one of the most respected journalists in Fleet Street. The man we want is just the kind of man who will not follow orders to the letter but someone who can think for himself, no matter how unpopular that little defect makes him with your old school chums.'

Cameron turned pink. He asked, almost in desperation, 'Do you know what the damn fellow does in his spare time?'

Godsell shrugged his shoulders.

'Writes poetry. He scribbles bloody verse.'

'So did Alexander the Great,' grinned Godsell.

CHAPTER SIX

Nicole McGragh, tormented by her secret, stood alone in front of the full-length mirror. It was a secret she could now no longer ignore, not here among the whores of the Château Beaupré as the gentle murmurs from the room directly above painfully reminded her.

Nicole tried to shut out these sounds as, moving mechanically, she unfastened the shoulder straps of her red slip and let it fall to the floor. Then, she unpinned her hair, shaking her head until the copper tresses tumbled free, and stepped out of her pants. There was a detached expertise about the way she undressed herself, which bore witness that it was a practice she was used to carrying out unaided. Alone; but then, it had always been like that.

She brushed her clothes aside with her foot and stood sideways-on in front of the mirror, its glass pivoted at an angle in its wooden frame. Nicole breathed in deeply until her breasts swelled as she pressed both hands flat across her drawn-in stomach. She moved her hands and smoothed her thighs. They were as firm now as they had been when she'd made her Paris debut at the age of seventeen.

The memory of that time still hurt deeply, for that was when she had come face to face with her secret. Now that hurt was made more acute by the sounds seeping cruelly through the ceiling. Those sounds were no longer gentle murmurs, they were rising and falling gasps of increasing urgency. They were taunting sounds from the lips of La Croix.

Nicole swung around. She glanced up at the ceiling in anguish but quickly lowered her eyes. Then, almost guiltily, she looked back over her shoulder at the rear-view image mirrored in the tilted glass. Reluctantly her hands were drawn from her thighs until they rested on her buttocks. It was of little satisfaction for Nicole to be reminded that she possessed the ripe, mellow body of a mature woman at the zenith of her sexuality. For she knew it was a sexuality which would never be fulfilled.

Nicole put her hands to her ears as she heard Clair cry out in pleasure. Then she flung herself onto her vast and empty bed.

Her eyes grew moist with a mixture of rage and resentment, and she called out the name that she still hated.

'La Croix.'

From the loneliness of her bed, she cursed its very sound and . the girl who now bore it.

'You could have been mine,' she said resentfully as, once more, she looked towards the ceiling and the sounds of an uninhibited symphony of sex.

'Mine, you little slut,' Nicole repeated, almost shouting. 'You should have been mine.'

Then as she heard Clair climax, Nicole felt herself become rigid as her limbs locked in terror. She was frozen by the fear which had haunted her since she was seventeen. That was when her world had fallen apart, the night she had become what she now was to those who adored her from afar. The unobtainable fantasy. If only she had been able to love with the abandon with which she danced. Yet it was not to be.

And because of that, she'd lost the first and only man she'd ever loved. He had been the stranger responsible for the bouquets which had arrived nightly, to the envy of the other girls in the chorus. The man who had taken her in his chauffeur-driven Facel Vega to wine her and dine her at Maxime's. The man who mocked her fear and left her alone and weeping because of it.

Nicole McGragh would never forget the bitterness of that night. The scene was still vivid in her mind. Nicole remembered how warm she'd felt after dinner, cosy in front of an open fire, her thoughts flowing pleasantly after the heady wine. At first it had seemed so gentle, his tongue on hers. The comforting strength in the way he held and stroked her. His words were as soothing as his caresses, just, she was sure, like the father she'd never known would have been; strong, kind and safe.

But then he'd touched her. There.

That was when she'd first felt the fear, the same one that now held her like ice.

Just as it had when his fingers rubbed at her through the silk garment he'd paid for. Then they were inside her, his fingers inside her body, twin intruders, prising her apart, stabbing her there. They had no right, not there, and she felt they were infesting her. Why was he doing this to her, this man she worshipped? Doing these things, like an animal?

Then it came. That thing instead of his fingers. That shaft slicing in and out of her. Pounding inside her. Inside there, soiling her.

Now, twenty-six years later, she could still feel him spend himself inside her.

She could also feel the sting on her cheek when she'd told him: 'I feel as though you have desecrated me.'

But it was the way he'd laughed at her that hurt more than the slap. The way he'd laughed, and said, 'You stupid little bitch. You're frigid, as much use as a bloody iceberg.'

Nicole McGragh had never seen Guy La Croix again.

She'd heard he'd married though. Guy La Croix had, within six months of walking out on Nicole, taken a wife. It was their daughter who had just finished making love to Major Rudi Helm in the room above Nicole's head.

Clair La Croix had gone to the top of the list which Nicole McGragh had prepared for Ulrich, simply because she was the daughter of the only man who'd learned Nicole's secret.

The following day, breakfast in the château was taken as usual. That meant it would last most of the morning. As always, the first sign of life was old Albert Boniface. His coughing and cursing would echo through the vast building as he began his daily tasks.

First, he would remove all traces of the previous night's activity from the salon, pausing only to ponder the weird wonders of the Aziz paintings. Albert would clean, dust, collect the glasses and stack the coloured chips neatly on the roulette table before drawing the drapes to open the windows.

Then he would wander into the gardens to complete the task that really irked him.

Cut flowers.

Madame McGragh insisted on fresh flowers daily. So, grateful he was unobserved, Albert would set out vases throughout the ground floor. He always left the dining room until last. There he would arrange the blooms along the baronial table, and help himself to coffee laced with finest brandy and have a smoke.

Then at eight-thirty, he'd amble into the vast entrance hall and pound the brass gong at the foot of the stairs which announced breakfast was ready. Heated dishes set out on the sideboard behind the dining table contained sautéed kidneys, sausages and a variety of smoked fish and eggs. The imported Spanish orange juice was mixed with champagne to make Bucks Fizz.

At intervals, the girls, on the arms of the officers with whom they'd spent the night, would graciously descend the winding stairs and make their appearance.

That morning Colonel Ulrich sat at the head of the table with Colette Claval at his side, watching carefully with unsmiling eyes as each couple made their entrance.

He saw Major-General Durring settle his ample frame into a chair halfway along the table. The Italian girl, Maria, sat next to him, feeding the general scrambled eggs from the tip of her fork and laughingly picking off the bits that fell onto his tunic with her fingers.

Ulrich's fingers opened and shut in a half-wave in Durring's direction and he returned the general's grin with a knowing wink.

He said to Colette, 'It's the happiest I've seen him looking for months.' The the tone of his voice changed, hardened, as he added, 'Which is more than I can say for you, child.' The word 'child' was emphasised.

He sensed the girl's reaction to his change in tone was one of sullen resentment. Soon, he decided, she would have to be taught a lesson. He could not afford to allow any dissent to affect the plan he'd so carefully laid for the officers and their whores at the Château Beaupré. They were far too important for that.

He looked down the table towards Eva Nielson. She wore a crimson velvet hacking jacket and a cream blouse tied with a lace scarf at her neck. She sat between two officers. It was the men who caught Ulrich's attention. Colonel Hans Hoffner, also dressed for riding, was a well-known devotee of Rommel's and always held to be a devoted family man with a wife from one of Germany's most influential families. The other officer was a Major Gerd Muller. He wondered how those smug aristocratic wives and families would react if they learned their noble menfolk shared a bed together with a blonde Danish whore.

He smiled at the thought.

That smile vanished the moment he saw Helm come through the door. The major's face looked concerned.

He watched as the major made straight to where Hoffner sat alongside Eva and said something in the colonel's ear. He saw that the colonel raised his eyebrows.

Questioningly Ulrich also raised his eyebrows as Helm walked towards him.

'What is it?' asked Ulrich.

'One of our soldiers has vanished during the night. One of Hoffner's men.'

'Vanished?'

'From the beach near Port-en-Bessin and Vierville.'

No one noticed Archie Smith board the London train at Portsmouth Harbour later that same day, clutching his battered brown suitcase. But then, no one ever seemed to notice Archie Smith, which was why his superiors regarded him as invaluable. He was so insignificant as to be almost perfect.

Very occasionally someone, usually a lonely old lady, would feel sorry for the seedy little fellow with the thin moustache and try to engage him in conversation. But Archie always had the answer to this unwarranted intrusion on his anonymity. He would open his suitcase to reveal his 'extensive range of brushes for every occasion'. He could talk endlessly and lovingly about his brushes which, it appeared, were his greatest friends on earth. They, he said, would never let you down. You could always trust his brushes.

Archie, it seemed, knew more about brushes than any man in England, which was odd considering he was not English. His case contained toothbrushes, shaving brushes, hairbrushes and heavy wire bristle broom heads guaranteed to banish dirt at a stroke. Pride of place in his collection went to a splendid cream and red lavatory brush. This was the showstopper. When Archie produced this sanitary masterpiece even lonely old ladies shrunk away behind the safety of their lace handkerchiefs and blushed silently.

During his years in England, Archie had learnt well. There were two kinds of people the English shied away from making contact with. One was the politician and the other the travelling brush salesman. That was one reason he sold brushes. The other was that it enabled him to travel widely through southern England without arousing too much suspicion. Archie Smith was also a very observant man, which was more than could be said for the station staff on duty that September day. When asked, none of them remembered the drab little man waiting for the London train, even though he made no attempt to catch any that left during the morning or early afternoon. Archie, on the other hand, was much more alert. He spotted Morgan the moment he walked onto the platform.

When Morgan's train left, no one noticed that Archie Smith had gone too.

Morgan was the sole occupant of the first class compartment which his rail warrant allowed him to use. He sat slumped in the corner seat next to the window, his feet resting on the seat opposite.

He watched the grey suburbs of Portsmouth slip by, as the train threaded its way through the scarred rubble of homes and factories reduced to ruins by wave after wave of air attacks from Hitler's air force. He noticed that, in places, weeds and flowers spread in green tentacles over the smashed masonry as if trying to draw it back to the soil.

Then, the outskirts of the town began to yield to the rural Hampshire landscape with its thatched cottages and neat haystacks. As the train rolled towards the New Forest, leaving a ribbon of smoke behind it, Morgan watched the barrage balloons over distant Portsmouth shrink to pin-pricks, then finally merge into the sombre clouds.

He lit a Capstan, inhaled deeply, and glanced up at the two photographs set into the compartment wall each side of the vanity mirror engraved with the motif of the Southern Railway Company. The first showed groups of bowler-hatted men with flourishing handlebar moustaches and watch chains, strolling with ladies in soft hats and long coats on a long pier which the photo caption boasted was Southend.

But it was the second picture which captured Morgan's attention. He did not need to read the caption. He knew the familiar curve of the promenade built on the granite sea-wall erected to defy the pounding of giant green-blue waves from the Irish Sea. In the background, he could see the funicular which climbed steeply to the top of Constitution Hill. As a child he used to stand on top of that hill and turn his back on the smug sea-front villas of Aberystwyth to gaze inland towards the wild Welsh mountains of his birth.

He was born in 1913, the first of his proud parents' five sons, in a remote cottage owned by the estate where his father worked as a stonemason. Until he was five years old, he neither heard nor spoken a word of English. Welsh was the language of this world whose inhabitants had resisted the imposition of the English tongue for eight hundred years of conquest. Morgan inherited this will of iron and a refusal to submit no matter how great the odds. He was from a race of mountain people endowed with the characteristics of formidable crags. Morgan was never to change.

His father christened him Rhodri, after a Welsh prince and poet, and his mother called him after the bible's Nathaniel, which is Hebrew for God's given. Morgan was a year old when his father left to fight in the trenches of France. When he returned five years later, his head was filled with stories of the riches to be earned in the booming pits of the South Wales valleys.

Three months later, the family joined his father in a terraced cottage in an Aberdare valley mining village. In this thriving Celtic Klondike, Morgan learnt his English at school sitting alongside the children of the immigrant Irish, Italians, Poles, Cornishmen, and English. But the language of the home was still Welsh and fireside evenings were spent reading the works of the old bards.

At the age of ten, his teachers marked him out as an exceptional pupil, and he became a familiar figure in the miners' library at the workmen's hall.

Then the slump silenced the pits and iron furnaces, and the mine owners slashed the colliers' wages. At fourteen, despite the pleas of his headmaster, the young Morgan left school and followed his father to assume the mantle of a human mole. It was underground that Morgan first met injustice face to face. They were to remain deadly adversaries for all time.

Then, one damp November evening, as he sat in a tin bath in front of the scullery fire washing off the dust and grime, there was a knock on the front door.

Emrys Puw, his former headmaster, thrust the folded newspaper in front of his face. Morgan rubbed the soap from his eyes and read the advertisement: 'Wanted. Junior Reporter. Good English essential. The Editor. *Aberdare Leader*.'

Three years later, Morgan stepped down from the Cardiff train at Paddington. In his pocket he carried a photograph of Bethan, the girl he was to marry, and a letter of introduction. It was from George Hall, the Labour MP for Aberdare, to the editor of the radical newspaper, *The Daily Herald*.

The *Herald*, the scourge of the establishment, and Morgan were well suited. His rise from general news reporter to specialist feature writer was rapid, and his articles soon earned him the respect of his professional rivals. It was during this time he became known as Nat. It was thought that Rhodri Morgan was too alien a by-line for readers to identify with. Nathaniel Morgan would take up too much space. Nat Morgan was created. He hated it, thinking it made him sound like a vindictive hornet, but it stuck.

Now, as the drab, smoke-blackened houses of South London flashed past the carriage window, Morgan's thoughts turned from the picture on the compartment wall to what his weekend leave held in store.

Debbie Forster. By some strange coincidence he had bumped into her when he was going through one of the black depressions that still engulfed him – even though Bethan's death had been almost five years ago. They all said time was a great healer. They all lied.

There had, of course, been other women since Bethan had died. But they were as meaningless as the creases they left on his sheets. Debbie was different. Morgan had begun to rebuild himself emotionally around the elegant brunette with whom he shared his bed and whose body soothed his sadness. In bed she performed with the abandon of an uninhibited wildcat, but it was the times afterwards that mattered most to Morgan: the times when they just lay in the darkness, her soothing fingers like tendrils on his chest as they talked. Debbie Forster was a very good listener.

As Morgan got down from the train at Waterloo Station, it was the first time in months that he had not thought of Bethan or the way she'd died, wasted from TB, in a sanatorium in the Brecon Beacons.

The obscure little salesman took his place in the queue a short distance behind Morgan, but close enough for him to hear the commando ask for a single ticket to Piccadilly Circus.

Thirty-five minutes later the little man climbed down the narrow stone steps leading to a small one-bedroomed basement flat in Goldhurst Terrace in West Hampstead. The name above the doorbell read: R. N. Morgan.

Archie Smith used a key to let himself in.

Morgan pushed open the door into the French House's single bar. It was half-empty.

Claude, the barman, was alone behind the marble-topped bar serving two girls sitting on the high stools. Both girls, Morgan noticed, were heavily made-up and eyed him as if he were the American fleet. Their smiles, like their clothes which they wore like a badge, were professional.

Morgan nodded back but made his intentions clear by walking to the opposite end of the bar.

Claude came over, drink in hand, and placed the brandy in front of Morgan.

'On the house, for a friend of Miss Forster,' he said.

Morgan said simply, 'Thanks.'

He did not like Claude. The Frenchman had an insatiable curiosity. As a former journalist, Morgan found that understandable; it was the nature of that curiosity that Morgan did not like. For a man who was obviously not a queer, the barman's questions were always a little too personal for Morgan's liking.

'Alas, no, m'sieu, I have not seen her tonight,' he replied to Morgan's question in a way the commando captain found ingratiating. 'Were you supposed to meet her here?'

'There he bloody well goes again,' thought Morgan but he said nothing.

It was none of the man's business, but then, neither was where Morgan lived, he thought. Morgan looked at his watch. Debbie was twenty minutes late.

Morgan finished his brandy. He must have cocked up the arrangements for meeting Debbie. He knew if she was not in the French House, she would be waiting for him at home, so he decided to leave.

As the door swung shut behind him, Claude, the barman, lifted the receiver from the phone on the shelf behind the bar.

The number he dialled was Morgan's.

It was the unmistakable smell of musk perfume Morgan noticed first. Debbie always wore it for very special occasions. He smiled in anticipation as he kicked the front door of his flat closed behind him, then dropped his holdall in the narrow passage and called out her name.

'Debbie.'

There was no reply. He called out again.

Morgan pushed open the lounge door but the half-spoken name stuck in his throat. His eyes widened as they saw the room was a shambles.

The contents of his desk and cupboards were strewn among the upturned furniture and books which had been swept from the shelves at the far end of the room.

'Debbie,' he yelled as he burst into the bedroom.

Then he saw her.

She was lying open-eyed on their bed and fully clothed.

Before he could control himself, Nat Morgan was sick.

CHAPTER SEVEN

Ulrich and Helm faced each other across the table, both men's faces burning with rage.

'It's obvious why the man vanished,' bellowed Helm.

'Rubbish,' shouted Ulrich, his eyes swollen. 'And when the man is caught, I will see to it he is shot out of hand like the treacherous little bastard he is. All his unit will learn first-hand what every deserter can expect.'

'That boy was not a deserter,' said Helm bringing his temper back under control. 'I believe, I know, he was abducted.'

'Major,' said Ulrich contemptuously. 'The man absconded.'

'He had no reason to do so,' said Helm quietly. 'No reason at all.' Helm's voice rang with conviction. He had spent the day talking to the soldier's officers and comrades at their base near Bayeux. It was early evening now and Helm was making his report to Ulrich.

The major waited as Ulrich pushed back his chair from behind the table and stood up. Helm wondered if the man had any other clothes than that pin-stripe suit and wide-brimmed trilby. Helm noticed the way Ulrich clasped his hands behind his back, tapping his fist against his open palm. How he despised the man and his whole kind: men who, by their total fanaticism, would destroy the land of his birth. To Helm, it was the land of Beethoven, not Belsen, and the talk of final solutions made him sick.

Helm tensed as Ulrich looked at him over his shoulder. Normally Helm would have felt pity for a man whose face bore the scars of battle as Ulrich's did. But in this case he did not. The major noted his superior used theatrical make-up to cover the blemish on his face. He also guessed that was why the colonel always wore the hat pulled down over his face and not regulation Abwehr uniform.

'What makes you so sure that this wretch did not desert his post?' Ulrich asked.

'Because,' said Helm, 'the boy was due for leave in two weeks. Before his posting to Calais. He was going home to be married.'

Ulrich snorted.

Helm ignored it. 'As far as I can see there can only be one explanation. He was abducted,' Helm said.

'By the Resistance, I suppose? Whenever that bunch of terrorists try to stage anything like that, they always make a great song and dance about it. But this time there hasn't been so much as a peep from the anarchist bastards.'

'I did not mean the Resistance.'

'Then who?'

'The Allies.'

'The Allies?' Ulrich's cackle almost choked him.

It was then Helm knew that the rift between them was unbridgeable.

'The Allies must know that we have fortified the beaches from their own intelligence reports and spotter planes. It would make sense for them to take a closer look at the beaches, especially if that is where they plan to land their invasion forces. That poor bloody sentry must have stumbled across a reconnaissance party.'

Ulrich said nothing, but Helm was aware of the man's eyes boring into him.

'Tell me, Major, why is it that you and your kind are so hell-bent on convincing anyone who matters in this Reich that Normandy, not Calais, is the invasion target?'

Helm was aware of a sinister sense of power radiating from Ulrich. The fanatic. He felt suddenly afraid. Not only for himself, but for Germany.

'I request that my fears about an Allied raiding party be included in the report on this matter to be sent to Admiral Canaris,' Helm said.

Ulrich turned. 'Your request is formally denied. I decide what Canaris does or does not see.'

Words failed Helm. He turned on his heel and stormed from the tiny office, slamming the door behind him.

Ulrich nodded knowingly.

'That's right,' he whispered to the walls. 'Run and bleed your heart out to that high-born whore. I can't wait to hear what you've got to tell her.'

When Helm arrived at the Château Beaupré, he looked like he felt. Exhausted. And worried.

He could see by Clair's face she'd noticed. She was wearing her kimono-style dressing gown with the dragon motif on the back, and sat cross-legged on the bedroom sofa, her knees drawn up under her chin. As Helm locked the door behind him, he turned and saw her uncoil her legs before rising and crossing the room towards him.

As she put her arms around his neck, Helm gave her a fond peck on the cheek. He felt just like a husband, glad to be home again after another hard and trying day at the office.

'Can I get you anything, a drink?' Clair reached up on her toes and loosened his tie, and he was aware of her long fingers affectionately fussing over the shoulders of his tunic, brushing away invisible dust.

Helm smiled his first smile of the day and patted her gently on the backside. 'I'd love a stiff brandy and soda.'

He sat on the edge of the bed and stretched forward wearily to remove his dusty jackboots. As he tugged on the boot, he felt Clair helping him. Helm looked up as she placed the two drinks on the bedside table. He leant back on his elbows as she sank to her knees and with mock grunts and groans, pulled off each heavy boot in turn and flung them carelessly aside.

The tension of the day began to leave him. He ran his hand through the long blonde hair spilling over his knee and thought that he at least could thank Ulrich for her.

She looked up and smiled at him. It was, he thought, as if Clair could read his mind and had understood what had gone on inside his head. She was always doing things like that. Once when he'd wanted a bath, she'd got up and run it for him without being asked. He had not said a word. But then lovers could do things like that and after just two months that was what they had become. Lovers.

She was the most beautiful creature he had ever set eyes upon. But it was more, much more, than that. They were so easy in each other's company that he'd felt as if he'd known her for years. It was the little things she did: the way she pronounced certain words in that husky voice that always made him smile; the way she always sat cross-legged on chairs. These things became momentous events for Helm to treasure. She was the sole inhabitant of a private, warm world where he could retreat from the daily reality of the shambles that was Normandy.

Maybe, he thought, these private worlds Ulrich had created are part of the problem; an anaesthetic to divert me, all of us, from the real problem facing the Wehrmacht. The defence of Normandy.

Helm ran his finger over her lips. Then he began to explain, recalling the state of affairs he'd found when he first had come to Normandy – the way the whole officer corps had been split into factions, the way some had questioned how the war was being waged.

He continued, 'Because I distrust everything Ulrich stands for, I had reservations about his plans for the Château Beaupré. But, in the end, I backed it because I felt it would help to improve morale and inspire the Normandy command to face the dangers that await us.'

He felt Clair squeeze his knee. Helm smiled, but the fondness in his expression was diluted by doubt. He said: 'I really believed it would improve morale. Now I'm not so sure anymore.'

'Why, my love?' asked Clair. 'Men like Durring and Hoffner seem to be having the time of their lives here. And just look at the way Captain von Beck chases after young Elaine.'

'Maybe that's the whole problem,' said Helm. 'We have all become too content. This place has taken our minds away from the issues. Nothing has really changed if the men I spoke to today are anything to go by.'

'I don't understand.'

'One of their comrades vanishes while on patrol, probably taken by the Allies, and Ulrich accuses them of all being potential deserters. Moreover, Ulrich has seen to it that only token gestures have been made to Rommel's plans to throw back an invasion force, while the beaches on this coast are not even mined.'

He placed his hands on Clair's shoulders and added: 'I fear not only for the future of Germany, but for us. Our tomorrow will vanish the moment the British and Americans gain a beachhead on French soil. We will all be finished.'

'What can you do?' she asked.

'I must try to talk to the old admiral.'

'An Admiral. I thought admirals were for sailors, not soldiers.'

Helm smiled.

'That's better,' said Clair.

'Idiot,' Helm said laughingly. 'Admiral Canaris is in charge of the Abwehr. The man who runs Germany's intelligence service. I have known him since a child. He's a man I respect and trust. A man who loves Germany as much as I do.'

'He can't be so great if he employs a pig like Ulrich,' said Clair. Her words made Helm run cold.

'So when will you talk to him?' Clair said, interrupting his thoughts.

'As soon as I have had a chance to talk to Hoffner and the others. They care about Germany too.'

Clair lit a cheroot and paused to pick a strand of tobacco from her lip before blowing a smoke ring in Helm's direction. 'If they care that much, then why don't they shoot Hitler or something?'

It had been asked with schoolgirl innocence, but the colour drained from Helm's face. 'That is the problem,' he blurted out before he could stop himself. 'I think they might try just that.'

'Oh,' shrugged Clair. 'I'm sure your great man, Admiral whatsisname, will know what to do.'

Helm's mouth opened, but his words were stopped by Clair's lips. They closed on his as she pushed him back onto the bed.

Helm kissed her on the nose and brushed back the curtain of blonde hair which had fallen over her face.

'How,' she asked, 'would you like a massage? It'll make you feel so much better.'

But before Helm could reply, he heard one scream first, rising above the sudden shouting. Then came the sound of breaking glass, and another scream, a different, familiar, threatening voice. It was a sound that made Clair leap to her feet, drawing the kimono around her. It sounded just like the night when she had been taken by Ulrich from the apartment at the rue de l'Eglise.

'You bastards,' the voice screamed in rage.

'Colette, Colette,' yelled Clair, running headlong down the corridor towards the sound of the screams that drew her like a drug.

Helm despondently kicked the door shut behind her. The closed door also shut out the sound of the screaming from the miniature microphone, the one that had been so carefully concealed behind the headboard of the bed, and whose single wire led to the old wine cellar in the château basement.

'You will all be taken from here to Gestapo headquarters in Caen and shot. All seven of you. There will be no exceptions.

'But I think you should all know that, before they kill you, your executioners will be at liberty to do with you as they will. I am sure by the time they have finished, you will all welcome death. You will greet the firing squad like a long-lost friend.'

Ulrich spoke calmly. He paused only to scrutinise the seven girls. They were lined up before him in the wood-panelled hall of the château. All stood in silence, their hands clasped on top of their bowed heads, eyes lowered towards the black and white tiles of the bare floor.

'So,' Ulrich continued, 'if there is any repetition of today's behaviour, then you will all suffer the consequences. If you choose to co-operate, then you can all pursue your roles here in the best traditions of the courtesans of the royal courts of France.'

As his voice trailed away, one of the girls began to weep. It was Elaine. Then two of the other girls lowered their hands from their heads, defying the order to get back in line, and moved towards Elaine. Colette Claval took one of her arms, Maria the other.

It was this trio who had earlier run amok, smashing everything they could lay their hands upon in a gesture of revolt. Nicole McGragh's fears about her problems had materialised in a trail of broken vases and windows.

They had then fled to the kitchens and kept the guards at bay with a non-stop hail of copper pots and pans. When they'd exhausted those, they'd used a garden hose.

'It seems warnings are wasted on you three.' Ulrich fixed them with his stare. 'You will remain here. The rest of you, return to your rooms until you are sent for.'

He watched the others turn and walk silently towards the grand staircase which led to the minstrels' gallery on the first floor. Then he saw Nicole McGragh standing in the shadows, watching, one hand on her hip as she drew deeply on the cigarette holder in her other hand.

Ulrich's hand reached inside his double-breasted coat. When he withdrew it, he held a Mauser. This he held out in front of him and walked towards the three remaining girls.

Elaine was still sobbing. Ulrich stood in front of her and placed the stub of the gun under her chin. He heard her wince as she felt the cold metal against the taut skin of her underjaw. Ulrich followed her eyes towards the high ceiling, and saw the painted, wild satyrs astride the snorting stallions pursue the fleeing nymphs above his head.

He said coldly, 'Do you ever want to see your baby again?'

Elaine nodded.

Ulrich sensed he'd won. Elaine would now do anything he asked of her, allow her body to be used in any way required of her, if it meant she would one day be reunited with her son, the last living link with her dead husband.

Ulrich took the gun from her throat and Elaine ran for the

stairs. As she went, Ulrich turned and faced Colette and Maria. He held out the gun, waving it in front of their faces. Then, in turn, he pointed it at each girl, allowing the weapon to linger menacingly before their eyes. He lowered the gun, spun round and noticed Helm had appeared. The major was standing at the far end of the hall.

Ulrich strutted across the vast hall, the sound of his leather heels echoing on the polished floor. He stopped outside the salon door, and glared at Helm, waiting for him to open the door. Then he marched into the room without turning, instructing Helm curtly as he passed: 'Bring the girls here.'

Inside Ulrich stood by the French windows. He waited until he heard the door behind him close, then he turned and faced the girls. He held out the gun as if it was an extension of his arm, pointing the barrel as if it was a finger.

He decided Maria would be the most difficult to break. Dressed in a full red skirt and off-the-shoulder white blouse that was half open, she stood hands on hips and head held back.

Colette on the other hand, looked confused and vulnerable, in a plain dress that emphasised her schoolgirl appearance, something which appealed strongly to him. His gun beckoned her towards him.

When she stood before him, Ulrich asked, 'Can you explain your behaviour?'

Colette closed her eyes and shook her head. It would be futile for her to try and tell him, she thought. He was not capable of understanding. This man who every night degraded her body, who kept her from the reassuring warmth of Clair. How could this man understand the sense of anger she felt whenever she saw Clair and Helm together, Clair laughing with him, Clair always hand in hand with the man who had taken her place.

Ulrich placed the tip of the barrel on the bridge of Colette's nose and pulled the trigger.

He heard Maria's scream behind him drown the single click. Ulrich smiled, then squeezed the trigger again. But again no shot came, only the mechanical click of the hammer on an empty chamber.

Ulrich tried again. Nothing.

Then twice more. Still nothing.

He looked over his shoulder at Maria. The look of horror on her face told him she knew this deadly game of roulette had run its course. He had reached the last chamber in the barrel. The final shot.

He cocked the hammer. As he did so a puddle of urine collected on the carpet between Maria's feet. He squeezed the trigger and watched as the Italian girl fainted and fell onto the carpet. He grinned, knowing he'd won.

Ulrich turned to where his gun was pointing. Colette had also fallen onto her knees. She was being sick. He smiled again. Then he snapped open the barrel and inserted a single bullet. The sound of the shot drowned Colette's retching. It filled the room.

Ulrich turned towards the door and waited for Helm to come bursting in.

'Right on cue, Major,' said Ulrich lowering the revolver. It had been pointing at the curtains dancing in the open windows.

'You can take this pair back to their rooms. I don't think we shall have any more trouble from them.'

He could see the disgust in Helm's eyes as the major stepped over the prostrate Maria and helped Colette, who was wiping the vomit from her mouth, to rise to her feet.

The next morning the town of Lisieux freed itself from the nightly curfew, stretched its muscles in the crisp air and exercised in the noisy rhythm of bustling activity. Street traders called out from behind their fruit barrows and arranged their wares ready for the day's business, then drifted off towards the smell of fresh bread coming from the kerbside cafés.

On the rue de la Gare, the curtains were still drawn on the third-floor window at the Hôtel Chloé. Anaemic rays of morning sunlight slipped through the narrow gap in the curtains and fell on to the bed in the corner of the room. Ulrich lit his first cigarette of the day and reached for the ashtray on the gramophone next to the bed. He lay back and stared at the ceiling.

A German orderly entered carrying a tray. On it was a pot of coffee, some jam in a china pot, a plate of croissants and four stiff brown envelopes.

'Put it over there.' Ulrich pointed to the table. He waited until the orderly had left, then got up and walked quickly to the table.

He picked up the envelopes and laid them out in a line on his bed. Inside the large envelope were spools of tape. On them were recordings of the previous night's conversations which had taken place between the officers and their whores at the Château Beaupré. The names scrawled on the envelopes were those of

General Durring, Colonel Hoffner, Captain von Beck and Major Helm.

Ulrich picked up the Helm tape first and separated it from the others. Then he went to the wardrobe, opened it and removed a large tape recorder which he'd concealed under a pile of linen. He set it up, lit his second cigarette from the dying embers of the first, then placed the Helm tape on the machine.

He sat on the edge of the bed, shoulders hunched, cigarette held tightly between his pink lips and stared maniacally at the slowly-turning spool.

'Can I get you anything, a drink?' The husky disembodied voice of Clair La Croix filled the room.

Ulrich turned off the tape.

The naked, hanging bulb threw rough shadows around the windowless room in the bowels of the Hôtel Chloé. It was a room known only to Ulrich. A telex machine stood in one corner next to a second table, smaller than the first. On it rested a plain black phone, its number inked out. That phone led directly to the unlisted Berlin number Ulrich often called, but only when he was alone. A number even Admiral Canaris did not know existed.

Ulrich placed the fat bundle of papers on the table. They were the verbatim accounts of the four tapes he'd transcribed a few hours earlier. He sat in front of the telex and began to punch out each tape with painstaking care. When it was finished, he wiped the sweat from his brow and crossed the room to where a simple washbasin was fixed to the wall. He turned on the single cold tap and rinsed his face.

As he dried himself he paused and looked in the mirror. He gazed at the reflected tattoo under his right armpit. It was in blue ink and made up of letters and numbers which denoted his service number and, more important, his blood group. If he was wounded in battle and needed a transfusion, the medics would know only Aryan blood could be used. This privilege was not accorded to other members of the German armed forces like the Wehrmacht or Abwehr. It was a right, an honour, only given to the elite members of the Schutzstaffel. The SS. Ulrich bent his head and kissed the tattoo.

The black phone rang.

Ulrich picked it up and recognised the voice of Brigadeführer Walter Schellenberg, the head of the intelligence service of the SS – Hitler's political knights of the Nazi round table, men who would lay down their lives to protect the Nazi ideal from all those who would threaten it – from without or within. And Ulrich knew there were threats from within. From the likes of Rommel, and those who followed him. Men who would betray the new order to save their own skins if the final victory looked in doubt. And Ulrich would see to it that the likes of them would not be allowed, either by design or misguided strategy, to prevent the German Imperial Eagle's final victory.

There would be just One Race, One Leader, One Reich. It would last a thousand years.

CHAPTER EIGHT

Nat Morgan looked down in horror at the figure sprawled on his bed. The fine and delicate features of the only girl who had ever meant anything to him since Bethan's death, had been lost beneath a pulp of black, bruised swelling. Her lips were thick and swollen and, like the side of her face, were caked with congealed blood from her mouth and nose. Her arms were outstretched and one leg was bent under the other. It looked as if she had fallen from some great height, but it was no fall which had done this to Debbie. The heavy bedside lamp, its flex torn and shade broken, was lying on the carpet, its base stained and red.

Morgan pushed himself away from the door and stumbled, rubber-legged, towards the bed. He knelt beside the girl and picked up the vanity mirror from amid the contents of her bag strewn across the bed. When he held it up to her mouth, a faint mist clouded the glass.

She was alive, just.

'Thank Christ,' Morgan mumbled, and jerked into action. He ran to the phone in the lounge, flinging aside an upturned chair which blocked his path. He stood, outwardly calm, in the shambles of his room and dialled for help. When the emergency operator answered, he spoke with tightly controlled clarity. There was no time for anger. Yet.

He called for the ambulance.

Then he went to the bathroom, ran a towel under the tap and returned to Debbie's side. She lay motionless, giving no sign she was even breathing. He took her cold hand in his and pressed his fingers against her wrist. There was no beat of life. He felt only his own heart, about to fracture his rib cage. He grabbed the mirror and thrust it in front of her mouth, watching anxiously, appalled by the clearness of the reflection. At last it came, slowly and faintly, the damp mist.

Gently he began to wipe away the blood with the damp towel, almost afraid to allow the cloth to touch her skin, lest it added to her pain.

Suddenly the broken face began to change. It was no longer bruised and swollen, but cold, white and wasted. The face from the death bed in Brecon's TB sanatorium.

'Please, not you,' Morgan whispered, driving the memory from his mind.

He cradled Debbie in his arms and began to rock slowly to and fro, speaking slowly, deeply. 'Don't die,' he chanted over and over. 'Don't die.'

It was as if by repeating the words there was somehow the chance that she might hear him, that she might respond to the urging of his will.

Morgan did not hear the ambulance men come into the flat. He only felt a hand on his shoulder and heard someone say: 'It's OK, mate. We'll take care of her now.'

Morgan, still numbed, looked up at the man's face. 'She must not die, understand?' he said quietly.

'Don't worry.' The man's voice sounded distant, as if he was talking to Morgan from another room. 'It always looks worse than it really is. You just wait and see, tomorrow she'll be as right as rain.'

'Come on now, sir, let's get to the lady,' a second man added. Suddenly Morgan realised that someone was trying to prise open Morgan's grasp.

'Looks as if you could use a drink, guv.'

Morgan shook his head. He released his grip and was on his feet.

He watched as they lifted Debbie onto the stretcher and strapped her in. He realised just how helpless, how lifeless, she looked and his numbness was replaced by anger. It swelled to fill the void inside him, and if he could have now laid hands on the man who had done this to Debbie, he would have set about his destruction with all the controlled butchery those years as a commando had instilled in him. Yet there was nothing he could do. Impotently he followed the stretcher-bearers from the flat towards the waiting ambulance.

As he walked behind them up the steps to the pavement, Morgan saw Debbie's arm fall over the side of the stretcher. She was wearing the bracelet he'd given her just a week before.

He recalled what one of the ambulance-men had said: 'Tomorrow she'll be as right as rain.'

But as they put her in the ambulance, Morgan knew his Debbie would never be right again. Ever.

The next morning the room still hung heavy with the smell of musk. But, for once, Nat Morgan did not seem to notice it.

He sat, slumped, in a wing chair and stared into the empty

grate. His fingers picked at the cigarette hole he'd burned long ago in the moquette arm, and strands of horse-hair dropped onto the newspaper scattered on the floor.

The flat was still a shambles. Morgan had made no attempt to clear the mess he'd found the previous evening. Everything, books, papers, furniture lay where they'd been strewn. He was past sleep now.

He'd spent the night pacing an antiseptic corridor at the Royal Free Hospital, waiting for news as the doctors fought for Debbie Forster's life.

Morgan could still hear the doctor's cold words, spoken without tact, clinical words from a weary man who'd failed, words which drilled into Morgan's brain.

'She'll live, but I'm afraid it won't be much of a life. The brain damage was too extensive. She might still be able to see, but if she does, she'll never recognise anything.'

The words were as cold as the headline, staring up from the floor: 'Bishop's Daughter Fights For Life.'

Morgan picked up the paper and re-read the story. It was just four paragraphs long and simply told how a bishop's daughter, now working as a secretary at the Foreign Office, had been attacked by a burglar she'd disturbed at the West Hampstead home of an army officer.

He let the paper drop. God, he was tired, so tired the words made his eyes burn. He rubbed them and once again surveyed the shambles around him. Everything he owned – which, except for his treasured books, wasn't much – tossed aside like so much garbage. This thief had turned Debbie Forster into virtually a living corpse for a worthless pile of rented junk.

Something was nagging at his memory. Suddenly it came to him. The realisation that it was not an ordinary burglary. It was all, somehow, because of him. But why?

He cursed aloud. Debbie had become a vegetable, and he, Nat Morgan, was in some way to blame. Morgan picked up the *Evening News* and tore it open. He read it aloud again. A common thief. A flat where there wasn't even a gas meter to rob.

He was furious with himself for not realising it before. A professional thief would have seen that there was nothing worth stealing the moment he came through the door.

'So what was the bastard after?' asked Morgan. There must have been something, something connected with him. And Debbie?

Morgan rose and began to pace the floor, picking his way between the litter. He ran his hand over the black stubble on his chin.

'Debbie must have known the man who attacked her,' he decided. 'Known the bastard.'

And because of that, he'd tried to kill her.

It must have been important that the man wanted no one to know he had been searching Morgan's flat.

'For what?'

Something so important that he'd tried to kill Debbie because she'd known him.

'But if Debbie knew him, then do I?' he asked himself. Was it someone they both knew, this man Debbie had found searching his flat?

His flat. Him. It was because of him.

The phone rang, its shrill bell breaking his thoughts.

He picked it up.

'Nat.' The rich Devon voice belonged to Georgie Hill. Georgie was fifty-five, drank and smoked far more than was good for him, and was the *Evening News* man at Scotland Yard. His by-line had been above the story in the morning's first edition.

It must have been at least three years since he'd seen Georgie. He'd put him in a cab after a drinking bout in the Olde Bell in Fleet Street during a half-remembered leave. Morgan warmed to the soft Devonian burr on the line.

'Nat, me dear,' said Georgie. 'I was sorry to hear about that business last night. I picked it up from the press bulletin this morning. How is the girl? The hospital are saying nothing.'

'She's in a bad way, Georgie, a bad way,' said Nat quickly, relieved to be able to talk to someone about it, even to a voice on the phone to whom the pale girl in a hospital bed meant nothing more than a headline. Four bloody paragraphs for a wasted life.

'Sorry to hear it, me boy. Were you ...' Georgie stopped himself and added, 'I meant, are you close to the girl?'

'Yes.'

There was a long pause on the line. Morgan knew from his own experience that Georgie was angling for something he wasn't really sure of, working out a way to broach the subject.

At last Georgie broke the silence. 'Nat, can we go off the record – strictly off the record?'

'Georgie,' said Morgan, 'I'm tired. Get to the point.' His voice was weary but his mind was racing. Why should Georgie Hill want to go off the record on a four-paragraph story?

'What's behind it, Nat? Who is the girl?'

'I don't follow you, Georgie.'

'Look, Nat me dear, you know what a story like this is worth.'

'Four paragraphs,' said Morgan bitterly.

'Right,' said Georgie. 'So why did the censor's office get on to my news desk after the first edition and tell us to kill the story? In the interests of security!'

'Georgie, I give you my word: I know nothing. Georgie, I'm tired. I'll buy you a beer when I'm next in the Street.'

Morgan hung up without waiting for a reply.

He slumped back into the chair. He'd already come to the dreadful realisation that because of him, Debbie had all but lost her life.

The phone rang again. 'Look, Georgie,' snapped Morgan, lifting the receiver, 'don't you ever give up? I have already told you I know sweet fu . . .'

The Home Counties accent cut him short. 'Captain Morgan, no profanities.'

'Who the hell is this?' Morgan barked down the mouthpiece.

'You'll find out soon enough, old man. Now just listen . . .'

'Now look . . .' Morgan's voice rose in anger.

'No, Captain Morgan. You listen. I'm afraid I have rather an unpleasant task for you. I want you to identify a body.'

The colour drained from Morgan's face. His lips, quivering, spoke the name.

'Debbie.'

'No. You will confirm what I am about to order you to do, by phoning the War Ministry, as soon as I've finished talking to you. A car will pick you up at your flat in exactly twenty minutes. It will take you to the mortuary in Hackney. There you'll find a body. You will be expected. All you have to do is tell us if you recognise the fellow. That's all we want to know.'

'And just who the hell are "We"?'

'That does not concern you at this stage. Just ring the War Ministry like you've been told, there's a good chap. Oh, and there's one other thing. See to it that it is the only call you make. If your phone rings, don't answer it. We don't want you talking to any more reporters.'

Then the phone went dead.

'The sod's got my phone tapped,' Morgan said. He began to

pace the floor again, fists clenched, trying to make sense of the last twenty-four hours.

He knew he was being used, but not why. He felt like a man being torn apart by unknown and unseen forces. But he would find out who was pulling the strings. For his sake. For – whatever good it would do her now – Debbie's sake.

He went into the bathroom and emptied the plastic beaker containing his toothbrush and toothpaste. Then he half-filled it with whisky and returned to the old wing chair and waited.

The car was an old Hillman saloon, painted olive green. It had bald tyres and worn sagging seats.

Morgan sat in the back, leaving the bench seat in front to the driver, who took up most of it. Her uniform, which looked about to split, was the same colour as the car – standard issue for civil service drivers.

What the woman lacked in conversation, she made up for in her driving. She pushed the thing as if she was Enrico Ferrari.

'There's no hurry,' Morgan protested above the shriek of the engine.

She shot through a red set of lights, forcing an open-top double-decker on to the pavement to avoid them.

'What are you doing?' Morgan yelled. 'There's no danger of the man I'm going to see leaving before we get there.'

'Yeah.'

She then jumped the next set of lights. The hard suspension cracked at every bump in the road, roads which had not seen a repair gang since Hitler's bombers had created more important tasks for council workmen. The empty shells in each street became more numerous as the little car sped deeper into East London.

Morgan had almost forgotten just how badly the city had been bombed. Now as they moved through Hoxton towards Hackney, he noticed that there were more bombed-out buildings than standing ones. The kids used them as playgrounds.

The car pulled up in the centre of a small yard, in line with the building's only door. It was badly painted in bottle green. The woman driver made no attempt to get out, or switch off the engine.

'We're here,' she said.

No sooner had Morgan let himself out of the car, than the car drove off, its bald tyres screaming as it bounced through the gates and vanished around the corner.

Morgan looked around the yard. It was empty except for one car, parked at the side of the squat building so as not to be visible from the road. Like the old Hillman, it bore government plates, but that was all they had in common. This was a large Humber saloon, a powerful car like the men who usually rode in them. Morgan wondered if it belonged to the man with the Home Counties accent.

He walked up to the door and rapped the iron knocker.

The door inched open, and a man who smelt of death and disinfectant peered at him through the crack. A thin, grey stubble sprouted from his pale face. Only the man's left eye moved to inspect the visitor.

'You are Captain Morgan.'

It made Morgan feel as if some great prophecy had just been fulfilled. The old man opened the door just wide enough for Morgan to slip inside and closed it quickly behind him.

The old man turned and shambled down the narrow passage towards a pair of rubber doors. Morgan saw him glance over his shoulder, as if to make sure he was following. As Morgan paced slowly behind the figure in the stained white coat, he heard only his own footsteps echo from the tiled walls. In the dim light he could just make out the old man's shabby pair of carpet slippers.

Morgan pushed through the flexible rubber doors. He swallowed hard at the thought of what lay ahead.

The doors opened into a high oblong room. The walls were lined from ceiling to floor with grey metal drawers, the cabinets in which they filed the dead.

His eyes followed the old man's finger to the centre of the room. There, under a single hanging lamp, were three marble slabs. The first was wet and empty, except for a coiled hosepipe, still dripping water from its brass nozzle. On the other two crumpled white sheets covered vague outlines.

Morgan looked at the old man, who nodded.

'See over there,' he said, then stepped back.

The commando moved forward, took the edge of the first sheet and pulled it back.

The old man's piercing rebuke filled the room, almost breaking Morgan's eardrums. 'No. No. No,' the man shrilled as he rushed forward. 'Not that. The other one.'

Morgan looked down at what he'd uncovered. On the slab was the body of a small boy, a child of about eight, with a mass of tight black curls above a forehead that bulged on one side.

'Not him. He was killed playing on a bomb site where he used to live. That'll teach him.'

Morgan thought of the kids he'd passed playing on his way to this place and glared at the old man.

'Not that, I said,' the man snapped. 'This is the one. This one here. Him.'

The man pulled the sheet from the corpse.

Morgan's eyes ran the length of the naked body before him. The man must have been in his early forties. Morgan studied how his ribs pushed against the skin; how his hands, the palms upturned, hung loosely at his side. The face was drawn and sallow. And unfamiliar.

Morgan tried to picture it in life. He wanted to see the pursed lips in a living context. Faces like the one before him belonged to the keepers of small corner shops: timid, frightened to offend faces that reserved their displeasure for small boys with sticky fingers, or flies that crawled over the bacon slices.

The corpse was unmarked. He bent forward and touched the face, placing his fingers on the chin. Morgan drew his breath as the head lolled grotesquely to one side. It was as Morgan thought. The man's neck had been broken. He knew it had been the work of an expert, a man trained to kill.

Morgan lifted one of the arms and let it drop. It fell heavily, slapping against the cold marble. Rigor mortis had not yet set in. The man had been dead only hours, perhaps even after Morgan had been summoned to identify a body.

'Well, Captain Morgan, do you recognise him?'

Morgan spun round and came face to face with the man who owned the Home Counties accent.

The man was dressed in heavy tweed suit, as if he had just come from a county game fair or point-to-point meeting. Yet, standing there in the morgue, he did not look out of place to Morgan. Despite the rustic glow on his face, Morgan knew that this man dealt in death.

'Who the hell are you?' spat Morgan, fixing the stranger with his contempt.

The man smiled, and in the gesture Morgan saw approval. It confused him.

'Godsell,' the man said. 'My name is Stan Godsell.'

Morgan placed his hand on the side of the corpse's face and pushed the head so that it rolled to face Godsell.

'Well, Stanley,' said Morgan, 'you can start by telling me why you killed this poor bastard. Now, before I beat it out of you.'

'I think that would be foolish.'

'I'll risk it,' said Morgan, moving towards Godsell. 'Who was he?' Godsell moved back as Morgan neared. The smile had gone.

'He was killed, Captain Morgan, because he was the "poor bastard" who roughed up our Miss Forster.'

Morgan stopped in his tracks. The words again danced through his mind. 'Our Miss Forster. Our Miss Forster.' His Debbie. Godsell's Miss Forster!

'Yes,' said Godsell, speaking more slowly now that Morgan was rooted to the floor, his face a mask of confusion. 'I'm afraid your loving little relationship was not quite what it seemed. You see, that chance meeting you two had in the French House, was not a coincidence. We arranged it.'

'Arranged it,' Morgan repeated dumbly.

He remembered his surprise at seeing her in the pub. A face from Paris, the British embassy. He even recalled what she had been wearing; the tailored navy-blue suit, the gloves and accessories which matched her ankle-strap shoes. Those green eyes looking at him from beneath the black net veil. Eyes as green as Bethan's. But unlike Bethan, she'd worn a painted beauty spot on her left cheek. Unlike Bethan who'd loved him. Then he recalled the delight she'd shown on meeting him again; the dinner dates that followed, the gentle lovemaking, the way she used to hang on his every word. The way she'd helped heal the wound of Bethan.

It was all a lie. A manipulated deception.

'As you must realise by now, our Miss Forster was more than just a secretary at the Foreign Office. In your case, she was invaluable.'

'My case?'

Suddenly Morgan felt as if a guillotine had severed him from Debbie for all time.

His case. He had been used. By Godsell. By Debbie. The last three months with her became for him at that moment a meaningless memory. As meaningless as the creases others had left on his sheets.

Godsell was standing next to Morgan now and he could smell the stale Scotch on Morgan's breath. His stubby fingers searched the inside pocket of his tweeds and finally produced an old leather wallet. 'We have a job for you,' he said, flicking open the wallet to display his identity card.

Morgan ran his fingers through his hair, then cupped his hands behind his neck and looked up at the blank ceiling, away from Godsell's face. A face he wanted to destroy.

Godsell was satisfied. One glance at Morgan was enough to confirm that, given the opportunity, the commando officer would have ground him into the carpet with no more concern than if he were a termite. He could sense the controlled fury Debbie Forster had spoken about in her reports.

Morgan was perfect.

'Pity about Miss Forster. A shame,' said Godsell. Morgan turned menacingly towards the MI5 officer. 'But I'm afraid it was necessary, Captain Morgan, for us to have used her, you both, in this way. It was necessary for what we have in mind for you.'

'Necessary,' yelled Morgan, bellowing at him with such venom that Godsell jumped back, dropping his wallet. 'For some fucking reason you Whitehall shits use me, send a girl to share my bed, share my whole life . . .'

'Exactly.'

'. . . and she ends up a living vegetable.'

Morgan turned and pointed towards the corpse on the slab. 'He did not do that to Debbie. You did. You and your bloody security games. And I want to know why.'

Morgan grabbed Godsell by the scruff of his neck and forced his face down until it was inches from the dead man's head.

'Why?' he shouted. Then he flung him away as if he could no longer bear to touch him. 'What about him? Why was he at my flat? What was he looking for? Why did he attack Debbie and who is he?'

Morgan spat the questions, adding, as Godsell picked himself up from the floor, 'I want answers and I want them now or I'll do for you what you did for him.'

Godsell dusted himself down and said: 'His papers describe him as a commercial traveller, named Archie Smith. Lies, of course. And he is dead because he had an unhealthy obsession with whores.'

'Whores? What have whores got to do with anything? I don't know any whores.'

'You will, Captain Morgan. You will.'

With that, Morgan saw the man from MI5 turn on his heels and walk towards the rubber doors.

Morgan looked down on the corpse, feeling nothing towards a man whom a few hours ago he would have willingly killed for what he'd done to Debbie Forster. But all he felt now was tired.

Exhaustion came over him in waves, making his head spin. He could only nod when he heard Godsell say, 'Please come with me, Captain Morgan. We have a lot to talk about.'

The Lord Privy Seal was Colonel Cameron's last hope. Seated in the Lord Privy Seal's office in the House of Commons, Cameron waited for Lord Beaverbrook to help him.

'I'll put my cards on the table,' he said. 'I've come to talk to you about one of the former reporters on the *Daily Express*. I'm afraid Whitehall is trying to foist him upon my department at SOE against my will.'

'You mean Nat Morgan?' the Beaver asked in the soft Canadian brogue Cameron thought the hallmark of slovenly speech.

'I do indeed. His file shows he used you as a reference to help him gain a commission in the Commando, which he might otherwise not have been granted.'

The Beaver smiled. 'He's given a good account of himself, so I hear.'

'Perhaps so.' Cameron smoothed the crease in his trousers. 'But my department at F-section is an entirely different matter. With respect, sir, I must ask you to think very carefully if there is any reason, no matter how trivial, you can give me for refusing to have him. Anything at all. For example, wasn't using your name to get his commission a little vulgar?'

'Vulgar,' Beaverbrook's voice rose slightly. 'Colonel, I was flattered. In those days at the Ministry, I had four phones on my desk. One was red. The number was known only to people like the Prime Minister and some service chiefs. When Nat rang to tell me, not ask me, mind, that he was using my name as a reference, he came through on that red phone. I don't know to this day how he got that number, but he got it. Now to my way of thinking that's initiative. He's just the kind of man you need at SOE.'

The old man chuckled. 'It was then, just after he'd hung up, I realised he'd never called me "sir" in all the time he'd worked for me.'

'Indeed!' Cameron snorted.

'Now look, Colonel,' Beaverbrook said impatiently. 'You should be glad you're having an easier time recruiting him than I did.' Cameron raised an eyebrow as Beaverbrook explained: 'He was working for that socialist rag, *The Daily Herald*, when I first noticed him. Then one day he walks into my office and lays down his own contract. It was watertight and gave him carte blanche to write without editorial interference. Anyone else I'd have thrown out. Him I hired. Then I found out he'd already resigned from the *Herald* over a point of principle.'

'Exactly, the man has no scruples,' said Cameron.

'Scruples,' echoed Beaverbrook. 'You know about his time in Spain with the International Brigade?'

Cameron nodded. 'Of all the many doubts I have about this man, that episode causes me most concern. You send him to Spain to perform a duty – report the war. As soon as he's there, he forgets that duty and throws in his lot with a bunch of ragamuffin misfits – half of them Bolsheviks, I shouldn't wonder. It casts great doubts on his character.'

'His actions were those of a man with scruples,' said Beaverbrook. 'Damn high scruples. The dispatches from Spain he sent were the best, bar none. And he kept sending them. Let me also remind you of whom he fought against. Fascists, Colonel. The same people we're fighting now.'

'That's different.'

'Read his cuttings. No one listened much then, but neither did they take any notice of what Winston Churchill said.'

Cameron thought: 'Foreigner.'

Beaverbrook answered his phone. He grinned wickedly. 'A message for you from Mr. Godsell. Captain Morgan is ready for you.'

Cameron rose to leave. He was furious, and it showed.

Nat Morgan watched the sun begin to slide towards the western skyline of the gnarled city, turning the River Thames into a slow-flowing stream of rust. From a top-floor window of the room where Godsell had left him, he could see the driftwood and jetsam bob helplessly in the murky waters.

He vaguely heard the heavy door close behind him, but he didn't move.

'Captain Morgan.'

The sharp voice filled the long empty room with hollow echoes, but Morgan placed his hands each side of the narrow window frame, and remained transfixed by the hypnotic movement of the river.

'Morgan.'

Just three hours earlier, Morgan would have reacted just like any other commando officer in the British Army. His response, although reluctant, would have been to spring to attention and turn to face the voice of authority.

But that would have been three hours ago. Not now.

Not now that he had been told that officially he no longer existed.

Captain Nat Morgan was missing, presumed killed, after a sabotage mission to a beach in Normandy.

'I'm sorry, old boy,' Godsell had told him. 'But that is the way it's got to be.

'Over the last few months certain snippets of information have begun to filter back from France,' Godsell had explained as soon as they had arrived from the morgue. 'It seems that certain well-known, even famous, ladies of the night have mysteriously vanished from their usual haunts in Paris. These whores, seven of them, are installed in the Château Beaupré, outside a tiny village in Normandy. Reports from one of the Normandy Resistance groups claim that some very influential German officers in the Normandy Command now have the exclusive rights to their services.

'SOE passed this information on to us and said it was of no interest to them. We thought there must be a reason why the Nazis have suddenly taken it into their heads to provide senior officers with whores, and if there is an explanation, we want to know it.

'And that is where you first came into the picture. Or rather, our Miss Forster brought you into it. She worked for us in Paris when you first met each other in your reporting days. That's why we assigned Debbie to really get to know you. It was all part of her job. She's done the same thing for us in the past with our American friends, as well as that lot in the Free French. We have to know what our allies are thinking. It's often not altogether in our interests.

'She told us more about you than we could find in all your non-too-complimentary army reports. But then, in this department, we often relish the qualities the army rejects.'

It was then Godsell stuck out his hand. 'Welcome to the club.'

Morgan had eyed him carefully.

'Get stuffed,' he'd said.

'I beg your pardon?'

'Get stuffed.'

As a reporter, Morgan had often come across the likes of Godsell, men who inhabited that shadowy world of information, and Morgan wanted no part of it. These men were vultures in suits who picked at scraps dropped by journalists in bars the world over. Men who would die for deception as if it were truth. Morgan was not of their world and never would be.

It was then that he saw Godsell could slip out of his rustic bonhomie as easily as he did his woollen socks.

'You, the late Captain Morgan, have no bloody say in the matter. Officially you went missing on a Normandy beach. We can make your permanent absence a fact. Like it or not you are in. The alternative, our only alternative for you at this stage, would not, I'm sure, appeal to you.'

'The alternative you gave Archie Smith, I suppose?'

'He had no alternative.'

'Is that why he attacked Debbie?'

'Oh yes, he knew her. You see, they trained together. Here in this very building. It was the British security forces who brought Archie Smith out of his native France. The idea was that he would work for us. You see the little bugger's name wasn't Archie Smith at all. It was Gaston Kranz. He was a French Jew and a loyal member of De Gaulle's Free French forces. The moment we finish training, he goes off and joins that lot. As you are no doubt aware, the Free French are giving the British and Americans a lot of trouble at the moment. They feel we should take them into our confidence and let them know everything we are planning to do to liberate their homeland.

'The Free French have also picked up the tittle-tattle about these whores from their own people in France. Then when they learned from some barman or other that Miss Forster had latched onto you, they decided to watch the pair of you.'

'How the hell can you know that?'

'Archie was good enough to tell us before he died.'

'For Christ's sake he was French! France was his country. He had a right to know what was going on. He had a right to know about these whores . . .'

'Right to know? We use the phrase "Need to know". It is a phrase I'm sure you'll get used to with us. As I said, welcome to the club, Captain Morgan.'

Morgan thought again about his 'official' position and, after all that had gone on that day, wished it were true.

'M-O-R-G-A-N.'

The voice ringing in Morgan's ears as he stared from the

window, was now at screaming pitch. He turned his head and looked behind him.

'Morgan. My name is Colonel Cameron and I am the one person you will call "sir". Is that understood?'

CHAPTER NINE

The little truant spotted them first.

'Germans,' he mouthed, his eyes growing with excitement. The boy stood on the hill high above Ste-Yvette, eyeing the two trucks hard on the tail of a staff car as it sped through the lane below. Young Roland could make out the uniforms of the soldiers in the back of the first truck, as clearly as the black cross on the car's side.

'Germans,' he blurted, out loud this time. Then he remembered his grandfather's warning.

Roland Pratt, flushed with childish exhilaration, had never run so fast in all of his ten years. His chubby legs moved like pistons over the tufts of grass, knocking the heads off the cowslips. His long, grey woollen socks fell in bunches around his ankles but he dared not stop to pull them up. He had to warn his mother, warn everybody. His speed increased at the bottom of the hill, and he flung out his legs to clear the ditch between the edge of the field and the road.

Father Marcel Delon stopped his bicycle in the curve of the road. He had heard the noise of the convoy gaining on him, and he had seen a flash of movement from the hill above. Then he heard a screech of brakes, and a shrill horn blast and saw Roland tumble through the hedge.

Horrified, he watched as the soldiers from the truck gathered round the boy. One was taking off his tunic to put over the motionless child.

Father Delon swung onto his bicycle and pedalled furiously, his cassock trailing behind him in the wind.

The village of Ste-Yvette was, for the most part, just one long street across which two rows of houses faced each other. Like the generations of the villagers who'd lived there, each house leant heavily on another for support: the oldest buildings, buckled with age, were held up between the newer, stronger structures. Other, more recent dwellings, stone cottages constructed in the previous one hundred and fifty years, were dotted at random in the surrounding fields of the men.

On the far side of the village, set well back from the road, was the twelfth-century Norman church of St-Samson. It was approached only by an unmade track that crossed the village green, coiled around the weathered churchyard wall, bridged a stream, and then meandered towards an abandoned farm on a distant hill. The churchyard was ringed by cypress trees, which had grown so high that only the battlements of the fortified bell-tower could be seen from the road.

By the time Father Delon had rushed up the dirt path to his neat house on the village green, the street lay empty in his wake. Villagers watched from hurriedly drawn curtains as the priest leant his bicycle against his fence and disappeared into the house. Then they turned their eyes back along the street and waited for the German troops.

Once inside Delon paused only to wipe the sweat from his brow.

'Madame Remy,' he called. But his housekeeper didn't reply. 'She's never here when I need her,' he mumbled.

He then caught the sound of approaching engines, took a book from the shelf and opened it at random. He placed his reading glasses on his nose and listened for the knock on the door. When it came, the priest, book in hand, opened the door with feigned surprise, and looked over the top of his glasses at Captain von Beck.

'Where does the gendarme live?' von Beck asked.

'Ste-Yvette has never found the need for one. Perhaps I can be of help?'

'Perhaps you can. It is too much to suppose there's a doctor in the village?'

Delon shook his head.

Von Beck turned towards the trucks waiting with their engines still running. 'Bring the boy in here,' he called to the driver, then swivelled to face the priest. 'He ran into my car. I don't think he's hurt too badly. I assume he lives in the village.'

Delon stepped back to allow von Beck into the house, then walked down the path to the truck.

The priest held out his arms and took the boy, still wrapped in the tunic, from the truck driver. Roland's face was grazed but his nose had stopped bleeding.

'Hello, Father,' he said weakly. 'My arm hurts.'

'I think it's broken,' the driver said.

'Do you know him?' von Beck asked as Delon came through the door. The German was standing in the passage, arms folded, blocking the priest's way to the study.

'Yes,' Delon said, offering no other information.

Von Beck made no attempt to move and let the priest past. Instead he took a document from the envelope. He read out two names.

'Serge Gironde and Gilles Arnaud. Where can I find them?'

'Try Paris,' Delon said quickly, his heart missing a beat.

'Don't try to be funny,' von Beck said. 'This says they live in Ste-Yvette.'

'Lived,' Delon replied flatly. 'They moved.'

Von Beck eyed the priest carefully. 'Father, I did not come here looking for trouble. Please do not make my duty any more difficult than it already is.' The German officer held out the document for Delon to see. 'This is an order conscripting these two men into the Todt labour organisation. They are wanted to work on strengthening the Normandy coastal defences.'

'They moved,' Delon said. 'To Paris.' The priest motioned towards his study door with his head.

'Now if I may see to the child.'

He moved towards von Beck, then stopped. Over the German's shoulder, he could see the ample outline of his housekeeper, a wicker basket of garden vegetables on her arm, hovering in the kitchen doorway. The priest hoped she'd been there long enough to have heard the conversation. He also offered a silent prayer that she had understood and knew what she had to do.

She did.

Madame Remy screamed.

Then she dropped her basket, held her clenched fists to her mouth and screamed again. Louder, much louder, this time.

Von Beck jumped out of his skin.

Still screaming, Madame Remy bolted for the open door, down the path, and straight through the crowd of astonished soldiers clustered around the garden gate. By the time she had crossed the village green and was running down the street, she had stopped screaming. Now she was shouting. 'The Germans have killed the little Pratt boy. The Germans are going to shoot Serge and Gilles.' When she reached the end of the street, she paused to catch her breath and then ran back the way she had come, moving more slowly but shouting more loudly. The words were the same.

Slowly the doors of the houses began to open and one by one, the villagers came out onto the street. Some of the women carried saucepans and began to beat them with metal spoons, others beat washboards. The men, all of them elderly, formed up behind their women carrying axes, meat knives from the kitchens and pokers from the hearth. They all took up Madame Remy's call until it became a chant. Hearing it, the younger men working in the fields around the village, straightened their backs and left the harvest. Armed with pitchforks and scythes, they headed for the throng. When they had been joined by the others, silent now but seething, the villagers moved slowly towards the priest and the troops, who fumbled nervously and inexpertly with their unslung rifles.

Von Beck, who was standing on Delon's doorstep, drew his pistol. He fired twice. Once above the heads of the crowd, the second at the ground near their feet.

But the villagers kept coming.

Von Beck scowled as Delon came to his side. The priest held out his hands and the crowd shuffled to an uneasy halt. He spoke with a firm, almost admonishing voice. But his eyes sparkled.

'Go home and don't be foolish,' he rebuked.

'What about little Roland?' a voice cried out.

'He was knocked down and broke his arm. He's inside and alive.'

'Knocked down by bloody Germans,' someone yelled.

Delon heard von Beck cock his pistol.

'What about Serge Gironde?'

'And Arnaud?'

'These pigs are going to shoot them.'

Von Beck stepped back and yelled to his men, 'Take up your positions and prepare to fire.'

His voice trailed off as Delon gripped his arm. 'Don't be an idiot, Captain,' he mumbled from the side of his mouth and then said to the crowd, 'The young officer was not aware that both men had left the village for Paris. Paris. He now knows that so no one is going to get shot, including you. Now go home.'

The crowd seemed to understand and, to the obvious relief of the outnumbered soldiers, began to drift back to their fields and homes.

'Father,' von Beck said, as he put away his pistol, 'I think that this village needs a policeman and I shall see to it you'll get one. Soon.'

Delon shrugged. Von Beck stormed towards his car but at the gate he paused, turned and said, 'About those two men: others will have to take their place on the fortifications. They will also be French.' Delon shrugged again.

'Captain,' von Beck's driver called out, 'some bastard has put a pitchfork through the tyre.'

Delon closed the door with a smile and went to his study. When he had made sure Roland was comfortable, he rang the chemist shop in Lisieux which the boy's grandfather ran.

'Hello, André? Listen. Young Roland's had a slight accident. It is nothing to worry about, but I would be grateful if you could come over as soon as you can; you see, the Germans are about to strengthen their coastal defences ...'

Later that afternoon, three miles from Ste-Yvette, the sun shone down warmly on the autumn-coloured grounds of the Château Beaupré and on three people strewn on its warm grass bed.

Eva Nielson smiled. Her eyes were closed and her head twisted slowly from side to side as her left arm swept over the grass until her fingers reached and sank into the soft velvet of the crimson hacking jacket. It lay on the lawn next to the silk blouse and long skirt she had been wearing earlier, when she'd left for her now customary afternoon ride with Colonel Hans Hoffner and Major Gerd Muller.

Eva's hips rose and fell, gyrating slowly to the feel of Hoffner's searching tongue between her legs. She flung out her arms until she felt the tight curls of Muller's head and pulled his face to her swollen breast.

Eva moaned, screaming for fulfilment. Hoffner responded by rising to his knees and Eva lifted her legs and draped her knees over his shoulders. She pressed the cold leather of her riding boots against the skin of his back. He cupped her buttocks, lifting her from the grass, and pulled her onto him. He groaned as he felt her damp muscles tighten around him, contracting with each eruption to drain the lifeforce from him.

Now Muller knelt astride her, his hands kneading her breasts until her features contorted in a knot of pleasure. Eva pushed his hands away and reached out for him, guiding him to her mouth.

As she took him, Ulrich gave a contemptuous sneer.

'Now you see the so-called gentlemen soldiers of the German army at play,' he told the young blond civilian standing with him in the derelict summer house. They were watching through gaps in the rotten wooden wall.

The civilian, Hans Voight, looked almost angelic, a choirboy who had grown up without ageing. He ran the Gestapo in Caen.

'I think we have got enough,' he said looking up from the Leica camera he had positioned on a decaying barrel.

Ulrich nodded. He dug into the pockets of his suit and produced a dog-eared note-pad. He took a pencil stub from his top pocket, sniffing the carnation in his buttonhole as he did so.

'What's the date?' he asked Voight.

'September 13, 1943.'

Ulrich wet the pencil and recorded the time and date with details of whom they'd just photographed. Voight countersigned it.

'When can I have the prints?' Ulrich asked.

'Tomorrow. What do you plan to do with them; threaten to show them to their wives unless . . . ?'

Ulrich laughed. 'I doubt if there is enough in Hoffner's family coffers to make it worth my while. Like most of his kind all he has got left is his bloody name.'

'Well, what then?' Voight asked, sounding puzzled.

'Hoffner is due to go before a selection board next Wednesday. He has applied for a staff officer's post on Rommel's command, when Rommel takes charge of Western Command later this year. No, Hans, not Hoffner's wife – the members of his interview board. Unless of course, Hoffner and I can come to some arrangement beforehand. And I am sure we can. It would be more than useful to Schellenberg and SS intelligence to control a man in the position Hoffner wants so badly.'

'Will he do it?'

'He'll do it,' Ulrich said emphatically. 'These photographs and the transcripts of conversations I've taped guarantee it. Hoffner and his kind never have had backbone. When it comes down to it, they'll do anything to save their own necks providing they can be seen to keep their good name.'

They walked back to the château by way of the rose garden.

'Why don't you stay for dinner?' Ulrich asked when they reached the terrace. 'Or longer if you can manage it.'

'I thought you'd never ask,' Voight smiled. 'Anyone you'd care to recommend?'

'Why don't you try Clair.La Croix. I'm sure our friend Helm won't mind.'

They laughed loudly.

Old Albert, ambling behind them clutching an awkward bunch of roses, watched Voight put something under the front seat of his car, parked outside the main door, before following the trilby-hatted figure of Ulrich inside.

André Pratt had brought the forged papers with him from his chemist shop in Lisieux. He rose up from the chair in Father Delon's study and moved closer to the oil lamp on the table. He raised his pince-nez on the chain around his neck and took a last look at the papers. 'Excellent,' he said.

Serge Gironde and Gilles Arnaud took the papers with thanks. Both men were dressed in shapeless second-hand suits, cloth caps and working men's boots. They carried small suitcases.

'Well, it really is Paris for you two this time,' Delon said. 'When you get there, go straight to the addresses I gave you to memorise. When you leave here, walk to the crossroads where Yves Estré will be waiting in his fish lorry. God go with you.' The priest kissed both men on each cheek.

Gironde and Arnaud nodded and were gone.

'Mmm,' Delon muttered thoughtfully. He unlocked the bureau where he kept his brandy safe from his housekeeper and half-filled two glasses.

'Thanks,' Pratt said. As he took the glass he caught the thoughtful expression on the priest's face and asked, 'Is anything wrong?'

'I can't make it out. The Germans seem to be going flat out to increase their slave labour force to defend this coast, yet look at the state of the troops they've got stationed here. They would be no match for the invading Allies. Their best men are all stationed in Calais because that is where they expect the invasion. So why are they spending a fortune on the defence of Normandy?'

'Perhaps there is a difference of opinion in the High Command as to where the British and Americans will land. You'd better mention it in your next report to London.'

'That's scheduled for midnight.' Delon looked at his watch. 'What is keeping Albert? He should have been here an hour past.'

'Does he really get anything of value to report from that set-up in the château?'

'Not really. Tittle-tattle mostly, but London have said they'll take anything we can give them on the place. However, so far all Albert has –'

'What the hell do you mean just tittle-tattle?' The booming

voice of Albert Boniface filled the room. Neither man had heard him enter the house.

'Don't look so jumpy,' Albert mumbled defensively. 'Besides, I've got more for you tonight than what you've got the cheek to call tittle-tattle.'

'Well,' Pratt said, 'we haven't got all night.'

'Rommel.'

'What about him?'

'He is going to come to Normandy and take charge of the defence of France.'

'Normandy!' Delon and Pratt said together. 'Are you sure?'

'That's all that bunch up in the château have been talking about all day. I keep my ears open, you know. They all think the sun shines out of his arse.'

'That explains the new coastal defence work,' Pratt said quietly.

'When?' Delon asked.

Albert appeared not to hear him. He was helping himself to a brandy. He took a sip.

'Dunno, yet,' he said. 'But I'll find out.'

Then he produced Voight's Leica and dangled it in front of them.

'Look what I found,' he said. 'It has given me a great idea. Listen . . .'

CHAPTER TEN

Weston Grange was a vulgar Victorian house bought by a tasteless family from Marlow after they had made a fortune from armaments in the First World War. They had lost it all in the Depression and had gladly sold the Gothic edifice to the first bidder. The government had taken it off their hands as a residential civil service college.

Now it was where SOE trained agents. Men and women from every occupied country in Europe went there to learn to create mayhem. They were then sent behind Nazi lines to wreak havoc and destruction through tightly controlled networks of Resistance groups. Most could be expected not to survive for more than three months.

Morgan was told that Godsell awaited him in a room on the third floor. When Morgan entered without knocking, Godsell looked up over his copy of *The Times*.

Morgan steadied himself as he looked down at one of the men who'd played a game with his life, who had had Debbie Forster destroyed, and who had wrung the little Frenchman's neck.

Godsell reached for the folder on his desk. 'Read this,' he said.

Morgan walked to the window seat and began to read the contents of the folder. He read slowly. For the first time he saw the names of the girls and began to think of them not as harlots but people. Prisoners. Like him, being used. He read of the raids and the scar-faced man responsible. Ulrich. Morgan paused to ask just one question.

'What happened to the girls on the shortlist who were not selected?'

'We assume they were eliminated.'

'Murdered,' Morgan corrected him. 'They were murdered by these bastards.'

Godsell smiled approvingly as he saw Morgan's outrage Morgan read on. He studied the names of the officers using the château. The names meant nothing; their ranks were impressive The file was composed of reports sent by radio from the Swordfish Resistance group. He nodded with approval at Father

Delon's suggestion that some of the girls could be approached to provide information about their German lovers.

'Has any approach been made?' Morgan asked.

'No. Any decision in that direction rests solely with Colonel Cameron. So far he has resisted any attempt to, as he puts it, dirty his hands with these girls.'

'Idiot,' Morgan thought and shook his head with exasperation. 'But this is a heaven-sent chance to get first-hand information about the thoughts and feelings of the Nazis using this place.'

'Tell that to Colonel Cameron.' Godsell eyed Morgan, then added, 'Then you'll have a real chance of spending the rest of this war sitting behind a desk pushing paper.'

Morgan's eyes darkened, and he looked away. There was no way he intended letting that happen. Not after what he had been through. He had been used enough. He thought of the girls. The way they were abused offended him. But much more, he saw the château as a means of hitting back at Hitler's creed, the creed he despised with all the loathing in him.

He turned to Godsell. 'I am going to France and you and Cameron are not going to stop me.'

Godsell smiled to himself.

Morgan's final week at Weston Grange ended like a night-mare.

'From now on you are no longer Morgan. You will not speak English at any time, only French, always. Your name is Paco, Henri Paco, and you are a plumber. We have stripped you of your identity and given you a new one. The one you will use when you get to France. If you get to France . . .' Godsell had said.

At first it was easy, almost like a dress rehearsal for an unscripted play. The set was two rooms arranged to look like a French home. Throughout the day the players, all French, came and went. They treated Morgan as if they had known him all his life – as Henri Paco. They ate with him, drank with him, reminisced over times and friends past as if they had actually existed.

After two days, even Morgan was uncertain of what was true. Every waking minute of the day he was Paco. But at night he would look at the ceiling before he slept and say: 'My name is Morgan.' One night he even dreamt he was Paco. After that the first thing he always said when he awoke was: 'I am Nat Morgan'.

Then he was betrayed.

'That's him,' the man pointed out. 'That's the one. That's Henri Paco.'

And the two other men led him out of the room blindfolded. They cursed him in German and took him to a windowless room. There day and night became one. Each man took it in turns to see he never slept. His eyes burnt under the glare of the single bright lamp.

'Tell us who you are and you can go,' they said.

'Paco,' Morgan said. Then they would beat him.

Twice he fainted from hunger and they fed him bread.

Then they would begin again.

'My name is Paco,' he screamed. Then they beat him again.

Then, behind him, a third voice, a familiar voice, an English voice said: 'Splendid show. You didn't let them break you. You are Henri Paco.'

Morgan looked up wearily from the chair where they'd bound him and saw Godsell's face.

Morgan thought: 'You dumb bastard, I lied. My name is Morgan.'

On a bitterly cold, sleet-driven morning in December 1943, Morgan, his training over, reported to the cramped quarters of number 64 Baker Street – the operations nerve centre of SOE. Morgan was to begin his duty under the malevolent wing of Colonel Ian Cameron.

Cameron glared at Morgan from the grey metal desk under the wall map of occupied France. 'I run a tight ship in F-section. I have neither the time or resources to waste worrying about the sexual habits of the German Western Command. You will go through the motions, read the Swordfish reports and note them where relevant. But any direct action by us is out. Understood?'

No. Morgan did not understand. Neither did the massive figure who rose to greet him when Cameron's secretary showed Morgan to his new office.

'Hello, I'm Arnie Connors,' he said, as Morgan grasped his offered hand warmly.

Connors was a balding, ex-Olympic skier on assignment as a liaison officer from SOE's American counterpart, the OSS. He was six foot five, looked bigger, and weighed around fifteen stone, none of it fat. He was in his thirties, with a friendly, fresh face and freckled forehead which swept back where the baby-like fair hair had once been. No one ever noticed he was bald on top. There was something about his pale blue eyes which defied you to do so. Before the war, he'd been a New York bouncer, a Montana National Park warden, and a New England ski instructor until he graduated from Princeton and settled down to teach English at Boston University near his home state of New Hampshire. His accent didn't sound obviously American. Morgan thought he detected a faint trace of Irish. But Connors dispelled Morgan's doubt by cursing the kind of oaths only Americans can curse. They described Morgan's feelings about Cameron perfectly.

'I could not have put it better myself,' Morgan laughed. He realised that it was the first time he'd done so since Debbie.

For his size, Connors moved nimbly. It took him three paces from his cluttered desk to the door. He locked it with a wink and took another three steps to the cupboard in the far corner. From beneath the bound bundles of reports, he produced a bottle of Jack Daniels.

'You do drink?' he asked, raising an eyebrow.

'Of course.'

'Good. I was brought up never to trust a man who didn't.'

The US major cleared space on his desk by sweeping the clutter onto the floor. He filled two tea cups, sat and put his feet up, leaning back on the chair.

'Courtesy of the PX,' Connors said as Morgan took the cup and drank, swilling the bourbon around his mouth before swallowing. He looked down at the mountain of papers Connors had swept onto the floor.

'It's all crap for the most part,' Connors said. 'Cameron seems to spend all his time shovelling it in my – now our, I guess – direction.'

'Look, Major . . .'

'Arnie,' Connors interrupted. 'That's how I was christened.' Suddenly Morgan felt better. Here was a man with whom he felt totally at ease.

'Arnie, what about the stuff that isn't crap?'

'You mean the hookers?'

'Exactly.'

Connors sipped his cup of bourbon, his eyes twinkling because he'd found an ally.

'What do you think of this?' The major dug into his drawer and handed Morgan a sheaf of typed paper.

'What is it?' Morgan asked as he flipped through the sheets.

'Two months ago, the caretaker at the château picked up rumours that Rommel was to take over the defence of France. They tell us now that the Nazis are using more forced labour to build their coastal defences. Yet the standard of troops they have stationed in Normandy is pathetic. They are either shell-shocked rejects from the Russian front or kids as green as apples.'

Morgan nodded. 'Why build defences if you don't have the men to man them?' he said, throwing his hands up. 'Somewhere someone is depriving Rommel of Panzers and crack troops. And these girls probably know more about the frustrations of Rommel's staff officers than anyone. If only we could turn some of them.'

Connors laughed. 'Don't you think I have not already suggested that?'

'And?'

'Nothing.'

Both men drifted into silence and gloom. At last Connors eyed Morgan over the top of his tea cup.

'You thinking what I'm thinking?'

'Yes. We have to do anything we can to get to these women.'

'Even if it means going around Cameron's back and risk getting our arses busted.'

'That's one way of putting it.'

The two men raised their tea cups of bourbon.

'To the whores of the Château Beaupré.'

CHAPTER ELEVEN

The rattle of the roulette wheel was followed by applause and laughter as Major Gerd Muller elbowed his way through the players around the table to claim his prize. He looked up at the three girls standing on the table and chose Annette Duval. She giggled as he took her around the waist and planted a wet kiss on his forehead as he lifted her down.

At the piano in the far corner of the salon, Elaine struck the opening chords of a polka and Muller and Annette began the dance. As he watched them, Major-General Durring placed his thumb on the neck of a champagne bottle, shook it and sprayed the laughing couple in a fountain of foam, causing Annette's hair to fall in wet curls. Then the general lunged at Maria and lifted her off her feet. He failed to keep his balance and they fell back on to the velvet sofa in convulsions of laughter. Durring stumbled to his feet and hauled Maria up to join the dance.

Madame Nicole McGragh would have preferred a more sedate celebration of her forty-third birthday. So, by the look of it, would Colonel Hoffner. He was standing alone hunched over a glass of schnapps. The bottle at his side was as empty as Hoffner was sober.

Nicole searched for Eva among the dancing couples cavorting noisily around the furniture. She was not there. Nicole moved discreetly to the ornate fireplace and rang the service bell concealed in the carved lion's head. Then, with a smile fixed on her face, she made her way to the large double doors to await Albert.

When she heard him clumping across the tiled hall, she inched the doors apart and peered at him through the crack. Still smiling, she said through closed teeth: 'Find Eva wherever she is and tell her I want her here now.' Then she pulled the doors closed and glided towards Colonel Hoffner. 'Come now, Colonel,' she said taking him by the arm, 'I will not allow anyone to look sad on my birthday. In fact I insist on everyone having the time of their lives.'

She let go his sleeve and clapped her white-gloved hands loudly. Elaine stopped playing and the dancers paused to look towards Nicole.

'Gentlemen,' she announced, 'tonight I shall have the pleasure of dancing with you all in turn, but first I shall have the honour of taking the floor with Colonel Hoffner. We shall all dance, including our gifted pianist.'

Elaine blushed as the dancers applauded.

'The captain shall see to the gramophone,' added Nicole.

The young von Beck bowed and wound up the machine on the antique sideboard.

'A slow foxtrot,' Nicole said, leading Hoffner by the hand. 'And please, will someone dim the lights?'

The record began and the couples, officers in uniform and the girls in evening dresses, moved slowly to the soft music as the glow from the log fire cast their shadows on the walls in the half-light.

As the dance ended the double doors opened, flooding the room with light from the hall. Albert had found Eva. She stood smiling in the doorway, her blonde hair falling over her bare shoulders. She looked breathtaking.

Nicole, a hand still on Hoffner's shoulder, smiled. 'Something to chase away the gloom,' she said.

Hoffner stared hard at Eva as she came, smiling, with arms outstretched towards him. 'Darling, have you missed . . .'

'Keep that slut away from me. I never want to clap eyes on the likes of her again,' Hoffner bawled.

Eva stopped dead in her tracks. The officers bristled. Nicole took her hand from Hoffner's shoulder. White-faced and furious, she took a step back. Then slapped Hoffner's face.

'How dare you! Get out. I never want to see you set foot in the Château Beaupré again,' she seethed. 'Ever.'

Hoffner took her firmly by the wrist. 'Then the privilege will be mine. I shall leave your whores to other fools.' He flung her hand aside and began for the door.

Eva, confused and shaking, stood in his way. Hoffner brushed past, knocking her out of his path.

'Hoffner!'

The colonel froze.

General Durring, red-faced and perspiring, strode towards the colonel with Maria at his heels.

'You will apologise.' Hoffner turned to face him. The general's fury was undisguised. 'Apologise!' he screamed. 'To the ladies concerned and to your brother officers for your outrageous behaviour which is unbefitting a man of your position.'

Hoffner felt weak at the knees. 'I cannot,' he said quietly, while thinking in black despair of his betrayal of them all, of the terrible tangle of blackmail he was in through Eva's charms.

'Then you shall face the consequences,' Durring said.

'It is a question of honour,' von Beck said removing his glove as he came forward. But before he could complete the challenge in the tradition of his class, another voice filled the room.

'Apologise, Colonel.'

It was Ulrich. An unlit cigarette dangled from his lips and his tie was askew. His wide-brimmed hat sat uneasily on his head and he clutched a half-drunk brandy bottle. At his shoulder stood Hans Voight, the Gestapo chief, his choirboy features expressionless.

The others moved back as Ulrich came into the room, and, bottle still in hand, he took Hoffner by the sleeve and walked him to the far end of the salon. 'You will apologise to all concerned: that whore, Madame McGragh, and those scum who claim to be soldiers. I still want you to patronise this place. It galls me to admit it, but you still have your uses. Apologise.'

Hoffner, his face ashen, nodded weakly as Ulrich's fingers sank into his arm. The photographs Ulrich had presented to him the day before his promotion board flashed through his mind. He felt sick. He was being a traitor to his cause and kind. But the alternative to leaking to Ulrich the information he wanted from staff meetings, was total ruin.

Hoffner took a deep breath and pulled his sleeve free from the bony fingers.

'I'm sorry. I hope Miss Nielson, Madame, and my brother officers will accept my unreserved and sincere regrets for my behaviour this evening.' He clicked his heels.

'Granted. You may go,' Durring said.

Hoffner bowed quickly and was gone.

'Elaine, please play for us,' Nicole said when Ulrich clicked his fingers in her direction. Embarrassed laughter rippled through the salon as Elaine's fingers moved lightly across the grand piano's keyboard, but when Maria led Durring to the floor, the others followed.

Nicole faced Ulrich. She noticed he was unsteady, slightly drunk. 'Colette is waiting. The usual place,' she replied to his question. He grunted and made for the door.

'Help yourself,' he said to Voight as he passed.

Voight made straight for Clair. The officer dancing with her stepped aside. The Gestapo officer took her hand without a word. They danced at arm's length.

'They deserve each other,' thought Nicole and rang for Albert to replenish the supply of champagne.

Five minutes later she angrily pressed the service bell again. But there was still no response.

Albert stood in shadows at the far end of the corridor. He took the unlit Gauloise from his lips and squinted through the darkness as Ulrich climbed the stairs under the disapproving gaze of the oil paintings on the wall.

As Ulrich approached, Albert pressed himself deeper into the alcove and held his breath. The German passed within two feet, his heavy tread echoing down the empty passage.

Albert watched the German fumble in his pockets outside a heavy oak door.The old man smiled when he saw him produce a key and turn the lock.

'That room! At long last he's using that room again,' Albert said softly to himself, as Ulrich pushed the door open with his foot and then kicked it shut. As the bang reverberated down the hall, Albert slipped from the recess, threaded quickly through the maze of passages, and bounded up the back stairs leading to his attic room with an agility remarkable for a man of his age.

After he had thrown open the door of his room and turned on the light, which was wrapped in a heavy cloth, Albert sank to his knees and felt under his iron bed in the half-light. A few moments later, his fingers landed on the parcel and pulled it free. He'd been waiting for this chance for weeks – ever since the package had been dropped by parachute.

Ulrich took a swig from the brandy bottle and watched his reflections grin back at him from the room's four mirrored walls. Then he focused his gaze beyond his multi-angled form and onto the large four-poster bed which stood in the middle of the room. Colette sat waiting, her back resting against a post. Both her legs were stretched out in front of her, the left one bent at the knee, and one hand rested between her thighs. As instructed, she was naked except for the net stockings held in place by the scarlet garter belt around her flat stomach. It was the first time in weeks he had insisted on this ritual.

As usual, Ulrich said nothing. He took off his hat and flung it aside, then sat on an oak chest and watched. He gulped from the bottle and motioned to Colette to begin.

106

Ulrich's heartbeat quickened as he fixed his eyes on the slight, but regular movement of the girl's index finger, which his nod had set in motion. She had rehearsed well. Her tongue wet her parted lips as she closed her eyes and moaned gently.

'Faster,' Ulrich barked, swigging freely from the bottle.

Colette obeyed. The rapidity of her finger movements increased as she jerked her hips and cried out in mock need.

When Ulrich ordered her to stop, Colette did as she was told. She rose and walked timidly towards him, hands held protectively over her breasts. When she was standing before him he rose, and she knelt down. After her slender fingers had unbuttoned his flies, he grabbed her short hair and pulled her face towards him, causing her to gasp in pain. Ulrich watched their reflections from every angle as she set about the task that revolted her, a task she carried out with the professional movement that belied her childlike innocence. Then she tasted him and cried out. Ulrich mistook it as a cry of joy and pushed her away so that he could undress.

When he had finished, he followed her to the bed and held the bottle while Colette gratefully drank the numbing brandy.

Albert focused the cine camera lens on the couple's faces. Ulrich was manoeuvring Colette into a kneeling position while studying their reflections.

'Small wonder he don't split her in two,' Albert mumbled from the tiny viewing room he had discovered built into the wall behind the two-way mirror. As Albert filmed, Ulrich wrapped his arms around Colette's waist and mounted her, thrusting with the frenzy of a bull. Then Albert thought he saw Colette yawn. He turned off the camera after a minute, lit a Gauloise and waited. London wanted faces, not Nazi backsides. By the time Albert had finished his third cigarette, Ulrich had exhausted his repertoire and fell back on to the bed.

As the couple took turns to finish the brandy bottle, Albert began to film again, concentrating on their faces as they talked. And as he thought about what he was recording, it dawned on him that the expression on Colette's face had not been one of boredom. It had been hate. Now that he recognised it, he realised he had never seen such contempt and loathing in all his sixty years on earth. Never.

When Albert had run out of film, he put down the camera and prepared to leave the tiny room. He was the only one who knew about that concealed chamber – a secret from his days as the late count's valet, a secret which even the old countess never suspected existed – but he had to be careful when entering and leaving for fear that someone might hear him. Albert pushed open the door which, from the corridor, looked just another panel in the wall. As he slipped out, camera slung over shoulder and empty cigarette packet in one hand, he heard footsteps approaching from the blackness of the unlit corridor. He quickly eased the panel back into place.

André Pratt, his odd pince-nez dangling from the chain around his neck, concealed his impatience with a tradesman's smile as he hovered around two old ladies who were burrowing through his decimated supply of cosmetics. He didn't give a second glance at Albert, whose entrance was announced by the jangling bell over the door and a rasping cough, the result of fifty Gauloises a day.

'I want something for my cough – those tablets that taste of disinfected horse dung will do,' Albert said, emptying his pockets onto the worn wooden counter.

The old ladies mechanically twisted their necks and glanced up with pursed-lip disapproval. As André gripped the cough drops impatiently in his outstretched hand, Albert spluttered and rummaged through the jumble he'd heaped onto the counter, before finally unravelling enough small change to pay for them.

As soon as he'd exchanged the money for the drops, Albert refilled his pockets and wheezed out of the door without so much as a thank you. When the old ladies followed timidly behind him, the old chemist picked up the slim package Albert had dropped behind the indigestion tablets. It contained the film clips.

Later that evening, André visited his young grandson Roland in Ste-Yvette. On his way home he stopped off at the church of St-Samson and knelt humbly, if briefly, in confession to Father Delon, while passing the strips of film through the grille.

It had begun to snow. Father Delon turned up his collar and increased his step. He held the heavy bible closer to his chest, lowered his head, and pushed on through the white night. The back streets of Caen were empty and the snow was settling thickly on the pavements. Ahead he saw the welcoming glow, pale through the swirling flakes, of Chez Hubert. He hoped the bar would be as full as usual, the patrons not deterred by the weather. There was only one free seat next to the window, which was always risky. He would have preferred somewhere in the corner.

Delon ordered a Calvados and as he sat down to wait, eyed his fellow drinkers. The customers were all male, dockers and market porters in the main; and the air was thick with smoke. There was no sign of Yves Estré. Delon opened his bible, at the page he'd marked with the slim brown envelope, placed the book mark on the table and read. Ten minutes later Yves Estré arrived and, taking a cognac at the bar, made small talk with the owner's wife until the three men at Delon's table finished their wine and left. Then Estré left his post to sit opposite the priest. Delon finished his drink, picked up his bible and walked out into the sub-zero temperatures of the night. When the shock of the cold hit him, he realised he was sweating.

An hour and two cognacs later, Estré walked back to his battered fish lorry and set off on his nightly run to the Breton port of St-Quay-Portrieux. His tobacco pouch was on the dashboard of his cab, the envelope tucked safely inside.

As usual, Yves drove through the night and arrived in time to meet the dawn return of the small fleet. He made his way through the bustle of arm-waving traders, and finally met up with Captain Jean-Claude Baptiste, weather-beaten master of *La Belle Hélène*. When they had completed their business, they sealed their transaction with a warm Gallic handshake and, after a heartening glass of brandy to keep out the cold, bade each other farewell. Estré had left his tobacco on a deck hatch-cover. Captain Baptiste flippantly tossed the pouch in the air and caught it again – carefully.

At midnight *La Belle Hélène* – named after Baptiste's wife – was riding silently at anchor on the fishing grounds 150 kilometres north-west of Brest. Just after two a.m. the crew heard the powerful thump of the twin Rolls-Royce Merlin engines of an MTB. From his bridge, Baptiste flashed the agreed signal at thirty-second intervals for exactly three minutes. There was a two-minute pause, and the MTB returned the signal.

With her engines throttled right down, the grey shape emerged from the darkness and came alongside the little fishing boat. Baptiste left his bridge and passed the package to a Royal Navy rating.

'God bless and a safe trip back,' the seaman murmured.

'Bon voyage,' Baptiste replied. 'And thank you.'

The rating nodded respectfully.

Less than a minute later the wooden bows of MTB 504 lifted

from the water to the whine of her aircraft engines at full throttle, leaving a semi-circle of boiling wake. With Albert's film safe below, she headed for the southern English coast and home.

Nat Morgan, alone in his untidy office at SOE, was in unusually high spirits. Albert's film had arrived by courier that morning. Morgan shuddered to think of the risks the old man must have gone through to comply with his request.

'Incredible,' he mumbled to himself. All he had done was act like some faceless administrator and pick up a phone from behind the safety of his desk, while others risked all to carry out the job.

Connors was in a building on the other side of Baker Street. It housed the Ministry of Information, which, among other things, produced government films. It also had processing labs and four viewing theatres. Earlier in the morning Connors, after telling Cameron he was going to a US staff meeting, had taken Albert's efforts to be processed and reassembled. If the film did not contain the shots Morgan wanted, Connors would destroy it. If it did, he would ring Morgan.

Morgan's phone rang at noon.

'Don't bust a gut, but I think this film is just what you asked for. There is a great ten-minute sequence of this Kraut Ulrich talking his head off,' Connors added.

Morgan beamed. 'What's the quality of the film like?'

'Bit fuzzy at times but not that bad at all. Just like a talkie without the sound track.'

'Sounds hopeful. Let's see if we can add our own sound and see what the man behind it all has to say for himself. I'll make a few calls to find someone who might provide the words, then I'll join you as soon as I can.'

Morgan dialled a Fleet Street number and was connected to the most comprehensive newspaper cuttings library in the world. If anyone's pronouncements on subjects ranging from Aachen to Zymaste has ever found their way into print, then the Press Association news agency and its sister company Reuters has it on file. It didn't take the duty librarian long to come up with the specialist Morgan had asked for.

'Name you want is Berry. Miss Maud Berry, 198 Aylmer Parade, East Finchley. Phone, Finchley 4434. She's the best in Britain.'

'Thanks,' Morgan said.

He rang the Foreign Office. They agreed to provide two interpreters, both security vetted. One fluent in German, the other in French. They also insisted their own man from MI6 should go along.

Morgan crossed his fingers and left SOE by the back stairs.

The smoke from Morgan's cigarette curled through the shaft of light that led from the projection room to the blank screen. Connors dangled his long legs over the seat in front.

'Christ, I hope this is going to be good enough,' Morgan said, stamping out his cigarette and lighting another. 'We've got to get this château thing out of the filing tray and onto the road fast, or I'm going to lose my mind stuck behind that desk.'

'Well, take a look and see what you think,' Connors said. 'Roll it, will you,' he called to the unseen projectionist, 'and just give us close-ups of them talking.'

The projector hummed in the darkness and the lower half of a girl's face filled the screen. Her mouth opened to take the neck of the brandy bottle held in someone's fingers. Some brandy ran down her chin.

'Not that,' Connors yelled. 'Move on to them talking – the section where they've just finished screwing.'

There was a loud click and the projector whirred noisily as a kaleidoscope of jumbled images flashed meaninglessly across the screen. Then stopped. Part of a man's profile, twenty times larger than life, turned quickly as the film moved on. He mouthed grotesquely, and the blotched skin of the side of his face, blown up on screen, emphasised the hideous scar.

Morgan started, gasping loudly, and stiffened in his seat.

'What the hell is it?' Connors asked urgently, sensing Morgan's horror.

'God, I don't know,' Morgan mumbled.

'OK, let's take it again,' Connors called when the sequence was over. They watched the re-run of the moving, wordless mouths in silence, Connors uneasily aware of the tension welling up inside Morgan. It was as if the man were watching his own ghost.

Suddenly Morgan was on his feet, his shadow blocking out the images. 'Stop it,' he shouted at the projectionist.

'What in Christ has got into you?'

'I've got to see the whole film. All of it.'

'Dammit it's only their mouths that are important.'

'Don't argue. Please don't argue,' Morgan snapped. 'Run the

whole thing from the very beginning,' he called to the back of the theatre, 'just as it was filmed.' Seconds later the film began.

The girl, naked except for garter belt and stockings, drank from the man's bottle. Then there was a rear view of the naked Nazi. The film went blank for a few moments until the next sequence began – a rear view of the man fornicating. Morgan was almost unaware of the sybaritic contortions as he watched the girl's face, reflected in countless angles from the mirrors on the wall.

Connors shifted uncomfortably in his seat. 'That's the little lesbian. Sure looks bored, huh?' Connors joked weakly, attempting to lessen the tension.

'That's not boredom,' Morgan said quietly. 'That's hatred. Pure hatred.' His mouth opened as he watched the man dismount and roll the girl onto her back. Then the man turned, grinning, towards the hidden camera. And Morgan saw his face.

'Cut it,' he screamed.

The frame froze.

Morgan stood, his knuckles turning white as he gripped the seat in front for support. The celluloid face leered at him from the screen. The same face that had leered at him through the Spanish rain. The man he thought he'd killed. The face he'd maimed.

Morgan ran his hands through his hair and closed his eyes. He saw the field of Spanish mud, George Williams, the long-dead miner. It all came flooding back: the soldier urinating over the disembowelled body; the SS officer he'd shot hovering over the slime of the foxhole like a black angel.

He felt Connors shake him, yell at him. Then he opened his eyes and again saw that face. Leering.

'What the fuck is it?' Connors whispered.

'I thought I'd killed that bastard.'

'Who? Him?' Connors looked at the screen. 'You thought you'd killed him? I don't get it.'

'I did that to his face. The last time I saw him he was wearing an SS uniform. He was part of the Condor Legion in the Spanish Civil War. I shot him after three of his men had slaughtered an unarmed, wounded man who hadn't the strength left even to cough.'

'Nat, are you sure? Think carefully, for crissake. This guy is an Abwehr officer,' Connors said urgently.

112

'He's no more Abwehr than you and I. The bastard is SS. Who is he?'

Connors shook his head and gave a long, low whistle. 'From Swordfish's description, that's Ulrich. Ulrich set up the whole château thing. If you're right and he's not Abwehr, then it means it's being run by the SS. Why? It isn't out of their concern for the sex lives of the German army, that's for sure. Cameron can't ignore it now we know the SS are in it up to their necks.'

'You want to bet?' Morgan said. 'We've got only my word that he's SS, but no proof. He'll want more than that.' He called to the projectionist. 'Run it again. Just their mouths in close-up. As big as you can get it.'

When it was over, Connors said, 'I think we have a chance. What time is this Miss Berry of yours due?'

'Not until two-thirty. Same time as the Foreign Office people.'

'There is a Miss Berry waiting for you in the foyer,' the Ministry of Information receptionist murmured in Morgan's ear.

Morgan turned to the three Foreign Office men sitting in the row behind him and Connors. The receptionist had escorted them in a few moments earlier.

'I'll go get her and bring her down. Excuse me,' Morgan said.

Several minutes later he was back with a demure middle-aged spinster. She was dressed primly in a tartan tweed suit. Her stiff grey hair was pinned tightly at the back of her neck, and a pair of round wire spectacles perched precariously on the tip of her pointed nose. She blinked as Morgan introduced her.

'These three gentlemen, whose names are not important, are from the Foreign Office. Gentlemen, this is Miss Maud Berry of the National Council for the Deaf and Hard of Hearing. She is the country's leading authority on lip-reading.'

Miss Berry blushed meekly and fiddled nervously with the corner of her lace handkerchief.

'Miss Berry ... umm ...' Morgan faltered. On the rare occasions Morgan was embarrassed, he had the irritating habit of tugging his ear lobe. He was tugging it now. 'As I've explained, what is about to follow will be most distressing and unpleasant ... umm ... for all of us. But it is very important.'

Over the next two hours, during which Miss Berry copiously took notes, the close-up sequences of the mouths were run and re-run. Sometimes she'd hold up her hand and ask for a sequence to be repeated several times. Then she began to compare her notes with the shapes the lips made on the screen, but before many of the close-up sequences had passed, she held up her hand to call a halt.

'There's something terribly wrong. I can't put my finger on it, but it's just not right. Not quite right at all.' She paused, and then added, 'I think I must really see it all in its entirety.'

Morgan tugged furiously at his ear lobe.

Thirty minutes later, she'd seen enough.

'Got it,' she said. 'I knew there was something. That man is drunk. I shall have to take into account that he is slurring his speech.'

Three hours later Miss Berry had finished.

'I am pleased to have been of help. I hope it will be of use, but for the life of me, I can't think how.'

Connors saw her out. At the door she said, 'What an awful shame about that poor young man's face. He could be quite dashing without those scars – just like Rudolph Valentino in a strange sort of way. Or perhaps not ...'

When Connors returned, Morgan asked, 'If the bastard was pissed, what language would he have been speaking?'

'His own obviously,' the man from MI6 said.

'We'll try German first,' Morgan said.

The German interpreter pored over the series of letter-sounds and began to fill in various permutations of letters between the sound symbols. Slowly a phonetic jigsaw began to take shape.

At midnight he handed Morgan a completed sheet of paper. It contained just four phrases. 'That's all I can say with any certainty,' he said, 'and then I'm not one hundred per cent sure.'

Morgan read:

They are all traitors.
Rommel cannot be trusted.
We shall stop him, ruin him.
The (uncypherable) invasion (series of uncypherables) too important to (uncypherable).

'Nat,' Connors said, 'I think you just might have what you've been looking for.'

'Wait,' the voice barked irritably.

Cameron did as he was bid, shifting his weight uneasily from foot to foot as he stood outside his warlord's office door. In his hands he clutched the Château Beaupré file.

'Come,' Churchill called after a few minutes which to Cameron seemed like eternity. The deep voice had an awesome ring of finality about it. Without waiting for another booming summons, Cameron pushed the door open with trepidation and entered. He'd never been so close to Churchill before. The room was filled with blue smoke from the smouldering Havana held in the Prime Minister's left hand. The fountain pen in his right moved furiously over the papers spread on the ornate Queen Anne desk. The fat cigar motioned Cameron to the simple chair in front of the desk.

Churchill did not look up from his papers. The colonel sat, crossed his legs and tapped his fingers nervously on the file in his lap.

'Stop that,' the old man lisped, his head still bent over his papers.

Cameron coughed softly and glanced quickly round the room. He'd often tried to imagine what Downing Street was like inside. Outside it looked so drab. The heavy curtains were drawn, blocking the crisp January sunlight which had shone brightly outside in Horseguards Parade. Except for the harsh table lamp illuminating Churchill's stubby fingers, only two wall lamps glowed softly. Cameron could not identify the gilt-framed portraits on the far wall, but there was enough light to savour the richness of the room. Disraeli, or perhaps Wellington, would not have looked out of place sitting on the exquisite, tastefully arranged antiques and sipping tea from delicate bone china cups.

'You've done well,' Churchill said theatrically, still not looking up, 'well indeed.'

Cameron noticed Churchill's steel helmet and gas mask on the Sheraton settee, and tugged at his collar. He'd put on his dress uniform for the occasion. It was stiff from disuse. His polished epaulets felt heavy on the shoulder; his medals looked as crass as the red stripe down the side of his trousers. Churchill looked as if he'd slept in his denim boiler suit.

'This year, 1944,' the Prime Minister continued, 'will be the watershed of our fight against Hitler. If we fail, the thought is too horrible to contemplate. As I speak to you, our troops are being held at bay at Monte Casino. But Italy is a side-show,' Churchill said, lisping heavily as he did on the wireless.

He's a ham, Cameron thought. But he was immediately ashamed of his irreverence. He wished he'd never thought it.

'It is France that counts,' Churchill continued gravely. 'That is why you and your department have done so well. You have unearthed SS dissatisfaction with our old adversary, Rommel, who has the task of defending the shores of France against us.'

Churchill looked up and stared pugnaciously at Cameron. 'How big is this split?' He added slowly, 'And what we are doing to widen it? Tell me succinctly what you plan to do on this Château Beaupré report?'

Cameron began to stammer and splutter. The old man couldn't be serious. He was baffled – and furious – as to how copies of Morgan's report had found their way onto so many influential desks. Response had been fast and favourable. Now he had to brief the Prime Minister himself. He wished he'd never set eyes on Morgan. But obviously the man's report had impressed Churchill. Cameron would now have to put into force Morgan's recommendation that Morgan should be sent to infiltrate the château. It galled Cameron to have to repeat Morgan's arguments as if they were his own.

But Churchill cut him short in mid-sentence.

'I cannot pretend I am too happy about us using the services, albeit indirectly, of prostitutes. But I agree your man should be sent to France and establish just what really is happening in this château. That would be best served by having a chat with one of the villains behind this set-up. Bring me one.'

CHAPTER TWELVE

Father Delon listened to the matin bells echo across the hills and then fade. Silhouetted by the evening sunlight, he watched from the church porch as the last of his congregation walked through the lych gate and vanished up the lane to the village. Then he closed the heavy wooden door and, in the chilly shadows of the vestry, removed his white cassock and hung it alongside those of the choir. He stretched, rubbed the stubble on his chin and, bent double, ducked through the rounded archway and slowly mounted the worn steps to the belfry. It was a long unlit haul to his radio transmitter-receiver. Once inside the small tower room, he inched two stones from the wall to reveal the set. The wire led to the weather cock which served as an aerial. He thrust his long arms into the gap in the wall and his fingers found the headphones. He sat on the stones he'd removed from the wall and placed the earpieces on his head. Then, after lighting a cigarette, he fiddled the dial until it rested on the agreed wave-band, and listened intently, pen in hand, for the messages to begin.

The BBC voice came through the crackling static in slow, deliberate French.

'The roses are now in bloom. The roses are now in bloom.'

After a few seconds' silence came the news, in French, that the Allies had taken Monte Casino and were moving towards Rome. Delon crossed himself. More messages followed. The fact that Uncle Harry wanted a new shirt was followed by the one the priest had been waiting for.

'The Dragon will leave its lair,' the voice said, and then slowly repeated the phrase.

Delon wrote it down frantically, flicked off the receiver and hastily replaced the stones. He hurried down the dark steps, through the long shadows of the church, and out into the dying glow of the pale winter sun.

Father Delon chained his cycle to the rail outside the Café Raymond in Lisieux. He waved to a policeman who was talking to two German soldiers, rifles slung, on the far side of the street. The policeman waved back. Delon never thought he would despise the French police force, but these days they had become nothing more than an extension of the occupying forces.

He could hear Albert arguing above the general hubbub. He was sitting, back to the wall, next to old André Pratt. Their bottle of Calvados was almost empty.

'Bring yourself a glass,' Albert yelled, waving as he shifted up the bench seat to make room. Delon sat. Albert filled his glass, then topped up his own.

Amid the verbal uproar, Delon took Albert by the sleeve and drew him aside. He spoke quietly in his ear, then did the same to André. 'The Dragon will leave its lair,' was all he said.

He was pleased with the vigour with which Albert and André, on the same side now, continued their discussions with the men at the next table. They had given no outward indication of the tension his simple sentence must have caused to well up inside them. Although they had all been expecting the message, its arrival was still unsettling. The risks they all now must face might mean death, not just for them but for their families. If the men at the next table had heard the sentence, it would have meant nothing. But to the priest and the two old men, it was simple: an SOE agent would soon be arriving.

Albert elbowed André and gave Delon a reassuring wink before he then left for work. He had a lot to do. Somehow he had to contact Colette Claval.

Clair was in her room. She had bathed, lingering until the scented water cooled, and put on her silk kimono. She was sitting at her dressing table, brushing out her hair, and her reflection reminded her just how content she felt, despite her role as a communal concubine. Her feelings for Helm overshadowed everything. She began to hum softly.

She did not hear the door close behind her. She gave a start when Colette's reflection suddenly appeared next to hers in the glass.

'I wish you wouldn't do that. It gave me a fright,' she said brushing her hair, not looking up.

'I'm sorry. I didn't mean to startle you.' Colette placed her hands on Clair's shoulders and looked for reassurance in the mirror. None came. Only a resentful stare. It made her feel redundant, and it hurt. But Colette could not, would not, begin to consider what life would be like without Clair's affection. It was the only human warmth she'd ever been shown.

'Let me brush it for you,' she said, reaching for the brush.

118

'There's no need. I can manage.'

Colette withdrew her hand quickly. 'But you always like me to brush your hair.'

'I said I can manage. Besides, I've almost finished.' Clair slammed the brush down and snorted angrily. 'Just leave me alone.'

Colette walked to the bed and sat down on it, cross-legged.

Clair opened a jar of nail varnish and busied herself painting her nails. She brushed quickly, raising each finger to her face after every stroke to inspect it. It diverted her eyes from Colette's reflection.

When she stole a glance, Colette was biting her lip. Part of Clair said, 'Go to her. Comfort her. She needs you.' But a louder voice told her, 'No. It's over. No use. You want Rudi Helm.'

She continued to brush her nails.

Colette asked, 'Is it anything I've said or done?'

'Don't be such a bore.'

The words stabbed Colette. She felt despair and then panic at being totally alone. She needed to be reached out to, touched. Held tightly, warmly. The gloom spread like spilt ink.

'Please, Clair, what has happened?' she asked.

'Nothing. Nothing has happened. It's just that at times you can be so damn trying.'

'It would be different if we weren't shut up in this place, I know it. If you feel you don't want me anymore, then it is only because we are locked up here. I hate it. I loathe this filthy, stinking, bloody place. They treat us like cattle. It's like being on a farm and led out of a cowshed only when someone wants you. When we are back in Paris, it will all be different. You just wait and see. Just like it was before.'

Clair thought, 'Don't make me say I don't want you any more.' But she didn't have to say it. Colette could read the words on her face.

'You've grown tired of me,' she mumbled.

Clair rose from the dressing table and faced Colette, but she had to turn away. 'I'm not tired of you,' she said softly. 'It is not as simple as that. I really do not want to hurt you.'

'Then what is it?'

'It is Rudi.'

'But that's impossible. You can't love him. Not that German. Please say that is not true. I could not face it here without you.'

'It's true.'

They fell into silence. Clair felt relief it was out, that at last she'd said it. She also felt guilt, remorse that she had hurt Colette. 'I'm a selfish bitch,' she thought. 'I don't want you to be hurt. Not you. Not Colette.' The voices inside her rose in conflict, and she felt only confusion.

Colette stood at the foot of the bed. Naked. Her simple blue dress lay rumpled at her feet. She was holding out her arms and tears streamed down her face.

'Share me,' Colette wept. 'It's all I ask, all I want. Share me. But please don't leave me. Not here. Alone.'

'I can't,' Clair screamed at the top of her voice. 'Why won't you understand that I can't?' She could take it no more. The pain and confusion were too much. She took Colette by the shoulders and shook her.

'Go. Go. Go,' she yelled and pushed Colette away. 'You must understand. Go, in the name of God, get out and leave me alone. I only need him now. Not you. It's over.'

Clair became hysterical. She took Colette roughly by the arm and threw her to the floor. 'I hate you. Understand? Hate you.'

Colette lunged and grabbed Clair's hair, pulling her onto the bed. Clair screamed as Colette sank her teeth into her shoulder. She broke free. Colette grabbed at the silk kimono and pulled her back. The silk, split in two, fell to the floor. Then they fell upon each other, rolling over the bed and smashing into the wicker headboard, splintering it. Their fists punched at each other's bodies, and their legs kicked wildly as they fell onto the floor, clawing at flesh they'd once caressed.

Clair stood up and gripped a handful of Colette's short dark hair, and Colette, kneeling now, tensed in agony as her neck bent back. Colette twisted her head and opened her mouth to scream and her lips brushed the inside of Clair's thigh. She bit deeply into the soft skin. Albert burst into the room just as Clair cried out in pain. He was a fraction ahead of Helm, who had bounded up the stairs when he heard the screaming. Together they parted the naked bodies which lay weeping on the carpet.

Helm wrested Colette to her feet. 'Get that out of here,' he spat in rage, flinging the naked girl towards Albert.

The old man caught her in his arms and held her to him, bristling as he saw the mark of Clair's talons on the girl's back. 'That,' Albert said with all the contempt he could muster, 'is a French lady. So mind your mouth.' Regard for his safety seemed to have left him, but Helm didn't hear. He had helped Clair up and she stood with her arms draped around his neck.

Albert snorted. He took off his jacket and slipped it over Colette's shoulders. It fitted her like a tent and reached just below her knees. She buried her face in her hands as Albert put his arm around her shoulders and helped her to the door. He smiled as he kicked it shut behind him. At last he'd made contact with the girl vital to his plan.

As the door slammed, Helm kissed Clair on the top of her head, lifted her, and walked towards the bed.

Then he stopped suddenly, staring in horror.

Dangling from the splintered wicker headboard was the metal head of a microphone. Fear swept over him. When he had poured out his troubles to Clair, poured out his fears to the girl he adored, his love and woe, someone had listened. Someone had heard everything. A glacial cold gripped him.

He sat Clair on the edge of the bed, knelt and raised his finger to his lips. Then as she watched, bewildered, he flew to the dressing table, picked up her nail brush and varnish, and painted the words SAY NOTHING on the mirror. He pointed to the microphone swinging on the length of flex.

Clair, baffled, could only nod.

Helm wiped the message from the mirror with Clair's stocking and went to inspect the microphone. The wire ran through an upright pole of the headrest. He lifted the bed. The wire passed into a hole drilled in the floor. His jaw tensed. Why was the room bugged? Someone's – Ulrich's? Perhaps it was Nicole McGragh's – idea of a cheap thrill? He doubted it.

Nicole McGragh's face confirmed it. 'What is the meaning of this,' she said from the open door as she surveyed the shambles caused by the two girls. 'I could hear the screaming throughout the building.' She pointed to Clair. 'You'll be punished for this.'

'She needs some air,' Helm said and handed Clair a dress from the back of a chair. 'We'll walk in the grounds.'

Then he took Nicole by the arm, manoeuvred her gently into the corridor, and shut the door. 'Who in hell's name gave you permission to place microphones in these bedrooms?' he barked.

Nicole was taken aback. 'I beg your pardon?' she said indignantly. 'And how dare you address me like that? Colonel Ulrich shall hear of this.'

'Who put them there?' Helm's voice rose. 'Who?'

'I don't know what you are talking about. And let go of my arm.' Nicole shook herself free. She eyed Helm carefully. 'It wasn't me,' she said slowly, her eyes glinting. 'So who was it?'

Helm sensed she was telling the truth. She was not party to any cheap thrill. That, he realised to his horror, left only Ulrich.

Helm felt weak at the knees. He feared the set-up had not only made men complacent. It also had compromised them. He felt sick again at the thought. What had the others told their whores? Von Beck, Muller, even Durring? Now Canaris at the Abwehr would have to listen to his doubts about the château operation. Canaris would have to take notice. He would ring him at once.

Helm apologised to Nicole, who was still nursing her arm where he'd gripped it.

Nicole smiled malevolently. 'It seems to be becoming a habit with senior German officers.'

'I must get you not to mention this incident to Colonel Ulrich,' Helm said urgently. 'I beg you. Please believe me.'

Nicole twisted her head and looked quizzically at him. 'Beg, Major?'

Helm could only nod. He waited for her reply.

'All right,' she said flatly.

Helm sighed. Then thanked her and returned to Clair's room.

Alone in the corridor, Nicole muttered to herself, 'If Ulrich has bugged your bedroom, then he's got his eye on you and that blonde bitch. Why should I spoil whatever he has in mind for the pair of you? Especially her?'

She turned sharply and took the stairs to her suite on the floor below.

Three doors down the corridor from Clair's room, Colette clung to Albert, her shoulders still heaving. He prised her from him and sat her on the bed. She shook her head, bemused. Albert sat next to her.

'Don't fret so,' he said with the assurance of a kindly grandfather. 'It is not worth it. Crying over someone like that snooty slut.'

'I love her.'

'Don't be such a silly girl. You can't love her. She's a . . . a . . . woman.' This was all a bit beyond Albert. 'You can't love a woman,' he reassured her as if she'd made a stupid, but forgivable, mistake.

'You're wrong. You cannot understand how I feel about her.'

He did not. 'She's a slut. She may talk like a lady with all of her fancy airs and chic clothes. But she's a slut. The way she makes up to that Boche pig. No decent French girl would do that.'

Colette smiled and brushed away a tear. 'She, all of us, have no choice, otherwise they'll kill us. Ulrich said so.'

'We'll see about that,' Albert snorted.

Colette sniffed, and smiled. She reached for the old man's gnarled hand and squeezed it.

Albert rose. He walked to the girl's wardrobe and rummaged through the clothes on the rail. He picked a floral dress, black with large yellow flowers. He handed it to her and turned his back.

'Put it on,' he said.

Colette was touched by the kind gesture. The only one a man had ever made her. She let the coat fall and slipped into the dress. As asked, Albert helped with the zip. His stubby fingers fumbled with the catch and he cursed. Then immediately apologised.

Colette laughed.

Albert said, 'You really hate Germans, don't you?'

Her smile vanished and the hatred he'd seen through the camera, and never forgotten, took its place.

'One day, I swear, I'll kill every one of the bastards in this place,' she said, eyes narrowing.

'Will you now, my little sparrow?' he said reprovingly.

'Yes. Every one of the pigs.'

Albert looked at the girl. Her threat was preposterous – but he knew she meant to try.

'Would you like to get away from here?' he asked, raising a bushy eyebrow.

'You mean it?' Colette gulped. He grinned. 'How? How can I get out?'

'Well,' Albert said softly, 'first there is a man I want you to meet.'

'Who? Tell me who, who, who?' She bounced on the balls of her feet.

'For the moment let's just call him the Dragon.'

Helm was beginning to lose his temper with the man on the end of the line. Even though he held the rank of Major-General.

'Fool,' he muttered and stubbed his cigarette, half-smoked, into the ashtray.

It was five minutes before General Dietrich Bekker, a top Canaris aide, came back on the line.

'It is totally out of the question for you to come to Berlin and see the Admiral in person. Quite impossible. He sends his regrets.'

'Look,' Helm pleaded desperately, 'you say this tape-recording system has been carried out without Abwehr authority. If Ulrich was not acting for you, then he can only be an SS plant.'

'The Admiral agrees with you,' Bekker said. 'He says if the SS had not tried something like this, he would have been disappointed. He'd have spent too much time overestimating them.'

'But that means that through these tapes of the whores, the SS must now have a complete picture of the strength and weakness of some of the top officers in Western Command.'

'I have already put your points to the Admiral,' Bekker said. 'And?'

'He says you should take no action.'

The phone went dead and Helm stared at the mouthpiece. It sounded as if Canaris wanted Rommel undermined, his arguments unheard. Surely he realised only Rommel could stop an invasion? Then a chilling thought came slowly to Helm. It was as if Canaris wanted Germany to lose the war . . .

He rang von Beck. 'I want to see you right away.'

Helm put down the phone. Von Beck was a good man.

Von Beck bit his knuckle and listened to Helm without interrupting.

'We must go straight to Rommel,' he said when Helm had finished. 'Bastards like Ulrich must be ground into the dirt, like all Hitler's scum.'

Helm shook his head. 'And tell him what? That you can't trust the officers on your command because they are being black-mailed over their sexual indiscretions? Think of the effect on morale if these men resigned, never mind were sacked. Disastrous!'

'It would be even more disastrous if we can't halt the invasion. Germany would be better served if we rid her of these Nazi weevils – right to the very top. Otherwise we're finished,' von Beck said bitterly.

'Talk like that is going to get you shot,' Helm warned.

'Someone is going to have to do it.'

'Be reasonable,' Helm said. 'You must go to Durring and tell him what's going on. I can't talk to the man, but he listens to you. He's also an old friend of Rommel's. Durring might just be the best man to make an approach to the Field Marshal. He's not much, but it's all we have.'

'Is it?'

'Just find him and tell him,' Helm snapped impatiently.

Von Beck rose in silence.

At that moment he had decided to become an assassin.

Major-General Franz Durring had been a great disappointment to his late parents. To achieve his present rank had cost them dear in money, influence and credibility. First it had taken all their well-heeled connections to secure a place in the military academy for their adolescent rake. And then it had taken every notable person they knew to keep him there. After graduation, Durring had received a prized Berlin posting. There he had set out to prove that the well of delights the city offered could be drained by pure Prussian dedication. But all that had been changed by that vulgar little man Hitler, and war. Nevertheless, Durring's connections and his ability to say the right things to the right people had meant rapid rise. Even now life had its compensations.

One was the Château Beaupré. Or to be more precise, the dark-haired Maria Luardi. She reminded him of his stern childhood nanny. All he ever asked was that she dress like Frau Hager and re-create the circumstances that made him, like other German children, such a great respecter of discipline. Durring's favourite scenario was a re-enactment of a boyhood episode during which he raided the pastor's orchard.

Maria also enjoyed the game. She delighted in shaking him by the jowls and spitting at him in punishment.

Maria had just made him confess for the third time that evening when the phone rang. Durring, a mouth full of stolen apple, answered it. As he listened, squinting with confusion, bits of apple dribbled down his chin. He swallowed hard to clear his mouth and tell his young aide just what he thought. But the line suddenly went dead.

He motioned Maria away and sat on the edge of the bed. Von Beck had to be joking. But it was in poor taste and dangerous.

'Young hothead,' he mumbled. Durring knew talk like that courted disaster, even among friends.

'What did the man mean: "We must act now. Remove them all"?' Durring asked Maria.

'How should I know?' Maria said, shrugging her shoulders.

Durring considered calling von Beck back. He had said that matters were so urgent they could not wait.

Then Maria stood before him. He reached out and placed his hands on her hips and buried his head in her breasts.

Von Beck could wait.

Ulrich was ecstatic. They wanted to kill him.

At last he had more than he'd hoped possible. At long last.

They thought they could kill *him*. The filth were going to try. Kill him. The bastards. And his Führer. Fools. That aristocrat Hoffner had no right to be on such a death list. Perhaps he should allow them to kill Hoffner, which would be sweet . . .

Ulrich was alone in the windowless basement of the Hôtel Chloé in Lisieux. He hunched forward over the tape and re-played the recording of von Beck's call to Durring. His eyes grew with pleasure as he leant closer to the slowly turning spools. It was a shame the pair had been cut short.

Ulrich transcribed the one-way conversation between the aide and his general – Rommel's general. Then he punched it out on the telex and waited for the phone to ring. It took four minutes.

Ulrich lifted the receiver, glowing with pride. Schellenberg had entrusted him to provide a good enough reason to rid his Reich of Rommel and his jackals. Now he had it.

'It's not enough,' Schellenberg said. 'It's good, but not so good we could nail Rommel. It will hang this von Beck from the highest tree – but I think I have a better use for him.'

'What more do you want?' Ulrich protested meekly.

'Don't be so disappointed. You have done well,' Schellenberg said reassuringly. 'Let me read your last message . . .'

Schellenberg read out extracts from Ulrich's tape:

'"I must see you at once, it's urgent and cannot wait. We must speak with Rommel as soon as possible. The time has come, there is no more left to waste. Hitler and those around him must be removed, for the honour of Germany. You know what must be done. It will have to begin here in Normandy with those who stand in Rommel's way: Ulrich, Voight, Colonel Schaffer, Major Kranck – even Hoffner – have to die. When we strike here the others in Berlin can follow. The army . . ."'

He stopped reading.

'Both you and I know they are plotting. But this as evidence is too vague. Durring didn't even speak. Except for this von Beck, we don't even have names. I want to know about all the treacherous bastards. There is shit in Rommel's nest but we have to make sure we can cover him with it. Ruin him for once and all. What you have so far is good, but only a start.'

'We can begin with von Beck. Pull him in,' Ulrich said.

'No. Leave him, he's small fry. A mere captain. The ball has been placed in General Durring's court. Tell me about him.'

'He's an aristocrat forced to play at soldiers – between pig-sticking parties in the Black Forest – and a close friend of Rommel's.'

'Will he break?'

'Yes.'

'Then break him. But it must be done carefully. Use the Gestapo and make it look as if they got the results on their own. Whatever happens, Rommel is going to smell like a farmyard.'

'What about von Beck?'

'Leave him. When we take Durring, he is going to have to run. Let's see whom he runs to. In fact I had better come to Normandy myself. No one, except you, will know.'

CHAPTER THIRTEEN

Morgan sat alone in a corner of the officers' mess at RAF Lyshan, cradling a glass of whisky. He wore commando uniform, the green beret folded into his epaulet. He was unshaven, and tense. In a few hours he would be in France.

He took a gulp of whisky to steady his nerves and looked round the room. He disliked the enforced bonhomie of messes, none more so the RAF's. The room was small and crowded. Under the propeller of an enemy Messerschmitt, which hung in triumph from the centre of the ceiling, a group of WAAFs crowded round a long table. At the end of it a young pilot, arms outstretched, was balancing a pint of flat beer on his head. The WAAFs, fresh-faced with bubble hair-dos and black stockings, were squealing encouragement.

Morgan felt in his pocket for the gold cufflinks. They were the traditional parting gift for SOE agents – a token of respect which could also be sold for hard cash should the need arise. He took another sip of whisky. His nerves were jangling.

Suddenly there was a loud shriek. He sat up with a jolt as the pilot spilled the beer, soaking one of the WAAFs, who spluttered and, laughing, wiped her eyes. Morgan caught his breath and the hairs tingled on the back of his neck. The girl could have been Debbie Forster's sister. She peered through her wet hair at Morgan.

'Do you always stare at girls that way?' She even sounded like Debbie, the same cut-glass vowels.

Morgan twisted uncomfortably as she came over to him. 'I'm sorry. I didn't mean to upset you,' he said.

'You didn't. On the contrary, I'm flattered.'

She even flashed her eyelashes like Debbie. It was uncanny. Morgan smiled sadly. 'It's just that for a moment I thought you were someone else.'

'She must be a lucky girl.' The WAAF smiled.

Remorse welled up inside him. He knew he was not entirely to blame, but if it had not been for him, Debbie would still look like that. Until now his mind had blocked out her image; he had thought of her only as a woman, his woman, the way she'd soothed him, made love. He threw back his whisky.

'Well, aren't you going to offer me one?' The girl sat at his table.

'I'm sorry.' Morgan stood.

'You really should not keep apologising. You know what they say ...' She clicked her fingers at the steward. 'Two more Scotches over here please.'

Just like Debbie.

'I always seem to remind people of someone. I must have a terribly common face,' she said.

'It's a lovely face,' Morgan said.

'She really is a lucky lady, this friend of yours.'

Morgan made no reply. The girl quickly changed the subject. 'Ooops,' she said. 'Sore point. Sorry,' then added in the same breath, 'Do you live in London?'

'Yes. A small flat in West Hampstead.'

'It must be super to be a commando, not having to live in some dreary barracks or other.'

'It has its advantages.'

'My parents have a house in Chelsea. I stay there when I'm on leave. You must give me a ring. We can do the town.' She scribbled a phone number and handed it to him. As he was putting it in his pocket, a young airman approached.

'Captain Morgan,' he said formally. 'Your things are ready. If you'd please follow me, sir.'

Morgan rose. 'Pity about the drink. No time,' he said to the WAAF.

'Don't forget to ring. You can always leave a message.'

Morgan smiled gently and turned to follow the airman.

When they had collected the two small brown suitcases from the property office, the airman carried them to a small room and left Morgan alone.

Morgan laid the cases on the single bed and opened them. One contained civilian clothes: a blue flannel shirt, brown trousers, denim jacket, underwear and peak cap. All bore French labels. He dressed.

He was now Henri Paco. His pockets contained the minutiae to confirm it: papers, cinema stubs and a rail ticket from Paris to Caen where he worked for a builder. The rail ticket had that day's date: February 2, 1944. Everything had been forged at SOE, perfectly.

Morgan felt the lining of his jacket and fished out a small envelope from which he removed two cyanide pills. He crushed them and washed them down the handbasin in the corner. The thought he might have to use them was too frightening to contemplate.

The second case contained a radio transmitter. Morgan sat on the bed and smoked his last English cigarette. Then he left the packet, along with his Zippo lighter, on the bed. He picked up the second case and made his way to the briefing rooms along the corridor.

There he was greeted by the pilot from 130 Special Operations Squadron (SOS) who would fly him to a small clearing in dense woodland near Lisieux. The man was a sergeant. Officers, more expensive to train, were never risked on such missions. Morgan took to the man instantly. He was craggy-faced with a shock of red, curly hair. He walked towards Morgan with a slight but noticeable limp.

'How do you do, sir. My name is Vigars. Sergeant Len Vigars.'

Vigars was a Cockney and proud of it.

Morgan loathed being called 'sir'.

'My name is Nat Morgan,' he said, breaking the strict SOE rule of anonymity. He decided Vigars had the right to know whom he was risking his life for, if not why.

'Welsh are you?' Vigars said cheerfully. 'Always had me holidays as a kid in Barry Island. Know it? Lovely place.'

Morgan remembered brown sea, donkeys on the sand, lost children and a loud funfair overlooking the coal port. He smiled.

'I loved it,' Vigars grinned back. 'Now, me old son,' he explained, 'I'm going to have to dump you right in the middle of these here woods by Lisieux [he pronounced it Lizyerks]. It might get a tiny bit hairy because of all the trees around it. They're a bit bleedin' high and the clearing ain't too wide at all. Just about seventy feet, maybe a bit more.'

'What's the wing span of a Lysander?'

'Only fifty-eight feet, so there's bags of room, providing we don't get a lot of side wind.'

Maths wasn't Morgan's strongest point but it did not take him long to work out there would be six feet of space between the wing tips and trees.

'Why the hell choose that clearing?'

'Safety, me old son,' Vigars reassured. 'It's miles from anywhere and all those high trees mean the Jerries ain't going to spot the fires the Resistance light to guide us in.'

Morgan nodded his approval.

'Now then, the form is that we can't use radio over the zone. When I see the fires, I put you down a bit rapid, keep the old motor running and out you get. But before you get off, you get a hold of the crate behind your seat. You hand that down to this bloke who will be waiting. But for God's sake, be bleedin' careful how you handle it and just don't sling it out any old how. Do it real gently like, because it's got enough high explosives in it to blow us all to kingdom come and back again. Got it?'

Morgan nodded slightly.

'Good on you. Questions?'

Morgan shook his head.

'Right, ready when you are. All I hope is that you haven't been putting away pints of beer. Lysanders don't carry a bog.'

Morgan laughed. 'Straight whisky man.'

'Light and bitter meself. It's lovely stuff but it plays hell with the old bladder,' Vigars added, crossing his legs.

Morgan watched him limp to the door leading to the runway and wondered how many times Vigars had risked his neck putting down in occupied France the stringbag waiting on the apron. For the Vigars of this world, Morgan had nothing but admiration.

'Len,' he called as he followed Vigars to the waiting aircraft.

'Second thoughts, mate?' the pilot grinned. 'Can't say I blame you.'

Morgan took the pair of gold cufflinks from his pocket. 'I'd like you to take these.'

'Gettcha,' Vigars said, waving his hand.

'Take them,' Morgan held them out, 'with thanks.'

Vigars hesitated for a moment, shuffling with embarrassment. He bit the inside of his cheek. Then took them. 'I really appreciate that,' he said, and meant it.

Morgan turned up his collar and walked through the drizzle to the waiting Lysander. It had been designed for towing aerial targets and its low stalling speed and short take-off made it perfect for landing agents in foreign fields. Vigars gave the plane an affectionate pat, mumbled something to it Morgan could not hear, and climbed aboard.

Morgan took the piece of paper with the WAAF's phone number and crumpled it into a heap. He watched as the wind blew it towards the puddles scudding on the tarmac and then joined Vigars. Two ground crew jumped nimbly aside as the propeller jutting from the stub nose sprang to life with a deafening roar.

Morgan put on his headphones in time to hear Vigars's conversation with the unseen control tower. 'Come on, lads, throw another Christian on the fire, and give us some bleedin' light.'

'Will do,' an Oxford accent replied.

Seconds later the runway lamps blazed in unison and lit a narrowing road which stretched into the darkness.

'Oscar Lima November, stand by for take-off.'

'Wish they'd get on with it,' Vigars said, turning to look at Morgan. 'We haven't got all bloody night.'

'You're cleared for take-off,' the voice said.

'Cheers, me old darlings. See you.'

The Lysander roared over the reflections dancing on the runway, lifted its nose and pushed steeply towards the clouds. When Morgan looked down, the runway had returned to darkness.

'Good luck,' said the voice on the headset.

'Cheers, mate,' Vigars replied, then mimicked the voice to say, 'Roger, over and out.'

Over Dorset they left the rain clouds behind, and flew steadily on in the darkness. Only the sound of the Lysander's engine could be heard. As they crossed the coast, Vigars closed on the throttle and lost height.

'We could ice up and that would be nasty,' he explained.

As they neared the French coast, Vigars yelled, 'Listen to that little lot. Just listen to them.'

Even above the steady hum of the old Lysander, Morgan could hear it. From thousands of feet above his head he felt vibrations shake the Lysander until every nut and bolt hummed in unison. It was a steady throbbing sound that pounded louder by the minute. Morgan looked up and saw nothing, yet the sound grew.

'What is it?'

'Wellingtons, bless them. Dozens of lovely Wellington bombers.'

As the formation flew directly above them, Morgan thought the Lysander would shake itself to bits.

'The bastards are really in for it tonight. Germany is going to get a right old hammering,' Vigars yelled, waving his arms in the air. 'Atta boys, give the bloody swines one for Anna.'

The formation passed them. Then, in the distance, they saw

132

a battery of searchlight beams stretch across the sky and heard the shore batteries pound in chorus, hurling red and yellow balls of fire exploding into the night.

'They'll never hit them at that height,' Vigars chuckled. 'Not in a million bleedin' light years. But they might get us, and that would never do.'

He yanked on the controls and the plane climbed steeply, veering south to avoid the flak.

'Hope you brought your winter woollies,' Vigars said.

Morgan huddled down in the seat. It got cold. Bloody cold. At last they levelled out.

'How much longer?' Morgan asked through chattering teeth.

'About forty minutes. Not long.'

'Len?'

'What?'

'Who is Anna?'

There was a pause.

'Was,' Vigars said.

'Was?'

'That's right. Was. My fiancée. Jewish, you know. What a little smasher. Lived down the Whitechapel Road. Father had a small tailor's shop. They was all wiped out in the Blitz. All of them. Grandmother and all. They came to London from Poland to get away from the likes of bloody Hitler and they still cop it. There's no sodding justice.'

Morgan said nothing. There was nothing he could say. He felt the old anger burn inside him as the two men lapsed into silence.

Then Vigars yelled, 'Oh frigging hell.' The engine was screaming at full power and suddenly Morgan's stomach moved to where his feet had been. The plane was somersaulting increasingly faster, and then it began to spin, boring through the night towards the earth below. Vigars was tugging frantically at the controls, first one way, then the other, all to no avail. The Lysander was completely out of control, gaining speed at a sickening rate. The box of explosives behind Morgan's rear seat catapulted forward and its corner smashed into his back, leaving him breathless. The box had wedged itself between floor and fuselage, pinning Morgan forward in his seat.

'What the shit's happening?' Morgan shouted as he fought for breath.

'We've bloody well iced up. We climbed too sodding high. The controls are frozen solid; I can't do a thing with them, they won't respond.'

As they plummeted, whirling uncontrollably, the side of the forward canopy shattered. Cold air raced in through the yawning hole in the perspex canopy, burning their faces, pelleting them with tiny drops of ice, like small slivers of glass.

Vigars whooped for joy as he picked up a large ball of ice, larger than a football, from his lap.

'Bloody great! The stuff's breaking off.' He threw it back through the hole it had made. 'Keep your fingers crossed, Captain.' He hauled on the controls and the plane curved to the right.

'We've got starboard control back,' he beamed.

'What about the others?'

'What do you want, chocolate sauce with it? At least we are going round, not down.'

Then more chunks of ice began to bounce off the perspex canopy. Both men yelled, as if to encourage more to break off.

Vigars wrested the controls again.

'It's getting better. We can now go in a straight blooming line.' He checked his compass and then nodded out of the cockpit. 'Look at that.'

The wings were sheets of ice.

'Is that bad?'

'I can fly her, but I'll never land her. I am going to try to head back for the sea.'

'The sea? I think I'd rather risk a crash landing. We've got no life rafts.'

'I don't plan to ditch the old girl, just thaw her out a bit.'

'I don't understand.'

'The salt air. It plays havoc with ice. When was the last time you saw a snowman on Southend beach?'

They re-crossed the French coast an hour later. Vigars had flown in circles at almost wave height and the brine gradually had turned the ice on the wings to water.

'I hope those Resistance geezers ain't got fed up waiting and buggered off home.'

'So do I,' Morgan said.

'We should know in about ten minutes. Keep your eyes skinned for the little fires.'

Morgan peered into the darkness, his anxiety mounting, but at last he saw them. One by one, tiny orange balls burst into life as the plane flew overhead. They formed two narrow – very narrow, Morgan thought – lines of light.

'Here we go,' Vigars said. The Lysander dipped with a sickening drop. 'Pray there's no side winds. I haven't got a clue which way it's blowing from those fires, they're going all over the shop.'

Morgan looked down. The glows were flickering in erratic dance. They raced towards them.

'Oops,' Vigars said as the fixed undercarriage clipped the tops of the trees. Then came a bump, and another. They were down.

The plane halted thirty feet from the end of the clearing.

'Thank God for that. Don't want too many rides like this one, thanks very much,' Vigars said. He wiped his goggles.

'Well, son, that's your lot. Better hop it.'

Morgan eased himself from his seat, opened the canopy and squeezed free of the box of explosives. He could see no one.

'Perhaps they've scarpered,' Vigars said.

Morgan prayed not. They were an hour overdue. What if during that time the Germans had stumbled across the Resistance group?

Vigars pulled back the throttle and the plane shook on its undercarriage. The engine was straining to go.

'I don't like it,' he said, 'but if we've got to pull out, we've got no chance of clearing the trees at the end of the strip. And it's not wide enough to turn around, without help.'

Then Morgan saw them. 'Over there in the trees,' he yelled as the figures emerged from cover. Morgan guessed there were about nine. Rifles in hand they fanned out around the plane, knelt in a semi-circle and raised their weapons. Another man emerged from the trees. He advanced brandishing a pistol, but Morgan couldn't make out his features in the dim, wavering light. All he was certain of was the gun pointed at his head.

'Don't move,' a voice said in English.

Morgan, unarmed, his mouth dry, cupped his hands and called out above the plane's roar, 'The Dragon flew tonight.'

Vigars was trying to swing the plane about but the Lysander's tail clipped the trees and he had to ease back the throttle. He could not turn without snapping the fuselage in two.

'The Dragon flew tonight,' Morgan, desperate, yelled again.

There was no response. The man moved forward. Morgan's hand felt for the dagger – his only weapon – tucked inside his sock. He found the handle, and drew it.

135

'Welcome, Dragon. You're late,' said the voice.

Morgan and Vigars let out sighs of relief.

'You have brought the explosives?'

'Yes.'

The man waved his gun hand. Two of the others lowered their rifles and ran to the plane. They raised their arms and caught the crate which Morgan handed down by its rope handle.

'Careful, lads,' Vigars pleaded.

Morgan took his radio case and jumped to the ground. The man tucked his pistol into his belt and thrust his hand forward.

'Scrélat,' he said.

'Henri Paco, pleased to meet you,' Morgan said, taking his hand and smiling. 'I believe you have a job for me.'

'Oi,' bawled Vigars, leaning out of his cockpit. 'Voulez-vous someone aidez-moi turner this bloody plane around. I'll never get home without the pissing tail.'

Morgan translated. Four men, straining and groaning, pushed the plane backwards until there was room to turn. With the rudder at right angles, the Lysander slithered on the damp grass and faced the other way.

Vigars gave a thumbs-up sign.

'Thanks,' Morgan called.

'Anytime, old son. Buy us a pint sometime.' Vigars then pulled the canopy shut and pushed the throttle forward. The plane bounced angrily, then screamed down the clearing and reached for the sky. A cloudburst of branches and twigs rained down as again the plane clipped the tree tops, and was gone.

The men moved along the lines of fires, extinguished them, and then, taking the case of explosives, vanished into the trees.

'What's that?' Scrélat asked, pointing to Morgan's case.

'Radio.'

'Dump it. Not worth the risk of being found with it.'

Morgan slung it into the undergrowth.

'This way, follow me,' Scrélat said over his shoulder as he moved quickly into the woods. 'The road is ten kilometres from here. We must get there by sunrise. The truck is waiting.'

When conditions permitted they ran at an Apache trot. When not, they jogged. They never stopped or spoke.

Twenty minutes before dawn, they sighted the dirt road where an old maroon Citroën was waiting. Painted on its doors in a flourish of yellow was: 'Scrélat Frères. Charpentiers': Scrélat Brothers. Builders.

When they reached the edge of the road, Scrélat grabbed Morgan's arm, stopping him in his tracks, and motioned him down with his hand. Crouched behind the hedge, Scrélat cupped his hand and gave two long hoots.

Silence.

Finally, two hoots were returned from the trees behind the truck.

'OK, it's safe. Let's go,' Scrélat said.

They ran to the truck. The other man met them there. He was wearing painter's overalls. Morgan was introduced only as Paco. He got into the front seat, and the other man sat in the back. Scrélat drove to the end of the dirt road and then they stopped for a few minutes to wait for dawn. When the sky turned crimson, Scrélat said, 'Curfew is over. Red sky in morning – shepherd's warning. It's going to be a bad day.' He jabbed the truck in gear, and the rear wheels spun, throwing up stones. They swung onto route Nationale 13 and headed for Lisieux.

Two German soldiers in greatcoats were manning a roadblock. When they rounded the bend, it was too late to try and turn back. They had come into full view. Rifles unslung, the two soldiers moved into the centre of the road and waved the truck down.

'Shit,' Scrélat hissed. He turned to Morgan. 'Pray they made a good job of your papers. Remember we picked you up from Caen station and stayed overnight because of the curfew. You've got your rail ticket?'

Morgan nodded. He felt the dagger in his sock, then crossed his legs and hitched his trousers slightly. The truck stopped.

The soldiers ambled forward. One placed a hand on the headlight and kicked the tyre. The other, younger and with a ginger stubble and bags under his eyes, walked around the truck. The first covered him with his rifle. Neither spoke. Scrélat fidgeted nervously. Morgan's hand rested on his shin, inches from the concealed dagger.

'Papers.' The soldier, who had completed his turn of the truck, held out his hand, while the other moved to Morgan's door, rifle in hand. He inspected Scrélat's papers and handed them back. 'Now yours.' He eyed Morgan who removed his wallet and gave it to Scrélat to hand to the German.

'We missed the curfew and stayed overnight in Caen.'

The German opened Morgan's wallet. He checked the identity card and compared the photograph with Morgan. Then he sifted through the contents. He looked at the railway ticket dated the previous day. From Paris to Caen.

'Train was late,' Morgan said.

Both soldiers moved as one.

Morgan felt the rifle barrel press into his neck.

'Get out.' Morgan, heart racing, winced. 'There was no train. Terrorists blew the line.'

Morgan thought quickly. They could offer no resistance. If they made the wrong move, they were dead. He took a gamble with his life. The line must have been destroyed between Paris and Caen. But where? If he picked a station the wrong side of the place the attack on the line had occurred, they were finished. He had no idea of the names of the stations along the track. But Scrélat would. Morgan kicked him on the ankle, and prayed Scrélat would pick up his cue.

'We know that. It was because of those bloody terrorists we had to spend the night in a bloody dosshouse in Caen. M'sieu Scrélat had to drive up the line to pick me up. The authorities should do something.' Would Scrélat pick a station not cut off by the blast?

The cold gunmetal still dug into Morgan's neck. 'Which station?' the German asked.

'Conches,' Scrélat said.

Morgan watched the second soldier's face for any hint that Scrélat had guessed wrong. He saw none. Then he felt the metal leave his neck. He turned. The soldier had slung his rifle.

'Besides,' Scrélat said pointing to the ticket in the second soldier's hand, 'why should we want to blow up a train with M'sieur Paco on it. I need him to work for me – labour is so hard to get these days. Everyone's being conscripted for defence work.'

The soldier grunted. He read the warrant giving Paco permission to leave Paris to work for Scrélat. It bore the seal of the German governor of Paris's office. He rubbed the bags under his eyes. It had been a long night and he wanted his bed. To check out the men in the truck would have meant only more paperwork. They had, after all, had their papers stamped, and there was the ticket.

He raised the red-and-white pole and waved them through.

The trunk clanked slowly up the road towards Lisieux.

'Thank Christ you guessed Conches,' Morgan said.

'I didn't guess,' Scrélat said. 'They are the only group in the area with any explosives. That's why we hoped you would bring in fresh supplies. We all ran out weeks ago.'

Morgan laughed softly and began to whistle just as the first rain drops splattered on the windscreen.

'Shepherd's warning,' Scrélat complained.

Twenty minutes later, the truck arrived at the red brick offices of Scrélat Frères, and Morgan followed Scrélat inside. They climbed some dusty wooden stairs to the timber store in the loft. Morgan saw an old man with a face which Rembrandt could have painted. On the crate beside the old man, was a bottle of rough red wine, a broken loaf and some cheese. When the old man saw them, he puffed out his chest, took a swig from the bottle and rose to greet Morgan.

'Allô,' he said proudly. 'I'm Albert Boniface.' He poured some wine into a cracked mug and handed it to Morgan, who took it with a grin and gulped it down in one.

'It's good,' he said politely, then coughed.

'It's terrible,' Albert said, grinning broadly. 'Welcome to France.' He then embraced Morgan in a bonecracking bear hug which Morgan returned. Remembering all that Albert had risked for him and for the war, Morgan stepped back and clasped the old man's shoulders. He could have squeezed him until the pips squeaked. 'Albert Boniface you're a gem ... I think you have a young lady who would like to meet me?'

Albert's eyes twinkled. He bent his fingers, pressed them to his lips and blew a smacking kiss into the dusty air.

CHAPTER FOURTEEN

Morgan was sleeping on a torn horsehair mattress in Scrélat's timber loft. He dreamed he was in a wet muddy hole in the château grounds. He was lying on his back, wounded and helpless, as a figure in a long black cloak and hood came towards him. The figure took off the cloak and a deformed face leered down at him.

Ulrich.

Morgan squirmed, but otherwise could not move. Ulrich, in Nazi uniform now, stood astride him and punctured his bowels with a bayonet. Then, with his jackboot on Morgan's stomach, Ulrich pulled out the bayonet and Morgan watched his own entrails slowly spill out.

Morgan screamed and opened his eyes.

'We are ready,' Scrélat said, as he nudged Morgan once more with his boot. He handed him a sten gun, freshly greased and smelling of oil. 'It's time for you to go to the Château Beaupré,' he said. Morgan took the gun and followed him. At the bottom of the worn wooden stairs, they were met by André Pratt and Father Delon.

'Do you still plan to see Ulrich's whore?' The little chemist's voice was full of concern, and he fidgeted nervously with the pince-nez hanging from the chain around his neck.

'We think meeting her in the château grounds is too big a risk. How can you be sure she will not betray you?' Delon asked.

'I can't,' Morgan said as he checked his sten, ramming back the catch. 'But, as we discussed last night, she is the only direct contact we have.' Morgan glanced at his watch. It was a quarter to seven. 'Now I must go. We are wasting time.'

Morgan, his eyes still heavy from an uneasy sleep, joined Scrélat in the cab of his truck. He placed the sten on his lap, released the safety catch, and covered the gun with an old sack from the floor of the cab.

It was not long after they had left the city and were headed along route 13 towards the Ste-Yvette turn-off, that they came upon about thirty men drawn up in small groups round two trucks parked on the side of the road. Some were smoking, drawing anxiously on their cigarettes. Others were shuffling uneasily, stubbing the dirt at their feet with their boot caps.

'Waffen SS,' Scrélat blurted, his face ashen.

'Keep going but don't accelerate unless they stop us,' Morgan said. 'Odds on they won't be concerned with the likes of us. They are the heavy mob.' Morgan recognised the tell-tale signs of men winding up for the fight. These men were ready for action.

'Don't be too sure. Those murderous bastards are not too bothered whom they butcher,' Scrélat spat.

Suddenly a man in a leather coat stepped out into the road. He raised his hand.

'Oh, Jesus. No.' Scrélat's voice was no more than a whisper.

The man in the leather coat beckoned them, and his arm movements quickened as he became impatient.

'Step on it,' Morgan barked. 'He's waving us through.'

Scrélat pressed his foot down.

Morgan smiled and touched his forehead in thanks as they passed the man in the leather coat.

'Someone is going to catch it this morning from that evil little bastard in the leather coat,' Scrélat said.

'He looked like an overgrown choirboy.'

'His name is Voight. The Gestapo chief in Caen.' Morgan's grin vanished.

Scrélat's foot was pressing the accelerator to the floor and the engine was screaming. The truck swayed from side to side as it hurtled down the road.

A huge elm tree signposted the Ste-Yvette turn-off. The truck pulled up beneath the naked branches, just as the school bus came up the lane. When the bus had turned on to the main road, Morgan, sten in hand, leapt down from the truck and ducked through a gap in the hedge and into a field. As the roar of Scrélat's truck faded into the distance, he edged along the field until he found the stream that would lead him towards Ste-Yvette and the château.

After following the stream for thirty minutes, Morgan finally saw the road where it circled the château boundary wall. When he had made sure that it was safe, he crossed it, running low, and plunged into the undergrowth opposite. He crawled silently through the bushes, skirting the wall. He stopped when he saw the small circle Albert had painted on the wall. It marked the place where he was to scale it. Albert was to have hidden the grappling hook and rope in the bushes directly in line with and across the road from the mark on the wall. He found them concealed under the highest hawthorn bush. From there, he could see into the grounds. He crouched and waited for Albert to appear on the terrace and give the signal. It would mean Colette Claval was ready to meet him.

The morning was dank and dismal. The only sound came from the muted cries of rooks perched high in the cluster of alders overhanging the high wall.

He heard Albert before he saw him, the old man's nicotine-oiled cough carrying on the still air. Then the old man came into view carrying a bucket in each hand and working a cigarette between his lips. He shuffled across the terrace and emptied his buckets into one of the bins near the wall.

Two soldiers, rifles on back, patrolled the lawns below Albert. When they'd passed, Albert removed his black beret and mopped his brow. The signal.

Morgan slithered on his backside down the slope until he reached the road. It was deserted. He launched the grappling iron above Albert's mark. It bit first time, and he shinned up the rope and hauled it after him. He sat astride the wall, concealed from the château by the cluster of alders. Only the rooks had noticed. They screamed angrily. Morgan lowered the rope, then dropped to the ground after it. He took the catch off his sten. Bent double, he broke for the derelict summer house and hurled himself through the narrow gap in the timber wall. His shoulder met the floor first and he rolled over onto his knees, sten held at chest-height in front of him. He swung it in a defensive arc around him. Nothing.

All he could do now was wait.

Madame McGragh picked at her scrambled eggs. Although she knew of no reason, she felt something was wrong. Perhaps Hoffner was responsible for the way she felt. They were alone, sitting at opposite ends of the polished baronial table, Hoffner sitting hunched over his reflection in the wood. His coffee, untouched, had turned cold.

Footsteps echoed in the hall and Nicole looked up to see von Beck, Elaine on his arm, in the doorway. The young captain acknowledged her with a polite nod, glared at Hoffner, and then walked out with Elaine.

Hoffner lit a cigar, drummed his fingers on the table. It got on Nicole's nerves. She coughed and Hoffner stopped.

Annoyed at the silence, Nicole got up and walked to the

full-length window. Maria and Durring should have joined them by now. So should have Helm and Clair. But the most obvious absentees were Ulrich and Colette. The colonel always made a point of taking breakfast.

Nicole opened the window, stepped out onto the terrace, and glided to the wall. Then she saw a figure in the bushes. Whoever it was was standing still, as if trying not to be seen. Then it moved. It was that wretched man Albert. She decided she had to do something about him. He was insolent. Nicole watched him go into the summer house. Out of the corner of her eye she caught another flash of movement from behind the ornamental rose garden.

Colette.

The girl stood motionless, her head turned towards the derelict building. Then she looked quickly around her, lifted her skirt, and ran after Albert.

Nicole stamped her foot in anger. 'What in the name of heaven are those two up to? They both know they are not allowed to fraternise.'

A guard rounded the corner, his boots crunching on the loose gravel chippings. Nicole called him.

'One of my girls is in the old summer house with that dreadful caretaker. Bring them both here at once.'

The soldier, hand over mouth, coughed nervously. 'I'm afraid I am under orders not to leave the château area. Major Helm has doubled the guard. It would be more than my life's worth, Miss.'

'Madame,' Nicole fumed. 'Then find someone else to go. The guards from the night patrol will be taking food in the staff kitchens. Send one of them. At once.'

Colette was nervous, as unsure of herself as she was of the man in front of her. Dressed in a dark blue denim jacket and a black roll-neck sweater, he carried a sten gun as easily as an angel carries a harp.

'I can only thank you for the risk you have taken by even agreeing to talk to me,' Morgan said gently. 'It's a great pleasure to meet you – and a privilege.'

His French was accentless but had a strange lilt to it; he could pass for a Breton. 'What do you want from me?' she asked.

'Your help.'

Albert nodded his head and smiled gently. The lines around his old eyes creased. Colette bit the inside of her cheek. When

143

Albert had first asked her if she'd like to flee the château after meeting someone he called the Dragon, she had been overjoyed. Then she'd thought about it further.

'Tell me who you are, and please don't say something stupid like "the Dragon",' Colette said.

'My name is Henri Paco and I'm . . .' Morgan's voice faltered. Colette watched as he ran his hand uncomfortably over the dark stubble on his chin. She wanted to look away from his face but his eyes held her to the spot.

'I am Nat Morgan. I am a British soldier and I want to know everything there is to know about what goes on at the Château Beaupré. I also want to kidnap a German officer and take him to England. I need your help.' He paused then and added, 'And I have just placed my life in your hands.'

'He didn't lie to me. He didn't lie,' Colette thought. She felt a strange twinge. Then she realised someone had asked her for something, not taken it.

'If I help you, will you get me out of this place?'

'Yes. I give you my word. And I'll see that you are safe.'

'In England?'

Morgan shook his head. 'I wish that was possible, but it cannot be done. But we will get you clear of Normandy – away from Ulrich. To Paris perhaps.'

Paris.

Once Colette would have jumped at the chance. But now Paris no longer seemed important. She shrugged, gesturing with her hands. 'I will help you. How?'

Morgan's reply was cut off by Albert's cry. 'Guards,' he rasped, the words sticking in his throat.

Two armed soldiers were walking briskly towards them across the lawn. Suddenly Colette's feet left the ground and she felt Morgan's arm around her waist. 'No one is going to harm a hair of your head,' he said, putting her down in a corner and standing in front of her, his sten gun at the ready.

Through the crook of his arm and the gap in the wall, she saw the approaching soldiers unsling their rifles and begin to run. Her heart was in her mouth. German voices were shouting from the terrace around the château. Then she realised that that was where the soldiers were running. Shaking, she cried softly.

She felt Morgan's arm around her shoulder. 'It's OK. Don't worry,' he said and then was gone. She took her hands from her eyes. Albert grabbed her by the wrist.

144

Nicole watched the guards at the gate leap for their lives, tumbling backwards onto the grass as the car raced through. Three SS men, their rifles at the ready, leapt from one of the trucks. Without stopping, the convoy sped after the Mercedes towards the château. When the car screeched to a halt, a uniformed figure climbed out onto the running board, a pistol in his hand. It was Ulrich. Nicole had never seen him in uniform.

'What the hell is going on?' she screamed, rushing back into the château.

Hoffner, head in hands, was slumped on the dining-room table.

Von Beck, followed by a white-faced Elaine, ran into the room, his pistol drawn. 'That's Waffen SS out there,' he said, his voice breaking. He lunged at Hoffner and pulled him to his feet. 'What's happening?' he screamed, shaking the colonel. 'Why are the SS here with Ulrich? Tell me! They are your bedfellows these days . . .'

Hoffner could only stare back.

Von Beck, panicked, pushed him aside and screamed for the château guards.

They poured from the basement doors and clattered across the vast hall, bumping into each other, pointing their rifles in all directions.

Von Beck yelled orders at the top of his voice: 'Guard the stairs. Protect the door. Is the rear covered? Someone get outside and find what's going on. Quickly.' But the guards continued to weave in and out of the hall in confusion.

Three bursts sounded outside, followed by more shouting. Then more shots – and silence.

Von Beck stood rooted to the floor, screaming for Hoffner.

Clair's face, blonde hair strewn over her eyes, appeared at the top of the stairs and Nicole demanded that she fetch Helm.

'He's not here. He went an hour ago,' Clair cried out above the din of more shooting.

The main doors flew open and Ulrich stormed in, Voight hard on his heels. They were flanked by Waffen SS. Seven château guards, their hands on their heads, followed. Two were bleeding, one from the arm, the other from his shoulder.

'Put down your weapons,' Ulrich cried to the guards inside.

'He has no authority over the army. Ignore him,' von Beck countermanded. 'He's only Abwehr. Get up those stairs and protect Major-General Durring.'

'Listen to the Colonel,' Voight called. 'Put down your guns.

This is a security matter that does not concern you.' When the guards made no move, the SS raised their weapons and moved forward.

'Captain von Beck is outranked. Do as Colonel Ulrich says,' Voight was shouting. 'Do it.'

Hoffner stumbled from the breakfast room. He jerked bolt upright when he looked into the mouth of von Beck's Luger.

'Well, Colonel,' von Beck said, 'order your men to protect the General – or I'll kill you.'

Nicole cried out in warning as Ulrich hit out with his pistol, but she was too late.

Von Beck's eyes were glazed before he sank to the floor.

'Put up your weapons. Do as they say,' Hoffner called desperately.

Ulrich and Voight were already climbing the stairs, the SS racing after them. When they reached the landing, they threw Clair aside, and continued down the corridor. Eva's head peered around her door but vanished quickly as Ulrich approached.

'How dare you,' Nicole called after him. 'This is inexcusable. Your superiors will hear of this.'

Ulrich did not look back.

Major-General Durring was struggling into his trousers as Ulrich and Voight flung open his door.

Maria hurled a half-eaten apple at the wall. 'Get out,' she shouted.

Durring, trousers in place, put a restraining hand on her shoulders and pulled her back to his side, making soothing noises. The general felt his colour rise.

'Out,' Ulrich barked.

'Have you forgotten who I am?' Durring protested. 'You will regret this insubordination. It is you who will get out. Now. That's an order.'

Ulrich laughed slowly.

'Ah, but no. It is *you* who are coming with *us*. And that is an order.'

'Us?' thought Durring. He tried not to show the fear rising from the pit of his stomach, but as two soldiers stomped into the room, his eyes were drawn to the hollow metal eyes on their tunics. The silver skull insignia. The SS. Durring went cold.

The Waffen troops seemed to slide into the room, apparently moving without using their legs. The general was speechless as the two SS men glided to either side of him, took his arms, and led him, dazed, from the room.

But when Durring looked down the stairs and saw von Beck, blood running down the side of his face, he flung his captors aside. 'Fetch the guards,' he shouted. 'Kill these bastards.'

Von Beck turned at Durring's call, but his face was met by the rifle stock of an SS trooper.

'Do something,' Durring called to Hoffner, as he and Nicole, side by side, came up the stairs.

To Nicole's horror, Ulrich kicked Durring's legs from under him, and as Durring fell heavily onto the carpet, Hoffner turned away and walked past him.

Durring, enraged, started to get up then, but Ulrich kicked him in the face and pushed him onto his back.

'Out. Out. Out!' Ulrich screamed, his voice reaching hysteria pitch. Scrambling, the SS men dragged Durring to his feet and, holding him in an arm lock, frogmarched him to the waiting Mercedes.

In a few moments, it was over, and Nicole, watching from her bedroom window, saw the motorcade speed down the long drive in a cloud of dust.

Hans Voight was pacing impatiently up and down the small room, his hands clasped behind his back. He paused, like a young schoolmaster, and looked down at the table and the three sheets of neatly typed confessions. He was waiting for Durring, who sat hunched on the other side of the table, to sign them.

'General,' Voight said slowly, 'I don't want you to be any more foolish than you have already been, so I will explain once more. Just once, do you understand?'

Durring, head downcast, remained motionless. Voight leant across the table and lifted the general's face. The swelling had now completely closed his right eye and the plum-shaped bruise had turned black.

'This first confession,' Voight explained, holding on to Durring's face and pointing to the typed sheet, 'outlines your own involvement in a plan to remove the Führer and those loyal to him. You will sign it.'

Durring shook his head. Voight released his hold and then punched Durring's bruised eye. The Gestapo chief took a folded sheet of paper from his pocket.

'This is a transcript of a telephone conversation you had. It is more than enough to send you to the firing squad.'

He shoved the von Beck transcript under Durring's nose. 'I want the names of the others involved with you and von Beck. The names,' he screamed.

After more silence, Voight picked up the second typed confession. 'This is an admission of your involvement with others. All you have to do is fill in the names. Then sign it. If you do, then the courts may go easy on you. You could save yourself by naming others.'

Durring's swollen lips parted. He whispered, 'Never.'

Voight shrugged. 'Up to you entirely.'

He then picked up the third confession. Even he was not altogether happy with this Ulrich masterpiece. He agreed with the other two the colonel had written for Durring to sign. But this was different. If Durring signed then there would be an accusation from a general, and friend of Rommel, alleging that the Field Marshal himself was plotting against Hitler. He read it out.

Durring looked up wearily. He said simply, 'You're mad. Quite insane.' Then he slumped forward.

Voight pushed him back in his chair. He then took a fountain pen from his inside pocket and unscrewed the cap.

'Are you left- or right-handed?'

Durring raised his left hand feebly. Voight took his right. The general's scream was long and agonising as Voight bent back three fingers until they broke. Durring rolled onto the floor and passed out.

Voight stepped over him and left the room to brief Ulrich on his progress. They took coffee and Danish pastries, and when Voight returned, he still had the crumbs around his mouth.

The guards had brought Durring round and he was now sitting back in the chair.

'Let's start with the first confession,' Voight said, handing Durring the fountain pen.

This time Durring signed.

When he had finished, Voight smiled and patted him on the shoulder. 'We shall talk about the second confession tomorrow. But for now,' he said, taking the signed version from Durring, 'thank you.'

Two days later Voight's patience had run out. His threats to make Durring sign the second confession had always been met by the same answer: a whispered, but dignified, 'Never.'

'General,' Voight said, 'I think it is time to extend and improve

148

your vocabulary.' He moved to the door, opened it, and signalled to someone outside.

Two shirtsleeved Gestapo came into the room carrying a wooden chair with leather straps fixed to the arms and legs. A third Gestapo carried a length of flex with a thong-like device at one end. Durring watched in horror as one man removed the light bulb from its socket and replaced it with the flex.

When the chair had been placed behind the table, Voight installed Durring in front of it. Two Gestapo held Durring's arms as Voight undid his flies. Voight took out Durring's penis and strapped the thong to it. Durring winced as he felt the naked wires against his limp flesh. While the two Gestapo strapped Durring into the chair, the third went to the door. He placed his hand on the light switch in the wall and waited for Voight to give the signal.

At Voight's nod, the general stiffened and raised himself slightly on his toes. His stomach raced through his intestines, his lips turned blue and a stabbing pain exploded in his chest. Then he slumped forward, open-eyed but lifeless, his body held in mid-air by the straps.

'The stupid old bastard,' Voight mumbled. Then he shouted, 'Fetch Ulrich. Quick.'

But Ulrich was already bursting through the door, racing to the figure sprawled on the floor.

'Shit.'

Ulrich wondered with trepidation what Brigadeführer Schellenberg would say. The SS intelligence chief was waiting eagerly for news in a room on the next floor.

It was just before dawn. Cold and damp. Schellenberg peered through the window bars into the yard. The wooden stake stood out starkly against the bullet-peppered stone wall, and the grey cobbles glistened with mist.

Schellenberg sucked his hollow cheeks. The collar of his full-length black overcoat was pulled up over the back of his neck. He looked over his shoulder at Ulrich, his eyes lined red with fatigue.

'What about Canaris?' Schellenberg said wearily, repeating his colonel's question. 'The man is finished anyway. It's only a matter of time before I nail the little Greek bastard.'

'But surely he might suspect something when he learns that Durring was exposed,' Ulrich said with astonishment. 'After all,

149

the phone call was intercepted in the château – the place his department sanctioned to improve officer morale.'

'He already has.' Schellenberg handed Ulrich a photocopy of a letter. 'My people intercepted this in Berlin the day Durring was taken. It is a request from Canaris to his old friend Rommel that Captain von Beck be moved to army headquarters in Berlin as soon as possible. From the SS point of view it is perfect, we can watch his every move. He will lead us to the plotters.'

Ulrich pulled out his lighter and lit Schellenberg's cigar. Both men looked down into the execution yard. It was time.

Voight entered the courtyard first, followed by two Gestapo hauling Durring's limp body by the armpits. The sound of Durring's boots dragging over the cobbles reverberated around the cold, dimly-lit yard.

As the Gestapo tied the body to the firing post, Voight fastened the head to the post with a blindfold to prevent Durring's head from drooping. Then he pinned a red square to the general's chest. The signal was given for the firing squad to march in through a door at the far end of the yard. They drew up in a line at the chalk mark and raised their rifles.

The dead body jerked in the half-light as the bullets found their mark.

Schellenberg turned to Ulrich. 'One day someone is going to die under questioning. It would never do if it was a general. Besides, traitors who conspire must be seen to be shot, especially when they roost in Rommel's nest.'

Helm raced up the stairs and threw open the office door.

'Hoffner?' he roared. 'Hoffner!'

Helm stood in the doorway and surveyed the shambles. Hoffner's desk was covered with piles of crumpled paper, and an empty bottle of schnapps lay half-buried on its side. The doors of the metal filing cabinets were open, and piles were strewn over the floor.

He went into the inner office and was confronted by Hoffner's popping eyes staring down at him. The dead man's face turned gently as the rope around his neck twisted slowly from the beam on the ceiling.

CHAPTER FIFTEEN

Colette lay alone and naked in the darkness of her room and wanted the loving warmth of Clair's bed. She would make sure that Nicole McGragh found out and prayed she'd tell Ulrich. Although Ulrich had said he'd beat her if she went near Clair again, she would have to do it. It would be her only chance of getting to meet Nat Morgan again.

She threw back the sheet, put on the light and slipped into a pair of pants and a long silk nightdress. She left her bedroom door open to increase the chance of someone seeing she was not there, and then walked along the passage to the top of the main staircase.

'Have you seen Clair?' Colette called loudly to Annette Duval, who was standing in the hall below.

Annette shook her head.

'Can you ask the others?'

Annette popped her head round the salon door and called to the girls inside. Then she turned and looked up at Colette. 'No one has seen her. She must be in her room.'

By the time Nicole, tight-lipped, had swept past Annette into the hall, Colette had gone.

Colette found Clair asleep, her blonde hair spilling over the pillow. She bent and kissed her on the forehead, and Clair opened her eyes.

'Forgive me?' Colette whispered.

Clair smiled softly and, reaching out, drew Colette towards her. When their mouths met, their tongues joined in a slow lingering kiss and Colette felt Clair's long searching fingers slide slowly down her stomach.

'My sweet love,' Clair said and pressed Colette's face to her breast. Colette could feel Clair's heart pounding, and she ran her tongue around the blonde's nipple until it stood out hard and erect. Then she took it between her lips and sucked it. Clair cried out and her fingers reached down to Colette.

The girls held on to each other for a long time, their arms and legs entwined. Then they made love again, uninhibited and endless, sometimes wild, yet warm and selfless.

At dawn, Colette left the sleeping Clair, kissed her on the cheek and returned to her own room to sleep.

The belt awoke her as it slapped viciously over the side of her face. Colette bolted upright and held her arms defensively around her as the next four swipes landed on her back.

'I'll beat sense into you,' Ulrich screamed at the top of his voice. 'I ordered you never to touch that La Croix again.'

Experience had not wasted its lessons on Colette Claval. As two more blows struck home, she knelt, arms on head, at the end of the bed. She then lifted out her arms in a gesture of mercy.

Ulrich squinted in a bloodshot rage and flayed wildly, the force of the blows sending her reeling. His next swipe spun her off the bed and she landed on her knees, her back to Ulrich. He was swinging the belt as if possessed, and Colette fell on her face, her back a scarlet mess of interwoven lines.

Ulrich stood back, raised his arm, then froze, letting the strap fall. He stumbled to the bed and slumped down on it, shaking, his head in his hands.

Colette turned her head and knew the time had come. She willed the strength back into her limbs and crawled towards the sallow-faced figure mumbling incoherently and rocking to and fro on the bed.

'I must not vomit. I will not be sick. I will not,' she urged herself. Then she took a deep breath and placed her hand on his knee.

'Dear Ernst,' she said. 'I'm sorry. It will never happen again.' Ulrich nodded and continued to mumble incoherently. Colette turned her head away as she took his hand. 'If only we could be together – away from this place,' she said soothingly. 'Perhaps just the odd night. It could be so wonderful, the two of us. Together. Alone,' she purred. 'It is not us; just this place. If only we could get away for no more than one night – your hotel, my love, instead of here. I will do anything you ask, there would be no diversions – like Clair.'

Ulrich, eyes glazed, still rocked to and fro, but a little smile twitched on his rigid face.

'You will sign the papers and tell Madame McGragh that I can come to your hotel to please you?' Colette added sweetly.

Ulrich nodded. 'It might save time when I'm busy.'

Colette clapped her hands. 'Oh thank you, thank you.' She kissed him on the forehead. 'It will be better for you; you wait and see.'

Three days later, a warm spring Friday, Colette used the pass Ulrich had given her for the first time. Ulrich had provided his Mercedes to bring her from the château to Lisieux.

It was almost a year since Colette had been outside her confines and once inside Lisieux, she delighted in seeing other faces, other sights. She noticed women's coats had got shorter. They looked drab somehow, but this was Normandy not Paris. She might even be back in Paris in a week – if things went well.

She fidgeted nervously in the back seat and tried hard to imagine how Clair would behave in such a situation.

She heard a voice say: 'Pull up here. We are early. I'll kill time and do some window shopping.' It was only when the young driver stopped and leapt out smartly to open the rear door, that she realised that voice was her own. She was thrilled she'd sounded so grand. Confidently she asked the way to Ulrich's hotel.

'Thank you.' Colette wondered if Clair would have given him a tip. She decided not. She waited until the car had driven off, then walked towards the basilica of Ste-Thérèse. Soon she spotted Albert standing on the steps, leaning against a pillar and reading a newspaper. He saw her and Colette smiled. Albert folded his paper and crossed the street. Colette followed, keeping at least twenty paces behind, but it was difficult keeping sight of Albert amid the crowds of women doing their weekend shopping. Colette, handbag held tightly, wove in and out of the shopping baskets, and dodged protruding baguettes in her efforts to follow Albert. Once she thought she'd lost him. She stood on her toes and craned her neck, trying to see over the advancing shoulders. Then she recognised the old man's rolling gait as he turned a corner. Colette hurried after him and passed through a smelly, litter-strewn alley piled with used fruit crates and cardboard boxes. When she had caught up, she saw Albert lighting a Gauloise in front of a chemist shop – André Pratt's, according to the lettering on the door.

Albert walked on and Colette pushed open the shop door, jangling its bell. Except for the old man behind the counter, the shop was empty.

'Yes?' the old man asked, looking at her curiously through his pince-nez.

'Have you anything to treat a burn?' Colette said quietly when she'd reached the counter.

'What caused it?'

'A dragon's breath.' Colette thought she sounded too foolish for words.

André walked straight past her to the open shop door, looked in both directions, then shut it and turned the key. When he had drawn the blind, he took Colette by the wrist and led her through a string-bead curtain at the rear of his shop.

'My handbag,' protested Colette. She'd left it next to the cosmetic display on the counter.

'No one is going to steal it, child,' André laughed.

Colette blushed as André led her up the stairs to his living quarters and then waited at the door to usher her in before him. Once inside, she saw Morgan, his back to her, looking out of the window. She coughed and Morgan turned, smiling, and winked.

Colette felt uncomfortable, strange. And when Morgan walked towards her, his hand held out, she stepped back uneasily.

'Who did that to you?' Morgan said, indicating with his chin the faint strap marks on her face and shoulders. His French, as before, was fast and accentless. His tone was threatening.

'Ulrich,' she said. 'Is he the one you are going to kidnap?'

Morgan clenched his fists and closed his eyes. Ulrich. The face that had haunted him for almost a decade. The man he'd sworn to wipe off the face of the earth.

'No.'

Colette's face fell. 'Why?'

'It's Helm I want,' Morgan said. 'I need your help to lure him to a place where we can take him without too much fuss.'

'The church at Ste-Yvette,' André Pratt suggested, as he handed out cups of coffee. Colette thanked him and sat on the sofa. Morgan lit two cigarettes and handed her one.

Colette exhaled slowly. 'And what happens to me?' she said.

'We can pay you well. We have the funds,' André said.

Colette's expression froze him. 'Do you really think I offered to help you for money?'

'There was no offence intended. Please accept my apol—,' André stopped in mid-sentence as the sound of someone pounding on the front door echoed through the apartment.

Morgan grabbed the sten he'd concealed behind the sofa and threw himself against the wall next to the window.

A BMW motorcycle and sidecar was idling in the street below.

'You were followed,' he barked at Colette, who sat transfixed, shaking her head numbly.

The pounding got louder and a voice called out in German.

'A two-man patrol,' Morgan said. 'Open the door and see what they want.' He cocked his sten and then drew a dagger from inside his jacket.

The pounding resumed and André bounded down the stairs. 'All right, all right, I'm coming,' he called out.

Morgan pushed Colette into the kitchen and closed the door. Then, holding the sten in one hand and the dagger in the other, he followed André down the stairs but stopped behind the bead curtain.

The old chemist was giving a distinguished performance of indignation as the soldiers stepped into the shop. They were carrying only sidearms, and their leather holsters buttoned down.

'Why was the shop closed?' one of them, who was grossly overweight, shouted, 'You are supposed to be the rota chemist open all day.'

André was by now behind the counter, and he peered at the soldier through his pince-nez. 'I have to eat, m'sieu,' he explained meekly.

'You don't have to take all bloody day about it,' the soldier said, pounding the counter. 'I've got toothache and it's killing me.'

André grinned broadly in relief and with pleasure at the German's pain. Morgan watched tensely as André produced toothache tincture from the medicine cabinet and moved down to the far end of the counter before offering it to the German. The soldier followed to accept the bottle from the chemist. He was now in knifing distance. Morgan drew back his dagger, still training the sten in his other hand on the second soldier who had not moved. Colette's bag was only inches from his hand.

'Next time you're on rota duty, make sure you are open all of your designated hours, or there'll be trouble,' the fat soldier snapped. He snatched the tincture.

'But I have to eat,' André protested again, 'and because I am a widower, I have to cook as well.'

'So you live alone,' said the other soldier.

'Of course, m'sieu.'

Morgan stiffened. André had made his first error.

'Then who does this belong to?' the soldier said, grabbing the bag and moving down the counter towards André.

'The girl who was in just before lunch must have left it,' André blurted. 'She'll be back. I'll look after it until she returns for it.' He held out his hand, but the German hesitated.

'What kind of girl would not miss her handbag for so long?'

Just then a terrible clatter of falling pans and breaking dishes came from the flat above the shop.

The fat soldier had André by the collar and was twisting his tie. 'Alone, huh? Take a look,' he barked at his companion.

'Nothing except empty boxes,' he said looking towards the deserted stairs.

Morgan had rushed up to the flat to find Colette panic-stricken and gesturing wildly in horror. He tugged her by the wrist, dragged her into the bedroom and threw back the covers of André's bed.

'Get your clothes off. Quickly,' he hissed as he tore off his jacket and shirt. He kept his trousers on but removed his boots and socks.

Colette, dumbstruck, stood rooted to the spot.

'Get that dress off,' he rasped urgently, but still Colette did not move. Morgan grabbed her with one hand as the other closed over her mouth to stop her scream. He then flung her onto the bed. This time he stopped her scream with his mouth. She began to kick and struggle but he managed to rip the dress from her.

Her eyes, round, large and black, were filled with terror. From the shop and stockroom below came the sound of a struggle, and soon they heard the soldiers reach the foot of the stairs. Their slow tread indicated they were climbing cautiously.

'Do as I say or we are dead. Do it.' Morgan took his hand from the girl's mouth, praying she would not scream. He placed his hands on her shoulders. 'We have been lovers for a month. I am André's nephew and he lets us meet here to make love in the afternoon.' Colette nodded meekly. She watched, still fearful, as Morgan left the bed and crossed the room to collect his clothes. 'Put on this and follow me,' he said, handing her his coarse denim shirt. It was about five sizes too large and her hands were lost in the sleeves. After he had quickly helped her to do up the buttons, he took her by the arm and pulled her after him.

Morgan feigned surprise as he and Colette came face to face with the soldiers at the top of the stairs. André stood behind them, his clothes dishevelled.

'Please,' Morgan said, 'we do not mean anyone any harm.'

'Over there,' the German motioned with his pistol.

'Where are your papers?' the fat soldier demanded. His fingers tightened around the Luger.

'In the bedroom. Top pocket of my coat,' Morgan said, grinning sheepishly as he tugged his trousers up. 'My name is Henri Paco, M'sieu Pratt's nephew. I am working on permit in Lisieux.' He hugged Colette around the shoulders and felt her tremble. 'This is my fiancée Colette. Colette Claval.'

The German sent the other soldier for the papers. Morgan smiled as the German inspected them, nodding like an idiot.

André continued to explain in German.

The soldier smirked. 'This French bastard is screwing a German colonel's woman,' he told his companion. 'Cheeky swine.'

Morgan kept a straight face as both men rejoiced that one of their officers was being duped.

'I can prove it,' André said. 'Let me fetch the girl's handbag.' The German nodded and the second soldier followed André downstairs. When they had returned, the German opened the bag and took out the pass Ulrich had signed for Colette. He read it aloud. Both soldiers went into fits of laughter. All officers were fools, they decided.

'What is it worth for us not to tell this Colonel Ulrich?' the fat soldier asked, yanking Colette from Morgan's grasp.

As André translated, Colette winced, and the German drew back Colette's shirt with the barrel of his gun.

'We will pay you to forget it. The Colonel will not thank you for making him look a laughing stock.' André translated Morgan's rapid speech, looking anxiously at Morgan. He produced the wad of banknotes he'd taken from the till.

The soldier opened Colette's shirt wider, exposing her breasts.

'If you touch that girl, who will the Colonel punish most – you or her?' Morgan blurted to André.

The soldiers stepped back and eyed the banknotes in André's hand.

'We are all in the same boat,' André said. 'No one will thank you whatever you do. Take the money and forget it. This is France. We have a different view about such liaisons. Perhaps they are not shared by your German colonel.'

The German snatched at the wad of notes and Morgan pulled Colette to him. Heart in mouth, he watched the German count the money. He stuffed the notes into his back pocket, then muttering something about all Frenchwomen being sluts, followed his companion down the stairs.

'We'll drink out on this for months,' he said, slapping his companion on the back.

Colette, both hands on the glass, huddled in a corner of the couch and gulped the brandy as if she were suffering from an enormous thirst. All the while she kept her eyes on the man seated in the chair opposite. She tried to imagine him without that gun he was always cradling. Where did he live? In one of those picture book cottages with roses around the door? Was he married?

She looked hard at him, hunched over his drink. He'd been as scared as she had. Although he'd tried not to let it show, she'd felt it, smelt it. Yet he would have killed for her. Or because of her.

'I know I didn't have the right to ask you to put your life at risk but there was no other way,' Morgan said suddenly, breaking the silence. 'I need you to help me get Helm.' Colette shrunk deeper into the enormous shirt that now enveloped her folded legs completely. 'It will be dangerous, I won't pretend otherwise, and if you feel you can't go through with it, I will understand. You have the right to decide. You have already risked a great deal. If you say no, then you are free to walk away from here as if nothing had happened. I will try to persuade the others to send you down an escape route – to Switzerland perhaps.'

Colette relaxed her grip on the cushion, and looked at Morgan disbelievingly. 'I need never go back to the château? Never touch Ulrich again? Ever?'

Morgan shook his head slowly.

'Never? Why?' Colette bit her lip. He looked, somehow, vulnerable, almost lost. His eyes were heavy, and, although he wore a faint smile on his lips, behind it she sensed a hidden sadness.

Morgan shifted uneasily, then stood and reached over to ruffle her hair. 'You wouldn't understand all my reasons,' he replied softly, 'and it would take too long to explain them. Let's just say Ulrich is one of them ...'

'But if I say no, will you still try to kidnap Helm?'

'Yes. It's important I get him. Vital. I'll just have to take the risks. We must know what's really going on at the château.'

'I can tell you that,' Colette said quickly.

'But you can't tell me why ... and I think Helm can.'

Colette fell silent. She got up and walked to the window. She bit her thumb as she looked down into the empty street. She knew then that she shared something with Morgan: she, too, wanted to bring the likes of Ulrich crashing to destruction. When at last she turned, she said to Morgan, 'I'm afraid I have to go – I'm going to be late for my appointment with Ulrich. Tell me what you want me to do.'

Colette looked at her watch, a gift from Ulrich, then down into the château courtyard. Except for the guards' truck, it was empty. Helm was due at any moment. She must get Clair out of the way before he arrived.

Colette looked at Elaine pleadingly. They were alone in the bedroom corridor.

'Please. Please.' Colette took Elaine's arm. 'I swear there will be no risk to you.'

Elaine bit her knuckles. 'It is not as easy for me as it is for you, because you have no one to care for.'

Colette's face fell.

'I'm sorry,' Elaine said gently, 'I did not mean to sound unkind. I meant that I have my baby to think about. You must understand. Ulrich has threatened I'll never see him again if I get into trouble. The only thing that keeps me sane here is the thought of my Alain's baby. Our son.'

Colette spotted Helm's Mercedes snaking through the lanes towards the château gates and her grip on Elaine's arm tightened. 'I beg you, please.' Elaine sighed and Colette thought Elaine was weakening. 'Please.'

'Are you sure there will be no risk to me?'

'Positive. I swear it.'

'Oh, all right,' Elaine said, sighing again.

'Thank you. You will never know how grateful I am,' Colette whispered hurriedly as from the window they saw Helm's car near the bend in front of the gates. 'Quick.' She pulled Elaine by the sleeve and they ran, silently, down the thick red carpet, towards Clair's room.

The Mercedes rounded the bend.

The girls, tight-lipped, tapped on the door and held their breath.

'What do you want?'

'It's important. I must speak with you outside,' Elaine said.

Colette, hidden round the corner, heard the bedroom door close and then the footsteps fade towards the back stairs. When she turned towards the window again, she saw Helm get out of his car, pause to say something to the driver, and then, gloves in hand, walk briskly towards the front door. Colette bolted for Clair's room and flung open the door. She made straight for the bedside table and rummaged desperately through the contents of the drawer. When she found the red leather writing set, she began to scribble furiously.

She wrote:

My Darling Rudi,

I fear for both our lives and dare not spend one more night under this roof. I know Ulrich plans to kill us both. I will explain when you come to me. I have sought refuge in the church at Ste-Yvette. Please come to me. All my love,

Clair.

Colette read the note and prayed Helm would not suspect it. The writing was barely legible. She placed the sheet in a matching envelope and addressed it to 'Rudi'. Then she sealed it, placed it on the pillow, and ran for the door.

'Stop.' Helm's voice caught her just as she was shutting Clair's door, and she froze. 'You little slut,' he said, grabbing her by the wrist and flinging her against the wall. 'You were warned to stay away from Clair. Now I catch you pestering her in broad daylight. This time you've gone too far. When Ulrich is through with you, you'll be finished, you little cow.' He pushed her away from him as if he could not bear to touch the girl who shared his Clair.

'I'm past bloody caring,' Colette yelled back and stamped her foot. 'And besides, whatever he'll do to me, he's said he'll do to her. Have you thought about that, you pig?'

Helm lost control and tore at her hair. 'I'll kill you, you little bitch,' he screamed, swinging her against the wall again.

Colette's eyes blazed, and she jumped sideways to avoid his jackboot. Before he could touch her again, she had fled.

'Clair,' Helm called out, finding her room empty. Anger in his voice, 'Clair, where are you? Clair?'

Then he saw the note.

The wooden gate creaked as Helm pushed it open with one hand. He walked cautiously along the path, the gravel crunching under his feet, the shadows of the cypress trees swaying in the wind. Watched by the eyes of the marble angels praying over the lichen-covered graves, he paused in the fusty portal and re-read Clair's note. He brought the scented paper to his nose and then crushed it into a ball. After looking around quickly, he turned the heavy iron latch and pushed open the massive, sighing oak door.

A priest knelt facing the high altar in the flickering light of the candles; the pews were empty. There was no sign of Clair.

The priest chanted prayers as the hollow echo from Helm's boots sounded through the still, cold church. He walked slowly past a wide, fluted stone pillar, worn with age, and then saw the kneeling figure, her head covered by the lace shawl he'd given her. He placed his hand on her shoulder and, squeezing gently, whispered her name. The figure turned, the lace sliding from her head.

'Thank you for coming so quickly,' Colette said, smiling as she looked up at him.

'Bitch,' Helm hissed catching her by the throat. 'What is the meaning of this?' As Helm's angry words rang through the church, he realised that the chanting had ceased. The only sound came from Colette as she fought for breath.

'That, Major, is not very wise,' the priest said, rising from his knees. He bowed to the high altar and turned, a Luger in his hands.

Helm released his grip on Colette and his hand instinctively fell to the black leather holster at his side. But he froze in mid-motion as two metallic clicks sounded from either side of him. His mouth dry, he turned to face Albert's leering grin. The old man had his sten at shoulder height, the mark of an amateur. Albert would certainly miss from that range.

'Allô, Major,' Albert said. 'I've told you before that's no way to treat a lady.'

Helm's eyes shifted to the direction of the second click. Sten waist-high, Pierre Scrélat glared back at him and Helm's heart sank.

'I'll see you all hang for this.'

Scrélat motioned Helm into the aisle with his sten, and with a second gesture told the major to raise his hands. As Helm did so, he viciously slapped Colette across the face with the back of his gloved hand.

Enraged, Albert dropped his sten with a clatter and clambered over the backs of the pews to get at Helm.

'Leave him.' The command filled the church and all eyes turned towards the shout. Morgan, silhouetted against the weak afternoon light, stood in the open doorway. He kicked the door shut behind him and marched forward until he stood toe to toe with Helm.

'Major Helm?' Morgan said, looking him straight in the eye. 'Major Rudi Helm?' Helm remained expressionless and glared silently at Morgan.

'I asked you a question,' Morgan said, his tone calm and polite. Only the same cold Prussian stare came back in reply.

Morgan swung at the German, doubling him over, and then swiftly brought up his knee. Helm folded into a crumpled heap on the altar steps.

'Let's begin as we intend to continue,' Morgan snapped. 'Get up.'

Helm clutched at the pulpit and, using it as a prop, hauled himself to his feet. Scrélat then seized him by the shoulder, removed his holster and instructed him to place his hands on his head.

'You have all signed your own death warrants,' Helm snarled.

'Keep your mouth shut,' Morgan spat. He nodded to Albert, who disappeared outside. Moments later he was back.

'It's here,' he called to Morgan and then vanished again.

At a signal from Morgan, Scrélat touched his sten to the small of Helm's back. 'Move.'

'You are all insane.'

'Move.' Scrélat stabbed at Helm with considerable force and the German stumbled forward. Father Delon, his Luger out in front of him, led the procession up the aisle. Then came Helm, hands on head, followed by Scrélat and his sten. Morgan and Colette brought up the rear.

When they reached the porch, Father Delon stepped aside to let the others pass and then, after closing the door on them, mounted the steps to the tower.

Outside the gate, an old green tractor throbbed noisily, its roar not quite managing to drown the sound of the dozen squealing piglets and the large black and white sow wallowing amid the straw in the animal trailer attached behind.

When the procession passed into the lane, concealed from the village by trees, Albert jumped, smiling, from the heart-shaped seat and opened the door of the trailer. He gestured Helm to get in. The German hesitated, looking around quickly for his car.

Scrélat hit him with the butt of his sten and barked, 'Get in and bury yourself under the straw.' As the piglets squealed in protest, Helm climbed into the stench and then knelt in the straw at the rear of the trailer. He looked helplessly at Scrélat, then covered himself until only his head showed.

Scrélat sat on the rear mudguard, watching. 'Your head as well,' Scrélat snapped. 'If I see as much as a square millimetre of German while you are in this trailer, I will empty a full magazine into it.' He tapped the sten in his hand. 'Understood?'

Without replying, Helm took off his cap and buried it, then pulled bunches of stained straw over his head.

Scrélat clung to the mudguard, his sten concealed by the jacket lying across his knees.

From the top of the church tower, Father Delon leant on the battlements and watched as Albert at last found first gear, and the tractor pulled away leaving Morgan and Colette at the gate. Soon after, André Pratt's old black Renault pulled up outside the church gate, picked up Morgan and Colette, and drove off down the lane and round the bend. Father Delon turned and climbed down to the belfry and his radio. Within the hour, Arnie Connors at SOE would know that Morgan had captured his German officer and needed a Lysander to fly him out. Quickly.

The desk sergeant, a normally placid man, flung his pencil stub aside and threw his arms in the air with frustration.

The little French farmer who stood chest-high at the Lisieux central police station counter was heaving with red-faced agitation. 'What kind of police force do you call yourselves if you can't find my tractor and pigs,' Emile Picard squealed. He banged the counter with a pink fist. 'They've been missing since yesterday.'

'All I can do for the moment is fill in the correct forms,' the sergeant yelled above the din. 'We have no time to put on a search. Take it up with the mayor of Caen if you like.

Morgan looked long and hard at Father Delon.

'We have lost radio contact with London. My message saying we'd got Helm and needed a Lysander to get him out got through, but since then the conditions have been dreadful. All I get on the radio at appointed listening times is static,' Delon said grimly. 'It's been almost thirty-six hours.'

'When do you think you'll be able to make contact again?'

Delon shrugged. 'There is no way of telling. It's in God's hands. But you should be safe here for a couple of days at least.'

'A couple of days?' Morgan's voice rose. 'Staying in one place is a hell of a risk. Can't we move on?'

'I'm afraid not. There is too much of a hue and cry going on for our friend in there. The Germans and police are stopping and searching everything that moves. They also think the girl has been abducted. So she is going to have to stay until the heat is off.'

'I'm going to have to question Helm myself,' Morgan said, 'just in case we can't get him to London. If I wrote a report could you get it to London?'

Delon nodded. 'But it may take time . . .'

'Then I'd better start right away.' He shook the priest's hand and walked towards André Pratt's Renault where Albert was waiting at the wheel. 'Keep trying that radio.'

When they had gone, Morgan walked around the roofless barn, its bare timbers rotten with age, and considered his tactics. Helm was an intelligence officer, a professional skilled in interrogation techniques. It wasn't going to be easy. But he was determined, and, ready now, walked towards the farmhouse, a derelict affair not much larger than a two-storey cottage. The roof sagged in the middle and looked as if it was about to slide into the weed-covered farmyard. Morgan squeezed through a gap in the door-frame, avoiding the door, which hung precariously on rusty hinges. The building reeked of decay. Dusty cobwebs hung everywhere and the walls were green with mould. In the room to his right he heard Colette and André talking, but he didn't stop, and climbed the stairs carefully. Some of the treads were missing, and those that remained were rotten.

Morgan acknowledged Scrélat, who was standing at the bedroom door, the sten under his arm, and a cigarette between his lips. Inside the empty room, Helm sat in a corner trussed like a turkey. His hands were tied behind his back and his mouth was gagged with a piece of cloth. He was asleep, his head resting on his chest. Morgan prodded him with his boot and he jolted awake.

'If I don't sleep, then neither do you,' said Morgan, squatting on his haunches to remove the gag.

Helm looked up, his eyes heavy but showing no fear.

'What do you plan to do with me?' he asked.

'Take you to London.'

'Why?'

'My people want to talk to you about the château.'

'They'll get nothing from me.'

'Want to bet?' Scrélat growled from behind Morgan's shoulder. He jabbed Helm with his toe cap and the German rolled over onto his side.

'Easy,' Morgan said. He pushed Scrélat back and sat Helm back up against the wall.

'Do you know Ulrich is in the SS?'

Helm's face replied with a look of distaste, but he said nothing. Morgan dragged Helm to his feet, held him by the lapels and, with all the force he could muster, smashed him against the wall. As Helm gasped to refill his lungs with air, Morgan slammed him against the wall again.

'Tell me.'

Helm said nothing and Morgan hurled him against the wall again. Morgan felt he was running out of time. He was also getting short on temper.

'Tell me how Ulrich uses the whores.'

Helm laughed in his face and Morgan hit him.

'Is that how you treat your prisoners?' Helm spat at Morgan's feet.

Morgan raised his fist again, then stopped himself. He realised that Helm was taunting him, trying to make him lose his temper. Anything to keep him off his line of questioning. He would rather be beaten than answer Morgan.

'Go on, hit me,' Helm taunted.

Morgan turned and walked from the room.

'Do you mind if I have a go?' Scrélat called after him.

'No,' Morgan said, hurrying outside as Helm's screams filled the house.

'It is her, isn't it?' The fat German showed his companion the kidnap poster with Helm and Colette's picture.

His companion looked up from the sidecar. 'Yes, I'm afraid so.'

'Then we must do something. We just can't ignore it.'

'What can we say? "Look, Colonel, we saw your woman the day before yesterday. She was in bed with a Frog painter, but he paid us to keep our mouths shut"?'

'Do you suppose he's the one who has kidnapped her and this Abwehr major?'

'Looks like it.'

'Perhaps the girl just ran off with the major and there isn't any kidnap?'

'Do you think so?'

'No.'

'Then what the hell are we going to do?'

'Let's not mention the painter. We can say we saw the girl go into the chemist. If they ever find her, she's not going to admit going there for an afternoon screw.'

The motorcycle combination swung around in the road and headed back towards the command post.

'Please?'

Colette reached out for a share of Morgan's cigarette and he took it from his lips and placed it in hers.

Morgan took the cigarette from her, leant on the barn wall and inhaled deeply. The harsh tobacco scorched his lungs.

'Helm can tell you little. I tried to tell you that on Friday at André's, but you wouldn't listen. You said you were not content to know just how the château worked, but why. Helm can't tell you that,' Colette blurted out suddenly.

Morgan held her by the shoulders. 'How do you know Helm can't tell me why?' he asked.

'Because of what Ulrich told me. He tells me everything. He thinks Helm's a treacherous pig.'

'What else has Ulrich said?' A look of slow realisation spread across Morgan's face and he slackened his grip.

'Lots of things. He hasn't got a good word to say about anyone. Sometimes it's hard to believe they are all on the same side. The things they say about each other ...'

'They?'

'Ulrich's not the only one. You should hear what Captain von Beck thinks. He'd shoot Ulrich if he had his way. He says people like him are trying to undermine Rommel and that Durring was only the first to go.'

'Did Ulrich tell you that?' Morgan's tone was one of total astonishment.

'No,' Colette said simply, 'Elaine did.'

Morgan closed his eyes tightly and began to laugh, banging his hand against his forehead. Although Colette did not share the joke, his laughter was infectious and she, too, began to giggle. Morgan lifted her by the waist and twirled her round and round. Then he put her down and they faced each other, still laughing.

At last Colette said, 'What's so funny?' Her eyes were wet with mirth. 'Tell me. Tell me please.'

'How would you like to go to England?' Morgan said flatly.

Colette stopped laughing and pointed to herself. 'Me?'

'You, the other six girls, Madame McGragh – all.'

'Please don't play games with me.'

'I'm not. I mean it.'

'Honestly? You can take me to England?'

'Of course.'

Colette threw her arms around his neck and cried with joy. But she stopped short when a piercing scream came from inside the house, and in seconds she and Morgan were running towards the door.

The desk sergeant sighed as he put the phone down. He felt as if he'd been living in a circus the past few days. 'Some kid says he found the trailer-load of pigs on an abandoned farm near Ste-Yvette,' he called to one of the other policemen. 'Can you check it out? A farmer called four days ago to report it missing. That's the day Helm vanished. You'd better check it out with the Germans.'

Morgan felt he was going to be sick. The German officer's broken face was twisted in pain as he lay groaning on the bare floorboards, his swollen lips hiding his splintered teeth. The left leg of his uniform trousers, torn in two, revealed the pulp which had once been his kneecap. The metal hammer, its head still wet with blood, lay beside him.

Morgan, furious, turned darkly and accusingly towards Scrélat. 'As much as I despise his kind, this sort of treatment only reduces us to their level. Can't you understand that?'

Scrélat pointed an accusing finger at Morgan, but he was interrupted by Helm, who looked at Morgan through a half-closed eye and sneered, 'I may be German but a Nazi, never.'

Ignoring Helm, Scrélat stepped towards Morgan and, punctuating his sentences with his strong, lethal hands, shouted, 'These days my people do not have the time to read the rules of war. A year ago today I cut my brother down from a tree after Germans had finished with him. They slit his wrists, hung him by his ankles, and watched him bleed slowly to death. So don't waste any time on him,' he said, indicating Helm with a sideways flick of his head. 'It's like I said: he's ready to talk to you now.' He prodded Helm with his toe cap. 'Aren't you?'

Helm closed his eyes. He screamed as Morgan lifted him under the arms and dragged him across the floor and sat him up against the wall.

Outside the hungry sow and piglets screeched. The noise filled the room.

'For Christ's sake, shut those fucking things up,' Morgan shouted furiously.

'They are hungry. That's all.'

Morgan turned angrily towards the voice to see Colette and André standing side by side in the doorway.

'We have nothing to feed them,' she said.

'Don't worry about them, concentrate on the pig that talks,' Scrélat said. He stood astride Helm, leaning with his hands on the wall behind the German's head.

Morgan watched the little scene. He could not condone what Scrélat had done – or might do. But he could not condemn it either. He tried to imagine how he would have reacted if Panzers, driven by gentlemen with no love for Hitler, had occupied his native Wales.

Helm, aided by an occasional kick from Scrélat, began to answer Morgan's questions. Slowly, painfully. He looked up wearily at Scrélat, whose face remained impassive. 'I fear Ulrich is using the whores to compromise and discredit some of Rommel's most trusted staff.'

'How does he do this? Does he pay or threaten the girls to encourage these indiscretions?' asked Morgan.

Helm grunted. 'He doesn't have to. He selected the girls carefully. We talk to them as if they were our natural choice of lovers – and Ulrich tapes our bedroom conversations. He knows everything.'

'And?'

'I'm not sure,' Helm moaned. Scrélat prodded him. 'But I think he uses this information to exert pressure on Rommel's senior staff.'

'Blackmail?'

Helm nodded, wincing with pain at the movement.

'How?'

'It's difficult to be precise. No one trusts anyone any more. I suspect that one of Rommel's staff officers...'

'Name.'

'Hoffner. Colonel Hoffner. I think he was forced to take an anti-Rommel line in staff meetings and then reported confidential defence decisions back to Ulrich. He couldn't live with himself because of it. He hung himself,' Helm said bitterly.

'Good,' Scrélat said.

'What about this General Durring?'

'Appalling,' Helm mumbled, shaking his head. 'Appalling. He was one of Rommel's closest friends. He signed – was forced to sign – a confession saying he wanted to remove Hitler.'

'Did he?' Morgan asked.

'That's not important. What matters is that some young officers, once loyal to Rommel, believe he did. Now even they are beginning to doubt the Field Marshal's will to win this war. And all because of Durring's confession. Guilt by association. The whole officer corps is split down the middle. That was what Ulrich always wanted – to discredit Rommel.'

'Why?'

'They think Rommel is not the Nazi he should be. They fear he might ditch Hitler if things do not go well for Germany.'

'Is that why he is going all out to strengthen the Normandy defences and bolster up the Atlantic Wall?'

'The Atlantic Wall!' Helm scoffed. 'It's a joke.'

Morgan smiled. He was right. Helm was just a bonus.

Two sharp reports, like gunfire, crackled in the afternoon air. It seemed to come from the farmyard below. Morgan dived to the broken window, and, carefully looking out, saw the two German soldiers dismount from their motorcycle and sidecar and walk towards the trailer of screeching piglets.

'Cover him. If he makes a sound, kill him,' Morgan whispered hoarsely, handing Helm's Luger to André. Helm stared back in terror as André placed it on the bridge of his nose.

Colette stood white-faced in the corner until Morgan hissed, 'Get down,' and she crouched, burying her head in her lap.

Morgan trained his sten on the soldiers as they eyed the trailer. One of them laughed loudly.

'Some bloody joke,' snapped Scrélat, who was at Morgan's side.

'Quiet,' Morgan hissed.

The piglets began to panic as the soldiers approached.

'I'll bet five marks this is the work of a bunch of black-marketeers on the look-out for cheap pork. They must have lost their nerve,' one of the soldiers chuckled.

'Keep thinking that,' Morgan muttered.

The other soldier turned to walk back to the motorcycle combination. Morgan closed his eyes tightly, willing the other man to join him.

The soldier sat astride the BMW, kicked it to life and revved the throttle. 'Come on,' he called to his companion, 'we haven't

169

got all day. Let's get back and report we've found the stolen pigs.'

The other soldier shrugged him off with a wave. Then he climbed onto the hitch joint and leant into the trailer. Seconds later he jumped back, waving something in the air, his words drowned by the frantic squeals from the pigs. Morgan's sten burst into life then, spitting flame, but the angle from the window was too narrow and the bullets slammed harmlessly into the yard, creating tiny fountains of dust and stone. Muffled by the crackle of gunfire, the front wheel of the motorcycle lifted from the ground as the rider kicked his bike into gear. In a blur, the other soldier dived full-length into the sidecar, and they sped off. As the machine broadsided to safety around the side of the barn, Morgan spotted Helm's cap clutched in the hand of the soldier trying to right himself in the sidecar.

'That fucking cap,' Morgan spat, kicking open the shutter and firing in vain.

Behind him Helm moaned and turned onto his side. He forced a smile through his swollen lips. 'That patrol has a radio. You are all as good as dead.'

'So are you,' Scrélat snapped. He leapt to his feet, then kicked the shutter open wide and fired wildly at the barn opposite. He paused, then squinted into the silence. It was broken by a single shot. The Mauser Gewehr 98's 7.92 calibre bullet fractured Scrélat's sternum, deflected through his heart and burst out through the back of his shirt. He sank slowly to his knees without a sound and fell backwards onto the floor. His eyes rolled for a moment before they fixed into the cold, fish-like stare of death.

Colette screamed. André dropped Helm's Luger and plastered his hands over his eyes. Morgan opened fire.

'You're all finished,' Helm said weakly.

'Shut up,' Morgan barked. He unleashed another burst. A shower of whitewashed plaster snowflaked off the barn wall. The Germans returned the fire.

'Get Scrélat's sten,' Morgan yelled.

The old chemist crawled across the floor and prised the weapon from Scrélat's cooling, stiff fingers. He knelt alongside Morgan. Then fired. 'You and Colette make a run for it. I'll cover you as long as I can,' André said above the chatter of the gun and the screams of the pigs.

Morgan looked over his shoulder at Helm, then at André.

'Kill him,' the chemist said. 'You don't need him anymore.'

The thought had already occurred to Morgan, but he knew he could not kill an unarmed prisoner in cold blood. Moreover, Helm might be useful as a hostage, something to bargain with. If they could only get clear of the farm then he might even be able to get Helm back to London.

Morgan crossed the room and cut Helm's hands free, then squatted in front of him, so close his knees nearly touched the German's chest. 'Unless you do exactly as I say, I am going to kill you.'

Helm nodded, and, rubbing his wrists, watched Morgan put down the sten. Then, as Morgan bent forward to haul Helm to his feet, Helm stabbed his fingers into Morgan's eyes, and Morgan, hands over his face, reeled back in agony. When Morgan recovered balance, the sten was trained on his chest.

A loud thwack almost broke Morgan's eardrums and a burning whistle flashed past his face. Morgan looked on in horror as Helm's body jerked upright and the sten spat crazily. Helm's head fell and a rose-shaped petal of crimson seeped through his serge uniform.

Morgan turned and looked past the smoking Luger to Colette's elfin face. Her eyes were squeezed shut.

'He was going to kill me. You had no choice,' Morgan said softly as he got up, and gently eased the pistol from her grasp. 'I owe you my life,' he whispered, putting his arms around Colette and holding her tightly to ease her trembling. Sobbing, she clutched at his arms, and her fingers sank into his sleeve.

He felt André jab him in the back.

'Get the hell out of here. Now. Before those bastards over there get more help.'

'You're coming with us. We can get across the field and be in the woods before they know we've even gone.'

'Maybe,' André said shrugging. 'But first give me a hand with Scrélat.' He noticed Morgan's puzzled look and added, his voice solemn, 'Please do as I say.' He turned to Colette and handed her the sten. 'Just stay down and keep shooting at the barn.'

While Colette fired off round after round, Morgan followed André's bidding and carried Scrélat downstairs. When he had laid him on the stone floor, André appeared with an armful of oil lamps he'd collected from the other rooms. 'Pierre has a wife and family,' he said, dousing the oil over his dead comrade. 'For their sake, and the rest of the group, it would be better if he was not able to be identified. They already know me.'

André lit a rag, then tossed it onto his friend's chest. He turned

171

away, his face a mask of sorrow as a fiery woosh filled the room with black smoke and the smell of burning flesh.

Upstairs, Colette screamed.

The two men bounded back to the first floor to find Colette pointing in horror towards the lane. The farmyard was swarming with German soldiers. Dozens of them, all running for the cover of the barn. Morgan tore the sten from Colette's hands and began to fire, as two more trucks and a snub-nosed armoured car growled up the dirt track.

Returning Morgan's fire, more soldiers leapt from the moving truck and began to fan out each side of the house.

André joined Morgan at the window. They fired wildly. Two soldiers fell. Within seconds, the farmhouse was being raked by return fire from rapid-action MG 34 machine guns.

Morgan caught a sudden movement from the corner of his eye and spun to face it. Colette was holding Helm's Luger to her temple. Morgan threw himself across the room, sending girl and gun flying in opposite directions. In an instant Colette was crawling frantically through the billowing dust and crumbling plaster towards Helm's gun, but again Morgan dived at her. Catching her around the waist, he threw her onto her back and knelt astride her.

'I want to die,' she screamed, pounding his chest. 'I can't face what those pigs will do when they lay hands on me.'

Morgan hit her, hard, with the back of his hand. Her mouth bled. He hit her again. She stopped screaming. He hauled her to her feet and shook her.

'You are going to England. Do you understand? England.' He was shouting at the top of his voice. She began to cry.

'England.' He shook her harder.

At last she nodded.

'Listen and listen carefully,' he said quickly, the urgency showing in the tone of his voice. 'You were with Helm when we abducted you both. You were on your way, the two of you, to Ulrich's hotel. You have no idea who we are. If you can convince them of that, then there is a chance you'll just be sent back to the château. It's the only chance you've got.'

Morgan felt Colette shudder and added, 'It will not be for long. Somehow Albert and the rest of the group will get you out. I swear it.'

Colette could only nod. There was nothing else.

Morgan took a handkerchief from his pocket and gagged her. He then tied her hand and foot with the bonds he'd cut from

Helm. André kept up a constant hail of fire, the old man's face a mask of panic.

Morgan took him by the elbow. 'Well, old friend. I think it's time to call it a day.'

André smiled sadly and shook his head. 'I am old and tired. I have been head of the Swordfish group for a long time. There are a lot of things locked away in there,' he said, tapping the side of his head. 'A lot of names and a lot of lives. It would not be fair to the others to give the Gestapo a chance of breaking an old fool like me.'

He rose and kissed Morgan on both cheeks, then smiled fondly at Colette. 'I'm sorry I let you both down.' He crossed himself, and then, sten in hand, walked from the room.

Morgan's eyes filled with tears and he knew he could do nothing. He watched from the window and cursed the futility of it all, as André stepped out from the door. The old man, his pince-nez swinging wildly from his neck, walked towards the barn splaying the blazing gun held out in front of him as he went.

In an instant, he was cut to pieces.

At that moment Morgan didn't care if he lived or died. He threw his gun down into the yard. His voice cracked with emotion as he called: 'I'm coming out.'

The Germans began to close cautiously on the house. Morgan stood, arms raised, in the doorway and watched them come towards him.

'My name is Henri Paco,' he said, 'and there is a girl in there. I don't know her name. We captured her with Helm. He's dead.'

CHAPTER SIXTEEN

Morgan opened his eyes. It was cold and black and he saw nothing except total darkness. He lay crumpled on the floor with the side of his face pressed against the damp flagstone floor. He ached agonisingly from head to toe. Feebly he tried to stand, but his legs were too weak to support him and buckled at the knees. He sank back to the floor and knelt, head bowed. Then he cautiously extended his arms and felt the darkness like a blind man. His fingers touched the wall which was covered in a thin film of slime. Unsteadily, both hands on the wall for support, he skirted the room. It was too narrow to stand with both arms outstretched. At one end he came to a metal door with no handle. He turned and, arms held before him like a sleepwalker, took four steps to the rear wall. He slid to the floor and huddled in the corner, his knees drawn up under his chin.

He wondered how long he'd been incarcerated. He closed his eyes and saw himself lying in the farmyard. German soldiers, who'd found Helm's broken corpse, were pounding him with rifle butts and kicking him mercilessly, baying like hounds. Suddenly a German officer, pistol drawn, was standing protectively over him and the kicking stopped. The last sound he heard before he passed out was Colette screaming with terror in the farmhouse behind him.

Now, alone in the darkness, he fought to stop himself passing out again. He felt utter desolation mixed with feelings of failure and guilt. He thought of Colette. What had happened to her? Would they kill her? Torture her? He blamed himself for letting her down. He had let everyone down. All of them. Once again he clutched at the wall and pulled himself to his feet. He retched, but no vomit came. His mind, at last, began to clear and it was then he realised the true hopelessness of the situation.

His mission had ended in disaster. He would soon be as dead as the others. He felt his bladder fill and tore at his flies to urinate on the floor.

But there was still Colette. The thought of her charged Morgan's mind. The thought of her being questioned by the SS or Gestapo filled him with rage. Morgan, his mind now in gear but his body still weak, stumbled to the cell door. He summoned what little strength he had and began to pound it with his fists and call Colette's name.

'You bastards, leave her alone. She is not the one you want,' he screamed with rage.

Suddenly the door burst open and flung Morgan before it. He reeled backwards, fighting to keep his balance. He instinctively lunged weakly at the shape silhouetted in the shaft of light in the doorway but fell feebly short of the German guard. Morgan's legs folded and he sank into the pool of urine on the floor.

A second guard appeared in the doorway. The two men moved forward and hauled Morgan roughly to his feet. They dragged him from the cell and slammed him against the passage wall. He heard the lock turn in his cell door, felt himself being pushed forward. He used the metal rail to drag himself up two flights of stone steps to the door at the top. It led to a small cobbled courtyard. And fresh air. It tasted wonderful and he felt the reviving effect the oxygen had on his bloodstream.

The yard was a small square set in the middle of a grim building. Some of the windows set in the high walls had bars, and a Nazi flag fluttered from a pole on the roof. As Morgan was led across the yard towards a green door, he realised he was in a barracks and noted his guards were army, not SS.

Then he was through the door and taken along a corridor. The floor was made from highly polished wooden blocks. He could hear the clatter of unseen typewriters; uniformed clerks eyed him darkly as they passed him with their sheets of paper. Morgan decided the building must be an HQ, probably Caen.

Morgan and his escort turned the corner into a large hall. There was carpet, deeply piled, on the floor. An enormous oil painting of a messianic-looking Hitler hung in a gilt frame above an ornate but empty fireplace. A young lieutenant waited at the foot of a curved staircase.

'Bring him straight up,' he snapped.

Morgan detected hate in the voice. Flanked by his guards, he followed the officer up the stairs and along a landing until they came to a polished oak door. The brass plate fixed in the centre announced it was the office of Major-General Gustave Hans Werner, Aide of the Military Governor of Caen.

Morgan was no longer afraid. He felt calm, even when the lieutenant manhandled him through the door into Werner's office. His legs felt they would no longer fold beneath him. He ruffled his hair, a smile almost appeared on his swollen lips, and he stood erect. He looked Werner in the eye and saw a man who bore the weight of concern. Concern, Morgan guessed, at what he'd learnt from Helm about the position of men like Durring, and perhaps, of Werner himself. Why else, he asked himself, would the governor's aide want to question him in person?

Morgan looked slowly around the room. It was large and elegant, sparsely but tastefully furnished. He turned to face Werner. The general, a distinguished silver-haired man, sat behind the large roll-top desk in front of a full-length window.

'So,' said Werner rolling his tongue, 'you are the terrorist called Paco.' He leant forward across the desk.

Morgan shrugged. 'That depends from which point of view you choose to look at it.'

Werner leant back in his leather chair. He picked up the pen from the writing set and rolled it between his fingers.

'Who are you?' he asked coldly. Morgan felt the chill.

'You've seen my papers.'

'They are meaningless,' sneered Werner, 'but we are checking.'

'Why bother? You bastards are going to shoot me anyway.'

'True,' said Werner, 'but first I want to know why you abducted, questioned by torture and then killed Major Helm.'

'We did what we did to remind you and the likes of that Nazi whore, that none of you are safe for so long as you remain in France.' Morgan glowered and added: 'Never.'

Werner pointed the pen at Morgan. 'Don't play games with me, Paco, or whatever your name is. I want to know, and I want to know now, why you interrogated Major Helm before you killed him?'

I bet you do, thought Morgan, and the longer it takes you to find out, the longer Colette and I live.

'Who said we interrogated him?' said Morgan.

Werner exploded. 'Do you people think we are all congenital idiots? You held the major for two days and tortured him to get information. I have seen his body. You people, so-called freedom fighters, would be a credit to the Gestapo.'

Morgan thought: 'You are a frightened man. There is no way you are going to hand me over to the likes of Ulrich. If I told you, you'd kill me on the spot.'

He said, 'Piss off.'

Then one of the phones on Werner's desk rang sharply. Werner jumped, then snatched the handset from the cradle.

'What?' he barked.

Morgan watched as Werner coloured with rage. Then, as

Werner bellowed down the receiver, Morgan felt a knot in his stomach tighten.

Werner shouted: 'Colonel Ulrich, this man Paco and the Claval girl are in army custody. Neither you, Abwehr or not, the SS or bloody Gestapo, will be allowed anywhere near them until I say so. Do I make myself clear?'

There was a long pause. Morgan could hear Ulrich's disembodied voice coming from the handset. Werner, he saw, winced, holding the phone away from his ear.

Then Werner interrupted the flow of invective. He said: 'It appears, Colonel Ulrich, you are more concerned with your whore than you are with the death of Major Helm.'

He slammed the phone down, wrung his hands, then picked up the receiver again.

'I don't want any more calls through. Understood? None.' He hung up. The phone rang again.

Werner grabbed it furiously. 'I said no more calls ...' He paused mid-sentence. Morgan saw his face tense and lose its colour. He dropped the receiver, half stood, his hands resting palms down on the desk. Morgan was aware the man was looking through him. He followed Werner's gaze to the door behind him, looking over his shoulder to do so.

The door opened without a knock. The young lieutenant who had met Morgan on the stairs and had remained in the room, sprang to attention and saluted the figure who swept through the door. So, Morgan noticed, did Werner, stiffly.

Although the insignia of Dietrich Bekker's Abwehr uniform showed he was of equal rank to Werner, Morgan noticed how the governor's aide tensed in his presence. Morgan thought the newcomer carried the extra air of authority of a man in daily contact with the very source of power.

'Is this the animal who kidnaps and murders unarmed officers from my department?' Bekker strode towards Morgan, ignoring Werner. The prisoner and captor faced each other toe to toe.

The man from Berlin raised his hand. Morgan thought he was going to hit him and turned his face involuntarily to the side. He felt foolish when all Bekker did was click his fingers. In response, Morgan saw an Abwehr captain appear in the doorway carrying a thin leather attaché case. He unzipped it as he walked across the room to Bekker's side. He took out a wax-sealed envelope and placed it in Bekker's outstretched and waiting hand. Bekker took it without a word or second glance.

Morgan watched with a growing apprehension as Bekker

broke the seal, his eyes still fixed on Morgan, his face expressionless.

They are going to hand me over to the Abwehr for questioning, Morgan thought. After all, Helm was one of them.

Bekker removed a single sheet of paper from the envelope and held it out for Werner. The aide moved forward and took it. He made no attempt to read it, but said: 'I assume you want Paco.'

Bekker nodded once.

'But with respect,' protested Werner, 'we have not yet had the chance to question him or the girl.'

Morgan sensed Werner's apprehension.

'The girl is of no concern to us and you can deal with her as you see fit. We are only interested in Paco. Like all captured terrorists, he is to be taken to Amiens prison at once,' Bekker said.

'But how can you be so sure he is important? We have not even established his identity,' Werner replied.

Bekker looked disdainful. 'It is the job of the Abwehr to be aware of such things. You should not take too much note of the smear campaign the SS runs against us. I suggest you read the warrant.'

Suddenly Morgan felt confused. How could a man of Bekker's rank state that Paco was of importance when Paco did not exist? And why was he being taken all the way to a prison in Amiens?

'But February the eighteenth is tomorrow. No one will have time to question him,' Werner said.

'I'm sure that won't distress you too much.' There was an edge of sarcasm in Bekker's voice as he took the warrant from Werner and thrust it at Morgan.

As he read it, Morgan's hands began to shake.

It was his own death warrant. Signed by Admiral Canaris. Morgan dropped it and it fluttered onto the floor. He leant forward, his hands resting on Werner's desk.

He heard Werner say: 'So he is to face the firing squad?'

'Along with ninety others,' Bekker said. 'A mass execution is the most effective way of showing the French public that these increasing acts of sabotage cannot, and will not, be tolerated any further.'

Morgan repeated the number to himself. Ninety. Trussed up and slaughtered like cattle. It was the hopeless indignity of such a death that disturbed him more than the prospect of death itself

Then he realized angrily that he would take the secrets of the Château Beaupré with him to the quicklime of an unmarked grave. Now it was all up to Colette, an old man and a priest.

'Smoke?' Ulrich asked.

Clair, white-faced and red-eyed, looked up nervously. She nodded.

Ulrich casually struck the match between his finger nails, lit the cigarette, drew deeply and exhaled through his nostrils. He did not take his eyes from Clair, who sat at the other side of the table.

'That's better,' he smiled as Clair reached up for the cigarette he now held upright between thumb and forefinger. Then, quickly, he stubbed it on the back of her hand. She screamed, clutched the burn and slumped down on to the table.

Ulrich lunged forward and grabbed a handful of her hair. He wrenched back her head and bent over her.

'Now,' he whispered, 'tell me once again why you wrote this?' He thrust a copy of the letter, luring Helm to the church of Ste-Yvette, under her nose. Ulrich had inked in the outline pressure which Colette's pen had left under the original.

'That's not my signature.' Clair began to sob again. 'I have never seen the letter before. I swear it.'

Ulrich's fingers tightened around the fistful of hair and twisted her face to one side. Then he hit her across the cheek with the back of his hand.

'Then why was it found in your room? Explain.'

'I can't.'

'You lying bitch.' He hit her again.

'I'm telling the truth,' Clair wept.

'Liar!' Ulrich released her hair and began to shake her by the shoulders. 'Liar,' he repeated as if it were an incantation.

Then he released his grip and stood back, hovering with glazed eyes above the convulsed figure on the chair. He swung out at her with his boot. The kick caught her in the kidneys with such force that it flung her onto the floor. She no longer had breath left to cry. He watched, hands on hips, until at last she rolled onto her side, then onto her knees. She placed one hand slowly in front of the other and crawled towards him. Ulrich remained expressionless as she clutched weakly at his trouser leg and looked up at him.

'Why?' she asked in no more than a whisper. 'Please tell me

why I should want to betray Rudi. Why?' She paused and drew breath. 'I loved him.'

Ulrich felt suddenly cold. He knew that was true. He looked down at the note and his hand began to shake. Whoever had written it, he would have to execute. If Clair had not lured Helm into the hands of the Resistance, then that left Colette. It was a possibility he refused to face. He looked down at Clair.

'Liar,' he mumbled and pushed her away with his boot. He turned and walked to the solitary window, peering through the bars across the rooftops of Caen. He could pick out the grey distinctive shape of the army HQ. Werner had held Colette and the man called Paco there for three days now, but there was still no word concerning the girl's role in Helm's death. No news was good news, Ulrich decided. Like Helm, the girl must have been a victim. He willed himself to believe it. He could not contemplate the alternative for the girl who had become as much an obsession to him as his politics; the Jew of his passion. She was his to respond to his every need. It was the only relationship he had ever had.

Ulrich considered the idea of German surrender as nothing short of treason. Germany had been a land governed by traitors where you needed a suitcase of banknotes to buy a loaf of bread, if you found a shop that sold any. Jobless, friendless, he had drifted to Munich. He had rediscovered his self-respect in the beerhalls among the men with slogans on their lips and a vision in their minds for a Germany free from the traitors who were sucking his fatherland dry. Among such men, he had found friendship for the first time in his life and had responded with undying loyalty to the cause they shared; it would rid them of their poverty and restore their glory. They had put food in his belly and a uniform on his back. He had marched with them to fight in the fields of Spain where he had risen from the ranks. Now he still served his masters well by wearing the uniform of an organisation run by men he despised. Scum like Canaris. Men with soft stomachs like Werner.

Ulrich, his thoughts still on Colette, did not hear Hans Voight come into the room. He turned when the Gestapo man coughed.

'Werner is on the phone in my office for you, Colonel,' said Voight. 'It is concerning the Claval girl.'

Ulrich's heart missed a beat.

'Watch that bitch.' Ulrich pointed at Clair curled up on the floor. He strode through the door and along the passage to

Voight's drab office. He marched straight in and picked up the handset from the table.

'Ulrich here,' he barked. His mouth felt dry. He feared what the governor's aide had learnt from Colette.

'You can pick up your whore whenever it suits you,' Werner snapped back. 'She is no longer important to us.'

'Good. Good,' Ulrich mumbled as he tried to collect his thoughts. 'And what about this Paco?'

Werner gave a short laugh. 'My dear Colonel, I thought you would have been informed since this whole affair now seems to be entirely an Abwehr matter.'

'I don't follow you,' Ulrich said curtly.

'The terrorist Paco has been taken to Amiens prison for execution. The order came straight from Berlin. It was signed by Admiral Canaris himself.' Werner sounded smug.

'Canaris.' Ulrich hissed the name through clenched teeth. 'Why should Canaris concern himself with this man Paco? What did you learn from him?' Ulrich's voice rose.

'Nothing,' said Werner flatly, then added, 'Or from your whore either.' He hung up.

Ulrich stared into the phone. 'Canaris?' he asked himself. He ran his hand nervously over the scar on his face, unaware that the man who had caused it was now on his way to the condemned cell.

Ulrich replaced the receiver. Then he felt his stomach tighten. He realised that the task of interrogating Colette Claval was being left entirely to him. He was the one who would have to decide if she would live or die.

'Tomorrow one of you will be dead,' Ulrich said quietly. Colette glanced sideways at Clair. Clair sat with her eyes closed. She bit her lip and sighed. Ulrich rose and walked slowly around the table until he stood behind Clair's chair. He placed his hands on the back rest, leant over her shoulder and whispered, 'Which one is it to be?'

Neither girl spoke. Ulrich straightened, then turned to Colette. She could smell the stale tobacco on his breath as he spoke to her for the first time since she had been brought into the room. During those twenty minutes, his wrath had been directed solely at Clair. For the most part his voice was pitched at a screaming falsetto as he waved the note he'd found in her room under her nose. Her denials were still firm.

'She would not harm sweet Rudi because she loved him,'

mocked Ulrich. 'So where does that leave you?' he asked Colette. She slumped deeper into the chair.

'You told the soldiers who captured Paco, you just happened to meet Major Helm in the street minutes before he was abducted. Do you expect me to believe that? Do you?'

Colette nodded. 'It's true,' she said quietly. 'They took us to a chemist's shop, then to the farm. You know the rest.'

Ulrich grunted. He began to pace behind the two girls. Colette realised how feeble her explanation sounded. She reached out and her fingers found Clair's cold hand. She clasped it tightly. There was no response from Clair, who stared straight ahead at the wall. Colette had not considered Ulrich would have had a copy of the note she'd written. She realised with horror she had placed Clair's life at risk. She also knew she did not want to die. In her cell the prospect had not greatly troubled her. She had convinced herself that André had done the only sensible thing. A quick death appeared then to be the best option. Not now.

'What do you know about this note and the church at Ste-Yvette?' Ulrich asked her, but he was looking at Clair.

'Nothing,' Colette said quickly. She could not involve Father Delon.

'I want the truth,' Ulrich shouted.

'That is the truth,' Colette yelled back.

'She is lying,' Clair said coldly, wrenching her hand from Colette's grasp.

Ulrich's jaw dropped. His gaze shifted from Clair to Colette, who groaned desperately as she bent her head in desperation. She realised Ulrich had no choice except to order her execution. Clair had left him no option, but, strangely, Colette felt no bitterness, only a vague sense of calm that, for her, it had now ended.

'The wretched child is lying through her teeth. It's preposterous to assume she simply bumped into Rudi by chance,' Clair continued with a haughty self-assurance. Her cool façade gave no hint of the anguish and emotion she felt building up inside her. 'She went deliberately to seek him out,' Clair added as she turned towards Colette, 'because I asked her to.'

Ulrich's eyes swivelled in their sockets. He could hardly believe his ears. It was much more than he could have hoped for.

'I wrote that note,' Clair continued. 'She had no idea what was in it and took it to Helm as a favour to me. I lured him into the hands of the Resistance. I betrayed him.'

Clair rose. She bent and kissed Colette, first on the forehead, then gently on the lips. 'You must understand,' she said as she placed two fingers to seal Colette's mouth, 'there is nothing left for me now.'

Colette began to cry softly. Clair held her head for a few seconds before she turned and faced Ulrich. With a composed anger she slapped his face. She spat at him before she turned and walked towards the door.

It was then that Colette noticed Clair wore the same blue dress as she had the day they'd first met. Clair's fingers lingered for a moment on the handle before opening the door. She looked back over her shoulder at the dazed girl in the chair.

'Goodbye, my sweet love.'

Then Clair opened the door and walked towards the waiting guards.

CHAPTER SEVENTEEN

The acrid smell of stale urine greeted Morgan as the heavy door thumped shut behind him. He surveyed the condemned cell where he would spend the last forty-eight hours of his life. The cell was long and narrow. At the far end, below the window, was a bare board which served as a bunk. It was fixed to the wall by chains. Morgan climbed onto it and looked out of the window.

He was in a block detached from the main body of the prison. The searchlights on the massive outer walls were trained on the prison yard. They were positioned between two control towers containing two German guards. Others patrolled the top of the wall. A barbed-wire fence ringed the cell block and within it roamed four Doberman dogs, who ran the length of the fence, barking at the shuffling line of civilian prisoners being herded by French guards from the workshops under the wall back to the main building.

Between the control towers, Morgan could see the majestic twin spires and the clock tower of the cathedral which dominated the ancient capital of the Kingdom of Picardy. The weak February sun sank behind the clock tower as it began to strike five. As if on cue, the searchlights came to life. Their glare dazzled Morgan. He dropped from the window and sat on the edge of the bunk. He reasoned that the Germans would have housed the ninety due to die in this same block, away from the other prisoners. Many would have been in captivity for months, and during that time must have found ways of using the prison system to advantage. Being Resistance, they would have a grapevine, a link to outside contacts, and even, a link to London.

The Nazis could kill him, but they could not destroy the information he now carried in his head. If he could make contact with some of his fellow prisoners, then there was still a chance he might be able to get this information out.

Morgan doubted if the condemned men would get exercise periods. That left meal times. When Morgan had been led to his cell, he had noticed the row of tables laid out in the centre of the floor. He would make contact then.

He ran over everything he had learnt and, like the newspaperman he used to be, began mentally to edit the jumble into a few easily memorised sentences which could be passed along a verbal chain to end at SOE. No one, he hoped, would forget the last line: the harlots are vital – kidnap them.

His thoughts were interrupted by the sound of a key turning in the lock. A French warder stood in the doorway and Morgan's hopes for a mealtime contact were dashed. The man had a tray in his hand. He knelt and slid it across the floor to Morgan.

Then, to Morgan's amazement, the warden made a Churchillian V for Victory sign and winked before he slammed the door shut. Morgan felt the adrenalin pump into his bloodstream. He could enlist the warden's help to make a contact; it would be too risky to trust the man directly. Suddenly Morgan felt better. He knelt by the tray. On it were a metal bowl of murky soup and a hunk of dry bread flecked with mould. The soup was cold.

A slight movement caught Morgan's eye. It seemed, just for a second, that one of the bricks in the cell wall moved. He put it down to a trick of the light, but it moved again. He watched as inch by inch, it began to slide out of the wall. Morgan grabbed it and helped ease it from its place. He laid it on the floor and pressed his eye to the gap. Another eye stared back. The eye vanished and was replaced by a pair of cracked lips.

'M'sieu Paco?' a voice croaked.

'Who are you?' asked Morgan cautiously.

'No matter, [the voice sounded like broken glass] but I have a message for the Dragon.'

The use of his code name took Morgan aback. It was known only to London and the Swordfish group, what was left of it. Morgan feared a trap.

'I don't know anyone called Dragon,' said Morgan.

'We don't have time to play games,' the man said.

'I'm not. I have no idea who you are. You could be a bloody German for all I know.'

The man snorted. His voice took on a sense of urgency. He said: 'The message comes from a friend.'

'Name?'

'Arnie Connors. He says there is still a bottle of PX bourbon waiting for you in the filing cabinet when you get back. The message said you'd understand.'

'I'll be buggered.' Morgan began to laugh aloud as he recalled Arnie's hiding place. No one else would know of it. As the man began to speak, Morgan cut him short. 'Look, is there any way

I can get a verbal message out of here and back to SOE? If they can contact you, you must be able to do the same to them.'

¡You can trust the guard who brought your food,' the man said, 'but with a little luck, you should be able to deliver it in person.'

Morgan could feel his heart thumping. He found it hard to believe his ears. 'You can get me out of here?' He was almost shouting into the gap in the wall.

'Not just you, m'sieu. All of us due to be executed.'

'The whole ninety?'

'Yes.'

'How? When?' There were a dozen questions Morgan wanted answered. But this time it was his turn to be cut short.

'Tomorrow,' the man said. 'Your airforce is going to bomb this bloody prison to bits.'

'Jesus wept,' protested Morgan. 'With us still in it?'

'Yes.'

The Doberman guard dogs were going frantic. Morgan, hands behind his head, listened to them as he lay on his bunk staring at the ceiling. Two of the dogs began to bay, ignoring the guards' shouts to be quiet. Morgan started as the brick fell from the wall onto the floor. He jumped up quickly and crouched at the gap it left. He saw the thick lips of his neighbour.

'It's almost time,' the man croaked.

'Did you pass on my message?' Morgan asked.

'I told my brother when he came to make his farewell visit this afternoon. He promised to pass it on to men who will relay it to London: but you could easily have told the guard. He can be trusted.'

'I never trust men who can be bought,' said Morgan.

'You are lucky you've never had to,' the voice grunted. 'I hope I'll see you after the bombing. If we are both still alive.' The lips vanished from the gap.

Morgan heard the cathedral clock strike, and, right on time, the searchlights bathed the prison in a powerful white light. It was as bright as day in the death cell. Morgan climbed on to the bunk and looked towards the sky which had begun to slip into night. Nothing, not even clouds. He looked down the two floors into the prison yard. The dogs were restively prowling along the wire fence isolating the special block from the rest of the yard.

Then Morgan heard them.

'Mosquitos,' he yelled joyfully, and scanned the sky for a glimpse of the RAF fighter-bombers.

The first plane came in so low and fast that Morgan almost missed it. The plane came screaming out of the twilight, its twin propeller blades almost slicing the tops off the chimney stacks. Two thin red lines of tracer fire spat from the wings. The guards patrolling on top of the outer wall ducked as the leading Mosquito swooped above their heads, its tracer shells pumping into the main prison building behind the special block.

Instinctively Morgan covered his head with his hands and bent double as the plane, throttles wide open, roared past the cell window so close it rattled the bars. Seconds later came the shrill sound of a bomb whistling through the air. Then an explosion. The blast threw Morgan off the bunk as the whole cell block shook, sending part of the ceiling crashing down.

Morgan picked himself up and leapt back onto the bunk. He grabbed the bars on the window and began to shake them, shouting with joy. One of the control towers had vanished. Morgan saw what was left of the wooden structure in the yard, among the mangled remains of the guards who had been in it.

Bullets from the second plane ripped through the yard, slicing through a group of German guards who were running, guns firing at the sky, from the main building. They fell like skittles.

In the corner of the prison yard, a truck burst into flames, then blew up, sending a fireball rolling in all directions. It engulfed the four dogs and the smell of their burning flesh and fur flooded towards Morgan's cell. A second truck caught fire as black smoke and flames licked through the broken windows of the main prison and hung over the carnage like a funeral pall. Inside the building, men began to scream after a bomb from the third Mosquito had taken away part of the roof and most of one wall. The blast had scattered the bodies of guards, prisoners and soldiers around the yard like so much litter.

Then a gas main exploded. A single giant flame leapt from between a crack in the yard's flagstones and burnt loudly like some enormous Bunsen burner.

The Mosquitos kept screaming out of the sky in waves, banking away at rooftop height, only to attack again and again as confused guards and troops swarmed through the blitzed prison.

The outer walls were breached by the fifth wave of attackers. Three bombs each carved a dusty canyon through the reinforced concrete and stone. Morgan could see the street beyond when the dust had settled over the rubble.

The lights had gone in the first few minutes. The scene was now lit by flames from the fires. More explosions followed and the heat seemed to suck the oxygen from the air. Morgan, his eyes streaming and throat full of dust, dropped, coughing, from the window. Suddenly there were no more planes. It was over. For a few seconds there was complete silence. Then, belatedly, a siren began to wail and alarm bells rang. Some men, including Morgan, began to cough. Others began to scream with pain, some wept.

Outside, in the yard, Morgan heard voices barking commands in French and German. He hauled himself to his feet and wiped his stinging eyes.

Then he heard gunfire. Further bursts told him the fire was being returned. He climbed onto the bunk and peered cautiously through the bars. He saw figures in the shadows, crouching behind the piles of rubble. They were raking the yard with fire.

'Christ,' mumbled Morgan, 'they are storming the prison.' The figures began to make inroads despite the returning fire.

He spun around as a deafening burst slammed into his cell door. Wooden splinters flew in all directions as Morgan dived onto the floor and rolled into the corner. He stood, fists open and boot raised like a Samurai warrior. The door was kicked open by a huge workingman's boot. Through the dust, Morgan recognised the familiar features of his cell neighbour. The owner of the voice was built like a small gorilla. He had a chest like a barrel and his arms dangled loosely from his massive shoulders. He held his sten gun like a toy rifle. He grinned at Morgan to reveal some broken teeth.

'Follow me,' he said.

Morgan bolted after him onto the metal balcony. It ran along all four walls above the well of the building where the tables were laid out. Rope safety nets, used to foil suicides, hung from the first-floor balcony.

'This way,' Morgan called after the big man and vaulted over the balcony. He bounced onto the net and looked up at a face peering over the rail. The man looked hesitant. 'It's quicker. Jump!' Morgan yelled. He swung to the floor and pointed to the spiral stairs leading from the balcony. Men were jostling frantically, pushing in panic, to reach the ground floor. Gun held firmly, the big man leapt. The net held and seconds later he stood at Morgan's side.

Outside, the gunfire intensified above the crackling flames and the odd gas explosion. The two men raced towards the door, the Frenchman launching himself at it with his shoulder. It flew open and he fell headlong into the yard. Bullets ricocheted from the ground in front of him. He clambered for the cover of a pile of rubble and motioned Morgan to stay put as more bullets bounced around the door.

To Morgan's left, a door burst open. He froze as a French prison guard leapt into view. Morgan noticed his gun first. It was a German MP 28 Bergmann sub-machine gun. And it was trained on his chest. Morgan's eyes moved to the man's face. He recognised the guard. The one who had brought his food. The one who had been bought for money. As he moved towards Morgan, he realised there was no way he could take the guard before the MP 28 ripped him apart.

The guard eyed Morgan for a moment, then said: 'Hit me.'
Morgan blinked.
'For God's sake, hurry man,' the guard snapped. 'Take the bloody gun and hit me hard before . . .'

His eyes glazed before he finished the sentence and by the time he hit the floor, Morgan was through the door. Bent double, he returned the fire from the main building as he ran towards the big Frenchman who, face twisted in concentration, was blasting at the prison.

Morgan could feel heat from the giant flame leaping from the ruptured gas main. It was intense. It also lay between them and the breached wall. Morgan dug his companion in the ribs.

'Make for the flame and on to the street,' yelled Morgan.
The man shook his head. 'You first. I'll cover. Those were my orders. You've got to get out first. Go.'

Morgan didn't argue. He ran headlong for the flame, covering his face with his arm. He plunged through. Seconds later, face black with smoke, the Frenchman was at his side.

Rifle fire came from behind them. Morgan spun round to face it. The shots came from behind the heap of rubble at the broken wall.

'They are Resistance,' the big man shouted. Morgan lowered the gun.

'Over here. Quickly,' a woman's voice called out from behind the rubble. The two men ran headlong towards it, leaping over stones to land on their backs. Morgan rolled quickly onto his stomach as two German soldiers came into view from behind the burning workshops at the foot of the outer wall. He unleashed two short bursts in rapid succession.

The first caught the leading soldier in the throat, tearing away half his neck. The second ripped into his companion's stomach, lifting him off his feet, through the shattered workshop window, into the fierce flames. The burst had emptied the MP 28's clip. Morgan cursed.

'We can make use of it,' the Resistance woman said. Morgan gave her the gun. As he did so, he saw more of the escaping prisoners running through the flames and smoke. Some were carrying wounded comrades. The group behind the rubble gave covering fire. The smell of cordite was overwhelming.

The woman looked over her shoulder at Morgan. 'You're in the way here. Get clear, fast.' Morgan turned and sprinted after the big man who was already on the other side of the street. They turned into a side alley with high walls on either side. There was a loud crash as the man charged through a row of metal bins, knocking them aside as if they were matchwood. Morgan had to leap to clear one which rolled towards him, as he fought to keep up with the pace set by the Frenchman.

Although the sky was tinged red from the glow of the burning prison, the alley, shielded from it by high wall and deserted buildings, was completely blacked out. Morgan followed blindly the sound of his companion's boots as they pounded the cobbles. The two men moved from one alley to another and through a succession of narrow, unlit, side passages. The sound of gunfire still crackled on the night air, echoing through the maze of alleys. Only when the echoes died, did they pause for breath, both men's hands on their knees, their bent backs against a wall for support. Five minutes later Amiens' cathedral clock chimed. It was half past six.

'Let's go,' the big man said. This time, they walked side by side through dingy back street after dingy street, all empty except for the lines of washing which hung between the silent, shuttered houses.

'What now?' Morgan asked at last.

The big man grinned down at him, looking deceptively oafish. 'You know I cannot tell you that. If we get caught, they can't make you tell what you don't know. Just stick close and trust me.'

Morgan grunted. He felt naked.

Suddenly he was aware of new sounds, car horns screaming

from the streets ahead, klaxons and sirens ringing out above angry voices. He guessed they were nearing a main thoroughfare. They turned into the boulevard de Strasbourg. It was chaotic.

'Our people must have blacked out the electricity supply before the raid,' the big man laughed.

Morgan followed him as he pushed his way through the throng of people on the wide tree-lined pavement. Men stumbled into each other as if they were blind. Just a few carried candles, which threw off scant and eerie light.

A few oil lamps glowed weakly from boulevard cafés where customers crowded together and talked excitedly. In the roadway, the traffic was at a complete standstill. Buses had collided, cars blocked bumper to bumper were slewed at crazy angles as the drivers ranted and raved at each other, standing beside their dented vehicles.

Morgan noticed the looters had been at work. Shop windows were smashed, shelves empty and their contents gone. Some had had their metal shutters torn down. Lost children cried as anxious parents called out as they searched for them. Morgan also noted there was no bomb damage from the raid. It had all been confined to the prison.

He caught his companion by the sleeve.

'There are no police or soldiers anywhere. Why?'

The big man laughed again. They were standing at a road junction now. He pointed down the rue Chabannes. One side was entirely taken up by a high brick wall, which looked just like the prison. Here traffic was also at a standstill. Outside the main gate, three buses had been overturned and set alight.

'We have had time to plan this raid,' he said. 'That building is the barracks.'

They crossed the road quickly, walked down a hill and through a railway arch. The Gare St-Roche was closed and a restless crowd milled outside the gates waiting for them to reopen. The two men pushed on and once again took the back streets. They turned a corner, both walking quickly now, when they were suddenly caught in a blaze of light. Instinctively Morgan covered his eyes from the glare. An engine was gunned to life and the headlights moved slowly towards the figures frozen in the beam.

It was an ambulance. A small man leapt from the passenger seat. He wore a white coat and quickly opened the back doors.

'Inside,' he snapped.

The two men jumped in quickly and the doors slammed shut. The klaxon rang out and the ambulance shot forward, throwing Morgan onto the stretcher bed.

'Pull the blanket over,' the big man barked. Morgan covered himself as the big man took off his jacket and put on a long white coat. He washed the grime from his face in a sink on the wall. Next to it stood twin oxygen cylinders and a rubber mask. The man tried the valve and gave a satisfied snort.

The tinted windows were the kind that enabled people to see out but not in. Morgan sat up and looked out. They were back on a main road. Traffic, although heavy, had begun to move again.

The klaxon screamed as the ambulance carved its way through the streets, going the wrong way around the bollards and ignoring road signs.

They were opposite the abandoned zoo, when Morgan saw the BMW motorcycle race past them and force them to stop. A soldier in German field grey got out of the sidecar as the rider killed the BMW's engine. The soldier carried a sub-machine gun.

'An emergency heart case. Collapsed in the blackout,' explained the ambulance driver.

'Open up. Let's take a look.' The German motioned with the gun.

'Then hurry, man, for God's sake,' the driver said as he got down from the cab.

The big man moved. He pushed Morgan down on the bed and grabbed the oxygen cylinders. He slapped the rubber mask over Morgan's face and turned on the valve.

'What the hell's going on?' he shouted as the rear doors flew open and he saw the German standing in the road peering in.

'Identity check,' the soldier barked. 'Who is he?' He pointed at the prostrate Morgan.

'How the hell should I know? He's not conscious and he's going to die if you stand there all night gawping.' The big man sounded furious. He glared at the soldier, as he climbed into the back of the ambulance. Morgan's breathing was snatched and irregular – his fear was certainly genuine. The big man knelt beside Morgan, his ear pressed to his chest.

'You can see he's fading fast,' he shouted at the soldier. The German hesitated, rubbing his chin.

'Right,' he said at last. 'You'd better follow us. Traffic is still in a mess.' He jumped from the ambulance and called to the motorcycle rider, 'Can we escort them some of the way?'

The rider kicked his machine to life, revved and nodded.

Klaxon ringing, the ambulance followed.

When they crossed the river Somme, the electricity had been restored and the traffic was moving freely. The escort waved them on up the hill to the hospital.

Two blocks later, the ambulance turned off the klaxon and turned left on route 16, the main road through the outskirts to Doullens.

The man removed the mask from Morgan's face. The Welshman was sweating furiously.

'What now?' he asked.

'A safe house. It belongs to a doctor. Another ambulance will pick you up after midnight and take you west into the country. There you will be handed over to another group, who will take you overland to a landing strip where you'll be picked up and flown out by Lysander. With luck, you'll be home for breakfast.'

The ambulance stopped just inside the city boundary.

'This is it?' asked Morgan. The man nodded.

As soon as he'd closed the doors behind them, the ambulance sped off. It left the two men standing at the side of some waste ground about a hundred yards from the rear of the doctor's house. They moved into the shadows and waited to make sure they had not been observed.

The sound of the ambulance faded and nothing moved. The trees at the side of the road were bare, their branches stark and damp in a pale moonlight which waned as a light wind drove clouds scudding across the sky. They moved silently through the wet grass towards the terrace of unlit houses. Morgan felt uneasy. There should have been noise, a radio, the sound of women in kitchens preparing dinner or washing dishes, children laughing or babies crying. A dust-bin lid clanged as a lone tom cat rummaged for food, then made off. Still no one turned on a light or came to investigate. Morgan's unease grew.

'Wait,' said Morgan, as the big man moved towards the rear garden gate set in a neat hedge. 'Before we go in through the back, I want to make sure no one is waiting outside the front.'

'Is is a safe house. No one suspects the doctor.'

'After what happened tonight, they'll suspect everyone.'

The man thought for a moment. 'This way,' he said and swung his arm like an Indian club. They moved stealthily along the rear of the unlit terrace until they came to the corner of the street. It looked deserted.

'Seems OK.'

Morgan shook his head and counted the number of chimney stacks silhouetted against the sky. Eight.

'How many houses from the end does our doctor friend live?'

The man sensed the urgency in Morgan's voice, and counted slowly on his fingers. He looked puzzled and counted again until he was sure.

'Eight.'

'Then let's get out of here.'

'I don't understand.'

With a flick of his wrist, Morgan called the man to his side.

'Look for yourself.'

The man's eyes scanned the street but his blank expression told Morgan he had seen nothing.

'The door and second-floor window.'

The man's face remained blank.

'Light,' said Morgan and slowly the Frenchman understood. Two thin shafts of light cut through the darkness, one from the door, the other from a window.

'That door is ajar,' explained Morgan, 'and no Resistance man is going to risk breaking a blackout by allowing light to show, especially when he is expecting us. If that door is open, it is because it won't close. Someone has kicked the lock off and that someone is watching through the chink in the curtain.'

They moved back from the road into the darkness.

It took them an hour to reach the abattoir. The big Frenchman had worked there up until his arrest by the occupation security forces. The road was wet and slippery, glistening after a short shower. It seemed deserted.

'We'll climb over the back wall,' the man said in a whisper.

'I'd prefer to lay low tonight and get out of the city in the morning, or tomorrow night,' said Morgan.

'If they have got the doctor, then the chances of anywhere else being safe is too much to hope for. They will have sealed off every road out of Amiens by now and they'll keep it that way for days. Your only chance is to do it my way.'

Morgan did not argue. Hands deep in his pockets, he followed the man up the street. Butchers' stalls, canvas flaps tied tight, were set out ready for the next day's business. Rain drops dripped steadily from the awnings as the two men approached the red brick wall in front of them.

'Halt,' a voice barked.

Both men froze. A flashlight shone in their faces.

'Raise your hands, slowly,' a second voice said behind them. A German soldier came out from behind a stall, rifle held at waist height.

Morgan raised his hands. The Frenchman followed.

'Big bastard, isn't he?' the soldier with the gun said as he moved forward. He jabbed the Frenchman. 'Papers?'

'Here.' The man went to lower his hands.

'Keep them up,' the soldier said and added, 'Take a look' to his comrade. He held the flashlight up to the man's face and, with his free hand, fumbled inside the man's pocket for the papers.

The big man bellowed like a bull. He flung his arms around the soldier, who dropped the flashlight and screamed as he was lifted from the ground in a bear hug. It was the last sound he ever made.

As the embrace of death tightened, Morgan heard the soldiers's rib cage crack. Then he moved. Morgan swung out with his boot. The heel caught the soldier in the groin. Before he could scream, the chop from the side of Morgan's hand shattered his windpipe. The second chop ruptured his aorta. He gurgled, then drowned as his own blood filled his lungs and tumbled from his mouth onto the wet street.

The Frenchman flung his dead German through canvas sheeting on a stall, tearing it cleanly. He turned and ran for the brick wall. His long arms stiffened as he flung himself into the air. His fingers curled around the top of the wall, and, slowly, groaning, he hoisted his enormous frame upwards until, at last, he sat astride the top.

'Here,' he croaked.

Morgan reached up for the dangling arm. He felt the grip tighten and was hauled upwards and dropped on the other side. Then they were together. They ran to a corner of the yard. 'Help me,' the man said and together they lifted the heavy iron manhole cover from its place.

'Inside. Quickly.'

Morgan clambered down the metal rungs into the darkness. He dropped the last few feet into the gushing waters of Amiens' main sewer. It came up to his waist and stank. The Frenchman joined him.

For his size, he moved with amazing speed. He swept through

the effluent like a battlecruiser with Morgan, arms aloft, in his wake.

They raced silently through the stench for twenty minutes. Then Morgan smelt fresh air. They were getting near the outfall where the sewer tumbled noisily into the river Somme.

'This is where I leave you,' the man shouted above the gushing sewer. 'A boat is moored and waiting for you in the middle of the river. Take it. I'll get word to the group who is to take you to the landing field. They will be waiting for you on the banks of the river about ten kilometres downstream. Good luck.'

Morgan grasped the huge hand warmly. 'Thanks,' he said. Then, as the man turned, he called after him, 'You never told me your name.'

The big man smiled. 'They call me the Slaughterman, because I worked in the abattoir. You understand.'

'I'll bet,' Morgan grinned as he watched the figure vanish back into the sewer. Morgan prayed the Slaughterman would make contact with the other group in time.

He waded to the end of the pipe, holding on to metal inspection rungs for support. There, as promised, he saw a small boat. It was tied to the end of a rope fastened to a ring on the wall above the pipe.

Morgan waited, watching for any sign of life from the silent buildings on the opposite bank. Above his head a prowling rat disturbed a pigeon, which flapped into the night.

He undid the rope, wrapped it around his wrist and jumped into the river. The cold robbed him of breath as he hauled himself along the rope towards the boat. He grasped the stern and the little craft needed no further urging. Hanging on to the side, Nat Morgan let the river take him west.

The black waters washed him from the city. Soon he could smell fields. Trees of all shapes loomed up from the banks. Morgan positioned the boat and hauled himself inside.

He picked up the oars from the floor of the boat. The blades cut through the water, and with powerful dipping movements of his shoulders, he was swept along with the swollen current. Morgan found it impossible to judge distance on the dark river which twisted and turned back on itself through the Picardy countryside. He guessed, and he hated guessing, it would take at least two hours to get to where the Resistance group would be waiting, if the Slaughterman had managed to get through to them. He would row flat-out for what he estimated to be an hour.

Then he slowed, just using the oars to steer, drifting with the downstream motion, desperately scanning the bank for any sign of the men who would take him to the landing field.

There was nothing. He began to get anxious. He thought of the light in the doctor's house. Poor bastard. The Gestapo would have him now. Morgan wondered how much of his escape plan the doctor would have known. Perhaps all of it. Perhaps he'd talk. Morgan also considered the possibility that the Slaughterman might have bought it. He put the thoughts out of his mind, concentrating on the sounds of a river at night.

He drifted around an ox-bow bend and quickly brought the boat to a halt. There was something, someone, on the bank. He heard a rustle from a clump of bushes. Then he saw the glow from the end of a cigarette. He knew no Resistance man would be that foolish. Then came a steady whirring noise and a gentle plop.

'A bloody poacher,' Morgan cursed. He could not risk being seen. He would leave the boat, skirt round the man and follow the bank on foot. He eased himself ashore and gently tipped the boat. It filled with water and slipped beneath the surface, leaving a mute trail of protesting bubbles.

Morgan moved in the fisherman's direction, silently, on the balls of his feet. He heard the twig snap behind him too late to do anything about it. Morgan's legs were suddenly kicked from under him and he crashed onto his back. His head caught a stone. Before he could recover, someone knelt heavily on his chest. He felt the tip of a bayonet at his throat.

'You move and you die.' Morgan froze. His assailant whistled and Morgan heard movement in the undergrowth. Rifle bolts were drawn and the bayonet left his throat. Morgan looked up and saw the fisherman in knee-length waders and rod in hand. The man with the bayonet stood up. He was flanked by three armed men. One of them raised his rifle and aimed it at Morgan.

'You have ten seconds to explain who you are,' said the man with the bayonet.

'That depends on who you are,' Morgan said quietly.

'Nine. Eight. Seven.'

'My name is Paco.'

'Any other?'

'Dragon.'

'Where are you going and who sent you?'

'The Slaughterman told me I was going home.' They lowered

their rifles. The man with the bayonet extended a hand and hauled Morgan to his feet.

'You were careless, friend,' he said.

Morgan rubbed his face. 'I didn't expect to see a fisherman with a fag in his mouth.'

The man laughed. 'I can't think of a better excuse to be on a riverbank at night, can you?'

'Your point,' said Morgan. 'Now what?'

'It's too late to get you out tonight. The Lysander's been and gone. He had instructions to wait thirty minutes – then leave without you. He'll try again tomorrow at ten. We'll take you to the field an hour before.'

'What happens in the meantime?' Morgan asked.

'We hide up in the woods. Anything else?'

'Don't suppose you've got anything to eat?'

The angler tossed him a fish.

As they moved off towards the wood, dawn began to break.

As the first rays of day dripped faintly through the grey clouds which swept over the Gestapo yard in Caen, a soldier knelt alongside the bruised and pale body of Clair La Croix.

The soldier drew his revolver and placed it at her temple. He glanced behind him as the firing squad marched away. He administered the coup de grâce. The girl's head lurched upwards, then what was left of it crashed back onto the damp stone slabs.

Ulrich let the curtain fall. He turned from the window and left for breakfast at the Château Beaupré.

CHAPTER EIGHTEEN

The field had been chosen well. It was long, flat and wide – far more suitable to accommodate a Lysander than the narrow cutting used when Morgan had arrived in the woods near Lisieux.

To the south, an unbroken vista of towering spruce sloped gently towards a meandering country road. The absence of livestock and smoke indicated the lack of farms or cottages. Only a sudden reflected glint of afternoon sun on a pair of field glasses revealed the presence of someone other than the nesting crows.

The German soldier holding the glasses to his eyes wriggled uncomfortably in the undergrowth at the far end of the field. A rustle from the bushes behind him, told him his replacement look-out was approaching.

'Anything?'

'No, except I'm almost pissing myself,' he said, handing over the glasses. He slid down the bank and urinated behind a tree before crawling back alongside his replacement.

'How are things back there?' he asked, nodding in the direction of the hastily erected tents camouflaged among the trees.

'Just the same.'

'They still don't know who the bastard is?'

'Only that he is a British agent, code named "the Dragon".'

'That all?'

'Right. That's all the Gestapo managed to get out of that doctor and his wife in Amiens. That, and the fact he is being airlifted out tonight from this godforsaken place.'

'Well, I suppose if that's all those sadistic bastards could get out of them, then that's all they knew.'

'Could be, anyway I'm off.'

The soldier turned, slid back down the slope and headed back towards the encampment. When he arrived, he noticed they'd finished assembling the field generators and cables. They were to provide the portable arc lights with enough power to banish the darkness from the remote hill twenty-nine kilometres from Amiens.

As darkness fell, the two men emerged from the thicket, crossed the track and made their way through the dense spruce to the field at the top of the hill. They cursed the half-moon that lit their path to the summit. Moons were fine for songwriters but were a menace for Lysander pilots. Normally, Special Operation pilots never flew unless the moon was down, but the importance of the information in Nat Morgan's head left no choice. When the men reached the top, they wished each other well. One of them slipped back into the night and Morgan was left alone with his sten for company.

He took two paraffin flares from his pocket and placed them eighty paces apart. He then moved back to the cover of the bushes and waited.

An hour later he heard the familiar drone. He looked skywards for the first sign of the Lysander as the drone became louder. It was almost directly overhead when he saw the pilot flash a signal with a torch.

Morgan moved. He sprinted and lit the flares. The Lysander banked, then dipped its nose and swooped in on the makeshift runway where Morgan stood waving his sten in greeting.

As the wheels touched down, an unseen German raised his flare gun and fired into the air. By the time the Lysander's rear wheel had hit the ground, Morgan was already firing into the bushes on the far side of the field.

Then the sky turned purple as the flare exploded into cracking stars. The top half of the field was suddenly bathed in a brilliant white light from the powerful arcs in the trees. Morgan, knees bent, began firing in the direction of their beams.

Two of the arcs exploded back to darkness as Morgan raked the trees. Then a third.

The Lysander slewed towards Morgan as the waiting Germans opened up with rapid fire from the bushes a hundred yards away. Then a row of headlights turned on in unison in the darkness at the far end of the field, and began to move slowly after the plane. It was now rolling broadside towards Morgan, then it straightened out on just one wheel. Morgan threw himself face down as the plane passed over him. It careered on up the field.

Morgan was on his feet. He ran in a zig-zag, firing at the line of advancing headlights. They had reached the section of the field lit by the remaining arcs. Morgan saw three heavy half-track trucks flanked by motorcycle combinations. In each sidecar sat a soldier behind a fixed machine gun. They were firing straight ahead of them at the Lysander, which had begun a tight turn. Chunks of fuselage and canvas flew off the plane in all directions.

From the corner of his eye, Morgan saw Germans swarm from the bushes and advance across the field. They too began to fire at the plane.

The trucks and motorcycles were nearer. Morgan saw there were more troops in the back of the trucks. He wished his sten were a more accurate weapon.

He decided to concentrate on the sidecar units. The burst was short, but enough. The blast lifted one of the machine gunners from the sidecar, and unbalanced, the combination veered into the line of fire. Flames from the explosion set off a chain reaction along the line of units and into the trucks. Human torches jumped screaming from the trucks. They ran in all directions, and some were cut down by cross-fire from their own men in the bushes.

Morgan turned for the plane.

The troops from the bushes had now formed a semi-circle around it. They knelt, firing rifles. Morgan began to shoot them. The bursts fell short. They were out of range. Behind them the sole remaining half-track began to close.

It was then the Lysander decided to fight back. It bounced angrily on its hard suspension, then taxied forward. The twin machine guns housed in the wheel spats burst into life.

Morgan rolled out of its line of fire, than ran towards the Lysander as it sliced through the kneeling men, fire spitting from the wheels. Morgan threw down his sten and sprinted for his life.

When Morgan reached the Lysander, he found the rear cockpit canopy already flung back. In the pilot seat he saw the grinning face of Sergeant Len Vigars. Morgan could have kissed it.

'Get a move on, my old son. Somehow I've got the feeling that little lot over there ain't pleased to see us.'

As Morgan clambered into the cockpit, Vigars opened the throttles and the force threw Morgan back into the seat. German soldiers were pouring across the field now, firing at the plane as it raced towards them. The lifting plane carved its way straight through them, leaving a trail of bodies lying in its wake.

Morgan wiped his eyes as the Lysander cleared the rising pall of smoke from the burning truck. He heard Vigars yell out, 'Oh Gordon Bleedin' Bennet!'

Vigars seemed to be almost standing up in the pilot's seat, as he strained to pull back the joystick to lift the plane's nose.

Morgan craned his neck to see what was responsible for the string of cockney oaths coming from Vigars's direction.

In front loomed the shimmering shape of more half-track trucks parked end to end in a bid to block their ascent. Metal crunched against metal and the plane dipped sickeningly to the right. Vigars wrestled with the controls in a combined effort to balance and lift the plunging Lysander.

Morgan saw the floodlit field tilt from right to left, then left to right and back again.

'Bloody Nora,' screamed Vigars as the plane straightened out and began to climb. 'Cop that little lot.'

Morgan looked down and saw the Lysander's starboard wheel bounce along the field and into the darkness of the bushes.

'That is rich,' laughed Vigars. 'We must be the only outfit in the whole RA bloody F that's got a pilot and plane both with a soddin' limp.'

'At least we are airborne,' shouted Morgan above the rushing wind as he pulled the canopy closed and put on the headphones.

'That isn't the problem now. The question is – how do we get down again?'

Morgan did not reply and for a while both men sat in silence – if the sound of the Lysander's fully revving Mercury 905 horse-power engine straining to its limits could be described as silence.

Vigars spoke first.

'I've no idea what you've been up to, mate, but someone wanted you out of that hole pretty bad. What have you gone and done? Bumped off old Rommel or something?'

'Nice thought,' grinned Morgan.

'Well, whatever you have done, someone, and that someone must be pretty high up, wants you back and sod the cost.'

'What do you mean, Len?'

'Night fighters, that's all, mate.'

'Night fighters?'

'That's right, a whole squadron of Spitfires to see us home, and what's more, they have even given us a code name.'

'Don't tell me,' laughed Morgan.

Right on cue, another voice came through on Morgan's headphones. It was Canadian.

'This is Winged Eagle leader to Stray Lamb. We have you in sight. Over.'

'Stray Lamb be buggered. Sitting Duck more like it,' mumbled Vigars.

'Winged Eagle leader to Stray Lamb. Come in, please.'

'Wotcha, mate.'

'Winged Eagle to Stray Lamb, can you increase speed and altitude?'

'You've got to be joking! It's a sodding miracle we're flying at all. We've had one wheel knocked off, got more holes in us than a colander and don't ask how much fuel we got because the pissing gauge has been shot up.'

'Take it you've been hit.'

Vigars exploded.

'What are you, Quiz King of Canada or something? Of course we're bloody hit. It's only my charm that's holding us together.'

The Lysander's progress was plotted on the giant map of Europe on the table in the control room at Manston aerodrome in Kent. It was watched with keener interest than normally shown by a man of Group Captain Spencer Stagg's experience. The phone in his hand was a direct line to the Prime Minister's bunker, and on it he gave a blow-by-blow account of the Lysander's flight to freedom to one of Churchill's aides. Such was the importance of the information carried in Nat Morgan's head.

On the table, the figures playing out the drama high above the fields of France were represented by coloured plastic counters. The counters were moved by pointers to match the changing position of the blips on the radar screen. The black counters were the Canadian escort fighters, the red – Vigars's Lysander.

The V-formation of yellow circles were German fighters.

'Radar reports enemy formation over Dieppe. They are changing to an intercept course. Speed and height indicate they are ME 109Es.'

'Unidentified enemy aircraft closing in from the Dutch coast.'

'Biggin Hill scrambling, sir – Spitfires.'

'Ringwood scrambling – Hurricanes.'

'Stray Lamb's altitude falling. Down to two thousand feet. Speed dropping. Situation critical. Escort aircraft say they are burning too much fuel while circling to keep in touch with Stray Lamb. They would face a real problem in combat situation.'

'Biggin Hill have engaged unidentified fighters.'

'Ringwood report contact.'

A line of new blips chased each other in single file across the screen.

'More bandits in pursuit. Heinkels.'

Stagg covered the mouthpiece of his phone. 'Get me RAF Cranton. Now.'

Seconds later. 'Cranton Duty Ops.'

'We have a problem,' explained Stagg. 'Damn it, man! I know you are only Air Sea Rescue, but you still fly bloody Defiants, don't you?' His voice rose in anger. 'I know the wretched kite was ditched as a night fighter because it was too slow. That's why I want the bloody things, and I want them now.'

'Cranton scrambled, sir. Estimated time of rendezvous, ten minutes.' Exactly ten minutes later, the Bolton Paul Defiants, unmanoeuvrable planes relegated from their fighter role after enormous losses in the Battle of Britain, replaced the Spitfires as Stray Lamb's escort. Their low air speed was ideal.

Four minutes later the whole Ops Room at Manston filled with cheering, everyone seemed to be on their feet, applauding wildly. The lone red counter had crossed the English coast.

'They are home,' said Stagg, 'and Lyshan emergency services are standing by to receive them.'

Churchill's aide breathed a sigh of relief and put down the phone.

The battered Lysander's engine cut out again. This time the plane's immediate loss of height was much steeper than before.

'C'mon my lovely girl,' urged Vigars from the back of his throat. The plane coughed, spluttered, tried and failed.

'This is Lyshan control. Your estimated height is now only four hundred feet.'

'Then it's a good job Salisbury Plain is as flat as a pancake, isn't it?' said Vigars with more than a hint of irritation.

'Roger,' replied the voice from the control tower, 'but the area you are overflying happens to be a minefield, old boy.'

'Thanks,' said Vigars flatly. He turned to Morgan. 'Right Job's comfort they are.'

'How far,' asked Morgan, 'before I can buy that beer I owe you?'

'There's the Red Lion near Bulford Camp. Car park's a bit

small for a Lysander though. No, seriously, it's about ten miles or more to Lyshan – if I can get this sodding engine to go.'

Indignantly the old plane responded. It wheezed, coughed again and this time spluttered back to life.

'Atta girl.'

'This is Lyshan control. Your air speed is down to ninety knots.'

Vigars turned and grinned at Morgan. 'She doesn't stall till sixty-five.' He patted the control panel affectionately.

'Lyshan control. Approach lights on.'

Below, in the distance, a narrow carpet of red and white light unfurled. The Lysander's design on its non-retractable undercarriage forced Vigars to make his one-wheeled approach run at an angle of 40 degrees.

'Or we'll just go sailing arse over tit,' he explained.

Second by second the rescue vehicles lining the runway seemed to get larger and larger. They began to fan out slowly and crawl, headlights on full beam, in the direction of the plane's run in.

The Lysander just cleared the perimeter fence. Vigars's face contorted as he struggled to keep the flaps down to the angle he needed.

Then he screamed out in anger. 'They are too bloody close.' The line of vehicles now racing along the runway only a few feet below the single wheel had narrowed the landing path to just a few feet.

'Unless we get down in a dead straight line, we have had our lot,' he yelled and wrenched the throttle back as far as it would go. The nose lifted and the runway vanished.

'Get those stupid bastard gits off that runway,' shouted Vigars as the plane overshot the airfield and climbed back into the sky. The engine began to miss again badly.

'Recommence your approach. Wind speed . . .'

'Bollocks.' Vigars cut the control tower short and concentrated all his efforts on flying the plane in a tight, dropping circle.

'Let's try the other end for luck,' said Vigars.

'Suits me.'

The moment the plane hit the ground, it pirouetted on its one wheel before the wheel snapped from the fuselage. The plane spun onto the runway like a revolving fan sending chunks of tarmac flying in all directions. It demolished a small wooden shed about a hundred yards from the runway, then buried its nose in the night grass, and, tail in the air, ploughed through the turf until it came to a halt in a shower of crashing bricks and glass against the outer wall of the main control building.

The line of fire tenders and ambulances, sirens wailing, lights flashing, all arrived at the scene together.

Both tips of the Lysander's single overhead wing dipped to touch the ground each side of the fuselage. Morgan's hand appeared from the rear cockpit, felt for a broken strut and clenched it tightly. He hauled the rest of him slowly into view as the rescue crews piled from the machines. He shook his head to bring back single vision, then clambered through the tangle of struts and wires and peered into the front cockpit.

Vigars's eyes stared back.

'It's my sodding leg,' he mumbled. 'Lend a hand.'

Morgan grabbed him by the wrist and pulled him up into a sitting position. Vigars groaned and turned his head. His glazed eyes picked on the shape of the fire crew – hoses in hands – rushing towards him.

His eyes cleared instantly.

'You dull load of buggers. Keep away from me,' he yelled.

The leading fireman stopped dead in his tracks. The others, prompted by the fury of Cockney abuse, did the same.

'But what about the fuel risk? The fire danger?' protested the fireman.

'Fuel. What fuel?' Vigars exploded. 'Thanks to you dull load of wankers I don't have any bloody fuel. I burnt what little I had left on the overshoot because you were right in the middle of the bleedin' runway. We bloody well glided in. So all of you, get out of it. Sod off.'

'Not you,' barked Morgan as the stretcher teams turned to follow the hang-dog fire crew. 'He's injured his leg.'

'Injured? I think it broke clean off,' mumbled Vigars. Morgan helped the sergeant unbuckle his belt as Vigars eased down the trousers under his flying suit.

'Foot's trapped,' he explained, fumbling under his flying suit. 'Got a knife?'

Morgan felt for his dagger and handed it to Vigars, who began to cut through the leg of his flying suit.

'Done it,' said Vigars. 'Help me out.'

The puzzlement on Morgan's face increased as he helped Vigars from the wreckage. Then the reason for the pilot's limp became clear – he wore an artificial leg. Vigars had cut his suit to unstrap it from the stump, as the foot had become wedged under a twisted strut.

'Ta,' said Vigars, and with his leg in his hand, hopped to the ground. Morgan supported him, full of admiration, as the little Cockney strapped his leg back in place and pulled the loose trouser leg over it. He left the remains of his flying suit on the ground. Before he joined Morgan in the jeep waiting on the runway, he turned and patted the plane: 'Thanks, old girl.'

'Group Captain Stagg at Manston would like to speak to you on the phone as soon as you have had your medical, sir,' said the airman driving the jeep.

'Medical?' said Morgan. Vigars began to chuckle.

'Medical,' repeated Morgan. 'I want a drink. Len, I think I owe you a light and bitter.' He put his arm on the pilot's shoulder and both men walked laughing towards the officers' mess, Vigars's tin leg clanking at the knee, which had twisted out of shape.

At the door to the mess, Vigars stopped. 'I am not allowed in there. It is for officers only.'

The fact he was a sergeant meant the rules forbade Morgan to drink with him in the same bar. Morgan bundled the protesting pilot through the door.

The mess conversation stopped. Morgan, still dressed in the clothes in which he'd been captured and his face smeared with blackout grease, led the limping Vigars to the bar. The pilot's face was flecked with engine oil.

'I want as large a pure malt whisky as you can get into one glass and the sergeant will have a pint of light and bitter.'

The barman hesitated.

A squadron leader was standing beside them, holding a telex message. 'It's all right, steward, you can make an exception this time. Serve them.'

The senior officer called Morgan aside. 'It's from the Prime Minister's office,' he said holding up the message. 'You are to report to him through Cameron tomorrow. A car will take you to Swindon station.'

'Thanks,' said Morgan, 'and thanks for helping with the drinks.'

'I think you both deserve it. By the way, he sends his congratulations.'

'Who? Cameron?' said Morgan in astonishment.

'Oh no,' said the officer, 'Mr. Churchill.'

When he'd gone, Vigars said: 'I don't know what you've been

up to, but I think it's me who should be buying the kitchen sinks.'

'The drinks are on me. I owe you.'

The men, who were to remain life-long friends, sat in the corner next to an open coal fire.

They both got stinking drunk.

CHAPTER NINETEEN

Morgan looked drawn as he stepped down from the Swindon train. He'd lost weight in France and the commando captain's uniform he'd left in the locker at RAF Lyshan on the eve of mission, hung loose around the collar. He adjusted his green beret and tucked the thin attaché case under his arm. It contained the mission report that he'd finished on the journey to Paddington.

It was Friday afternoon and the station was crowded. A crocodile of evacuee children, wrapped in woollen overcoats and scarves, trudged along the platform. They wore their gas masks like school-bags and their names and addresses were on large cards pinned to their coats.

'All this talk of V-bombs has caused a new scare. This lot are for the Hereford train,' a WVS lady explained to the porter.

Morgan pushed his way through a group of sailors sitting on kit-bags. The queue for the tube train stretched around a corner. Many of those waiting clutched bundles of bedding and small metal primus stoves to brew tea. In the underground stations they could avoid the V-bomb threat, and were making sure of good places on the platform. Morgan walked to Praed Street and hailed a cab.

Only the Stars and Stripes flying from the wrought-iron balcony distinguished the house from the others in the Georgian terrace on the north side of Grosvenor Square. He rapped on the heavy brass knocker. A white-helmeted US marine opened the door.

Morgan entered the headquarters of General Dwight D. Eisenhower, Supreme Commander of Allied Forces in Europe.

The marine checked his identification.

'This way, sir.'

Morgan followed the marine up a curved, red-carpeted staircase to the first floor, and along a corridor. Paintings of past US presidents hung on the walls. The marine tapped on a polished oak door next to one of George Washington astride a white charger. The marine opened it without waiting for a reply. Morgan went straight in.

Sitting alone at the head of a long polished table was Cameron. He greeted Morgan with an icy stare.

'Well,' he said slowly, 'you made a complete bloody hash of that little lot.'

Inwardly Morgan began to fume.

'You think so.' His tone made it clear the reply was not a question. Then without being asked, he sat down at the far end of the table and faced the colonel.

'Do sit down,' said Cameron.

'Thanks,' said Morgan, lighting a Capstan Full Strength. 'Could you pass the ashtray?'

Cameron stiffened, leant forward and slid the heavy cut-glass bowl towards Morgan, who stopped it with the upturned palm of his hand.

'Let's not beat about the proverbial bush, Morgan. You failed. The object of your mission was to bring back a German officer so we could assess the extent of any split in the Reich's Western Command since Rommel's arrival in Normandy. From that we hoped to establish how serious the arguments were about which route our invasion would follow. Instead an officer was killed and so was Swordfish – an invaluable Resistance leader who had served us well.'

Morgan bent and opened the attaché case at the foot of his chair. He took out the brown paper folder which contained his report and pushed it the length of the table towards the colonel.

Without a trace of the anger he felt, he said: 'I think, with all due respect, you'll find more in that report than you or Godsell's associates would have got out of Helm in a month of Sundays. It's all there, all you need to know about what anyone who matters in that Nazi shithouse of a Reich is thinking. From the way they are deploying troops and armour, they think it is Calais.'

Although he did not show it, Cameron bristled with indignation. He could do without insolent buccaneers like Morgan in the tight ship of his section. He arranged the folder in front of him with apparent disinterest, making no attempt to open it.

'So all our reliable sources seem to indicate,' he said rolling his tongue over the word reliable, 'but nevertheless, Morgan, a German officer – your prisoner – was shot. Murdered. We wanted him brought back to England alive. As I said, a complete bloody hash.'

Morgan leapt to his feet. 'Murder?' he yelled. 'Murder. Look, since we seem to be sitting right in the middle of your pissing proverbial bush, let's get a few things straight. As I see it my mission was about a brothelful of whores, who put them there and why. Now we know all of it. In the end these girls and a couple of wheezing old men are going to mean more to us than some herrenvolk professional soldier hell bent on making a career out of honourable martyrdom.'

'Major Helm was a fellow officer . . .'

'He was what?' interrupted Morgan. 'I'll tell you what he was – a soldier in a Nazi army fighting to preserve Germany, to preserve Hitler's fucking Reich and all that goes with it. The swastika on his lapel said it all as far as I'm concerned. There was no split in the ranks when things were going well. It's only now, when they think there's a chance they are not going to win, that people like Helm and Rommel are having second thoughts about Hitler. To me the issues of this war are straightforward. You wear Hitler's uniform or you don't. Helm wore it.'

'You are becoming emotional, Morgan. Some leave perhaps?' said Cameron. The offer had nothing to do with the strain Morgan had been under. Once he had this man out of his section, he could keep him out.

But Morgan continued as if he had not heard. 'If you got out from behind your desk and saw some of these Nazi bastards at work first-hand, you might even get emotional too. So before you start bleeding for brother officers, read my report – then decide whose life is more important, his or the Lisieux whores, that is if they have not already been shot. And tell me: would that be murder too – or just an act of war?'

Cameron ignored the question, his fingers flicking at the corner of the unopened file.

'Being wrong is getting to be something of a habit with you,' said the colonel, sifting through some typed sheets of notepaper at his elbow. He picked up a sheet and held it out. 'It appears they have just dealt with one of these prostitutes, a creature called, let me see, Clair La Croix. According to the Swordfish group, she was shot.'

'And Colette? Colette Claval? What about her? Is she safe?' asked Morgan, the concern detectable in the urgency of his questions.

'It's Colette, is it?' said Cameron raising one eyebrow. 'As far as I can gather, she is still on her back doing her bit for army morale. She's been handed back to Colonel Ulrich.'

Morgan went cold. 'You'll find that report ends with a recommendation,' he mumbled.

'Really,' Cameron said flatly.

'I recommend we lift the lot, madame and all, and bring them back to England.'

'How gallant of you,' said the colonel. 'But quite absurd.'

'I don't think so,' snapped Morgan. 'These girls could tell us more about the strengths and weaknesses of the men who will face the invasion of France than all your pin-striped poofs in MI6 put together.'

'Utterly out of the question.'

'You forget the SS set this little lot up. If we bring these girls out, then we have the instruments of their intelligence, and not only would we learn how Rommel's staff were thinking but how much the SS knew about the way they felt, and what they were doing about it.'

Morgan waited for the reply, watching as Cameron ran his finger to and fro slowly over his clipped and greying moustache.

'No,' he said finally looking at his watch.

'Why?' There was a note of desperation in Morgan's voice. 'Why?'

'If these ... women are everything you claim, then they are of more use to us where they are. I want you to arrange through the Swordfish group that this Claval girl and her friends ensure the time they spend fornicating is as profitable to us as it is to the SS. The Resistance must run them as an extension of their group. You, Morgan, will exploit them.'

Exploitation was exactly what Morgan hated. He clenched his fist, denying the urge to hammer the table, his eyes blackened at the injustice of it.

'They already know enough to make them a vital – integral – part of our intelligence build-up towards the invasion. If we risk the action you suggest, then the SS will guess our interest in the whores is more than voyeuristic curiosity. It will focus attention on the fact that we consider Normandy important. Damn you, you are not only risking the lives of these girls, but the invasion itself.'

'These harlots, as useful as they are, are simply what the Romans called impedimenta – baggage, camp followers. Nothing more. They are simply the spoils of war,' the colonel said.

The colonel rose and tucked Morgan's file under his arm. He

turned and walked to the door, avoiding the dark-haired man's glare.

'It's time we were at the briefing. I want you and Connors there to represent the section.' He paused and added, 'So far as I'm concerned the matter is now closed. Is that clear, Morgan?'

The red glow of the oil lamp through its glass bowl cast a large flickering shadow of Ulrich's profile over the entire wall. He was drawing hard on the cigarette held tightly between his stained fingers. The reflected image was split unevenly by the corner of a wall as he leant forward to stub out the cigarette in the already overflowing ashtray on the woven cane table next to the bed. He looked down at Colette.

She lay completely naked on the bed. Each ankle was tied firmly to the posts of the brass bedstead by her black silk stockings. Her hands were roughly bound together above her head by Ulrich's uniform tie which was knotted to the centre post in the ornate headboard. The bonds were too tight and when she squirmed, it made it worse. Her back was raw where he had punished her for Clair.

Ulrich's anger had swung full circle. Now he was sorry. It was just sometimes he could not help himself. It was not that he regretted things he did, like painting his tortoise as a child, but sometimes he did wish he could have more control over his impulses. Yet those he served would not have had it that way.

He moved closer to the bed and knelt beside it. He would show her he could be kind as well as firm.

Colette felt his lips working their way up her outstretched arm. Ulrich genuinely believed she was panting with ecstasy.

Then the magic of his moment was broken by a frantic pounding on the bedroom door. Ulrich cursed.

'What is it?' he snapped.

'An urgent telex has arrived from Berlin. It's marked "Top Secret", and for your eyes only.'

'I'll be right there,' he shouted. He sat up and sighed loudly with frustration. He hurriedly put on his trousers and tunic, and stepped into a pair of carpet slippers. He checked Colette's bonds, then his fingers slid gently down her cheek.

'I won't be long,' he smiled. 'I promise.'

He closed the door softly behind him, so as not to disturb her. He took the stairs quickly to the basement telex room, whistling as he did so. He dismissed the telex operator with a snap of his fingers and locked the door behind him. He punched the code to Berlin which meant he was ready to receive, and watched the tape in anticipation.

He watched, eyes widening, as the machine began to chatter out its message line by line. He tore off the print-out, unable to believe his eyes.

It read:

> TOP SECRET. MAXIMUM PRIORITY.
> FROM: SCHELLENBERG. SS. BERLIN.
> TO: ULRICH. LISIEUX.
> CANARIS REMOVED FROM OFFICE TODAY. AB-
> WEHR ABOLISHED. TO BE REPLACED BY SS
> INTELLIGENCE SECTION IN ALL ITS FORMER
> FUNCTIONS. RETURN TO BERLIN AT ONCE.
> FEB 19. 1944.

Ulrich closed his eyes and clenched his fists. 'At last,' he said softly, 'at long last.' The delight swept over him. He tore the message, stuffed the pieces in his top pocket and bounded back to his room. His eyes had glazed over. For once, he seemed totally unaware of the girl still bound to his bed.

'Please,' she called to him, 'untie me. I can't feel my fingers.'

Ulrich paid no attention, appearing not to hear the plea. It was as if he was in another place. He walked straight past the bed to the wardrobe at the far end of the room. He let his Abwehr tunic fall to the floor. From the top shelf he took down a suitcase, laid it on the floor and unlocked it. He opened the lid and ran his hands reverently over the contents. Then he carefully lifted the black uniform and laid it on the table. His fingers caressed the death's-head insignia.

At last, with the Abwehr abolished, he could wear it as a right. He could show the world he was an SS colonel. No longer would he have to pretend he belonged among lesser men.

He dressed. Proudly, he regarded his reflection. He remembered the first time he'd worn it. The huge flags, the song of a thousand voices raised in praise. The chanting, getting louder by the minute, until it seemed all Munich shook. What a night.

He turned to the bed and raised his arms. 'How do I look?' he asked. Suddenly the spell was broken. He moved quickly to the foot of the bed and untied Colette's bonds. He leant over her and released her hands. She eased herself into a sitting position and rubbed life back into her ankles.

'We shall have to wait for another time. I have been called to Berlin. Forgive me?'

She nodded, biting her lip. He ruffled her hair, then was gone. She heard him yell for a car to be brought. She felt totally desolate and sat staring down at her feet. After a while her eyes moved to Ulrich's tunic. She wondered if he had left any cigarettes. Colette picked up the jacket and opened the top pocket. She removed the torn telex and knelt on the floor as, puzzled, she began to piece it together again.

'I cannot read German so I do not know what it says, but it is important. The moment he received it, he left for Berlin – and he was wearing an SS uniform,' said Colette handing the copy of the telex message she had taken from Ulrich's pocket to Albert.

'Mmmm,' he mused thoughtfully rubbing his chin, spreading the message out on the kitchen table, smoothing the creases where he had glued it with the palm of his hand. He raised his hand and stabbed at the message with a stubby finger.

'Now he,' he said leaving his print over Canaris's name, 'is famous. Very famous.'

'Give Father Delon my love,' called Colette and blew him a kiss. She stood in the kitchen doorway and watched as Albert wobbled unsteadily down the château drive on his rickety old cycle.

Puffing and panting, Albert leant the cycle against the church wall and took out his red and white spotted handkerchief to mop his brow.

But as he walked through the portal, a black Mercedes rounded the bend and drew up behind him. Two German officers sat in the back, the driver was a private. One of the officers got out, said something to the driver then walked up the path after Albert.

There was nothing Albert could do except keep walking, but his old bow legs began to shake as the German's footsteps got nearer. He held his breath as the officer drew alongside, but he strode right past without giving him a second glance.

Albert's first thought was for Father Delon, who had now taken over from old André as Swordfish. His second was to turn and run for it, but he saw the second officer get out of the car and light a cigarette. The old man with a telex in his pocket so secret that no more than a dozen men yet knew its content, felt his time had come. There was nothing for it, except to keep going. Any sudden change of action would arouse the suspicion of the German watching him from the road.

As Albert reached the door of the church an old lady, dressed in a black shawl and bent with age, hobbled past him with the aid of a walking stick.

The German was closing the door of Father Delon's confessional box behind him. Albert snatched the beret from his head and dived into the nearest pew, closed his eyes and prayed.

He dared not open them, even when he heard the door of the confessional open and close again. He tried to guess how many pairs of footsteps he could hear walking up the aisle, but the echoes confused him. When he heard the thud of the main door closing, he rose and cautiously made his way to the confessional. He pushed open the door and whispered: 'Allô, Father Delon, are you there?'

'Where else do you think I'd be but at confessional?'

'But ... the German ... I thought ...'

'He was Austrian in fact.'

'Bah,' said Albert, screwing up his beret and hurling it to the ground. 'An Austrian. Well, let me tell you, Father. Hitler, he is an Austrian too.'

'Calm yourself, Albert Boniface, calm yourself,' said the priest soothingly. 'Now. What do you want with me? It would be too much to hope it had anything to do with asking our Lord for forgiveness – like that Austrian has just done.'

Albert snorted like a carthorse, and rubbed his nose. He took the telex from his pocket and pushed it through the grille in the wall which separated him from the cleric.

'Colette thinks it might be important. It's something about Canaris,' said Albert. He heard the unseen priest give a long, low whistle.

'She was right,' said the priest, who realised he would have to risk breaking broadcasting procedure and transmit the contents to London without delay. He asked Albert to thank Colette.

The old man mumbled and stood to go, then hesitated and bent down until his lips pressed against the grille.

'Holy Father,' he said, 'I confess to wanting to kill Germans.'

The cypher clerk looked annoyed when the corporal handed him

Father Delon's unintelligible message. The clerk, a private in the Royal Signals, was at his wits' end. More than half of his shift, F-section, were off work with the flu, his wife was ill too, which meant he'd had to cook his own lunch. He'd burnt the chips.

Now this.

He looked up hopefully at the corporal. 'Play the game, mate,' he complained pointing to the pile of messages in his overflowing in-tray waiting to be decoded. 'Some of those have been waiting for hours, bloody days, even. Can't this one wait?'

''Fraid not, Ginger. This one's a Priority Red from the Swordfish group. Colonel Cameron's office say it's got to be done right away.'

The clerk tossed aside the message he was working on and picked up the one sent less than thirty minutes earlier from the church in Ste-Yvette.

He picked up the relevant code book, glanced up at the clock on the wall and realised it was almost time for his tea break.

'Thank God for that,' he mumbled. It had been a bloody awful day.

He picked up his pencil, licked the stub, and began.

The cypher clerk who had decoded Father Delon's message forgot about his tea break.

'Jesus wept,' he said. 'Someone had better get a copy of this to Cameron before he leaves the briefing for the PM's bunker. Fast.'

Cameron faced the crowded briefing room. He had just given the assembled top officers the two new code words. 'Overlord' meant the invasion of Europe. 'Neptune' indicated that the invasion would take place in Normandy.

Cameron stabbed the pointer at the map on the wall. 'This stretch of coast was, before the Ice Age, part of the continental landmass of Europe, which means it has retained the topographic characteristics of the beaches which now form Normandy.

'Here, in South Devon, the Slapton Sands are identical in every respect to the beaches south of the town of Marsalines. They have been given the code name 'Utah' and it is there the US Fourth Infantry Division will make its assault on D-Day. They will have the advantage of being familiar with every inch of the ground because of the full-scale dress rehearsal they will be fortunate enough to carry out at Slapton.'

Cameron eyed the men sitting along both sides of the table. The British to his right, their US counterparts opposite.

'There's enough brass here to sink the goddamn landing craft,' Connors said behind his hand as he fanned away the heavy smoke in the air. Morgan grinned back.

'What did you say, Major?' boomed an American naval commander at the top end of the table. He was a small thin man who chewed on a fat cigar. All eyes turned towards Connors. He coughed to clear his throat.

'I asked about landing craft, sir. I'll be on one as an observer.'

'Make sure it ain't mine,' growled the commander.

'I think I can answer that,' Cameron said diplomatically but firmly. The commander bit on his cigar. Morgan winced.

'There will be eight in all. Aboard will be the entire United States Fourth Infantry Division and the First Amphibian Engineer Brigade.

'The engineers will hit the beach first. Their task is to rid it of obstructions and give the tanks a clean run inland. We shall be using Sherman amphibians . . .'

'What else,' an American colonel quipped. 'They work.'

Cameron and his British team did not join in the laughter.

'By the way, gentlemen,' Cameron drolled, 'we shall be defending the beach with the Canadians. We shall be using live shells and ammunition to do so. They also work.'

The laughter died.

'The Deputy General of the assault force, General Theodore Roosevelt and Commander Ben Skahill will be on board the command ship. The assembled forces will leave Plymouth under darkness on April 28. The assault will begin at H-Hour on the twenty-ninth. Then the entire force will be guarded by the Royal Navy.'

'What strength's our cover?' the commander with the cigar asked.

'HMS *Azalea*,' Cameron said.

'And?' the American navy man's voice rose.

'The *Azalea* can cope. She's deemed to be sufficient.'

'What is she?'

'A corvette.'

'A damn what? These landing craft are irreplaceable.'

Uproar broke out on the American side of the table. Senior officers huddled together, mumbling their discontent.

'That's crazy,' Connors told Morgan.

'Seems like it,' he said.

No one noticed the dispatch rider. Still wearing his crash helmet and goggles, he marched straight up to Cameron and saluted.

'Sir,' he stamped loudly to attention. The room fell silent as all eyes turned to Cameron.

'Thank you,' he said as he took the envelope and read the message inside. He rubbed his moustache and frowned.

'Gentlemen,' he announced quietly, 'the Abwehr, it seems, no longer exists. It's been abolished and replaced by an SS team led by Brigadeführer Walter Schellenberg. There is no news as to the fate of Admiral Canaris, I'm afraid.'

Cameron's American counterpart sensed the colonel's concern.

'What does it all mean? Is that bad about Canaris getting the chop?'

'It means,' said Cameron, 'that things are going to be a lot more difficult for us in the trying months to come. Damn difficult.'

At the far end of the table, Morgan leant across to Connors.

'That was the bastard who signed my death warrant and sent me to Amiens.'

Cameron's eyes bored into Morgan.

'Exactly,' he said sadly, 'Exactly. Things won't be quite as easy next time.'

He walked from the room.

CHAPTER TWENTY

Are you serious?'

Arnie Connors's voice showed his incredulity. Morgan was sitting on the sofa in front of the book-lined walls of his living room. The air was dense with smoke and a half-drunk bottle of Scotch stood on the card table next to an empty one. The ashtrays were full but both men were cold sober, despite having drunk their way towards dawn.

Morgan leant forward and handed the glass he had just filled to Connors, whose pale blue eyes glinted with interest.

'Deadly serious,' said Morgan.

'Who in hell are you going to get to sanction a plan to lift this cat-house full of hookers back to England? Cameron bust a gut when you suggested it at the briefing. He almost gave himself a coronary.'

'Churchill.'

Connors spluttered, showering the smoke haze with whisky.

'Don't waste it,' grinned Morgan, then added earnestly, 'I am sick to death of the way people are being manipulated in this bloody affair – on both sides. We are all being shunted around like pawns. First of all the Nazis just pluck these girls from their homes and friends and incarcerate them with no regard for their rights or feelings. Then I'm duped and deceived by the likes of Godsell.'

He downed his Scotch and pointed towards the bedroom door with the glass. 'They turned Debbie Forster into a vegetable in there, playing their fucking war games. They are all obsessed with charades, both sides, Ulrich on the one hand and Cameron on the other. Everyone has become so concerned with who exploits whom to the best advantage, that they have lost sight of the real objective.'

'And that is?' asked Connors quietly.

'To win the war against Hitler and restore some kind of dignity to this insane world. These girls have a right to dignity from us too, but what is equally important is that they have the knowledge and information we must have about the men who will face us on the beaches of Normandy. That's where the whole thing will be won or lost.

'Now, Cameron plans to use some of the girls as an extension of the Swordfish group, but all the information they send back, first has to pass through us. Although it would grieve the bastard to admit it, he does not have a monopoly on duplicity.'

'Nat,' said Connors, 'are you suggesting we rig these reports?'

'If need be, yes.'

'For want of a better word, that's treason.'

'To whom? My first loyalty is to people, not to those who enslave them, no matter whose uniform they wear.'

He watched Connors wrestle with the dilemma of what he was being asked to do. It was certainly subterfuge which could bring down the wrath of accepted practice on their necks.

'Arnie,' said Morgan, 'can I count on you?'

The big New Englander, his face set in determination, nodded. 'What do you want me to do?'

'Turn a blind eye to my analysis of the reports and help me prepare.'

'Prepare?'

'That's right. This is not going to be easy. Just three, perhaps four of the girls from what I gather from Colette, will risk all to go along with us. The others may take a little persuasion.'

'Kidnapped sounds more like the word I'd use.'

Morgan smiled wearily. 'Semantics. But whatever word we use, it is not going to be easy to lift these ladies, not now the SS have taken over openly.'

'Getting out of Normandy with a harem of screaming whores is going to be even harder.'

'That's why I want your help to prepare.'

'I've said you can count on it.'

Morgan blew the ash from the cover of the notebook sandwiched between the ashtrays on the card table. He found a virgin page and wrote the name Mike Byrne, his instructor during his earlier training as a commando officer.

'This man,' said Morgan, 'I can trust. When the time comes, he will help select a small team of good men. Men who won't need to be told what they have to do – they'll know. To carry out a raid on the Château Beaupré, I'll need ten men – eleven if you want in.'

Connors said: 'I want in.'

Morgan's smile indicated his deep-felt appreciation. 'Thanks,' he said. 'Now we need men whose rank is not going to count a shit. They can be any colour of the rainbow, any nationality, and soldiers, sailors or airmen. It does not matter. They can be anything as long as they are trained – and can handle women. They are going to have to be able to charm the pants off a frigid nun; men who understand women because I want no one who is going to use force on these ladies. No one.'

Connors uncoiled himself from the chair and refilled both glasses. He frowned as he handed one to Morgan.

'Nat,' he said, 'I feel the same way as you do about this whole affair, but there is one thing that bothers me. From this moment on, both our heads are on the block and, as there is no going back. I just want to know how much this Ulrich character has to do with the way you're acting.'

Morgan took the glass and cradled it in his hands. It was shaking as, for a moment, he closed his eyes, then steadied himself. He hunched his shoulders, pressing his elbows into his knees.

'Arnie, wiping him out is a bonus. Hitting back at what he stands for is a reason. But whatever, I'm going to kill him, for what he has done to people, many people, not just me.'

Connors raised his glass.

'Let's drink to it.'

Morgan responded.

Father Delon would never understand the British as long as he lived, he decided angrily. Then he re-read the message he'd just decoded in his study and sighed with exasperation. It was from London and signed 'the Dragon'. Delon poured himself a brandy and sat thoughtfully in his club chair. He wondered how Albert would react to the news. Enthusiastically, no doubt.

'Old fool,' he thought and immediately regretted it. It was just that he thought the old caretaker should take more heed. They all should. Pack the whole thing in when they were all still one step ahead of the Gestapo. Too many had died already, Pratt, Scrélat, the girl. And for what? Nothing really, he thought bitterly. The Germans were still in France.

Now this latest message from London wanted them to do more. It was ironic that the plan the Dragon wanted carried out had been his idea in the first place. It might have worked then, now he had great doubts.

'It's him.'

Madame Remy's voice startled him. She sounded frosty.

'He can see it's me,' Albert growled, 'and I'm sure you can find some work to do.'

Madame Remy banged the study door.

'You look worried. Trouble?' asked Albert.

'Could be,' Delon said. He handed the message he'd transcribed. Albert smiled slowly.

'I knew they'd see it our way in the end,' he said. 'We should have done this in the first place, just like I told them.'

'Perhaps.' Delon pressed his thumbs to his lips. 'But now?'

'Of course. We can't say no. It wouldn't be fair. We must do what they ask.'

'Like André, or Scrélat, I suppose.'

'That was different,' Albert protested.

'They died,' Delon said flatly, 'and if we go ahead with this, so could a lot more of us, including you.'

Albert helped himself to the priest's brandy. He pulled up a chair from the table and sat in front of Delon.

'Look, Father,' said Albert. 'I knew you when you were knee-high. It's a long time ago and by now you must have guessed I'm not that good at always saying what I mean. That's why I make a lot of noise, so people say. But I'm not stupid. This was a good idea in the first place and nothing has changed that.'

'Albert,' the priest interrupted, 'everything has changed. The Swordfish group was almost wiped out, the Germans, that man Ulrich, knew there was a connection between the group and one of the girls at the château. It was only fate that he got the wrong one. Poor child.' He crossed himself.

'Or the will of God,' Albert said. 'The others are still there, so are we. Now, all London is asking is that we ask the girls to provide us information on those scum who use the place. If they agree, then so must we. Besides, the Dragon says it might help to get them all to London.'

'You don't believe that,' Delon said contemptuously.

'I believe the Welshman will try,' Albert retorted. 'Now, can we?'

Delon thought for a while. 'It must be up to the girls,' he said at last.

Colette watched Albert totter uncertainly on the kitchen stool as he reached inside the earthenware pot on the top of the dresser in the château kitchen.

'Got it,' he said at last.

Colette gave him her hand and the old man jumped to the floor and took the long tube of ash that had been a cigarette from his lips. He was holding a brown camera case. The one he'd stolen from Voight.

'This,' he marvelled, holding up the case in triumph as if he did not quite believe it himself, 'is a Leica camera. A German production by an idea by a great Frenchman called Daguerre.'

'Incredible,' Colette mocked gently.

Unabashed, Albert explained, 'It is simplicity itself to use.'

He held the viewfinder to his eye and clicked the whirring shutter, which purred in response to his dabbing finger. Then, muttering, he fumbled with the catch and, with some effort, showed her how to load it.

'See,' he said, 'easy,' bending his knees like a true professional. Colette brushed her hand through her hair and pouted, posing like the models she used to admire on the front of Clair's fashion magazines that littered the apartment at 17, rue de l'Eglise. Albert hugged her.

'Now, Colette, as Nat Morgan explained in his message, we must get the information he needs to justify bringing all of you to England. Can you get this camera into Ulrich's room without being detected?'

'I can try.'

'Good. Does he keep a diary, papers, anything of use you can photograph when you are alone?'

Colette's dark fringe bobbed in acknowledgement. 'I'm sure he does,' she said.

'Good. The question now is, who can we trust?'

Colette frowned. 'All the girls, because of what we must endure, have become like sisters and would be with us in principle. Maria and Eva would give practical help, so might Elaine. I am not too sure about Benedit and Annette. Although they hate it here as much as we all do, I think all they want to do is to be able to return to Paris. I cannot say if they would be prepared to risk their lives. Madame McGragh has far too much to lose; she would never agree.'

Albert struck a pose, like the statue of some civic dignitary, his hand clutching his lapel. He revelled in the role of decision-maker, the controller of his very own ring of prostitute spies.

'I'll leave it to you to sound out the others,' he said and handed the Leica to Colette. He crushed the stub of his cigarette underfoot, and sparks flashed as the hobnails struck the flagstone.

Elaine Bisset sat at the polished writing table next to the open lattice window. She was wearing a demure, pink dress with long sleeves and a lace collar and cuffs. There was a cut-glass bowl of spring daffodils beside the once-a-month letter she was allowed to write to her parents in St-Denis. As usual she wrote about nothing except how she longed to see her baby son, Alain, again. Someday. She did not seal the envelope as the censor would have to read it first.

Colette's head appeared around the door and Elaine looked up.

'Can I talk to you for a moment?' Colette sounded nervous.

Elaine put down her pen and smiled.

'What can I do for you?' she asked.

'It's perhaps what I can do for you. What would you say if I told you I could get you to England?' Colette watched anxiously for any reaction. Elaine laughed lightly.

'Only if you provide a wagon-lit on the "Flèche d'Or" and a suite in Claridges, or is it the Savoy? And I made you promise you'd never make me drink the tea.'

'I'm being serious,' Colette said firmly. She took Elaine's wrist and held it firmly. 'Deadly serious.'

Elaine's smile vanished. She pulled herself free and stood up. 'Please go,' she said.

'Just listen,' Colette pleaded.

'I've listened to you before,' Elaine said bitterly, 'and look at the trouble you caused. Just leave me alone. I don't want to end up like Clair. Get out.'

'There's no risk to you,' Colette protested.

'Ah,' Elaine snorted, 'I seem to have heard that somewhere before.'

'What is it?' Colette shouted. 'Do you enjoy being a Nazi whore?'

Elaine slapped her face.

'How dare you. You know that's not true.' She was on the verge of tears. 'Do you think I enjoy being passed from one bed to the other like a used pillow case? Do you think I enjoy sitting with the pigs at dinner when they discuss how good I've been? How they love to do this or that. You must be sick. I hate them.'

'Then help me. Help yourself. Get back at the bastards.'

'It's not that easy. If it was just me then I would. But I have a child out there. Don't you understand what that means?'

'Yes,' Colette said quietly, 'I'm sorry. I should not have asked.'

She turned to go.

'Wait,' Elaine called.

Colette turned.

'What is it you want?' the former teacher asked.

Colette hesitated. 'I need someone who's had an education, like you. I want someone to help me get Ulrich's papers and things and tell me what they say. That's all I can tell you.'

'I'm afraid I'd be no use. I don't speak German that well. Just the odd word I've picked up since we've been here.'

Colette looked blank. 'But I thought you were a teacher.'

Elaine gestured. 'I taught eleven-year-olds, and music. That's all. Why don't you ask Eva? She is supposed to be good at languages.'

It was true what they said about Eva Nielson. She was never happier than when she was working. As Colette pressed her ear to the Dane's bedroom door, she could hear Eva was very happy indeed.

Colette retreated to the end of the corridor and sat on the wide window seat and waited for Eva to satisfy herself. It was a long wait.

When at last the weary Panzer commander emerged, he looked exhausted, his eyes glazed with delight. He thought the girl who had ridden him like a mare in what was the most uninhibited session of lovemaking he had ever experienced, was truly remarkable. Why couldn't his own wife be as interested in his work as that whore? His own dreary Inga had never, in all the time they had been married, ever shown the slightest interest in tanks or his theories on how battles were won or lost.

As he rounded the corner with a courteous smile for Colette, she slipped down from the window seat and walked towards the open bedroom door.

Eva, standing with one foot on the bed, finished fastening her stocking top to the suspender and looked up. Colette had a finger to her lips. Eva smiled and followed Colette into the gardens. She listened to Colette's proposal with interest.

'With Denmark being such a small country, every Dane has to be a linguist. I speak and read German fluently. It is not that different from Danish anyway.'

'So you will do it?'

'But of course,' came the reply. 'It will be a pleasure.' Colette smiled and shook her head. She would never understand Eva.

The Dane read her expression and said, 'I have told you before, in bed a man is a man to me and I will take everything they have to offer – and more if I can get it. That is me, the way I am. But when they leave my bed and put on that uniform, they become German soldiers again. The soldiers who also occupy my country. That is why I help you.'

'Maria has also agreed to help us,' said Colette. 'Ulrich will be away for three days as from tomorrow. I don't know where, just that he said he wouldn't be able to see me for a few days. It may be the only chance we get.'

'Oh,' said Eva casually, 'I can tell you where he is going.'

'You can?' blinked Colette.

'Yes. He is going with Rommel and some staff officers on an inspection tour of the Western Defences. That sweet man I was with earlier is going too. He thinks it is all a complete waste of time.'

A look of complete satisfaction spread like sunshine across the smiling face of Colette Claval.

Later that night the other girls would come to her with all the tittle-tattle they had picked up between the sheets during the day. Some of it was relevant, some of it not. No matter. From the tower of his church, Father Marcel Delon would radio it to London, and to the Dragon.

There was only one thing that Colonel Ernst Ulrich and Captain Helmut Lang, the thirty-six-year-old aide to Field Marshal Rommel, would ever agree upon, and that was that the invulnerability of Hitler's Atlantic Wall was a complete and utter myth.

But in Normandy, Rommel was now in charge. He was improving defences out of all recognition.

That evening, Ulrich was to leave Lisieux for Caen where he would join Rommel's party to inspect these defences. Ulrich finished packing for his trip and was sorting through his papers, which would have to wait for attention until his return. Of all the communications he had received in the past weeks, one was causing him particular concern. No matter how hard he racked his brains, he was still no nearer to the solution.

'Overlord? Neptune? I have no idea,' he said to himself shaking his head. He put Foreign Minister von Ribbentrop's cable in the top drawer of his bureau.

To lessen the risk of anyone – let alone his US superiors at OSS or Cameron – finding out the nature of the bizarre letter, Arnie Connors typed it himself.

Five thick green lines were printed on top of the page to draw attention to the legend 'THIS DOCUMENT IS THE PRO-PERTY OF HIS BRITANNIC MAJESTY'S GOVERNMENT'. Then came three phrases, all printed in red-lined squares below each other. They read 'Most Secret', 'Restricted Circulation' and 'Bigot'.

The men who would receive this letter, were of such authority that they would recognise at once the significance of the phrases. It was reserved for documents of the highest classification. The odd word 'Bigot' meant the sender was one of a very small, privileged group of people. A person privy to plans to invade Europe.

It was on this paper that Connors duplicated eighty-six copies of the letter he had written. Any doubts that the commanding officers who read the letter might have would be dispelled by the security rating. Without question, they would pass details of the strange request in the letter down their respective lines of command.

Within the next week, three of the recipients of the letter phoned Connors at SOE, each following the instructions that nothing was to be put in writing. The callers, one Royal Navy, one British Army and the third US Airborne Division, all had the same problem. They had men in mind who might fit the bill, but the men were all in the cells for misdemeanours of one kind or the other.

'What were the charges?' Connors asked.

'Bigamy,' replied the Royal Navy officer. 'The man's name is Martin. A good chap really, first-class Marine until all this business came to light and he blotted his copy book. Pity, actually.'

'What's involved?'

'One wife in Portsmouth, another in Manchester and a third in Sicily. But he has a fine fighting record which includes Crete and North Africa. But it seems that, no sooner than he hits the beaches, he is unable to keep the ladies at bay.'

'What was his name again?'

'Martin. Nigel Basil Martin.'

Connors burst out laughing. 'Nigel Basil, for Christ's sake. With a handicap like that, he can still make women take him seriously? Send his file to Sergeant-Major Mike Byrne. Then wait until you hear from me. Meanwhile keep Martin on ice.'

The British Army officer was more puzzled by it all. 'I have three men who seem to be the kind you are looking for, but I can't see for the life of me why their reputation as ladies' men should have anything to do with anything.'

'You don't have to see anything beyond the security rating at the top of the page,' snapped Connors, who found this particular breed of British Army officer a pain. 'Just tell me why they are in the can.'

'Taylor went over the wall.'

'Forget him. No deserters.'

'Then, there's Appleby. He is in civilian custody for the non-payment of paternity orders. It's not that he had welched on his obligations. It is just the payments, at the moment, come to more than he earns. He has a good service record, though, one of the last out at Dunkirk.'

'And the third.'

'Machen. He is being held by the civilian police as well – on a charge of housebreaking.'

'A thief?'

'Could not wish to meet a more honest man, but you cannot blame the Brigadier for insisting on the charge, after he found the cad having it off with his daughter on the old boy's tiger skin rug. Just not the thing.'

'I want both those men out of police custody right away and confined to barracks. Their army records will be sent to Sergeant-Major Byrne at the address in the letter.'

The US officer had two problems. One was homosexual and the other was black.

'His name is Ellis, he's a Nigger and he's charged with assaulting an officer,' drawled the Southern lieutenant.

'Are you seriously offering me a man who has hit an officer?'

'Just a technical offence, Major, sir. The officer in this case was a woman and they were found in bed together. She's been charged with fraternising with other ranks and Ellis with assault. Personally I'd have had the black bastard shot for what he did.'

Connors knew it would have been pointless to argue.

'What rank is Ellis?'

'The bum is Private First Class.'

'What about the other?'

'Name of Crowski, in for fraud. They caught him making free phone calls to his mother in Nebraska.'

'So what?' said Connors irritably.

'Well, sir, the boy had to charm every girl on the Plymouth telephone exchange to get those calls put through for free.'

'Just charm?'

There was an embarrassed silence from the lieutenant who came from Alabama where they burnt people for using such words.

'Well, sir. He's a goddamn faggot.'

'A queer?'

'Yes, sir, but the telephone girls loved him, just could not resist him by all accounts. Now the army has to pick up the tabs for the phone calls. It runs into hundreds of dollars.'

The lieutenant, as instructed, although at the time he thought it irregular, sent both men's files to a Limey NCO called Byrne.

Eight days after sending out the letters, Connors had obtained Morgan's list of possibles. Cameron, whose attention was focused on preventing Morgan from outflanking him by building up a case for abducting a brothel-load of whores, had not noticed a thing. Morgan's initial delight was, however, to be short-lived.

The two rota clerks on duty in the outer office, next to Ulrich's office in the basement of Lisieux's Hôtel Chloé, could not believe either their luck or their eyes. Women, like the visions standing, smiling, before them, did not often wander into their world of endless memos where figures meant numbers in dusty ledgers. Creatures like these did not spend their time over wash tubs rinsing out socks or enjoy nights out on clerk's wages in beer halls, nor were they yours to take on a spread-out raincoat in a dark alley. These women were fantasies, like those who pouted from the passenger seats of fast foreign cars and appeared in the glossy magazines read by the wives of lesser men. It was men of power, not intelligence corporals, who displayed apparitions of beauty like Colette, Eva and Maria, as standards of their success.

Colette was already familiar to the men as Ulrich's private property, although none dared give her more than an envious second glance for fear of incurring the colonel's wrath. Even when he was away she was untouchable, even by a lingering look of envy.

But the two girls with her. It was more than the men had ever dreamed.

'Why did I not get any message to say the colonel would not be here?' said Colette trying to sound haughty. 'And when will he be back?'

Both men shrugged their shoulders. Although they knew, they dared not tell her.

'Then I shall take the things I need from his room myself,' she said and flitted from the office, leaving the soldiers alone with Eva and Maria.

Colette openly used the front staircase to reach Ulrich's room. She fumbled in her handbag and produced the key to let herself in. She felt a strange excitement, the thrill of stealth. Once safe behind the closed door, she removed the Leica camera and three rolls of film.

She placed them on the large double bed and began to empty the contents of Ulrich's desk and bureau, spreading them out, sheet of paper next to sheet of paper, on the bedspread.

All she needed now was for Eva to read them for her so she would know what to photograph. She lit a cigarette and waited, moving only to fetch an ashtray from the bureau, and blow off some ash she'd carelessly dropped onto the von Ribbentrop cable. Luckily the ash left no mark.

Maria moved slowly towards the older soldier, a moon-faced man whose breath smelt of cheese, and placed both hands on each of his shoulders. She let them linger there for a moment, then slid them over his chest to the knot of his loosened tie. She began to fiddle with it suggestively, pressing her breasts against his chest as she ran her knee up and down the inside of his thigh.

Her lips glistened as she whispered, 'Do you boys have a room in this hotel?'

He gulped and nodded.

'And when do you get off duty?'

'In one hour,' said the two clerks together.

'What a pity,' said Eva as she undid the top two buttons of her white blouse. 'It is very warm in here. I need a long drink and somewhere to lie down.'

'So do I,' said Maria, 'but we only have an hour, then we must go.'

The younger soldier's eyes turned to the shape of golf balls as Eva undid the third button on her blouse to reveal more of her ample, marble-white cleavage, forced upwards by her low, cupped bra. She moistened her lips as she noticed the enormous bulge growing at the top of the man's uniform trousers. He noticed she'd noticed and, as Eva smiled her invitation, he began to sweat. None of the boys would believe him when he told them.

Then both soldiers seemed to read each other's minds. Without taking his eyes from the deep valley between Eva's breasts, he said, 'Someone must be here to man the office at all times, it's regulations.' He began to stammer. 'But no one would miss just one of us for half an hour. Then when one comes back, the other can slip out . . .'

'I can't resist a man who can make decisions,' said Eva moving towards him. She began to rub her hand softly over the throbbing bulge bursting from the man's trousers. He closed his eyes and trembled. The boys would never believe it.

He opened his eyes in time to see Maria lead his comrade through the door towards the stairs, playfully twisting the open-mouthed man's tie.

Eva's hand slid down the top of his trousers and the young soldier felt his knees buckle as her fingers closed around his erection.

'I can't wait half an hour for a drink,' she purred. 'Do you have any in your room?'

The man shook his head weakly. Eva's left hand tightened and he gave a gasping squeal. Her right hand was outstretched and waiting.

'Buy some wine from the café down the street,' he said pressing a fistful of francs into her open palm, 'and take it up to my room. It's on the second floor.'

Eva released him, and flicked her head so her long blonde hair trailed behind her like a veil. She blew him a kiss.

'I could never resist men who make decisions. In half an hour then . . .'

Eva used the back stairs and went straight to Ulrich's room. She knocked four times. Colette let her in.

'I've got about twenty minutes if we are to be on the safe side,' Eva said. Colette had removed papers from Ulrich's desk and arranged them on the bed in neat piles.

'I think we'd better start with the diary,' Colette said, taking the camera from her bag. She turned on the bedside lamp and focused the light on the table. Eva began to flick through the diary.

'Hurry,' urged Colette impatiently, as Eva began to fumble the pages.

'I can't read his bloody writing,' she snapped.

'Come on,' said Colette, glancing with fear at the door.

'This,' said Eva, selecting a page at last.

Colette laid the page open on the table and photographed it.

'And this.'

Click.

'This.'

'Click.'

It took four minutes. 'That gives us only a quarter of an hour left.' Colette sounded worried.

'Don't panic,' Eva said.

'I'm not,' Colette replied. But she knew she was. 'We've got to do all those files yet.'

Eva began to go through them. She would break off only to hand ones she felt were important to Colette.

Colette cursed.

'What is it?'

'Run out of film.' Colette tore open the back of the camera and wound up the reel. She put it in her bag.

As she opened a new roll, the phone on Ulrich's table rang. The girls stared at it, open-mouthed. It rang again, longer this time.

'What do we do?'

'Answer the bloody thing,' Eva said.

'We can't. What if it's Ulrich?' Colette felt sick.

'Colonel Ulrich's room,' she said brazenly. Colette went white. Eva bit her lip and crossed her fingers as she waited for the reply.

At last she said, 'No, I am afraid the Colonel is out.' There was a pause. 'I have no idea when he'll be back. I'm only the chamber maid.' Eva hung up, and went back to the papers. 'I'll just take the ones marked secret,' she said, handing a batch of stamped sheets to Colette over her shoulder. Colette was still fumbling with the new film. Eva snatched the camera from her.

'I'll do it,' she said. 'You just give me any paper you see with this red stamp on it.'

Colette wiped the sweat from her palms and went back to the bed. She was shaking now.

'How much more?' asked Eva.

'Hundreds,' moaned Colette.

'We've no more time. I'll have to go.' She put down the camera.

'Just this one. It has got that funny stamp.'

'It will have to be the last. You put everything back,' said Eva, and took the von Ribbentrop cable.

Not even a Buddhist monk could have ripped himself from the grip of Maria's thighs, and a clerk, whose breath smelt of cheese, had no chance at all.

After thirty-five minutes, the ache of anticipation in the young soldier waiting alone in Ulrich's outer office, was almost unbearable.

After forty minutes, he wrung his hands in frustration and started pacing the floor, leaving a trail of expletives behind him.

When forty-five minutes had passed, his frustration became unbearable. They could send him to the Russian front for all he cared. He bolted from the office and took the stairs to the waiting Eva three at a time.

Colette, sitting alone in the foyer, watched him go. She gave him a minute, then, with a brisk assurance, walked straight into the unattended office.

She was only to photograph papers marked ... what was it again? Colette took out the note on which Eva had earlier scribbled the all important phrase. The small French girl could not even pronounce it.

'Sehr Geheim' – Most Secret.

Ten minutes later, a fresh roll of film used, and she was finished. She slipped the camera into her bag and walked calmly back to the foyer. She sat cross-legged on a sofa under the shade of a hideous potted plant and lit a long cigarette. She felt terrified.

Maria and her flushed soldier returned as the hotel clock chimed the hour. When they reached the foot of the stairs, Maria walked straight towards Colette without giving the soldier a second glance. For a moment he stood gawking after her, then, as the realisation dawned upon him, he turned, red-faced, and tucking in his shirt, galloped back to the office.

His panic subsided when he saw all was in order.

'Ach,' he said. 'Who is going to know anyway?'

As it turned out, the replacement clerks were twenty minutes

234

late themselves. When they arrived, he asked them, 'Where the hell have you been?'

'Sorry, we got held up.'

'That's no excuse. You know I could not leave until you arrived. This office must never be left unmanned. Never.'

As he left for a much needed beer, he noticed the girls had gone. All in all, April Fool's day 1944 was a date two German clerks would never forget. It was the most exciting day of their lives. Figures would never seem the same again.

CHAPTER TWENTY-ONE

Connors waited alone in Morgan's flat. On the table was an uncorked, but untouched bottle of red wine. Next to it was a neat bundle of foolscap sheets of paper. They contained the names and brief service records of the men Sergeant-Major Byrne considered suitable to carry six whores and a madame off into the French night. Rather than risk discovery by sending them to SOE, he had mailed them directly to Morgan's home address.

That morning, Connors had never seen Morgan in such jubilant mood – despite a stand-up row with Cameron which had rattled every window in the Baker Street office. The big American did not share his Welsh friend's optimism. As Connors saw it, Morgan's plan had completely backfired, and he could not understand his jubilation.

Every report which had landed on Morgan's desk over the past six weeks had been subjected to all of his not inconsiderable journalistic skills. Phrases had been subtly and swiftly sub-edited to alter emphasis; paragraphs moved in the narrative order to either heighten or lessen their impact; meanings changed by the addition or omission of key words. Morgan had not worked for the *Daily Express* for nothing. As a public relations exercise on behalf of his ladies from France, it was faultless. But, as Connors had forecast, he had done too good a job.

When the batch of photographs, including details of the Atlantic Wall and the von Ribbentrop cable mentioning Overlord, had arrived in London via the Breton fishing boat *La Belle Hélène* and a Royal Navy MTB, Morgan had been over the moon with undisguised joy.

Armed with these facts, with air reconnaissance pictures which indicated the Germans had moved the crack Panzer Lehr division to within striking distance of the beaches of Normandy, and with a confident smile, Morgan stepped into the dour Scottish colonel's office.

He argued, soundly, that the intelligence indicated the Nazis were having second thoughts about which route the invasion would take.

'I agree with your deduction that there is something in the Normandy wind,' Cameron told him, 'and I also agree that if they had tumbled Overlord, then your ... women could conceivably know about it. But the fact that von Ribbentrop seems to be cabling all and sundry screaming for an explanation to the meaning of the Overlord and Neptune codes, indicates they are still in the dark.

'As you have said, Morgan, these girls are of vital importance, and that is why they are staying where they are. For the duration.'

'What about those fucking Panzers?'

'Simply a sop to Rommel. That would be my guess.'

'Guess?'

The stakes – the chance that the whole move to liberate Europe could flounder on the beaches – were too high to wait any longer. Morgan decided to enlist the help of the most powerful man he knew. He was not to know that the man had attended a Downing Street cabinet meeting the previous day. Among the items discussed were the invasion and the Château Beaupré. The decision to continue using the whores as an instrument of policy later had been struck from the minutes. After all, the Lord Privy Seal, Lord Beaverbrook, knew and trusted the judgement of the man whose reports emphasised just how vital the girls were.

The expression on Morgan's face the moment he came into the room, told Connors everything he did not want to know. He poured the wine and Morgan took the glass before he slumped disconsolately into the chair. He did not say a word; his expression said it all.

'Well?' asked Connors in response to the Welshman's silence.

'Beaverbrook's exact words,' said Morgan, 'were "no dice" to a raid, which I assume is Canadian for get stuffed.'

'Even with the von Ribbentrop cable and the Panzer Lehr pics?'

'The old man quoted Cameron at me: "A question of priorities and probabilities." The girls are too important to be taken out.'

'I guess there is no way we are going to need these,' Connors said, looking at Byrne's lists on the table.

Morgan's eyes sparkled.

'Great. I knew Mike would come through. Let me see,' he said eagerly. Then like the reporter he once had been, he began to sift through the papers with amazing speed, periodically holding out his glass for a top-up. Soon there were three distinct piles.

Probable. Possible. Not a cat's chance. Connors leant back on the sofa and shifted his formidable 240-pound frame.

'Jesus, Nat, don't you ever give up?'

'Mmmm,' said Morgan still sifting, 'it's the Celt in me.' By morning, he would have his team.

'Forget it, Nat, and good night,' said Connors, rising.

'Where the hell are you going? There's a pub down the road called the Britannia. The landlady is Welsh, and she's keeping me some malt whisky.'

''Fraid I am going to have to take a rain cheque.'

'Why?'

An expression of bloodhound gloom trickled over Arnie Connors's face. On this earth there were two things he hated. One, because they devoted the energies of a lifetime to mediocrity and trivia, was clerks. The other, because as a child one had overturned almost resulting in his death by drowning, was boats.

'Nat,' he said sadly, 'the two greatest phobias of my life have joined hands to conspire against me. You and I know a secret which will change history – and what do army clerks christen us – Bigots.

'Now, next week Connors, a Bigot, heaven forbid, is going to have to board a damn ship to report on the Utah Beach rehearsal at Slapton Sands.'

'When is this?' said Morgan.

'Next week, on April 28.'

'But,' protested Morgan, 'that's my birthday.'

'Have a happy birthday,' mumbled Connors adding, 'Ships, one day, are gonna be the death of me.'

'If only,' thought the German naval commander, 'they had given us homing torpedoes like this two years ago, we would have won the Battle of the Atlantic.'

He stood impassively in front of the radar screen at Cherbourg Marine Control watching the line of blips, changing so slowly they hardly appeared to be moving at all.

'Convoy and single escort vessel,' called out the rating with the headphones, 'and maintaining a strict radio silence.'

The commander remained motionless, except to move his eyes towards the clock on the wall.

It was 22.35 hours.

'They have left the Solent, sir, and are heading west. The

convoy is hugging the coast and steaming towards Portland Bill,' reported the rating.

The commander picked up the table-top phone.

'Launch the raiders.'

As the second hand on the wall clock reached midnight, the ninth and final E-Boat slipped its moorings and purred gently in the wake of the rest of the squadron.

Two miles from the shore they manoeuvred into formation, engines barely ticking over, and bobbed on the still sea like the tip of a deadly arrow. Then, as one, their mighty engines sprang to life and churned up the calm sea into a broth of boiling water. The nine sharp bows lifted as one and sliced through the still water – towards the English coast of South Devon's Slapton Sands and the single line of the ships that blipped helplessly across the radar screen on the leading E-Boat's bridge.

It was Winston Churchill who later said, cussedly: 'The destinies of two great Empires ... seemed to be tied up by some goddamned things called LSTs.'

LST was some clerk's abbreviation for Landing Ships – Tanks. They were three hundred and twenty-eight feet long and had a draft of only thirteen feet which allowed them to get as close inshore as possible. But with a top speed of just eleven knots, they were slow craft, unmanoeuvrable and, even on the stillest sea, rolled like reeling drunkards.

On the bridge of LST 531, Arnie Connors leant over the safety rails and willed himself not to be sick.

Even though the moon was bright, none of the approaching ships showed a light, and all remained invisible from the shore. It was only by the moon-glow that Connors could see the tiny British corvette *Azalea* slip through the darkness. She was the only escort ship.

He strained his eyes at the luminous dial of his watch. It was 01.40. Then the sky lit up with what he took to be unexpected streaks of lightning.

He could see the ship ahead for the first time. The legend on her stern read LST 507. A voice, somewhere behind him, called out: 'Troops and tank crews standing by at assault stations.' Then a scream: 'Tracer fire.'

Before the distant sound of the pumping E-Boats' guns caught up with the javelins of light streaking towards the line of ships, the first torpedoes ripped through the hull of LST 507, sending

239

a rolling ball of flame through her bowels, cremating the men who stood in its path.

'Torpedo port bow.'

'Hard a port,' yelled 531's skipper.

It was too late. Connors heard a dull – almost soft – thud. He felt the ship lurch and there was a second muffled thump. The ship tilted forward, as if she was trying to balance on her stub nose, and her twin screws lifted from the water, screaming at full revs.

The blast which followed sucked the air from Connors's lungs and, as if in a dream, he felt himself rolling slowly through the air. Below him, as his head followed his heels in unhurried succession, he saw the grey hull tip onto its side. Then the red-lead of the water line came into view, followed by darkness and the icy taste of salt water.

His head broke the surface. The water was black, sticky and pungent. Oil was pouring into his lungs and stomach and he could hear men screaming. In the distance, he saw the beam of a searchlight scan the bobbing heads of the splashing survivors.

Connors's vision began to blur, and then, for some reason, he remembered it was Morgan's birthday.

That night, it was as if the Allied Supreme Commander sensed there was something very wrong. General Dwight Eisenhower had tossed and turned until dawn in the tiny bunk of the caravan parked in the stately grounds of the historic Southwark House near Portsmouth. He had moved there from London to be closer to the heart of invasion force Overlord, which he planned to launch in eight short weeks.

On the table next to his bunk there were three phones. The black one connected him to his Chiefs of Staff, the green one was a direct line to Churchill at Downing Street, while the red phone was used only for 'scrambled' calls to Washington.

When the black phone woke him from his troubled sleep, he knew it meant disaster. The caller was General Betts, Assistant Chief of Intelligence at Supreme Headquarters, a man not in the habit of waking his superior at six a.m. unless it was with news which could alter the outcome of the war.

'The German Navy has attacked the invasion rehearsal force. It looks bad, damn bad.'

'Casualties?'

'So far LST 507 confirms two hundred dead and LST 531 has lost an estimated four hundred men.'

'What about their identities?' asked Eisenhower urgently.

'Still checking them out.'

'I want a complete news blackout.'

'You have already got it,' replied Betts.

Eisenhower put the phone down. In eight damn weeks, he thought, we were supposed to be in France.

He picked up the green phone.

Churchill was already working at his desk when Eisenhower's call came through on the scrambler. His grey jowls sagged with concern as he listened to the Supreme Commander's explanation.

Eisenhower concluded: 'So we have no way of knowing if the E-Boat attack was just a matter of chance or not.'

Churchill paused ominously before replying.

'So,' he said, 'in just fifteen minutes, the US Fourth Infantry Division has lost six hundred men, three hundred more are wounded, some so badly that they will die. And as I understand it, you have left me with no bloody reserve LSTs.'

'That, I'm afraid, is the position.'

'And we don't know why the attack took place?'

'No, Prime Minister, we do not.'

'How many of the dead were Bigots?'

'Nine, sir,' Eisenhower's voice began to falter, 'and five are still missing.'

'Ike,' said Churchill deeply, 'I want every one of those bodies found and accounted for. Every single one. Only men like these and God know what we plan for Hitler. God won't tell, these men might. We must find them.'

The news of the fiasco hit F-section at SOE like a bomb. To his credit Cameron reacted swiftly, and Morgan arrived in Portsmouth just after noon. He went straight to the US Military Hospital where the survivors had been taken.

'Connors, Connors,' the nurse repeated, running her pencil down the list of names. 'Ah, yes. He is in ward seven. That's down the end of this corridor and through the second door on your left.'

'Thanks,' said Morgan and took off down the corridor. He saw a doctor come out of the ward, turn and walk in the opposite direction. Morgan ran after him and caught him by the sleeve.

'Major Connors, Major Arnie Connors, how is he?'

241

'He has only just regained consciousness. But he'll be fine now we have pumped the oil and water out of him.'

Morgan's sigh of relief could be heard all over Portsmouth.

'Can I see him?'

'Only for a moment, he's still very weak.'

'Thanks,' Morgan grinned. It was impossible to associate the word weak with Arnie Connors.

In less than a minute, Morgan was back in the doctor's office at the head of the ward.

'I need to use the phone. It's a matter of the highest security,' Morgan said.

Without being asked, the doctor rose and left the office, closing the door behind him. Morgan called Cameron first.

'Look,' he explained, speaking quickly to prevent interruption, 'this cock-up down here is far worse than anyone first thought. After the attack, those E-Boats did not run for the French coast as the *Azalea* reported. Connors saw them cruise through the wreckage – and they were picking up survivors. This means that men who were taking part in a full-scale run through for the Utah Beach landing are now in the hands of the fucking Gestapo.'

Then, as soon as he had finished, Morgan made a second call.

Only the thin tube of neon light fixed to the low ceiling betrayed the fact that Cameron was not walking along the passageway of one of Lord Nelson's wooden ships. The heavy timber walls smelt of the sea, which was not surprising, as they had once been part of the English admiral's battleships of the line which had served their country so well against another European dictator. Now they lined the four-feet-thick concrete walls of the passage leading to Churchill's War Room beneath the streets of London.

The room's metal door, as thick as a bank vault, was open and Cameron saw Churchill was alone at his desk. He was dressed in a dark blue boiler suit and working furiously on the papers spread out like litter in front of him. Without looking up, he took the saturated stub of the Havana cigar which had been clenched between his teeth, and tossed it expertly into the empty waste-paper bin beside his chair. He continued writing, but with his free hand he picked up the security file with the words 'Château Beaupré. Lisieux' typed in bold red letters on the brown cover. He held it up towards Cameron without looking up. The colonel took it nervously.

'Fetch them,' growled Churchill.

CHAPTER TWENTY-TWO

'You want what?' exploded Cameron. 'Who in hell do you think you are to demand anything?'

'All I'm asking,' said Morgan, 'is your word that these girls will not be treated as prisoners of war or as enemies of this country. I want your assurance that every one of them will be treated with the respect they deserve and given their freedom.'

'Prostitutes,' bellowed Cameron, 'that's all they are. Prostitutes, not bloody Joans of Arc.

'Morgan,' he said, 'it is bad enough that you have got your way. Make no mistake, if Mr. Churchill had not asked for you himself, I would have put you on a charge. You defied my express orders to drop this idea and when I tell you that you have just fourteen days to assemble this ragamuffin crew, you tell me that you can do the whole thing by the weekend because, behind my back, you have selected the men you want. So don't push your luck. Now get out of my office and get out of my sight.'

'All I want is your word.'

'Get out,' ranted the colonel, 'and this time see to it that you manage to return with what you were sent for.'

But Morgan was gone. The colonel kicked the door closed. Ever since he had taken Morgan's phone call from Portsmouth, he had feared the mission would have to go ahead. He was professional enough to accept that if the Germans learnt anything from the men they had plucked from the Devon sea, then it was odds-on that the girls would know about it. After all, they were the lovers of some of the most powerful and influential men in Hitler's army, and if the secret was out, then the whole outcome of the war would be affected. D-Day, as planned for months in meticulous detail, would be cancelled and there might never be another chance. All this Cameron accepted, but what rankled most was that Churchill's idea for the raid matched Morgan's to the last details. What Cameron was never to know was that, after phoning him from hospital, Morgan had placed another call. It had been to the office of the Lord Privy Seal. Beaverbrook had been immediately available and had listened to the plan with interest. He promised to mention it to Churchill.

Morgan had not needed Mr. Godsell to point out how

244

politically embarrassing it was for the British Government to use prostitution as an instrument of policy. Which was why the thirty-six men who arrived that night at the Hampshire commando training base, did not bear the same nationality. Their uniforms, all identical, were not those of the armed forces they served, and bore no rank or insignia. Fourteen of the men were British; the greatest number, sixteen, were American, one was Polish, two Canadians and the other from New Zealand. Two had been sent by a bemused Free French commander, who thought all the men in his unit capable of seducing a stone statue. They were all highly trained in the act of killing, with or without a weapon.

They were met on arrival by the man who had selected them. The final choice of the team who would raid the Château Beaupré was, however, to be left to the man standing alongside Sergeant-Major Byrne – Nat Morgan.

The men, none of whom had any idea why they were there, were split into nine groups. Each group of four was allocated a sergeant. Each sergeant was an Advanced Royal Marine Commando Training Instructor, hand-picked by Byrne, who believed them to be the best that the British Armed Forces had to offer.

The men then piled into waiting trucks and were taken with the instructors to four different locations in the New Forest. They then followed their instructors back through the night in a gruelling cross-country run, completed with full pack. On return to base, they were then permitted sleep, all two and a half hours of it, until the sun reared its unwelcome head. Then came the first part of Byrne's scheme to, as he explained in his broad Irish brogue, separate the bucks from the real fighting stags. What followed that Thursday morning before breakfast did just that. Although all the men who took part were battle-hardened veterans, the exercise made them fearful for their lives. The importance of the mission, a mission about which they were never told, demanded it. For it was with these men and the girls they would abduct from the clutches of the SS, that the decision whether it was necessary to cancel Operation Overlord lay. They had to be simply the best there was.

That was why the knot in Morgan's gut tightened as he watched what followed from the second-floor window overlooking the barrack square. One unarmed man from each group faced his instructor. Each sergeant was armed with a six-inch commando knife.

'And,' Byrne informed them from the whitewashed sidelines, 'unless you take that knife from him, the sergeant will kill you with it.'

When, ninety minutes later, the last man had finished trying, twelve were on their way to a Bournemouth hospital with stab wounds. Three of them with the kind of injuries medical spokesmen describe as 'serious'.

The men who survived were then allowed breakfast. Unlike Byrne, few of them could face what was put in front of them because they still felt sick.

As Morgan watched the big Irishman work his way along the toast rack, he wondered how he could ever have been so foolish to have thought it was generals who ran armies. They did not; they simply planned strategies; it was sergeant-majors like Mike Byrne who called the shots. He had a face like a nineteenth-century Dublin bareknuckle prize-fighter.

'Nat, my boy, will you pass the marmalade? You must be up to something that's really terrible to get this stuff laid on – it's rarer these days than the smile of a Belfast preacher.'

'Mike,' said Morgan, 'there is no way I can tell you what's going on at this stage of the game. Except that what I want these boys for is not going to be a picnic. I would appreciate it if you'd consider coming along. It can be arranged – if after what you put them through this morning, you feel you could trust them not to blow your head off the first chance they got.'

Byrne's face cracked into a wrinkled smile. 'There'll be no chance of any such thing. It's important that these lads become a team, that much you've said. If I can unite them in their hatred of me, then I've done my job for you. As for the other thing, you surely know that I'll be with you all the way. Whatever it is. I always said you were one of the best I ever had pass through me hands.'

Morgan rubbed the jaw which the man sitting opposite had once fractured in two places.

'Do you want in?'

'You've got such a nice way of asking, how could I say no to you?'

'Good,' said Morgan, 'now we've got three.'

'Three?'

'You, me, and the man who wrote the letter, Arnie Connors of OSS.'

'How many men is it you'll be needing in all?'

'Ten – and us three.'

'Now then, as I see it, that makes thirteen in all.

Morgan laughed. 'Why, are you superstitious?'

'Jesus, no. Not at all.' But Morgan noticed he touched the wooden table three times as he said it.

During the next session it was the turn of the men to be given a dagger. The instructors wore protective jackets which had two-inch strips of cork sewn into the canvas material. They were also armed with a revolver containing two bullets. They faced each other over a distance of twenty feet.

'Now, you men,' roared Byrne in the best traditions of his rank, 'the sergeants will fire the first shot, and they'll be aiming at the dirt between your feet. Your task is to put that knife into the protective jacket – and I mean the jacket – before he can let off his second shot. Where he aims it is being left entirely to each sergeant's own good sense. If any man wants to back down, now is the time.'

Only two men took advantage of the offer.

This time Morgan watched from the side of the barrack square. From where he squatted on his haunches, he was not sure which came first, the spurt of dust in front of the Negro's legs or the sound of his dagger quivering in the instructor's cork-lined jacket.

'What's his name?'

'The black fellow's called Ellis.'

All came through unscathed and, in fact, the only other injury of the day was claimed by one of the instructors, who had his arm broken in the no-holds-barred unarmed combat session which followed the shooting range tests.

By the time Connors arrived from Portsmouth, Morgan's selection was almost completed. Over the limp kind of stew only army cooks seem capable of producing, the three men pored over the list of names. Connors was the only one to doubt one man's possible inclusion.

'Crowski – that faggot with irresistible urges to phone his mother?' blinked Connors.

'If Byrne had not stepped in, that instructor would have ended up with more than a broken arm,' grinned Morgan.

'Well, I hope you make it clear there are no phones where we are going.'

Next morning, just after dawn and Morgan's departure for London, Byrne eyed the row of weary men in front of him.

'When I call out your name, step two paces forward.'

Appleby – British 4th Commando.

Ellis – US 82nd Airborne.

Crowski – US 101st Airborne.

Davies – Welsh Guards.

Machen – British 2nd Commando.

Martin – Royal Marines.

Romeau – Free French Forces.

Rosetti – US Marines.

Scott – 1st Canadian Parachute Battalion.

Travers – US Marines.

'Right, first of all I'd like to thank you all for volunteering. Now I'm going to have to try to knock some shape into you. I've never seen anything so horrible in all me days.'

Morgan had his men. As Byrne, who considered them among the toughest he'd ever seen, marched them away, Morgan finished drafting the coded message for transmission to a village priest in Normandy. He smiled at the mental image of Albert Boniface when he learnt of Morgan's request for his help. Then his thoughts turned to Colette, his feelings muted by the spectre he pictured standing over her. He saw the face of Ulrich.

CHAPTER TWENTY-THREE

As Father Delon sat that same evening, listening through the headphones to the messages from London, he suddenly felt older and greyer than other men of forty-three years. But then other men did not wear the mantle of Swordfish. Since he'd assumed it, it had taken a heavy toll.

The messages crackling in the headset were all meaningless, except to the people for whom they were intended. Already he felt the beginnings of the faint throb which meant another headache. They seemed to get more frequent these days and he wished his role would soon be over. He did not think he could take much more.

He was sitting on the slab of stone which, when he was not using it as a seat, formed part of the wall which hid the radio equipment. The priest felt numb and shifted his position to ease the feeling. His foot brushed the storm lamp on the floor which fell over, and a pool of burning oil spread out behind it as it rolled across the granite floor. From the oak rafters above his head, the wings of dozens of sleeping bats flapped into life as the needle-toothed rodents took to the air, squeaking in circles of panic. Only when he'd beaten out the flames with a sack were they again still, watching as he re-lit the lamp's wick, replaced his headset, and listened.

In an instant the fatigue had vanished. There, crackling through the static, was the message he had been expecting. He held the words he'd just written above the lamp and checked them as the distant voice repeated the message.

It was on. And he had work to do.

An hour later the priest, dressed in the hat and robes of his faith, cycled past the Gothic façade of Lisieux's St-Pierre cathedral, past the Hôtel Normandie on the rue du Char and, with a shudder, past Ulrich's requisitioned Hotel Chloé towards the Café Raymond.

As unobtrusive as the sombre garb allowed, he settled himself behind a glass of Calvados in a corner seat, as far from the door as possible.

'Why,' he thought, 'is Albert Boniface always late?' It was not in Albert's nature to disappoint. When he eventually arrived, the priest was on his third glass of Calvados. As usual the old man was puffing, coughing and cursing.

'You smoke too much,' said Delon as Albert plonked the bottle of rough red wine on the table between them.

'Bah,' said Albert, and dismissed the slander against his temperance with a flick of the wrist, took a hefty swig of wine, and belched.

'Always you worry too much. No wonder you are getting to look old,' he said looking over his shoulder, taking in the scene with his one open eye.

'Don't do that,' hissed the priest through clenched teeth.

'It's healthy to belch, good for the digestion.'

'I meant looking over your shoulder. You are always looking over your shoulder,' said Delon, sounding irritable.

'Bah,' snorted Albert. 'Like I said, you worry too much.'

By the time Father Delon had finished relaying Morgan's message, Albert had half-finished the bottle of wine. He had just one question.

'All of them?'

'All six girls, and the madame,' confirmed the priest. 'But the main problem is going to be time and transport. The Dragon wants to be in and out before anyone has time to realise what has happened. He wants us to select the spot where they can land by submarine . . .'

'A submarine,' Albert interrupted in awe.

'Yes,' snapped Delon, 'but we have to provide the transport to take them to and from Beaupré to the coast. It's about twenty kilometres.'

One by one Albert's teeth came into view, as his lips parted in a huge grin. He took the priest by the arm and again glanced over his shoulder to make sure the world was watching. He puffed out his chest with pride and beamed, 'I have it.'

Then he hunched furtively over the table and began to speak in a stage whisper from the corner of his mouth. Father Delon kicked him under the table and, if looks could have killed, Albert would have breathed his last. Albert took a swig of wine before he plunged his finger into the glass, then he began to draw a liquid map on the table.

'Here,' he explained, using the stub of his Gauloise, 'is the Château Beaupré.' Dipping his finger into the wine again, he drew a straight line. 'This is the main road from Lisieux to

Deauville.' He dug into the ashtray and produced another cigarette stub. 'This,' he proclaimed proudly, 'is a quarry.'

'Now look . . .' said the priest irritably.

'It was a quarry,' Albert interrupted. 'But now the old offices are used as a German command post from which to patrol the beaches and control three gun emplacements. Here. Here and here.'

He placed three more stubs on his map of wine. 'There is always transport; cars, trucks, motorcycles – the lot. Now if Morgan and his men come ashore here,' he stubbed his finger on the table, 'voilà, nothing but a few dead Nazis between them and fast transport to and from the château.'

Father Delon began to nod his head.

'It might just be worth a try.'

'What do you mean might?' boomed Albert. The priest motioned with the flat of his hand for Albert to keep his voice down. The whole café seemed to be turning in their chairs, all looking at Albert. The old man hunched his shoulders even deeper.

'Bah,' he hissed, 'you always worry too much. It'll be the death of you.'

When Albert broke the news to Colette, she flung her arms around his neck. He put his hands on her tiny waist, lifted her feet from the floor and waltzed her around the room in a dance of joy.

'It's true. You are all going to be taken to London,' he smiled.

'When? When? When?' The words tumbled from Colette. 'It is all too fantastic to be true. At last, away from this place.'

She reached out and clasped the gnarled old hand, then, lifting her dark eyes, kissed him on the cheek.

'Albert,' she said, 'thank you for everything.'

He drew the back of his hand across his face. 'Bah. It's Nat Morgan you should thank. Now let's get down to details. Will any of the girls be unwilling to go?'

Colette bit her lip. 'None of them want to stay here . . . but to go willingly to England . . . I cannot say.'

'Some of them will have to be told. The question is who?'

'Certainly Maria, and Eva – if they have men in England, that is.' They both laughed and Albert lit two cigarettes at the same time. He passed one to Colette and watched her, waiting for a reaction, as she slowly blew a smoke ring from her pursed lips.

'What about Elaine Bisset?' he asked.

Colette drew deeply on the cigarette and held the smoke inside her before exhaling.

'There is no doubt she would be with us, if it did not mean leaving her baby. Of all of us, she is the one I feel most sorry for,' she said.

Albert put his arm around the small girl's shoulder, raised his eyebrows slightly, and tilted his head in a half-shake of disbelief.

'Then she cannot be told.'

'But,' protested Colette, 'what about her baby?'

'This war will soon be over. Europe, France, will be free again. She will have a lifetime left with her baby. Trust me. These Nazis are done for.

'And the madame,' Albert spat the word, 'that Breton bitch, the one with the high and mighty sounding foreign name.'

'Your guess is as good as mine. But she is always saying what a survivor she is. She will not want to be on the wrong side when the time comes.'

'Then, you must do one last thing before you go to England. Get to her and find out how she feels. We must know.'

Colette agreed. When Albert had left, the girl, arms outstretched, yelled at the top of her voice, 'London.' She pirouetted, repeating it to herself. Nat Morgan had kept his word. She was going to London. Freedom. She collapsed, giggling, on to the bed. Suddenly the expression of delight turned to one of puzzlement.

'Why?' She felt afraid.

Next day, she told Maria and Eva.

'Why?' replied Maria with a rolling hand gesture of Latin contempt. 'Who cares why.'

Eva said: 'All that matters is we are getting out. London, I'm told, has a lot to offer.'

Then, together and armed with the reassuring thought of what they thought lay ahead, the trio knocked boldly on Nicole McGragh's door.

She was reclining on a deep-red velvet chaise-longue, thumbing through an invitation list of a party she planned to throw the following week. She eyed the girls coldly.

'I was about to send for you,' she said. 'You are going to

entertain some of the finest troops in Germany at a little party I plan to give next week. They are from the Panzer Lehr who have just been stationed in Normandy, at Caen.'

'Oh,' said Colette, her mind racing with curiosity. 'Why?'

'If you display a little more than your usual disdain on the night, you might ask them and find out,' she said flatly, not knowing that the glances exchanged between Colette and Eva meant they had already decided to do just that. That night, Eva would be even more co-operative than usual.

Judging by the expression on Maria's face, Madame McGragh realised she could not depend on the same devoted assistance as Eva seemed prepared to give. Hands on hips, Maria flung back her mane of hair.

'Tell me, Madame McGragh, when this war is over and the Germans have gone, will you be shot as a collaborator?'

For once the red-haired former actress was at a loss for words. When she regained her poise, she raised her eyebrows and said: 'I beg your pardon?'

'Will they shoot you?' Colette repeated Maria's question, and, with a year's pent-up contempt, blurted: 'They might just shave our heads but we wondered what you thought would happen to you for helping Germans.'

'Shoot!' said Nicole McGragh, her voice rising in non-theatrical anger. 'With talk like that, you are the ones who run the risk of facing a firing squad. Now get out, all of you.'

'Shot,' echoed Colette, 'just like Clair.' The room flooded with the bitterness which she felt at that thought.

'No, not like Clair,' the madame's lips pursed tightly. 'I do not plan to allow anyone to lay a finger on me, no matter what.'

CHAPTER TWENTY-FOUR

The submarine's grey belly dropped on to the sea-bed with a jolt, churning up the sand and shingle. She was three miles from the beaches of Normandy, lurking under the waves and waiting for the rain-lashed dusk on the surface to thicken into night. When it did, her master trimmed the tanks and took her to periscope depth. With the incoming tide, the sub began to slink towards the shore.

Supporting a traditional submariner's beard, Lieutenant-Commander Bryan Dickensen ordered the periscope up, and the greased pole in the centre of the command deck rose slowly. Dickensen took both handles and brought the eye-piece down to his level. Legs bent slightly at the knee, he turned the viewer in a full circle and grunted his approval. Then he stood back and gestured for Nat Morgan to take a look.

Beyond the black sea loomed the hostile cliffs of occupied France. Morgan swivelled the periscope and, to the north, he picked out the shape of the first gun emplacement, then he followed the line of the cliffs until he spotted the second gun positioned to defend the small beach. It lay at the mouth of a valley, the only break in the sheer wall of limestone rising out of the hissing sea. Further south was the third battery of guns.

'How far can you take us in?' asked Morgan.

'Within half a mile,' said Dickensen. 'Are your men ready?' Morgan nodded. 'Prepare to surface.'

Minutes later the sub broke the waves and loomed on the ocean surface, an avenger from Neptune. At the foot of the conning tower ladder, Morgan's men lined up behind him in single file. They were all dressed alike in dark-green combat suits and black woollen caps. Their heavy boots had rubber soles and all, even Ellis, had smeared black grease over their faces. No man bore the badges of rank or regiment and no man carried anything that would have identified him.

The weapons they carried, pistol, sub-machine gun, and dagger with knuckle-duster handle, were an assortment of those taken from captured enemy prisoners in Italy and North Africa. Among the commandos, Machen, the former Newcastle welder with a taste for brigadiers' daughters, carried a Russian anti-tank weapon. Crowski, who could offer the women who adored him nothing but a smile, and Scott, a wiry Canadian, carried a wooden case containing its shells on to the wave-washed deck. There Morgan stood scanning the coast with night glasses. Only he and Connors knew the target. The men only knew that they must not be taken alive. If found, the weapons they carried would only confuse the Germans.

As the men lined up on deck, the crew lowered the three rubber inflatables in which the Royal Marines would paddle them ashore. The commandos took their place in the dinghy allotted to them, all except Crowski, who still stood on deck holding the ammo case.

'I'll still bet it's that Rommel we're going to hoist,' he shouted down. 'He's just like our Patton – a real general.'

'Shurrup,' barked back Byrne, who also thought that the reason for the raid.

'Come on, why in the hell else would we be going?' asked Rosetti.

'You are not in the American army now,' growled Byrne. 'When I say to be quiet, I mean it. The next one of you who opens his mouth, I'll tear his tongue out.'

The instant silence showed that they had learnt their lessons. But, as Crowski handed the case to Scott, the sub lurched and with arms swinging in an effort to keep his balance, he fell headlong onto the men in the dinghy below.

'Goddam faggot,' mumbled Connors, as they set off for the shore.

By the time they reached the cliffs, the rain had ceased. The dinghies bumped silently against the jagged rocks as the men's hands reached to grab an outfall, a ledge, anything they could grip which would steady the bobbing craft rolling in the vicious, rising swell.

Morgan, his face solemn and taut, looked at the Negro from Detroit.

'Right,' he said.

Ellis bent and picked up the grapnel from the floor of the dinghy. He twirled it above his head until it whistled, then he let it fly. The three-pronged hook vanished above him into the darkness, uncoiling a plaited rope behind it. When the rope was spent, Ellis tugged. It had made good first time. He tested its hold by hauling himself off the boat's deck. His ivory smile said it all.

A minute and a half later, Nat Morgan knelt on the wet grass of the Normandy cliff top. He had returned, with the fate of the D-Day invasion plan hanging on his shoulders. He took out his dagger, cut the rope from the hook and tied it around the trunk of tree which, due to the prevailing wind, grew inwards at an angle from the sea. One by one the men, bouncing off the limestone cliff, followed him up the rope.

Then the Royal Marines returned to the sub and as soon as they were aboard, she dived. She would re-surface an hour before dawn, which left Morgan just six hours before he returned with his very important human cargo.

His men squatted around him in the darkness on the cliff top as he went through his priorities. He needed first to ensure that their path of withdrawal was secure. That meant that the three gun emplacements had to be eliminated. He divided six of the men into groups of two – allocating each an emplacement which, according to the whores he was about to abduct, each contained five men. Their removal would be a simple grenade job from behind. No problem, he said, and selected Appelby and Davies; Machen and Travers; Rosetti and Martin.

Then, if the Swordfish group's information was correct, there were the shore patrols to be taken care of. Nine Germans each guarded a third-of-a-mile stretch of coast including the small beach which was heavily mined. Connors and Crowski would work from the north, Byrne and Scott from the south. They would meet at the beach then move inland to cover the road leading from the command post in the quarry.

Morgan, Ellis and Romeau, the Free French Legionnaire, would take that out and acquire the transport which Albert said would be there for the taking. Because all phone and radio messages – both to the gun emplacements and defence control – passed through the command post, this would be the first target.

'Synchronise watches,' said Morgan. It was 22.15 on May 11, 1944. 'You will take out the emplacements in exactly one hour. We will then rendezvous on the road out where I'll be waiting with the transport. You'll cover our approach from the ridge above the road. Elimination of the shore patrol begins now. Anyone not at the rendezvous by midnight is on his own. Understood?'

There was silence.

'Good,' said Morgan. 'Move.' They vanished into the night.

Morgan inched towards the rim of the quarry on his stomach. It was a giant semi-circular crater hewn out of the limestone. The open end was lined with a wire fence and the command post, housed in old offices, stood in the very centre of the crater one hundred feet below. Morgan's heart sank as he took in the scene. He saw that there was only one truck parked in the compound, not the fleet of vehicles Albert had promised. And there were two guards on the gate, not one. The whole raid could be blown before it had even bloody started. His plan had been to take out the one guard, then the command post. But with two men at the wire gate, the chances of the alarm being raised had doubled. And where was the fast transport?

'Just one sodding truck,' he muttered. He looked over his shoulder at Romeau who put down the anti-tank gun Machen had given him.

'Pulley,' said Morgan. Romeau nodded and removed his back pack and coil of rope from his shoulder. To his left stood a telegraph pole. Without being asked, he shinned up it and fixed the pulley to the single arm, then dropped silently to the ground. Morgan took the ends of the rope threaded through the pulley and tied them. He slipped the loop under his arms, then stepped over the edge of the quarry.

Ellis and Romeau strained to take his weight, the rope burning their hands as they fed it out to Morgan who bounced his feet off the sheer face until he reached the ground. The anti-tank gun and shells were lowered down the hoist, followed by Ellis and Romeau. Then, one at a time, they sprinted to the rear of the command post. Morgan knew he must lure one of the guards away from the gate so Romeau could take the other without being detected. Only with the guards out of the way, could they launch a surprise attack on the post itself.

'But how?' he thought desperately. Then he edged to the side of the building up to the window. The heavy blind was drawn and he could hear voices inside, arguing.

'If you want to smoke that thing, then smoke it outside. It's stopped raining.'

Morgan moved back. As ordered, Romeau drew his dagger and began to circle the quarry face until he was in striking distance of the sentries.

The front door of the command post opened and a school-masterly, bespectacled soldier stepped into the shaft of light. He lit his pipe.

'Close the bloody door,' a voice complained.

'Shut it yourself. You were the one moaning about the smell

of my pipe.' As the door closed, Ellis crawled through the darkness in the direction of the ambling German puffing contentedly on his pipe. Suddenly Ellis leapt out in front of him and held his finger to his lips.

'Shh,' he said. The soldier's face showed his surprise. He recovered his wits but as he was about to yell out, the tip of Morgan's dagger pressed into the side of his throat.

'Cry out and you're dead,' said Morgan, as he backed the soldier towards the truck. 'What are the guards' names?'

'Faber and Kranker.'

'Call Faber over here,' said Morgan.

'Why, what is it?' Faber shouted.

'Come and see for yourself over here, behind the truck.'

The moment Faber rounded the back of the truck, his companion tried to call out a warning. Within the same second they both died, and so, a minute later, did Kranker at the gates. which were now unlocked and open.

When Morgan walked through the command post door, he did so with the confident air of a man going into his own home. None of the five soldiers playing cards round the table looked up at first. By the time they did, Ellis and Romeau were at his side, their sub-machine guns held waist high.

'If anyone dies, it's going to be your fault,' said Morgan pointing his pistol at the young lieutenant in charge. 'The rest of you can get up slowly and stand facing the wall with your hands on your heads.'

They rose like one. Morgan called the lieutenant and pointed to the radio transmitter.

'Call your control and tell them the phones are out of order,' said Morgan, providing the reason why no one would hear from the command post again that evening. They would not use the radio for fear that communications would be picked up by the Allies' monitoring network.

'But my regulations state . . .' protested the officer.

'Call them,' said Morgan menacingly. He never ceased to be amazed at the reverence Germans held for regulations. When the officer had finished, Morgan smashed the set to pieces and Romeau tore out the phones. And with that, the link to the outside world.

'Bind them, hand and foot,' said Morgan. But before either Ellis or Romeau could move, the sound of distant gunfire crackled through the night. The men lined up against the wall moved in all directions at once. The lieutenant grabbed his Luger from the table and one of the soldiers struggled with the bolt of the rifle he'd snatched from the arms rack in the corner.

The room rattled with sub-machine-gun fire. Ellis fanned the smoke from his eyes and said, 'The stupid, dumb bastards.' The lieutenant lay sprawled across the table where one of his men had fallen on top of him. The others lay in a tangled heap of arms and legs piled against the wall.

Morgan moved quickly, nervous energy sparking from him like static electricity. The sound of fire on the night wind meant he had a fight on his hands. He could not afford to waste a second. Morgan took two grenades from his belt, tied a length of string to the firing pins and wedged the grenades behind the door. As he closed the door behind them, he dropped the loop over the catch. The first man into that office would be blown to bits.

More gunfire echoed from the direction of the beach as Romeau collected the anti-tank gun and ammo and deposited them in the back of the truck.

'What the hell is going on back there?' said Ellis turning his head towards the sea. The question was rhetorical.

Less than a minute later the report of three explosions followed each other in rapid succession.

Morgan, sitting in the front seat of the truck between Romeau and Ellis, looked at his watch and said, 'It's 23.15. There go the gun emplacements – right on time. Let's go.'

'Oh Christ,' moaned Romeau, 'the ignition keys must still be in that booby-trapped building.'

Ellis smiled. 'Got a brother who once made a living out of crossing ignition circuits,' he said, getting out of the cab.

The engine fired at the second attempt and the truck moved off through the open gates and up the winding track towards the beach road. At the rendezvous point they pulled up, kept the engine running and waited for the others. It was 23.30 hours.

They had been waiting for a couple of minutes, all yearning for a smoke, when Ellis glanced up. He froze, for snaking along the valley road were three points of light, and the vehicles behind them were moving fast.

'Out,' yelled Morgan, and the three dived for cover in the roadside bracken, still heavy from rain. They watched as the motorcycle and sidecar pulled up in front of the staff car, their headlights trained on the abandoned truck. The rider dismounted, and followed by his passenger, drew their pistols and moved cautiously forward.

Morgan glanced up towards the silent ridge and wondered if the shooting from the beach meant no one had made it back to cover it as planned. Then two sharp cracks rang out to fell the advancing soldiers. The ridge was covered.

Then a figure stepped out of the blackness behind the car's headlights. It was Byrne. In one hand he held a bloodstained dagger, in the other his revolver. The German officer at his side, white-faced with fear, had his hands in the air.

When Morgan reached the car, he saw the driver slumped over the wheel. He had been stabbed through the throat.

'Scott bought it on the cliff,' said Byrne as Connors and Crowski came down from the ridge. Then Appleby came running along the road. He was alone.

'Where's Davies?' asked Morgan. Appleby just shook his head.

Connors pointed to the German officer and asked: 'What do we do about him?'

'He says they were alone. There aren't any more of them,' said Byrne. He looked at Morgan and raised his eyebrows. Morgan answered with a nod.

'Move,' said Byrne, nudging the man forward into the darkness. When he returned a minute later, he was alone. He rested against the roof of the car and vomited.

The breathless Martin was next to arrive. 'Rosetti's coming,' he panted.

He arrived just ahead of Travers and Rosetti. Then Machen made it. 'That's it,' said Byrne. 'We've lost two men but got the transport.'

'That's two men too many,' said Morgan heavily, 'and it's just gone midnight.'

They concealed the German bodies in the bracken and Travers kicked the motorcycle into life. Byrne, sub-machine gun on his lap, sat in the sidecar. The others piled into the truck which Romeau drove, and with Ellis and Morgan in the Mercedes staff car, they set off towards the Château Beaupré.

It was an hour later, and they were lost for the third time. This time the convoy had followed Travers left at the crossroads and up a lane which petered out into a rutted farm track. They had to reverse to a clearing where Morgan pored over the map unfurled on his knees.

'Guess we should have turned right here,' said Connors, his fingers on the red line representing the crossroads. Morgan shook his head, trying to re-create a picture of the countryside he could relate to his last visit when he'd learnt the château's secret. Slowly it formed.

'Balls,' he cursed, 'we're miles out – only a few miles from where I was first dropped in the Lysander. This, here, is the main road from Caen to Lisieux – route 13.'

'It's that old number again,' said Byrne, pressing his face to the half-open window.

Morgan's expression darkened. He felt things were beginning to go wrong. If they doubled back, it would take them thirty minutes to pick up the point where they had first got lost. Then, if everything went smoothly, another thirty minutes to reach the château, then ... He stopped thinking. He would have to risk using route 13 which could save an hour. It could be crucial time – the difference between success and failure. He got out of the car and gathered his commandos around him.

'We'll have to use the main road. Unless we run into a patrol there should be only one problem – the roadblock. As I remember, it is a simple affair: a sentry box, two men and a pole barrier. Those men's uniforms could be a blessing in disguise,' said Morgan.

Crowski, a Polish American, began to intone the Lord's Prayer in Latin. 'Pater noster, qui es in ca ...'

'That's enough of that fucking blasphemy, no call for it,' said Byrne angrily.

'We should never have brought ... that ...' muttered Connors, looking sideways at Crowski, then taking his eyes away quickly, as if they had been offended by what they saw.

'So,' continued Morgan as if he had heard none of it, 'we take out the roadblock, the men – and their uniforms.'

The convoy moved off again, this time led by staff car followed by the truck and, safe from the glare of headlights, Byrne and Travers on the BMW motorcycle with their blacked-out faces and combat uniforms.

The vehicles turned left on route 13. Resting on the roof of the truck's cab, as Morgan ordered, the stub of the anti-tank gun's barrel poked from beneath the front flap of the canvas hood.

At that moment, Albert Boniface wiped his nose with his sleeve and crushed the stub of his Gauloise into the mounting pile of spent cigarette ends at his feet. He was standing in the shadows outside the château's boundary wall. As he lit another Gauloise, he too sensed things were not going to be as straightforward as he'd planned. No one had bothered to tell him there was going to be a party. That red-haired Breton bitch had to choose this night of all nights to welcome the new Panzer officers, he thought. There were a dozen inside, the drivers who'd brought them as well as the normal guard. This latest lot had been drafted into Normandy from Poland, or so Eva had told him.

'Crack troups, my sow's arse,' mumbled Albert. He would soon see just how good they were. That's why he had dug his old World War I rifle out of the attic. A bit rusty, he thought, but still a good gun. He, Albert Boniface, the hero of Bapaume and the Somme, had shot Boche with it before. He smiled at the thought that tonight he might get another chance. If only Morgan and his commandos turned up in time.

Suddenly he cocked his head at the sound of a motorcycle engine. He sniffed the wind, like an old spaniel, and moved back into the shadows.

'This could be them now, and about time too,' he muttered.

It was not.

The German curfew patrol rode straight past him and on up the country lane – towards the main Caen to Lisieux road. Route 13.

The roadblock was just as Morgan remembered from the first time he'd seen it from the front seat of Scrélat's truck. The wooden barrier between him and the whores upon whom the invasion of Europe decision lay was about a hundred yards ahead. The road was straight and lined each side with tall poplars.

As the Mercedes and the truck slowed, Travers swung the motorcycle onto the grass verge and killed the engine. The sentry moved back to join his comrade, who raised the barrier and waved the approaching vehicles through.

Ellis ducked down under the Mercedes' dash and Morgan removed his woollen cap and, burying his head in his shoulders, hunched over the wheel. He drove through the roadblock at thirty miles an hour with the truck following at half that speed. Standing on the tailboard were Connors and Machen. When they reached the sentries, both men pounced as one.

Machen missed his man but Connors broke the other's neck before they hit the ground. Romeau's foot smashed down on the brake and behind him he heard Travers kick the BMW motorcycle to life.

It bounced and skidded back onto the road, revving wildly.

Travers straightened the machine, pushed the throttle wide open and turned on the headlights to full beam. In the spotlight he saw Machen resting on one knee beside the sentry box. The German soldier had picked himself up and, when he saw the single headlight screaming towards him, he turned and ran in sheer panic.

He saw the staff car stop and could hear himself screaming for help as, arms waving, he ran after it. He raced past the truck and stumbled on towards the waiting car. There, he thought, lay his hope of deliverance from the nightmare in which his friend Gunther had been killed.

The truck kangarooed forward as Romeau stabbed it into first gear and pressed his foot to the floor. The wheels spun as Romeau engaged second, then third, his foot still hard down. He saw the soldier fall, then pick himself up and glance over his shoulder, his face a mask of fear as he wove from side to side. The truck followed his erratic patterns like a magnet hunting a stray iron filing.

The heavy bumper caught the soldier in the small of the back and the force catapulted him on to the bonnet before he bounced off the roof and into the ditch.

When the motorcycle unit took up its place back in front of the convoy, Byrne and Travers wore the serge greatcoats of the Third Reich. On their heads – the dead men's steel helmets with their swastika emblems.

The sight of those uniforms in front of the Mercedes made Morgan's skin crawl. It was the same loathing he'd felt on a moonscape of mud in northern Spain. He remembered the SS private urinating beside the corpse of a disembowelled Welsh miner, and in his mind saw the thin dead face of George Williams lined with the blue scars of the pit. For a moment he thought he heard the sound of the wheezing breath of a lung ravaged by silicosis coming from the seat beside him. He turned and saw it was Ellis hissing through his drawn lips.

'That's it,' he said as the motorcycle in front swerved to the left. Morgan noticed the sign nailed to the trunk of the towering elm tree. It read: 'Beaupré. 10km.'

'So,' said Ellis, 'Bow-prey is just ten kilometres away. What's at that place?'

'A château,' grunted Morgan.

'Say, is anything bothering you?' asked Ellis sensing Morgan's mood. The Welshman shook his head.

'Nothing,' he said, 'except I hope the place is crawling with SS bastards.'

'Thanks a million,' said Ellis. Then he sat up, the whites of his eyes rolling. They had come to a straight stretch of road wide enough for only one vehicle to pass. At the other end was the motorcycle patrol, which had earlier passed Albert. As Byrne slipped back the catch on his sub-machine gun, he saw the German rider stand up from the single heart-shape saddle. Byrne moved the angle of his gun, hidden under the greatcoat draped over his shoulders.

'Easy,' said Travers soothingly, 'he's calling us through.' He eased back the throttle, and as they passed, acknowledged the German patrol with a wave. Then they turned right along Route 13. It was 02.30.

At 02.45, the motorcycle patrol reached the deserted roadblock. The driver slammed on his brakes.

'What is it? You almost threw me onto the bloody road,' the passenger complained.

The driver pointed towards the deserted roadblock, the pole pointing towards the sky like a warning finger.

'Think something's up?' the passenger asked.

The driver drew his pistol. 'Cover me,' he said. He jumped into the dry drainage ditch which ran along the side of the road. He crouched low, gun held out in front of him, and moved slowly towards the roadblock. He'd almost reached it when he tripped and fell headlong. He'd fallen over the body Romeau's truck had knocked into the ditch. The corpse was dressed only in its underpants. They'd taken his uniform.

The driver rushed into the sentry box.

They had forgotten to cut the phone wire.

The driver lifted the receiver.

CHAPTER TWENTY-FIVE

Madame Nicole McGragh glittered. She floated through the crimson velvet opulence of her salon with assured sparkle. The continuous popping of champagne corks indicated just how well her reception was going. In different times the occasion would have merited a mention in the social columns. Her girls danced to the strings of the uniformed military quartet. They were playing Strauss. As the girls waltzed, Nicole McGragh thought they looked simply beautiful, as did the whole scene. She was very happy with her creation.

The dance ended with a flourish and the Panzer Lehr officers, in full dress uniforms, bowed graciously to their partners, politely clapping their white-gloved hands.

A monocled major sitting this one out nudged a fellow officer.

'Which one takes your fancy?'

'I'm told we can take any. All that is except,' he twisted his neck, '. . . where is she?'

Then he spotted Colette. She was sitting with Ulrich in the far corner of the room, wearing a simple black dress, with a rose in her hair and white pearls around her neck. Ulrich clasped her hands, gazing at her with anticipation, unaware that the man who had vowed to wipe him from the face of the earth was at that moment standing outside the château gates.

'Brandy,' he said, picking up his glass from the arm of the sofa and handing it to Colette. She took it obediently, fortified by the hope that, tonight, she would kill him.

As she made her way to the long drinks table, covered by a white tablecloth of Breton lace, the Panzer officer took the monocled major by the arm.

'Her, that's the one,' he said. 'Any girl but her we can have. She is strictly forbidden fruit. That hideous SS colonel has exclusive rights.'

'Pity,' said the major, 'she is quite lovely in a schoolgirl sort of way. The kind of girl who brings out the worst in a man.'

The quartet struck up again.

'Well, I think I'm going to take my chance with the tall blonde,' said the major, adjusting his monocle.

'Told she's hot stuff. A man of your age must take it carefully,' quipped the officer.

'At forty, a man is in his prime,' said the major laughingly and made his way towards Eva.

Colette, who had given Ulrich his brandy, praying it would rot his liver, brushed past the major as she made her way to the door. Nicole McGragh saw her, and, excusing herself from the company of a charming young captain, followed her. She caught the girl firmly by the arm.

'Where do you think you're going?'

Colette tore herself from the madame's grip.

'For some fresh air,' she snapped, 'the atmosphere in here makes me sick.'

'Don't be too long. Otherwise Colonel Ulrich may think it ungracious,' returned Nicole.

Colette closed the double doors of the salon behind her, crossed the tiled hall and climbed the curving stairs which led to the first floor and Eva's room.

The moment she entered, Colette noticed that although the bed was made, the pillow was still creased and warm. Eva was never one to waste time. A brief smile fleeted across Colette's face. She liked Eva, even valued her, but despite the resemblance to Clair, the blonde Dane did not arouse the same yearnings. No one did. Except Nat Morgan. She thought of him as she picked up the pillow. Just as Eva had promised, there was the Luger she'd stolen from her last bedmate. When Colette picked it up, she thought it seemed a lot heavier than the pistol she'd used to kill Helm.

Colette slipped the cold gun into her dress and was about to make her way back along the corridor towards her room, when she heard voices. It was Eva leading the unsuspecting monocled major to his fate.

Looking as guilty as Adam's Eve, Colette pressed her back to the wall outside Eva's room and looked towards the carpeted floor. As the Dane and her prospective lover passed, the blonde turned and smiled at Colette.

'Did you get my present?'

The dark girl nodded, looking afraid.

'Good,' said Eva, and led the major to her room.

As soon as they were inside, the major asked, 'What on earth is the matter with her?'

'Oh nothing. She's just a bit odd, that's all.'

'She looked as if she was waiting for something.'

266

'A bus, perhaps?' They both laughed as Eva pushed him towards the bed.

Colette's lips brushed the barrel of the Luger, and she thought of the promise she'd made to Albert the day she and Clair had fought over Helm. She gripped the gun until her knuckles lost their colour.

'I will,' she breathed and repeated her threat to kill every Nazi in the place. Including Ulrich.

Yet when she followed the sound of the quartet back to the salon, he had vanished.

'He has gone to investigate a terrorist attack on the roadblock on route 13. The authorities phoned him here,' explained Nicole McGragh.

'Terrorist?' answered Colette, lifting a glass of champagne from the long table.

This time it just had to be them, thought Albert as he stepped into the road brandishing his old rifle. When he saw two Germans in a motorcycle he almost had a heart attack.

He fumbled with the bolt, cursing loudly, until he saw Morgan step out of the Mercedes: then he held his rifle high above his head with one arm waving free to greet him. The two men embraced warmly, and then Morgan took a pace backwards. 'What the hell is that?'

'My old army rifle. I am going to blow a few German heads off with it,' said the old man proudly.

'The only head that is going to be blown off, is going to be on the shoulders of the man who pulls the trigger,' said Morgan taking the rifle from him.

Morgan, Connors noticed, was becoming tenser by the second, as if he was being wound up by a large invisible key of bitter hatred. The men, now squatting in a semi-circle around Morgan and Albert, sensed it too.

Morgan, despite Albert's persistent attempts at interruption, finished briefing his men on their targets. 'Like you, the girls do not know the reason for their abduction. It is too important for anyone to be told, just believe me when I say the outcome of the war may depend upon this raid.'

He was pleased the only response from the commandos was the sound of fresh magazines being rammed into the sub-machine guns – and of Ellis spitting on the wet road.

Albert, however, was still tugging at Morgan's sleeve. 'Listen to me for God's sake. The place is crawling with Panzer Lehr officers and their escorts tonight for a special party. It is not just the usual guards and the odd visiting officer.'

Morgan's heart sank, although he dare not show it. He just said, 'That means we can use their transport back to the coast. We also don't have to risk being spotted getting this lot up the drive. Dump them in the bushes.'

As the car and motorcycle unit followed in the wake of Romeau in the truck, and ploughed through the undergrowth opposite the château walls, Morgan and Connors followed Albert towards the huge wrought-iron gates. Albert fished in his waistcoat pocket and produced a large key. But no sooner than he had lifted the padlock, he let it drop and jumped back.

'There's a car coming down the drive,' he gulped, his eyes bulging.

Connors was already bent double, running for the cover of the bushes, motioning the others to follow. Albert galloped after them, snatching back his rifle from Morgan, who drew his hand gun and remained just feet from the gates, pressed up against the wall in the darkness and invisible in the night.

He saw the faint glow of the dimmed headlights halt on the other side of the gate, then came the sound of someone unlocking the giant padlock. The gates creaked open and the bull-nose of the Horch staff car inched through until the car was clear of the gates.

Sitting in the back was Ulrich.

Morgan went cold, washed by a nausea of hate and loathing. The man he was hunting was just feet away, so close he could make out every line on his face, as Ulrich studied the map with a flexible navigation light. It would only take the one shot. A shot Morgan dared not risk so close to their target. He felt the frustration bite at him as he watched the car pull away.

Morgan turned as, one by one, his men appeared from the bushes and once again the massive gates bearing the Beaupré crest opened.

'Rosetti, take the tank gun and cover the gate. Anything that comes up or down that drive, blow it to fucking bits,' said Morgan.

Then the rest of the commandos followed Morgan and began to fan out through the shrubbery towards the château and the distant sound of a string quartet.

It was playing the 'Blue Danube'.

CHAPTER TWENTY-SIX

Morgan crawled on his belly towards the cobbled courtyard, followed by Connors and Byrne.

'It is 03.05,' said Morgan when they reached the end of the shadows. From the damp lawns they watched the lit yard and counted six staff cars, four of which were Mercedes and the others Horch. They were parked next to two open-top Auto-Union armoured cars and a motorcycle unit identical to the one Travers had dumped outside the gates. Two guards, rifles on shoulders, leant chatting on the last of the line of neatly parked cars. They were both smoking.

Their unseen watchers slid backwards to where the others were waiting on bended knees, almost not daring to breathe.

Albert, his old rifle pointing to the sky like a Zulu spear, said, 'If there are two guards in the courtyard, then it means that there are two more patrolling the grounds somewhere. I know where the bastards will be.'

'What about the staff car drivers and escort?' whispered Morgan.

'Probably pissing it up in the servants' quarters in the basement,' croaked Albert.

Morgan, from his earlier visit on the day they captured Helm, knew that this meant an attack mounted through the kitchens at the rear of the building and getting past the courtyard patrol unseen. Damn.

But he just handed Albert a torch, adding, 'You understand what you have to do?'

Albert grunted and took the torch. He inspected it as if it was a wonder of modern technology, rolling it in awe between his stubby fingers. Satisfied he could make it work, he then pulled the stub-neck bottle of Calvados from the poacher's pocket inside his crumpled jacket. This, he felt more at home with. He confidently drew the cork with his teeth and spat it out noisily. Byrne winced, clenching his teeth. Albert took a swig from the bottle, smiled as the drink burned its way to his ample stomach, wiped his mouth with his sleeve and burped.

Morgan adored him. He gave him an affectionate tap on the shoulder, a mock punch with a gentle fist.

'Let's go.' Albert adjusted his beret proudly, puffed out his chest, took another swig of Calvados, then set off clutching the bottle and swaying towards the derelict summer house, where Morgan had once hidden and where he knew two lazy Boche would be cowering from the night over a flask of schnapps.

Behind him floated the shadows of Morgan, Ellis and Romeau.

As soon as the motorcycle patrol's message had been passed to him at the château, Ulrich had gone straight to the roadblock on route 13.

The two patrolmen had been joined by a detachment of Waffen SS led by two officers. They were gathered around the two dead sentries who lay covered by greatcoats on the side of the road. The troops parted to make way for Ulrich as he marched briskly from his car towards them.

Ulrich knelt over the bodies in turn and pulled back the coats.

'Murdering terrorist bastards,' he hissed. He began to shake with rage. He strode back to his car.

'Come with me,' he told the SS officers, who followed respectfully. Ulrich made room for them in the back seat. He searched his pockets for a cigarette. One of the officers gave him one of his, the other lit it for him. Ulrich inhaled deeply, his anger almost uncontrolled as he blew out the smoke between his clenched teeth.

'Well?' he said.

'The patrol found them and called us. We called you. An obvious terrorist attack.'

'Brilliant,' Ulrich sneered. 'What have you done about it?'

'We have set up roadblocks on all main routes. I don't reckon they will get far. We acted as soon as we heard. Our people have orders to hold anyone remotely suspicious.'

'We'll get them the moment they try to get through. They cannot get out,' the first officer added.

'Except they won't use a main route,' Ulrich said flatly. Both men coughed and shifted in the seat.

'But, Colonel,' one protested, 'it would be impossible to cover all the roads. We just don't have the men.'

Ulrich paused. 'I will not permit outrages like this to take place. They must be stopped in this area for once and all. They are an affront to the authority we must be seen to represent.

'These people must be taught a lesson for once and all time. Where is the nearest village to the roadblock?'

An SS officer took out a road map. He lit his lighter while the other studied it.

'As the crow flies, it would be Ste-Yvette.'

'Ste-Yvette,' Ulrich repeated. 'You two come with me back to my hotel in Lisieux. We are going to have a busy night ahead. So are the villagers of Ste-Yvette.'

As Albert moved unsteadily towards the summer house, Connors and Byrne edged silently towards the line of parked staff cars and the two men who guarded them.

On the lawns below them, Albert took another swig of Calvados. Then he began to sing the French national anthem at the top of his voice. 'Allons enfants de la Patrie, le jour de glaire est arrivé. La La La La . . . La La La La La. Boom Bom Ba Bom Ba Boom Ba Boom . . .'

He rolled forward, pausing only to take another swig and adjust his jacket.

'Hey, hey you in there,' he slurred. 'You bastard Boche, come out and fight. Let's see what you're made of.'

Then he sang his anthem again, only louder than the first time. The two bemused guards peered through the gaps in the jagged splinters of the rotting wooden wall. Albert shone his torch at them.

'I can see you. You're both yellow,' he hiccupped loudly, taking yet another swig. 'Come on out and fight, you Boche pigs.' The soldiers grinned at each other, put down their rifles and stepped out into the open through the gaps in the wall.

In the shadows of the terrace, Connors and Byrne both cursed as the guards moved their position to see what was going on below. They were now standing in the full glare of the shaft of light flooding from a château window. As long as they remained there, they were safe. One of them called down to the commotion below: 'What the hell's going on?'

'Nothing,' called back the nearest soldier to Albert. 'It's only that crazy old odd-job man. He's drunk, pissed as a newt.'

'Well, shut him up. We've got all the top brass up here.'

'We'll bring him up and you can lock the old goat up until he's sober.'

Albert raised his fist. 'You,' he said as, between swigs, he squared up to the soldiers, 'you and whose army, eh? Hitler's? Bah.'

271

Both torch and bottle fell to the ground as the soldiers each took an arm, turned him, and began to frog-march him towards the château terrace. They had barely started, when the razor-sharp garrotting wires sliced into their necks.

As Albert bent to pick up his bottle, he noticed one of the dead soldier's legs still twitched in involuntary spasm.

'Pick up the torch too,' said Morgan, balancing on the balls of his feet and looking towards the terrace. He saw the soldiers still in the safety shroud of light.

'Bring the old fool up,' called one. Morgan dug Romeau in the ribs, and Romeau said, 'Ja.' It was the only German he knew, gleaned from watching a Noel Coward movie on the evils of Nazi Germany.

'Let's have another chorus,' said Morgan handing Albert the torch. The unsteady beam dipped and swayed as it neared the terrace. They made their way to the end furthest from the light. Only feet from the dividing line of darkness, the guards saw the light fall to the ground and go out. Then the singing began again, louder than ever.

'Christ,' cursed one of the guards, 'can't they keep the buffoon quiet?'

'Let's give them a hand to get him inside,' said the other. Connors and Byrne waited until they had moved from the light, and then sprang.

It was now 03.20 and less than one hundred minutes from the May dawn. The raid on Lisieux was one hour forty minutes behind schedule.

Ulrich knew it was going to be more bad news the moment he walked into his office at the Hôtel Chloé in Lisieux. He could tell by the expression on his night clerk's face. Ulrich motioned the two SS officers from the roadblock to sit and he took the phone. He sat on his desk.

Seconds later he was back on his feet, eyes wide and mouth open. He listened, screwing up his lips. He said just one word.

'Bastards.'

Then he slammed the phone down.

'What is it?' asked the SS officer.

Ulrich was shaking. 'I'll decimate them.'

'Who, sir?' Both officers were standing strictly to attention as they spoke.

'Those fucking troublemakers from the Resistance have murdered the entire command post and patrol units between

Houlgate and Villiers-sur-Mer.' He added with disbelief, 'And they used weapons stolen from us to do it. Our own men killed with German weapons. Two dead at the roadblock was bad enough – but now this – an entire coastal command post wiped out. They will pay dear for this.' His voice fell to almost a whisper. 'I shall teach them a lesson they will never forget. We will show them who are the masters here.'

He picked up the phone. 'I want as many men and as much hardware as you can spare, sent to the area between Houlgate and Villiers-sur-Mer. Replenish the command post and scour the whole area. I want these terrorists dead or alive . . . of course you can take bloody tanks if you think you need them. Move.'

He turned to the SS men. 'You, contact your garrison. I want a complete detachment of troops and I want them now.'

'Yes, Colonel. Where will they be needed?'

'Ste-Yvette.'

It was 03.24.

The moment the first SS trooper's feet hit the cold stone floor, every phone in the Château Beaupré went dead. Then Appleby rejoined the others and put the wire cutters back in his trouser pocket. Then, without being asked, all of them checked their weapons. Connors tutted his contempt as Crowski fiddled all fingers and thumbs to load his Luger.

'Ready?' said Morgan. The silence meant yes, and the men divided into groups. Morgan guessed, and he hated guesswork, that all the girls, except Colette, would be in the salon with the madame and the twelve Panzer officers. They would be taken by Connors, Crowski, Machen and Martin.

The escort and drivers, he hoped, would be getting pleasantly drunk in the basement servants' quarters; some, with luck, might even be asleep. They were the job of Byrne, Appleby, Romeau and Travers. First they would lob in grenades followed up with rapid fire, then double back to reinforce Connors.

Morgan and Ellis would be first into the château through Colette's window and work their way down to the salon. At 03.25 Connors would burst into the salon; ten seconds earlier Byrne would pull the pin from the first grenade. That, anyway, was the plan.

They synchronised watches, then moved off towards their allotted targets, leaving old Albert to stand guard.

'Look-out be buggered,' he said indignantly, waddling in the wake of Connors and his men.

Morgan tossed a handful of gravel at the lighted third-floor window. Inside the room Colette shoved the Luger under the pillow and moved to the lattice, undid the catch and flung open the window. It was time, at last. She looked down and saw two unrecognisable shapes, then a rope snaked through the window and curled on the floor behind her.

She fastened the slip knot onto the bedpost. It began to slide slowly towards the window under the strain of the man scaling the wall outside. Then she saw Nat Morgan standing on the window sill.

Colette, her heart pumping with delight, rushed to him, wrapped her arms around his waist and pressed her head against his chest. He bent and kissed her dark hair, holding the trembling little figure tightly until Ellis was standing beside them. Nat lifted her chin and brushed his lips along her forehead. 'This,' he said without looking at Ellis, 'is a lovely lady called Colette Claval.'

She blushed.

'Are all the others in the salon?' asked Morgan.

Colette shook her head. 'Eva, Annette and Benedite are ... entertaining in their rooms,' she said.

Both men drew their guns and moved towards the door.

'Show us,' said Morgan.

Byrne's party had reached the back of the château. He looked at his watch, took a pin from the grenade, counted for five seconds, then hurled it through the window. As he did so, Romeau kicked open the door and Travers and Appleby dropped on to one knee each side of him. They all squinted instinctively as the grenade rolled towards the men sitting around the large wooden table. The grenade came to rest against one of the legs. Nothing. It failed to explode. Then Appleby and Travers opened fire.

A German on the far side of the table, leapt to his feet and turned it onto its side. The five soldiers who had been sitting nearest the door were now lying dead on the floor, cut down by the raking gunfire, as was the first man who had managed to open the door which led to the stone passage beyond. The soldiers behind the table were using it as a shield and dragging it towards the passage door and safety. These men were also giving as good as they got in the exchange of fire. Although Byrne's men were flooding the room with non-stop rapid fire, they were kept outside the building.

Then Byrne, seemingly oblivious of the return fire, appeared in the doorway. In one hand he held the smoking gun, his finger pressing the trigger, and with the other, he lobbed a grenade underhanded behind the table which now barricaded the passage doorway. This time the hand bomb exploded in a flash of noise which filled the air with blood and innards.

When it cleared, two men dangled grotesquely over the gore-stained table. But fresh automatic fire was now coming from the passage beyond.

'Sweet Jesus,' cursed Byrne. 'We are never going to get see these old whores, never mind getting them all back to England. It's a fine mess.'

At the first sound of shooting, Nicole McGragh screamed, dropped her champagne glass and held her hands to her cheeks. Behind her, the string quartet fell backwards off their chairs, and were struggling to free themselves from the tangled mass of arms, legs, violins and cellos, as Connors burst through the door. He sprayed the air as a warning, but it only added to panic and terror sweeping the room as whores and officers scattered in all directions.

From the corner of his eye, Martin caught a movement which he swung round to face, firing his sub-machine gun wildly from the hip. Four unarmed musicians slumped back to the floor.

Connors knocked Martin's arm upwards and the fire brought the heavy glass chandelier crashing down in the centre of the room, crushing the Panzer officer standing beneath it with his hands in the air.

'You'll hit the girls. Don't hit the damn girls, for Christ's sake.' Machen and Crowski were now in the doorway.

Crowski was yelling, 'Nobody move,' at the top of his voice, but he was too late. Four of the seven Panzer officers had already fled the room.

It was utter pandemonium.

At the time when Byrne had first pulled the pin from the dud grenade, the monocled major was lying back on the bed with a contented smile as he watched the vision which was Eva slip into her lace panties and clip tight her matching black bra.

He leapt from the bed at the first sound of gunfire, but it was, for him, already too late. Eva had closed the heavy oak door and was turning the key in the lock from the corridor outside.

As the officer tugged vainly on the handle, Eva turned and saw

Ellis walking towards her. The major was now bellowing his head off for Eva to unlock the door.

Ellis motioned Eva back, drew a grenade and pulled the pin with his teeth and counted up to five. He then unlocked the door, which flew open, and the major, still tugging at the handle, fell sprawling backwards.

Ellis rolled in the grenade then slammed the door shut and locked it. The major, his eyes popping with terror, crawled frantically towards the grenade. He picked it up, brought back his arm to hurl it through the window. Then it exploded.

'Right, lads, in,' shouted Byrne, emptying his magazine into the passage. The men dived for the cover of the upturned table and pushed away the two corpses. Byrne joined them and he could hear the sound of the screaming and shooting from the salon upstairs. He prayed he was not going to be too late. If Nat Morgan said these girls were vital, then vital they were. One thing Morgan never did was to exaggerate, but Byrne still hadn't a clue why anyone should want to kidnap these ladies of the night.

'Sure, there's more than enough working Dublin docks without having to come all this way to get us some more,' he thought as Romeau fired a burst down the passage. The fire was not returned.

Appleby made to rise. Byrne pulled him back roughly.

'Stay put, you idiot.' No sooner had he spoken, than one of the bloodstained heap they'd left for dead on the kitchen floor behind them began to move. He eased himself from under the body of his dead comrade, and felt his face where the flesh had once been. His whimper turned to a scream and he leapt to his feet.

As he did so, a burst of automatic fire spat from the passageway, and the German, a boy of no more than eighteen, died instantly.

'I told you so,' said Byrne to Appleby and pulled the pin from another grenade. 'Now after this one, I'd like to introduce you to some very important young ladies. The type you'd be proud to take home to meet your Ma.'

He hurled the grenade. The passage was now clear.

As the gunfire echoed through the château, Colette led Morgan to Annette's room. He kicked open the door without ceremony, and saw the girl, fully clothed in a long evening dress, standing in the corner holding her clenched hands to her mouth and screaming hysterically.

Her bed mate was halfway through the window onto the balcony beyond. When he saw Morgan, he redoubled his efforts but the moment the balcony took his full weight, it crumpled like rotten timber. A scream ended with a sickening thud. Morgan stuck his head out of the window and saw the twisted figure lying motionless on the terrace below.

He turned and saw Colette trying to calm Annette. Her efforts were futile and Morgan moved to the bed and shook the pillow from its case. He tried to soothe the girl and said reassuringly in French: 'We are here to help you not hurt you. Please, love, try to keep calm.'

Annette, engulfed with terror, was beyond reason and although it pained him, Morgan was forced to slip the pillow case over her head and tied it with her dressing-gown cord just below her breasts. He then fastened the cord to the bedpost, apologised, and left her sitting on the bed wailing her heart out.

The moment he stepped out into the corridor, he froze. His hand motioned Colette to move back to the safety of the room.

At the far end of the corridor was Ellis. His legs were bent slightly at the knee and both his hands gripped the handle of the pistol which he held out straight in front of him like a police marksman. Backing up towards Morgan was a Panzer officer. One arm was locked around the throat of Benedite Philippe. The other held the pistol pressed against her right temple.

From where he stood, Morgan could have willingly blown the back of the Nazi's skull apart, but he knew that the man's reflex action would trigger the shot and the girl would be killed. He placed his gun on the carpet and unsheathed his dagger, calling Ellis forward with his hand to ensure the German kept backing towards him.

Ellis inched forward, the barrel of his revolver pointing at the centre of the German's retreating forehead. Morgan could hear the girl's fight for breath, and shifting his weight to the balls of his feet, raised his right hand until he was sure it was at exactly the same level as the wrist of the German's gun arm. He dropped his left shoulder to add to the momentum he would need for the dagger's upward thrust.

Slowly, very slowly, Ellis, the whites of his rolling eyes widening, crept forward, his gun steady as a rock. Morgan dare not breathe as the soldier's wrist moved nearer the open hand he held as steady as a steel claw.

Now. The flame from the German's pistol singed a frizzed path through Benedite's hair as Morgan twisted the man's wrist upwards in a vice-like grip. By the time that the bullet sent a shower of plaster down from the ornate ceiling, Morgan's dagger had found its mark.

Morgan picked up the trembling Benedite and led her gently towards Annette's room. The moment she saw the hooded figure on the bed next to Colette, she, too, started to scream. This time it was Ellis who bound her.

As soon as he finished, shots rang out from below and echoed up the stairwell towards them.

It was, as Albert later proudly claimed, only his presence in the main doorway clutching his faithful rifle that prevented the pandemonium in the salon turning into an absolute fiasco. Because he blocked the main exit, the fleeing officers turned and ran up the stairs in the centre of the grand hall. Halfway up, these stairs broke to the left and right from a small landing to join the minstrels' gallery circling the first floor.

Albert's first shot was wild; the second succeeded only in bringing down an antique collection of two spear-tipped axes and an oval copper shield from the wall of the half-landing. For the third shot, he carefully picked his spot on the gallery, took aim, and waited for the running officer to come into his sights. Then he squeezed the trigger. At first the man seemed to raise his hands in a gesture of surrender, then he turned and folded neatly over the balcony rail, crashing onto the black and white tiles at Albert's feet.

A rapid burst from Machen sprayed the stairs and brought down the second man, but the third drew his pistol, let off a shot, before disappearing around the corner. He ran in the direction of a screaming girl and a single shot.

Connors, with Crowski as his unlikely ally, were hard on the heels of the fourth man, a young captain with a reputation for valour. As he scampered up the stairs, he felt Connors's breath on his neck and turned to swing out with his jackboot. It caught Arnie Connors square on the chin and sent him sprawling back down the stairs to crash into Crowski on the half-landing.

'Fuckin' faggot,' cursed Connors, picking himself up and launching himself back up the stairs, taking them on all fours. Two steps from the top he half-straightened and saw he was facing the barrel of a Luger pointing at the bridge of his nose. From the corner of his eye, he saw Crowski's sub-machine gun bump down the first flight of stairs and smack against the tiled floor of the hall.

'This is it,' he thought as the German moved back, his knuckles whitening as his finger closed around the gun in his hand.

Then a blur flashed past Connors's ear, and he saw the German's eyes widen in agony as a flood of blood and vomit gushed from his mouth, killing his death scream of pain.

The spear-tipped axe had passed straight through his solar plexus and impaled him to the wooden panelling behind him. The heels of his jackboots swung like a slow pendulum.

Connors turned back towards Crowski, who stood mouth agape, taking in what he had done. The men's eyes met, and they both nodded.

A burst of machine-gun fire came from the direction in which the other officer had fled.

'Guess Morgan has just made it four,' said Crowski.

Connors closed his eyes. 'Crowski, I thank you,' he said.

'Oh, my,' came the reply. They turned and walked back down the stairs, Crowski pausing to pick up his gun.

Albert, marvelling at what he'd just seen, was almost knocked off his feet when the door to the basement flew open. It was Byrne who was quickly followed by the others. They scanned the carnage through the film of smoke rising from their glowing guns.

'Too late,' said Albert. 'You have missed it all.'

'Is that a fact now,' said Byrne. 'Where are the others?' Albert pointed his rifle towards the now closed double doors of the salon.

As he swung them open, the first thing Byrne saw was the crushed body which still lay sprawled under the chandelier. Standing in front of the upturned drinks table amid the broken glasses were the remaining officers holding their hands in the air, their faces masked in disbelief.

Trussed up on the floor with the pillow cases still over their heads were Annette and Benedite. They still lay kicking and screaming where Morgan and Ellis had dumped them.

'We'll have to gag and bind them. They are beyond reason,' said Morgan. Even Crowski's soothing charm had failed to calm them and now he carried out Morgan's instructions.

Morgan moved to the Regency-style settee where Elaine Bisset sat wringing her hands and mumbling incoherently with shock. He knelt in front of her and said softly, 'Listen, you're safe now, and free.'

'That's right,' said Maria putting her arm around the girl's shoulders to comfort her. 'They are going to take us all to England.'

Elaine came to her senses as quickly as if she had been doused with a bucket of cold water. She jumped to her feet. 'No, you must not take me, I can't go. I won't go, not without my baby.'

She began to pound her fists against Morgan's chest. 'My baby, I want my baby. I won't leave my Alain, I won't.'

Morgan, saddened by what he was about to do, turned to Crowski and said quietly, as if words offended him, 'Gag and bind her.'

As Crowski led Elaine away, Maria, eyes flashing, moved towards Nicole McGragh. 'That's what they do before they shoot people who deal with the Nazis,' she taunted.

Connors was now at Maria's shoulder. He pointed to the Breton. 'What about her?'

The madame went white. 'Don't you dare lay a finger on me.'

'Lady,' said Connors, 'for a part-time brothel-keeper, you sure put on the style.'

'Will you please cut that sort of talk out in front of the lady. There's no need for it at all,' Byrne said as he pushed between Connors and Nicole.

'God save us from the Irish,' mumbled Connors.

'There's no need to ask which side of the family you got that old temper from, now is there?' Byrne's face cracked into a smile of a thousand lines. 'You sound just like me cousin Catlin. As fine a looking girl, too, by the looks of it. You should have been on the stage.'

Nicole could not help the smile.

'Now that's a lot better than all this fighting and feudin'. God knows we've seen more than enough of all that thing already.'

'Are you going to kill me?' Nicole sounded frightened and glanced at Maria, who stood glaring at her.

'Whoever heard of such a thing. But I can tell you what. Those German fellows might just do that,' Byrne said.

'And you say the English won't harm me, any of us,' said Nicole.

'And who are you calling English now. Even the man in charge over there isn't English, what more could you ask for.' Byrne grinned again.

'You give me your word no one will harm me. Your word personally.'

Byrne tweaked her cheek. 'On the grave of St. Brendan.'

He moved towards Morgan.

Then Nicole said to Maria, 'You see. I survive.'

'Slut,' snapped the Italian.

'That's enough. Shut up,' barked Morgan who turned as Colette came into the room. She was ashen-faced, and carrying the Luger she'd hidden under her pillow. Colette turned towards the German officers, raised the pistol, and said calmly, 'I'm going to kill you filthy bastards. For Clair.'

Open-mouthed, they all stepped back as one, and Connors moved quickly and grabbed for the gun, knocking Colette's arm upwards. In the time it took for the deafening report to echo away, the German officers broke line and made a bolt for the windows leading out onto the terrace. Machen and Appleby's machine guns spat fire and cut the fugitives to pieces.

'Oh God,' mumbled Connors.

'We could not have left them alive anyway, sir,' said Byrne, 'and I think it's time we were on our way.'

The hooded girls were all struggling furiously as Martin, Travers and Romeau hoisted them over their shoulders and followed the others to the waiting cars.

As they piled the girls into the back of two Mercedes, Ellis asked, 'Where's the blonde?'

Eva was missing.

'Find her, quick,' said Morgan, and Ellis turned and ran back into the château of silent death. He stood at the foot of the corpse-strewn stairs and listened to his voice echoing her name.

Then she appeared on the balcony of the gallery above him. She was still wearing only her bra and panties.

'You told me to stay in Colette's room,' she explained.

'Come on and get your ass down here,' yelled Ellis.

'You like it?' pouted Eva posing in a half-turn.

'Best I've ever seen. Now come on,' urged Ellis. As she walked down the stairs, Ellis removed the jacket from a dead officer.

'Put this on,' he said. Eva turned and held her arms out and he slipped the jacket over them. It was about three sizes too big, covering half her thighs and most of her fingers. Ellis buttoned it for her.

'You English?' she asked.

'American.'

'I like Americans very much,' she said, slipping her arm through his as he led her towards the door.

Seconds later the cars moved off, led by Byrne at the wheel of one of the open armoured cars. Albert, proudly clutching his rifle, sat at his side as navigator.

Still at his post, Rosetti turned as they approached. He heard Crowski sing: 'Don't shoot now, it's only us.'

'Shurrup,' snapped Byrne. Rosetti slung the anti-tank gun over his shoulder and climbed into the armoured car alongside Crowski.

'Oh shit,' he complained, 'I really wanted to be able to tell my kids that I hoisted a real live general, an' all we got ourselves is some hookers.'

'Oh but they're so cute,' said Crowski.

'And bloody important,' said Byrne, 'and I don't want to hear another word until we get everyone back on the submarine.'

It was now 03.40 hours.

'I will concede,' said Ulrich looking at the map he'd hung on his hotel office wall, 'that the leader of this Resistance group is a man to be reckoned with. The raid on the coastal command post was quite brilliant and I, personally, shall be the one who puts a bullet through his skull. But before he and his terrorists die, they will have learnt the price of their stupid gesture. I can't wait to see if this man thinks the cost of his night's actions are worth it.'

'The car is here,' said the junior SS officer.

'Good,' said Ulrich, adjusting his cap as he made for the door. 'Let's pay the good people of Ste-Yvette a visit and see how long it takes to flush this Napoleon of guerrilla warfare into the open. In Spain, our friend Franco had just the right approach towards such scum.'

Morgan, in the back of the first Mercedes, reached out and clasped Colette's hand.

Thanks to Albert's knowledge of the winding Normandy lanes, they were making up on lost time as they sped through the vanishing night towards the beach. The girls he was taking there on their way to London, would influence the decision whether, in less than a month's time, British troops would hit the shore three miles from their departure point or not. The Overlord code for those sands was 'Sword'.

He noticed the car's windscreen wiper was fighting a losing battle against the mud thrown up from the Auto-Union armoured car in front. Morgan knew the feeling; he put it down to his self-defeatist Welshness. No one ever beat the Welsh, he thought. They didn't have to. The Welsh themselves could always be relied on to do it for them. The worst just had to be behind them. Even though he had not come face to face with Ulrich, he had only lost two men, Scott and Davies, and had taken all the girls – and he had Colette. He was on the last lap home where his men would split up and he'd probably never see any of them again. He would get them all pissed, they deserved it.

There were only about three miles to go and the low black blanket of cloud kept the first rays of the rising May sun at bay. He knew the Marines waiting in the dinghies to ferry them aboard the sub would not turn tail, yet the melancholy still spread over him like spilt ink.

Colette completed the sense of rising doom when she looked up and said: 'We forgot to bring the tapes.'

Ulrich's taped treasures were still at the château. On them the voices and fears of all the now dead Panzer Lehr officers, drafted to Normandy from Poland.

'Uffern!' Morgan conjured a Welsh curse from the pit of Satan's flames. His mind began to race through the options but he found he had none. There was no way he could go back, which made it now more important than ever to get the girls back to London. The tapes may still have been in the château basement, but there was much more in the heads of the girls, now sweeping towards the rendezvous with a submarine.

'What's that?' said Ellis turning his head from the driver's seat.

'Uffern? Nothing, it's just Welsh for . . .'

'Not that,' said Ellis, '. . . that.'

Morgan saw the glow of light from the quarry. The armoured car in front had already stopped and Crowski was clawing his way to the top of the ridge towards the track leading to the command post. They had destroyed it only hours before, yet it was now glowing with fresh light. Romeau, on Byrne's orders, was sprinting after him, chased by Morgan, who dived onto the wet grass beside them.

He saw the quarry bathed in an unreal white light beamed from the generator-powered arc lamps to the wire fence and cliff top above the excavated hole housing the command post offices. Four dead men sprawled on the steps leading to the office – they'd opened the booby-trapped door. Dozens of armed troops milled around the compound in apparent confusion and, spaced at regular intervals along the track to the road, were three Tiger tanks – armour of the Panzer Lehr at Caen.

The sound of barking dogs came from the direction of the cliff-top gun emplacements, which meant the whole area was crawling with searching soldiers who must have found the bodies of Scott and Davies.

'Get Appleby and Byrne up here. Move,' Morgan told Crowski who vanished down the ridge, passing Connors on his way up.

'Krauts,' intoned Crowski, 'there are hundreds of them crawling all over the place, big tanks too. All for some hookers.'

Connors, tearing at the turf, kept going until he lay alongside Morgan and Romeau. 'Looks as if someone is pretty anxious to keep us from getting out of here – and that is something we didn't bargain for,' he said.

Morgan bit his lip: 'Why? How did they know we were here? The phones and radio were taken care of.'

'Maybe a routine patrol.'

'Unlikely.'

Connors agreed.

Morgan wasted no time when Byrne and Appleby arrived. He asked Byrne first, 'Was Scott dead when you left him?'

Byrne's nod was enough.

'Davies?' he asked Appleby, 'what about Davies?'

'Must have been.'

'What the fucking hell do you mean "must"?'

'Well, there was blood and guts everywhere. He took it face-on, stomach and chest. No chance at all.'

'But was he dead when you left him? Did you check?'

'I didn't take his pulse, if that's what you mean. But he wasn't making a sound. No moans, nothing. He was just lying there, poor bastard.'

'But you weren't sure he was dead.'

'It was like I said.'

Morgan paused, his face lined with concern, then asked: 'Appleby, why did you think we came on this raid? The truth.'

'I thought we were going to lift Rommel, or some other high-up general.'

'We all did, that's for sure,' echoed Byrne.

'Looks like they do too,' said Connors indicating with his head at the army of ants below.

'We must have missed or just wounded one of the patrol and he could have found Davies, who was not dead,' said Morgan.

'He looked dead,' said Appleby, 'no sound or nothing.'

'OK, Appleby,' said Morgan, 'not your fault. Get back to the others.'

As he moved off, Morgan looked at Byrne: 'What would you do if you were amongst that lot down there?'

Byrne thought before answering. At last he said: 'I'd sit tight and wait for us to come walking back, then ... bingo.'

'That's about it,' agreed Connors.

'And exactly what they are going to do,' said Morgan. 'They'll have the beach and cliffs covered, waiting for us to walk into their hands. But they can't have arrived long, otherwise they would have had this ridge and the road covered. That means they can't know about the château yet, or how many there are of us and how much firepower we've got. That's why they've brought in Tiger tanks. They are not sure what's happening. Fetch Albert and that anti-tank gun up here.'

Romeau vanished and minutes later returned with Albert and the Russian weapon.

Albert flopped, wheezing, onto the grass, and held out his hand to fend off any questions until he had caught his breath back. At long last he managed to croak: 'We have, I think, a slight problem,' and mopped his brow. Morgan appreciated the classic gift of Gallic understatement which the French always use to illustrate a point.

'It is,' added Albert, 'going to be a little difficult for you to make it to the submarine – no? – for the present, at least.' He put away the lucky red and white spotted handkerchief he used to mop his forehead.

Morgan sank on to his haunches, plucked a blade of grass and sucked it slowly to savour the dew.

'Cool bastard,' thought Connors, who by now was beginning to get worried. After all, they had the girls in whose minds lay the fate of Europe ... and they were caught like rats in a trap. He looked up in desperation and saw in the sky the black clouds were beginning to grey in face of the advancing dawn. His anxiety would have multiplied if he could have known that aboard the submarine waiting offshore, Commander Dickensen had given the order to pull out. As far as he was concerned, watching the flood of light on land through his peeping periscope, the mission, whatever it was, had failed.

Morgan would never have accepted that. He turned to the old Frenchman and said: 'Albert, it is vital, absolutely vital, we get all of these girls back to England, more important than you realise.'

'Perhaps,' shrugged Albert. 'Perhaps not.'

'We,' said Morgan emphasising the word heavily, 'need somewhere to hide these girls as it is now obvious we are not going to get out tonight. We need time, maybe a day or two to think, just until the hue and cry dies down.'

Albert loved responsibility and rolled his tongue over his lips. 'What about the church of St-Samson at Ste-Yvette? We can, using my route, be there in less than half an hour.'

'What about the risk of us getting spotted?' asked Connors.

'That's why Romeau is going to stay here with me for a while to keep the anti-tank gun company. Leave us the armoured car and the rest of you go with Albert and, with a bit of luck, I'll see you for breakfast.'

As Connors and the old man moved back down the hill to seek refuge with the girls, Morgan took in the scene below him. Ideally he would have liked to knock out the Tiger tank nearest to the beach road first, but it was the only tank without its crew inside. The men standing around it were chatting. The other crews were in their machines, which meant they could move and fire back immediately. Morgan chose the tank parked in front of the quarry gate as his first target. It would block the exit and keep the soldiers trapped inside the compound until they could tear down the fence.

As soon as he heard the engines of his hijacked staff cars make their run for freedom, he fired at the tank. The shell smashed into the Tiger's tracks, and, seconds later, a second shell punched a jagged hole through the armour plate. The turret hatch flew open and men leapt for safety as a pall of black smoke poured out, followed by flames and the fierce rip of the exploding ammunition. The compound was now sealed off.

The turret of the middle Tiger swung towards its attacker and the barrel of its giant KWK 36 gun scanned the ridge like a deadly finger. Its shell could pierce armour three inches thick from a distance of a thousand yards. Morgan and Romeau were just one hundred yards away. Then fifty-six tonnes of tank jerked back under the momentum of its own firepower as its shell ploughed a deep furrow in the ridge twenty yards from the two commandos. At that moment Morgan's attention was focused on the crew of the unmanned tank, who made an inviting target as they scrambled aboard. They never made it, vanishing in the midst of a direct hit from the ridge.

Now there was just the one remaining tank, and it was lumbering up the hill towards Morgan and Romeau, the sound of the machine gun housed under the mighty main barrel drowned by the din from the screaming V-12 Maybach petrol engine at full throttle.

Morgan and Romeau ran crouching towards it, both men aware they would only get one chance. Then Morgan knelt on one knee, the gun steady on his shoulder, as Romeau sprinted to his left followed by the accusing KWK 36, which swung after him. Then, as the metal monster reared to clamber over a fallen log, Morgan fired at the soft casing of its underbelly. The steel crab died with a moan like rolling thunder.

When the men reached the top of the ridge again, Romeau took the anti-tank gun from Morgan and angled it at sixty degrees so that shells dropped from the sky like mortars into the quarry compound. Then, the two men ran for the road.

As the snub-nosed armoured car crashed through the undergrowth to the lane which led to Ste-Yvette, Morgan noticed the grey edges of black clouds were tinged pink. He was not sure if it was caused by the first rays of the rising sun or the glow of burning tanks.

As the sun's rays turned from pink to orange, Father Delon sat alone fingering his rosary in his favourite leather armchair in front of the two red and white china dogs guarding the unlit fire. He was a man deeply troubled by worry and doubt. Less than five minutes earlier, he had agreed to Nat Morgan's plan that the whores and the men who had abducted them could claim the sanctuary of his church belfry. Morgan had been honest about the risks of reprisal the Germans would wreak when the full extent of the mayhem became clear, but Delon thought it his reluctant duty to help.

The knock on the door which broke his thoughts was a gentle one. He rose, still clutching his rosary, and shuffled down the passage. He opened the door and saw Ulrich standing on the doorstep flanked by his two SS minions. They brushed past the cleric without saying a word and, as Father Delon closed the door, he saw the SS troopers pouring from the trucks which had parked in the village square.

So this was it. As Swordfish, Father Delon had often wondered how the end would come. For his predecessor, André Pratt the chemist, it had been quick and heroic in a hail of bullets. Now they had come for him, and it was all so ordinary. The three Germans could have equally just dropped by for a cup of morning coffee. The scene seemed so mundane it was unreal, not at all like the nightmare he had feared onc day he would have to face.

Someone, Delon guessed, must have seen the commandos with blacked-out faces carrying the struggling girls into his church, followed by Albert and the others. Someone must have seen – and betrayed them. He felt sad that anyone could do a thing like that.

Ulrich and the others had still not spoken a word. They all stood side by side fixing the priest with their glares. Because the priest could think of nothing else to say, he asked, 'Shall I make some coffee?'

'Priest,' Ulrich growled, 'I have not come here to discuss cold-blooded murder over a cup of coffee. Last night terrorists killed the sentries at a roadblock and wiped out an entire coastal command post. Probability suggests these murdering bastards came from, or were supported by, the people of your village.'

Father Delon gave up a silent prayer of thanks as his nimble mind began to function again. Ulrich did not yet know about the château. There was still hope for Morgan's whores.

'If the Resistance did what you say,' asked Father Delon, 'how can you be sure that the people of Ste-Yvette are involved?'

'The word is "terrorist" and I have not come here to debate semantics, but to teach you French scum a lesson you will never forget. What you will do, priest, is hand me the murderers by noon today. In the meantime, you will select twelve of your precious flock and take them to the church. If you do not hand over the terrorists by noon, then I shall shoot one of the villagers you have selected every thirty minutes until I have the killers responsible. Understood?'

Father Delon felt his legs buckle and leant on the table for support.

'You place me in an impossible position. We know nothing of the men you are hunting, yet you ask me to choose twelve innocent people to die. I cannot,' said Delon with dignity.

288

'Then, Holy Father, you'd better ask your god for help in finding the killers. My men will withdraw to the outskirts of the village for just two hours. By that time you will have selected my dozen hostages. If not ...' Ulrich tapped the palm of his black-gloved hand with his baton, '... then I shall take thirty – to begin with. Good day.'

Four minutes later Father Delon knelt alone in front of his high altar and prayed for guidance. The decision he faced was the most difficult of his life. Either he handed over the fugitives concealed in his belfry, or he signed the death warrant of innocent men, women and children.

Father Delon rose slowly and followed the echo of his lonely footsteps as he climbed the spiral stairs to the tower of his church. He opened the belfry's tiny door to the accompaniment of the safety catches being drawn back on the waiting guns beyond. In the cobweb gloom, his heavy eyes picked out the four hooded women bound together by their wrists in the corner, one of them still sobbing convulsively. He acknowledged Colette, who sat alone and cross-legged on the floor. Her head was bowed as if in meditation, her hands clasped tightly around the Luger in her lap. Eva slept, her head resting on Ellis's shoulder, and behind them stood Maria, her arms folded defiantly.

The commandos lowered their guns and Nat Morgan moved forward and thrust out his hand with a smile. The priest wrung it as he repeated Ulrich's threat. He was heard out in total silence and when he finished only Connors spoke. He said: 'Oh, my God.'

'That bastard,' broke in Morgan who now knew the tables were turning full circle. The spectre that was Ulrich was now stalking him, using the lives of children to lure Morgan into the open.

'I am afraid even if you left now and risked making a run for it, that would still not prevent the executions,' said Delon. 'Ulrich wants his vengeance.'

'Father,' said Morgan slowly, 'I want you to refuse to pick any hostages.'

The priest protested, 'That means more than a dozen will die.'

'It means that we have an extra few hours, more, by the time he has rounded up his thirty victims. By that time someone is going to go looking for the missing Panzer officers, and when they get to the château, no one is going to be looking for members of the Resistance. They will be hunting us.'

Then Colette looked up. 'That will not stop the madman. I know him. He will delight in what he is threatening.'

Morgan's black eyes burned resolutely. 'He is going to be too busy with other things on his hands. Trust me, Father, go home and wait.'

'I'll always trust you,' replied Delon. 'But what happens when the time comes? Who dies, my people or you? That is the choice.'

Then the priest turned and left quietly to return to his prayers.

Morgan called his men around him. His voice cracked with emotion as he said: 'I must ask some of us to sacrifice our lives . . .'

CHAPTER TWENTY-SEVEN

Major-General Max Salmouth looked out of the salon window at the corpses which were laid out in three neat rows of army stretchers in the château courtyard. Parked along the drive stood the line of military ambulances with their distinctive red crosses painted on the roof and sides. Leaning against the back door of the last vehicle was the young Panzer Lehr private who had helped lift down his commanding officer from the gallery wall. He had still been pinned to it by the spear-tipped axe impaled through his body. The boy was still retching and the bile from his now empty stomach burnt his throat like acid.

'Butchers,' murmured Salmouth, and moved away from the window. 'Animals. I want them caught.'

Behind him, his aide put down the re-connected phone.

'I am afraid the position is even worse than we feared,' he said grimly. 'They have created havoc on the beach. We have lost three of our Tiger tanks and a lot more men. But they have failed to escape.'

Salmouth clasped his hands behind his back and paced the bloodstained carpet.

'That is some consolation. It is only a matter of time before we catch them. Now, what about this fool of an SS Colonel Ulrich?'

'We have still been unable to raise him on the phone.'

'So he still does not know about the carnage here?'

'No. He still thinks he is chasing a bunch of thugs from the Resistance, tying up valuable time and men in Ste-Yvette.'

'The fool. Can't he see we've got an enemy raiding party on the loose who just attempted – and failed – to kidnap the cream of the Panzer Lehr corps? The man is an idiot.'

Morgan finished outlining his plan: 'It's the greatest price I can ask you to pay but I cannot tell you why it is so important we must – must – get these girls back to England.'

Appleby rose and rubbed the stubble on his chin. 'The way I see it, it's mostly down to me we are still all stuck here. If I'd made sure Davies was dead, we all would have been home by now. Besides, I think we have got a fighting chance out there.'

Then Machen stood up and added, 'The chances do not look so good, even if I stay here, and there is no way I'm going out waving a white flag – not after what we've done.'

'Ah well,' grinned Travers, 'I don't see why this should be an all-Limey show. Guess I'll go along with it. At least the Krauts aren't going to expect us. That's something anyhow.'

'Thank you,' said Morgan grimly and handed Appleby the map. He knew that their chances of making it back to England were negligible, which was why he'd overruled Byrne and insisted on volunteers.

'What I want you to do,' he explained, 'is to double back to the woods where we dumped the transport and take an armoured car and two Mercedes. With all the luck in the world, you might last two or three days during which time you must use both minor and major roads in all directions to create as much destruction as possible.

'Remember, it is essential for you to allow yourselves to be seen and chased. Your mission is to create a false trail and make the Nazis concentrate all their forces on following you, while we move in the opposite direction – towards the Breton coast. You must stay alive for at least three days – that's May 15 – after that you are free to try to contact a Resistance life-line. You must not be taken alive.'

The three men nodded grimly.

'I will leave the details of when and where you strike to you, with one exception. Your first target must be, as soon as possible, to draw the heat from this village and the people who live in it. We owe them at least that after what we have brought them.'

'Can we take the anti-tank gun?' was Travers's only question.

Morgan nodded, and turned to Rosetti. 'Get up on to the roof of the tower and see that Ulrich is where he said he was going to be.'

Crowski cupped his hands to lift Rosetti towards the trap door leading to the ancient battlements, but as Rosetti slid it back, the belfry filled with bats squeaking in terror as the morning sunlight flooded in through the gap.

Maria screamed first as the claw tip of a skin-stretched wing brushed her face; then Colette, as a cold pink nose touched her cheek, dragging a sleek and oily coat behind it. The men and screaming girls collided, waving their arms above them in a bid to fend off the bats, who dived at their heads like flying rats.

'Shut those girls up, for Christ's sake,' bawled Morgan, clamping his hand over Colette's mouth as he shielded her with his body. The bats bounced off his head in grotesque sequence. 'And Rosetti, shut out that fucking light.'

'One of the little mothers bit me.'

'Shut it and cover the roof, or I'll bloody well bite you,' said Byrne.

Seconds later, the belfry returned to gloom and one by one the bats returned to the claw-clinging perches on the rafters and hung in a one-eyed uneasy sleep.

'All he got to worry about is a bite,' said Travers, picking up the tank gun to follow Appleby and Machen down the winding stone stairs.

As they left, Morgan looked agonisingly at Connors, who said: 'That is a suicide ride.'

'Don't you think he fucking well knows that,' snapped Byrne. 'Sir.'

An hour after their departure, Father Delon returned. His haggard features told Morgan everything he did not want to hear.

'I have come to ask you to surrender. As Swordfish leader, I am going to give myself up – as a priest, I am pleading with you to do the same,' said Delon, his voice tinged with strain.

At first Morgan thought the man had simply lost his nerve. He was wrong.

'Look, Father,' said Morgan reassuringly, 'I know and understand how you feel, but just give me a little more time, that's all I ask. When they discover the château, they'll . . .'

'They have. Ulrich has just been informed on his car radio. He still insists it was the work of the Resistance,' said Delon, cutting Morgan off in mid-sentence. 'Ulrich has also found the armoured car you left in the field on the outskirts and he is now ranting and raving, more convinced than ever that Ste-Yvette is the centre of the attack. He is already rounding up people. The executions will start in just one hour.

'Nat, he plans to kill the whole village. Everyone. It pains my soul to say it, but I must give you all up. What could be more important than the lives of my people – little children, some still at the breast?'

Morgan buried his face in his hands. He could not tell Father

Delon what was more important. He turned and looked at the elfin face of Colette Claval. Her eyes were filled with tears.

'We must give ourselves up,' she said and began to cry. 'The price of freedom is too high.'

Morgan enveloped her in his arms and pressed her to him tightly. Then he heard the single metallic click of a gun being cocked. Morgan turned and saw Romeau raise his gun. He was pointing it at the priest.

The former Free French Legionnaire said, 'If no one in this village is guilty of lifting a finger against the Nazi occupation, then I am ashamed to be French, but none of us here is going to die because of it.'

'My son,' said Delon calmly, 'today I am going to die. It may be with my people, it may be with you, or by your hand. I would rather it was with my people; the other two alternatives are no longer important.'

Colette moved to the priest, knelt at his left side on the cold stone floor and grasped his robes. She looked up at Romeau and shook her head so her fringe bobbed, and said with a soft defiance: 'No.'

Morgan glanced at Connors and Byrne and his slight nod was hardly discernible. Both men raised their sub-machine guns to shoulder height. The others began to back slowly to the walls and out of the line of fire, Eva standing behind Ellis. On the floor, the bound human bundles trembled.

Romeau looked at Byrne, who said soothingly, 'Now why don't you put down that thing, like a good old fellow. It's only going to take the sound of one little shot and it's up the road for us all, and that's a fact.'

Romeau paused, then lowered the gun. Ellis moved forward and took it from him.

Father Delon shook his head sadly and moved to the door, beckoning Morgan to follow. He paused on the stairs at the first arrow-slit window in the thick twelfth-century wall.

'Look,' he told Morgan.

Morgan could see the two open trucks parked tailboard to tailboard on the village green. Each contained two belted MG machine guns and, sitting in their shadow, cross-legged with their hands on their heads, were twenty-one children, aged from three to twelve years old.

'They are to be first,' said Delon. 'Ulrich has divided the whole village into three groups: men, women and children. He thinks the chances are greater of getting the results he wants if he starts with the children, but no one, except me, knows anything.'

'Please,' pleaded Morgan, 'give me time.'

'We don't have any. When the church clock strikes the hour, he will start shooting. I cannot let that happen.'

Major-General Salmouth watched the ambulances ferry his dead slowly down the drive towards the yawning château gates.

'That was never the work of a gang of patriotic thugs,' he said to his aide. 'While Ulrich and his damn SS are strutting around threatening a bunch of French peasants, an Allied raiding party is probably halfway back to England.'

'Ulrich does not seem to think so. He is still convinced the whole episode is a Resistance plot. He seems to think that by carrying out his reprisals, he can get his whores back,' said the aide.

'Whores,' spat Salmouth, 'who gives a damn about the whores? These raiders must have been after our officers, who gave their lives rather than be taken prisoner. The whores probably just fled in terror. They'll all turn up sooner or later. It is these butchers we should be after.'

'But Ulrich is insisting the whole thing is an SS security matter. He is adamant that the army must be kept out of the whole operation.'

'Does he think we are all pimps? Try to raise me Schellenberg in Berlin again. I'll sort this whores nonsense out with him.'

Whores were also the chief concern that May morning of General Dwight D. Eisenhower. He was sitting in his caravan in the grounds of Southwark House, Hampshire, with photographs of the Normandy beaches spread out on the table next to his untouched breakfast.

Whores had taken precedence over even a rare treat like bacon and eggs the moment he had taken Churchill's call on the green phone.

'Ike,' said the warlord, 'the raid on Lisieux is blown. The commandos failed to make the rendezvous with the submarine.'

'Where the hell does that leave the invasion plans? In just twenty-five days, we are scheduled to hit those beaches.'

'I would be glad if, as Supreme Commander, you would inform me where it leaves us, so that I can inform your President,' replied the Prime Minister formally.

At the time that Churchill was replacing the receiver, Appleby hit the brakes of the Mercedes and a farmer towing a hand-cart of poultry dived for the safety of the roadside ditch. The car's wheels locked as the fender hit the road, sending sparks into the blue air. Travers, in the snub-nosed armoured car, swerved hard to avoid running into the back of the Mercedes, and smashed through the cart, leaving a shower of feathers and fluttering chickens. Appleby saw Machen flash past in the other Mercedes, hooting the horn and grinning. In his rear-view mirror, he could see the farmer waving his fist through a cloud of dust.

They turned left off the main Lisieux road onto route 834 and headed towards the town of Lieuréy. It was on this road they came upon a long queue of waiting French vehicles. They, too, slowed, and at the head of the line of traffic saw two army trucks parked side-on, partially blocking the road, and the German soldiers searching the stationary vehicles.

Travers felt for the strap of the anti-tank gun, and positioned the barrel on the windowless rim alongside the steering column. Then, followed by the two Mercedes, he accelerated at the trucks as he squeezed the trigger of the anti-tank gun. One of the trucks lifted from the ground in a convulsive jerk and crashed in flames on to its side. There was no sign of the soldiers who had been standing in front of it. By the time their comrades, who had survived the spray from Appleby's and Machen's sub-machine guns, reached their weapons, the attackers in their German machines were out of range.

Twenty minutes later, the news of the attack reached General Salmouth, just as he was preparing to leave the château for Ste-Yvette. He was determined to convince Ulrich that he should release his SS troopers to hunt the raiding party. Now there was no time. He had to try and get the SS Colonel on the car radio-phone, which so far had been impossible.

'Try him again,' Salmouth snapped to his aide, 'and tell him that the soldiers who were responsible for the raids have broken through a road check at Lieuréy, killing five more men. They are heading north – towards the coast.'

'Damn line is still busy.'

'Keep trying, man, keep trying.'

It was at that exact moment Morgan decided that both he and Father Delon must die. There was no other option left him, and he consoled himself with the thought that, before he died, he would kill Ulrich first. He would carry out at last the vow he had made on a field of Spanish mud. His plan was that he, with Ellis and Romeau, would storm out of the church of St-Samson, firing as they went. The others, led by Connors and Albert, would take the girls and, in the confusion, reach the dense woods behind the church. It would be up to Albert to make contact with Resistance groups, who would pass men and girls down escape lines to either Switzerland or Spain. Their chances of making it back to England were slim, but they were better than Morgan's. What would happen to the villagers outside awaiting the firing squad was anybody's guess. Morgan dared not think about it.

Of his men, Morgan noticed that Rosetti seemed to be cracking badly under the strain. Connors had ordered him to go in advance of the others and check that their exit to the woods was clear.

'Come on, Rosetti, move it,' said Connors for the second time.

'Don't you talk to me like that, you smart-assed, mother-fucking son of a bitch.'

'What did you say, soldier?' said Connors, tensing his massive frame.

'You deaf as well as dumb?' Rosetti was wringing his hands and pacing in small circles of agitation. As he swung out with his boot and kicked the wall, Ellis placed his hand on his shoulder and said, 'Hey, take it easy, man. At least you've got the chance to get out of here.'

Rosetti grabbed the hand, and his face contorted in a grimace which made the tendons stick out in his neck. A thin film of saliva bubbled from the corner of his mouth.

'Nigger,' he breathed, 'take your filthy black hands off me.'

As Byrne drew his dagger and circled the wall, Rosetti slumped to the floor unconscious, his eyes rolling under their closed lids.

It was then that Martin, who had been keeping watch through the arrow-thin window on the stairs, burst into the belfry.

'It's too bloody late,' he gasped, 'we've had it, look.'

Morgan leapt after him to the window. He saw Father Delon walking down his neat garden path towards Ulrich, who was talking into his car radio-phone. The priest and the colonel exchanged words, then Delon followed Ulrich back into the house.

'He's gone and bloody well shopped us,' said Martin.

In less than a minute, Ulrich reappeared and bounded down

the path, yelling orders to his troopers, who broke ranks and ran after him across the village square.

Morgan raised his gun and took aim, fixing Ulrich in his sights.

'I'll drop the bastard where he stands,' he said quietly.

'Wait,' said Martin, 'he's getting into his car. The buggers are pulling out. They are leaving.'

Morgan lowered his gun and closed his eyes. 'Appleby,' he said, 'I love you.'

CHAPTER TWENTY-EIGHT

Eva, her blonde hair hanging long and still dressed in the uniform jacket, took it in turns with Colette to mop Rosetti's brow. He was still unconscious and running a high fever. Only Byrne half-guessed what was wrong, and he said nothing. At least when Rosetti was out cold, he was quiet.

Although the search was spreading, involving more and more soldiers, because of the weaving trails of chaos caused by Appleby and the others, Ulrich had still left a handful of troopers in Ste-Yvette. It was not until late afternoon that Father Delon decided to risk returning to the church.

When he arrived, Morgan said: 'I'm afraid I was going to kill you.' The priest bowed his head.

'And I was going to betray you, if it had not been for that phone call. It was from a General Salmouth. He had been trying to reach Ulrich on his radio-phone, but Ulrich was using it so they put the call through to me, as I have the only phone in the village. Your men are doing a good job. Ulrich left like a mad dog.'

Morgan turned and pointed to Rosetti. 'Can you get us something for him? He's got a fever. We cannot move out with him like that.'

'If the worst comes to the worst, you can leave him. I can get him into a convent hospital. But the danger seems to have passed for the moment. Tomorrow, or the day after, perhaps it will be safe for you to move.'

'Thanks, but time is not on our side. When I said our mission was more important than even the lives of the villagers, I meant it.'

'I know you did,' said the priest. 'I'll see what I can do,' and with a half-smile, turned to leave.

Then, on Morgan's orders, Ellis and Martin used their daggers to cut the bonds of the hooded girls. Martin helped Elaine up, and Crowski lit two cigarettes. He gave them to Annette and Benedite, who rubbed their wrists and ankles ruefully.

'I'll be brief,' said Morgan. 'If the Germans catch you, then you'll be shot. If you do what I say and give me your support, then the chances are we won't be caught. It is all up to you. If you agree to come with us willingly to England, then there will be no need for any of this.' He tossed one of the pillow cases into the corner.

Nicole McGragh was the first to react. 'We have done nothing to anger the Germans, why should they shoot us?'

'Ask Clair, you bitch,' snapped Colette.

'And when we get to England?' asked Annette, taking the cigarette from Crowski, who had sandwiched himself between her and Benedite.

'You will just answer a few questions about the château and your time there, then you will be free to go. I give you my word that you will be well rewarded and, as soon as France is liberated, we shall see you can return. Life will begin for you where it left off before you were taken to the château. For your help, I am giving you the freedom to do what you want when the war is over. Can I depend on you?'

The four women paused, then mumbled their consent. But Elaine Bisset, yearning for her child, under her breath said: 'Never.'

From Ste-Yvette, Ulrich had driven to his hotel in Lisieux and wasted no time in setting up a hunt headquarters. It did not occur to him in his rage to wonder why the whores had been taken, only who had dared to do it. As his eyes bulged at the map on the office wall in front of him, he conceded that the raiders' leader was a considerable foe. He rubbed his aching scar. The hunt had now become a duel between him and this unknown adversary.

He began to stick flags into the map to denote known places where the raiders had been. He started at the coastal command post, then the roadblock, the château, Ste-Yvette and the checkpoint at Lieuréy. Then his brown, stained finger followed the lines of the roads as he projected the likely routes the raiders would take in their flight to the coast, and he selected his sites for roadblocks and ambushes.

'I'll get him,' he said as he gave his orders and waited for the traps he'd set to spring. But, two hours later, he flung his glass paperweight at the map in a blind rage.

The stolen Mercedes and armoured car had been found abandoned with empty fuel tanks, and three fresh vehicles – all Horch – had been stolen in a hijack. Three more soldiers had been killed. Now the raiders were heading east, inland.

By his next reported sighting in early evening, Ulrich's confusion was complete. Now the raiders were heading north towards Rouen. At least the security forces had managed to kill one of them. But the dead man carried nothing to identify him. He was dressed like a commando but not in the uniform of any known army, his sub-machine gun Italian, pistol Russian and grenades German.

Ulrich rested his hand against the stump which had once been his right ear.

'Whoever is behind this,' he screamed, 'I want him dead.'

He could not know that the man he was tracking to the grave had an even greater thirst for vengeance, which he had sworn to pursue even to the tomb.

That man now slept in the belfry at St-Samson where the priest whom Ulrich had planned to kill just a few hours earlier, knelt in a prayer of thanks.

Father Delon also asked his God to forgive the sinners of both sexes, hiding in the roof of his Holy Father's high house.

'Sinners,' he repeated, his eyes widening as if he had received the divine guidance for which he'd asked, 'sinners they are indeed which is why no one will be looking for little saints.'

He rushed chuckling from the church towards his house and phoned his sister. He spoke in Latin, but then his sister, now a Carmelite mother superior, was a great scholar in such unworldly things.

As Delon spoke, Colette, her arms wrapped tightly around Morgan's neck, dreamt her dreams of England. Morgan shrugged himself awake and saw it was Byrne's hand shaking his shoulder. He eased himself from Colette gently so as not to wake her, and crept after Byrne to the stairs beyond the door.

'It's Rosetti,' whispered Byrne, 'come on.'

Morgan followed Byrne silently down the stone steps to the main body of the church. From the shadows of the still-flickering candles came the sound of mumbled grunts, sounds such as those made by an animal in pain. Morgan strained his eyes and saw Rosetti's shape dance on the wall in the reflected candlelight. His arms dangled at his sides and his head hung at a strange angle on to his chest.

'He's delirious,' said Morgan, as he and Byrne crouched forward between the silent pews, and his whisper seemed to ripple through the church. As Byrne shook his head, Rosetti's eyes rolled after the whisper as it floated past his ears. He turned to face the man who'd spoken it, then bared his teeth in a snarl as his fingers curled like talons.

'Easy now,' said Morgan and moved towards him. He hissed

at Byrne, 'What the hell is the matter with him? I've never seen anything like it.'

'I have,' said the Irishman, 'in India and Egypt. The poor bugger's got rabies. He's done for.'

'So are we, unless we can stop him getting to the village. That SS patrol is still here.'

'We must do something fast,' said Byrne, and sprinted up the centre aisle to block the door. He drew his dagger and inched towards Rosetti, forcing him back towards the advancing Morgan. The demented Rosetti pawed at the blade, and spat like a puma. Then he spun around and threw himself at Morgan, bowling him over onto his back and sitting on his chest, fingers pressing his neck, until Morgan's tongue jutted from his mouth and he turned blue.

Morgan fought to draw breath as the grip tightened, Rosetti's nails cutting into his neck. Suddenly Rosetti's fingers slackened and the animal noises ceased, to be replaced by the awful sound of the air leaving his lungs for the last time, as Byrne pulled out the dagger he'd embedded between the soldier's ribs. Rosetti, a line of foam on his parted lips, died instantly.

They buried Rosetti in a shallow grave they tore from the damp earth of the bank of the stream, running behind the rear of the churchyard, watched over only by the praying marble angels keeping vigil over silent graves.

When they returned to the sleeping church, Byrne said: 'I think I'll stay down here a wee while.'

Morgan clasped him by the shoulder and left him sitting in front of the altar. He returned to the belfry, where he found the others asleep. Rosetti, he decided, had just volunteered to remain behind to cover their escape. That's what he'd write to the man's wife back home in New Jersey.

Then he lay down beside Colette and, unable to sleep, he wept.

Father Delon arrived at the first light of dawn, with breakfast and a mother superior.

Ellis opened his eyes first and his eyes popped at the sight of the nun's smiling face. He fumbled under the blanket to button his flies and nudge Eva awake. She did not bother to button up the uniform tunic as she rose.

'Good morning to you. How do you do?' she said in her thick Danish accent as she shook the nun vigorously by the hand.

Then, one by one, the other sleeping figures stirred, blinking at the sight of the serene nun. She clicked her fingers, and two pyramids of black and white tip-toed into the belfry, and behind these triangular mountains of clothes came two tiny and embarrassed little nuns, swaying under the weight of the habits piled high on their outstretched arms.

The prostitutes followed Father Delon's instructions without question and swiftly donned the nuns' habits, tucking the flamboyant hair styles firmly out of sight under stiff and starched white bonnets. As Delon said later, they became instant little saints, all a picture of purity and walking innocence.

There was, when they'd finished dressing, just one spare habit.

'Crowski,' growled Connors, 'put it on.'

'Why, certainly,' he smiled, adding as he dressed, 'Gee, I bet I look cute.'

Byrne winced, but all the girls roared with laughter. Already, Morgan noted with satisfaction, Crowski had become camp mascot, adored as much by the camp followers of the Third Reich, as he was by the girls on the Plymouth telephone exchange.

Ten minutes later, one SS guard noted with total disinterest, the nuns – one shambling awkwardly – who followed the mother superior and puffing driver to the bus, with the notice proclaiming it to be the transport of the blessed convent of Ste-Thérèse.

Once behind the wheel, Albert ground the ancient, spoke-wheeled bus into gear and it bounced up the lane out of Ste-Yvette in a cloud of hissing steam. Father Delon waved it a fond goodbye.

Half a mile from the village, the bus jolted to a halt and Morgan's commandos followed him from the hedgerow into the bus. They had left, unseen, by the back of the church, run along the river bed and cut across the fields to rejoin the road. Concealed by the flowing habits of the demure nuns, the commandos lay on the floor under the seats as Albert ground the gears.

The broad-shouldered nun sitting opposite the sliding door, held a sub-machine gun under her black flowing cape as the bus turned right on route 13 and drove towards the convent at Avranches, which was set in the rugged and wild Brittany coastline, overlooking the splendid bay of Mont St-Michel.

During that entire journey they encountered only one roadblock. The sentry, a bored man whose hobby was catching butterflies, took just one look inside before waving them through with a respectful smile. But, as the bus pulled away, he scratched his head for a moment, then decided to forget it. A red admiral had flitted into the sentry box. It alighted on his report book, which lay open at page 135, with the date, May 15, printed at the top. The sentry pounced – but missed it.

CHAPTER TWENTY-NINE

This time Ulrich, alone in his office, was convinced he had the man who had stolen his whores. It was only a matter of time before he would personally annihilate him.

He placed the blue pin flag in the map on the wall on the site of a farm three miles inland from Fécamp, on the coast of Normandy. The farm had been under siege for six hours, and, although there had been heavy firing, the SS major who had pinned down the fugitives had instructions not to storm the building. The farm was surrounded, and every available man was on his way to Fécamp. It was only a matter of time before the commandos ran out of ammunition and then Ulrich would meet face to face the man who had caused all his problems.

When they'd finally exhausted their reply of fire, Ulrich's SS would move in and take them – alive. But so far, according to the reports phoned to him on the hour, every hour, it was a hard fight. The commandos were fighting to the last. They had replied to calls to surrender with a shower of anti-tank shells.

But now, as their ammunition ran out, the sub-machine gun fire had ceased. There was just the odd shot from a pistol.

At long last, Ulrich's phone rang. He picked up the phone to answer the call he'd been waiting all day to receive.

'What, in the name of God, do you mean there were only just two men . . . and they have shot themselves?'

He would never, ever, learn Appleby's and Travers's names. His confusion complete, he tore the map from the wall in total rage.

Just before dusk, as the sun slipped like a bright orange into the Mont St-Michel bay, the double heavy wooden doors which kept the world from the nuns of the convent at Avranches, opened to allow an old fish truck inside. It parked next to a gentle stone fountain set in a tranquil lawn, flecked with flowers.

Behind the wheel sat the craggy shape of Yves Estré. He ran his hand through his wild beard before adjusting the jaunty angle of his denim peak cap to something more respectful and in keeping with his surroundings.

'Old Albert Boniface,' he said, as he applied the handbrake to his truck. It was a name he associated with good humour – and danger. The last time he'd worked with Albert for the Swordfish group, poor André Pratt had been in charge. He had taken some film from Albert to Captain Baptiste, master of *La Belle Hélène*. It all seemed so long ago, he had quite forgotten how he'd felt then.

The knot of fear in his stomach an hour later reminded him all too well. His truck bumped over the cobbles outside the white-walled convent and rattled west to the port of St-Brieuc. This time, however, his cargo in the back was human. He was first to dump his cargo in a safe fish cold-store and then take Albert and Morgan to meet Captain Baptiste.

The girls whom he'd seen file from the convent, flanked by nuns and commandos, were dressed as Breton fish cleaners, complete with overalls and turbans. All that is except two, Colette and Elaine, who were dressed as boys and wore caps identical to Estré's.

As the journey progressed, Crowski's incessant chattering was beginning to grate on Connors's nerves but his debt to the man forced him to keep quiet. Crowski and Martin were both trying to outdo each other to impress Benedite and Annette.

'I knew the moment I set eyes on you, that you both must have been something special, but real movie actresses! Now me, I always wanted to be a star like you girls, but in the ballet. My Mom talked me out of it and I ended up in a bakery, but you ladies have given me new hope. How was it you keep your nails so nice again?'

Connors shut his eyes. He decided Crowski was winning hands down. Byrne and Nicole McGragh were cosseting each other in the corner, delighting in each other's Irishness.

'Tell me more about the Abbey Theatre again?' she said. 'Is it as wonderful as they say?'

'A fine old place and my mother has a brother who is the actual stage manager, and you, with a patriot for a father, should have no trouble at all.'

'Do you mean that?'

'Would I lie to a lovely Irish girl like you? Of course I mean it. Mr. O'Casey was a patriot, too, and they do all his plays.'

'When the war is over, you will go and live back in Dublin?'

'Ah,' said Byrne, 'there's not really all that much there for me now.'

'There could be.' She moved closer to him. He began to

colour. She went on: 'Are you sure there'd be no problem about residence?'

'I'll see to it myself.' Byrne smiled as she rested her head on his shoulder. He tapped her hand, as if she was playing Joan to his Darby.

'That's right,' sneered Maria, sitting next to the silent Elaine, 'she should feel at home there. The Irish don't fight the Germans either.'

'Shut up, you two,' said Morgan, 'and keep away from each other's throats. A fight between ourselves is all we need now.'

Colette nestled closer to Morgan. Every mile was taking her further from the nightmare of the last eighteen months. The rape, the beatings, the humiliations of Ulrich were slipping away like the telegraph poles on the side of the road. She rested on Morgan's chest and his steady heartbeat reminded her of the clock on her bedroom mantelshelf when she was a child. She felt as safe and warm now as she had then, under the featherbed with her doll, dreaming dreams of Paris.

Now she dreamt of Morgan and Wales. The ghost of Clair had been laid.

'Tell me again about your home?' she asked.

Morgan smiled. 'Rugged and warm.'

'I can't wait to see it,' she said, as the truck swung into the cold-store.

Eva smiled as, somewhere in the darkness of the truck, Ellis groaned again.

In the aft cabin of *La Belle Hélène*, Morgan shook the hand of her master.

''I will pick you up in the dinghy at ten tonight, at the cove near a village called Binic,' said Morgan, refusing a third glass with a wave of his hand. 'The others are waiting.'

As he ducked through the cabin door, he turned. 'Captain, you will never know just how important, how vital it is to get these girls back to England.'

Connors and Byrne were waiting amid the lobster pots piled high on the quayside. Morgan joined them and they turned into a narrow alleyway to make their way back to Estré, who was waiting in the truck.

'Halt. Your papers.'

They turned and saw two German soldiers walking up the alley towards them.

The German sentry with a passion for red admirals, read the circular again and the description of the dangerous fugitives. Then he thumbed through his log until he came to the entry he had marked 'Bus/nuns – cleared'.

'I'll probably get put on a charge for time wasting,' he thought, as he called the number on the top of the circular. It was Ulrich's office in Lisieux.

'So, what is odd about a bus full of nuns?' snapped Ulrich.

'Well, Herr Colonel,' stammered the sentry, wishing he'd never bothered in the first place, 'three of the nuns were smoking cigarettes.'

As Ulrich hung up, his eyes glistened. He went straight to his desk and found the latest situation report on the hunt for his whores. Two German soldiers had been killed that morning in the port of St-Brieuc while they were on a routine check. Ulrich went to the map on the wall and found the checkpoint where the bus had passed. It was on route 175. His finger followed the red line of the road until he came to the port of St-Brieuc. He began to laugh softly, then louder and louder, until the sound of his hysteria rattled the windows.

'This time, I know it is them. I have trapped this bastard who thought he could outwit me. I have him. At last.'

Then he placed a call to the SS commander at St-Brieuc. 'I want a complete radar check on the whole Breton coast as from now. I want you to have E-Boats standing by at St-Malo to intercept any craft which tries to slip out of French waters.

'I also want cliff patrols to begin at once. Mobilise every SS unit you can lay your hands on, and position them on coast roads within striking distance of the beaches of Brittany.'

Four hours later, Ulrich arrived at the hastily organised search centre at St-Brieuc, and waited.

The call came through in less than forty minutes.

'Sir,' said the lieutenant, 'St-Malo control reports an unidentified vessel has just left the fishing fleet which sailed this evening from St-Brieuc. It has changed course and is heading back towards land. If she maintains her present course, she'll come ashore near the village of Binic. Estimated time of arrival is two hours.'

'Got them,' said Ulrich in triumph. 'Take me to Binic.'

He swung out of the room, ready to exact his long awaited, personal retribution on the man who had caused him such trouble and humiliation – the man who also thirsted for a just vengeance. Ulrich and Morgan were set on their collision course.

The ladies of Lisieux huddled together for warmth under the cliff-face, as a wild wind whipped in from the Atlantic. It gusted over the parched bracken and heather of the moor, which dipped to the road a mile inland. Crowski, slapping his arms and hugging himself to keep warm, walked down the beach to see if he could see the others on the moor. He then walked back to the girls and undid the headscarf binding Elaine's ankles together.

'Now you promise not to try and run off again?'

Elaine nodded as Crowski sat beside her on the shingle, pulled up his collar and scanned the white horses leaping from the crests of the ocean's waves. There was still no sign of *La Belle Hélène*.

From the top of the craggy tor halfway between the steep path to the beach and the road, Martin watched the SS column snake along the road. It was the third to do so in the last hour. This one, however, stopped.

Morgan saw Martin wave his long gun three times, as did the others concealed in a defensive arc amid the bracken. Morgan ran crouching through the ferns and scaled the tor to join Martin. He counted twelve enemy troop trucks with a staff car at the head of the column. Morgan looked over his shoulder towards the empty shipless sea.

'How many men in each truck?' asked Martin.

'One hell of a lot more than us, and the whole coast is crawling with them. It means they know we're on the coast – but not where,' said Morgan. 'When they do, let's pray this wind is still up.'

The wind was Morgan's last hope. Arnie Connors had cursed it, but Morgan had blessed the squall, along with the tinder-dry bracken. Sheer weight of numbers and a depleted supply of ammunition ruled out a successful shoot-out. But he had pleaded with Estré for the two five-gallon fuel cans which he carried in his truck for his return run, and now the invisible arc through the bracken where the men lay reeked of petrol. At the first sign of trouble, he would have a wall of fire between his whores and the advancing SS. Again Morgan blessed the wind and, keeping low, ducked back through the waist-high ferns until he reached Albert and Romeau.

'Are you both sure you don't want to come with us on the boat?'

The ex-Legionnaire gave a half-nod. 'We will be more use this side of the Channel when the time comes. Besides, if need be, we can cover your pull-out. We can move along the beach till dark. It's you they'll be after and not us.'

'You have my thanks,' said Morgan, and clasped Romeau by the hand. He then turned to Albert, and the old man winked at him, then set off on all fours beckoning Morgan to follow. At what Albert considered a safe distance, he flopped into a sitting position and panted. He held out his hand to forbid any thanks. Morgan clapped him on the shoulders.

'I want you to take care of yourself, you wicked old bugger. I hope to see you much sooner than you think.'

'Nat, my son,' he said slowly, 'I know.'

Morgan went cold. 'Know what?'

Albert nodded. 'I've known from the moment you first came. The whole plan to invade France – or not – hinges on how much they have learnt from the German lovers, eh? You see, I only play the buffoon, but I was the only one who knew why you would have sacrificed Ste-Yvette for these girls. Not even Delon guessed, eh?'

The old man, his eyes twinkling with mischief, placed his stubby finger to his lips and said: 'Shhh, not a soul.' He relished the look of total amazement on Morgan's face. 'Promise me just one thing?'

'Anything.'

'Look after Colette. You are all she has left.'

Before Morgan could answer, the air sang to the sound of Martin's gun. The SS troopers were swarming from the trucks and plunging into the bracken, firing as they ran.

Their fire was returned by Morgan's commandos, who sprayed the fern with wide sweeping bursts. These along with the grenades Martin hurled from the top of the tor, held the SS to within twenty yards or so from the road. Then the Germans began to fan out to draw the intensity of fire and started to close in. Morgan turned in desperation towards the sea. It was still empty, and the advancing SS were moving steadily forward. Martin hurled his last grenade, quit his craggy perch and moved backwards through the bracken, shooting as he went.

It was the wind which carried Crowski's urgent shouts from the beach to the cliff top. He was waving his arms above his head and pointing to the headland. *La Belle Hélène* had rounded the point. As she dropped anchor offshore, Morgan saw Captain

Baptiste scramble over the low stern in the ship's lifeboat – and with a rubber dinghy in tow – cast off and head inshore.

Morgan ordered his men to pull out and yelled to Martin, who was still firing, to get back as Byrne and Ellis let fall their lighted rags.

Martin was lost from view behind a wall of dancing and swirling flame. He had exhausted the clip in his sub-machine gun and hurled the weapon aside as he ran headlong towards the spreading inferno devouring the bracken in its path. With his hands shielding his head and face, he took a deep breath and plunged into the licking flames in a bid to reach the others. All the others heard as they sprinted for the beach was the cracking report of the ammunition pack around Martin's waist as it exploded.

Morgan remained on the cliff top, firing into the flames, until he saw Albert was safely up the beach and following Romeau out of sight around the headland. The women and men were piling into the boat and dinghy, when Morgan saw a black shape coming at him through the smoke and dying flames around his feet.

'Martin,' yelled Morgan, and turned back to help his comrade. Covering his stinging eyes with his arm, he moved back across the black, burnt earth towards the man engulfed in the flames. The man rolled out of the fireball, tearing the wet handkerchief from his face, and displayed the full horror of his mutilated features.

Ulrich looked into the smoke-blackened face of the man standing in front of him. Recognition was immediate.

Ulrich raised one hand slowly and pointed his finger at Morgan, feeling the side of his face with the other. 'You,' he said in disbelief, 'you are the one.'

Suddenly Morgan felt freed. Standing, at last, face to face with his enemy, he felt a strange peace. He had no hatred left; it was all spent. Behind him on the beach, he was aware of voices calling him. He half-turned as if to go, to turn his back on the evil hissing at him just feet away.

Then he suddenly launched himself at Ulrich.

Ulrich's taunt died in his throat as Morgan dived at him, his knee taking him in the balls, his fingers meeting under the skin of the Nazi's neck. Morgan shook him with such fury it seemed Ulrich's head must leave his shoulders. Morgan heard Ulrich's neck snap as he hurled him onto the charred soil. It was as if he watched himself raise his boot in slow motion to waist height, and bring the heel down on the hated face below him. The heel landed just above Ulrich's eyebrow and a jagged slice of bone, that had once formed part of his forehead, caved inwards and pierced his brain. But Ulrich was already dead, and Morgan left him to the flames.

He sprinted to the beach, flung himself headlong into the waves and struck out after the dinghy. But the moment Connors and Ellis hauled him on board, he heard Crowski yell, 'For Christ's sake, stop her.'

Morgan looked up and saw Elaine standing on the seat of the lifeboat towing the dinghy. She paused for a split second, then threw herself into the sea and began splashing wildly towards the ball of fire raging on the cliff top. She was calling the name of her baby son.

'Alain, my Alain.'

Crowski and Ellis plunged in after her as Connors fought to hold Morgan back from joining them, as the tears ran down his face.

As Crowski almost reached the girl, a wave lifted her from his grasp, then dropped the girl in its trough. She had gone. The men swam in circles, calling her name. But there was no sign of her.

As soon as they were back on board, the boat swung about and headed for the open ocean and a rendezvous with the waiting destroyer four miles offshore. They were almost there.

CHAPTER THIRTY

As the dawn came up over the English Channel, Pilot Officer Norman Cole looked down from the cockpit onto a trawler below. He tugged on the controls of his plane to take a closer look and the Beaufort – nicknamed 'Whispering Death' because of its silent engines – swooped down towards the little boat pitching on the swell.

Then Cole saw the fishing boat lift from the water and tilt at a crazy angle to starboard. The bridgehouse had disintegrated as the giant geysers of spray erupted around the listing boat and a mushroom of flame billowed from stem to stern. The pilot saw a human torch fling himself into the sea.

'E-Boat,' barked Cole and threw the plan towards the sky.

'Was it them?' said the number two. 'If it was the one we are looking for, then they had no chance.'

The bomber's observer, encased in the plane's perspex nose, yelled: 'Three E-Boats, bows out of the water, making for the trawler.' Cole made his run at sea level. The claws on the Beaufort's underbelly opened on command and released its single 1605-pound torpedo.

It homed in on the leading E-Boat like a deadly barracuda tracking down a wounded sprat.

From the *Belle Hélène*'s bridge, Morgan saw the distant flames and smoke of both ships' death rites. The giant fire on the horizon dwarfed the flames from the tiny trawler.

A sea-sick and green-faced Connors scrambled into the wheelhouse from the cabin where he'd left the girls.

'What the hell is all that?' he asked Morgan pointing to the pall.

'An E-Boat has just sunk a boat. They must have thought it was us,' replied Morgan, as Baptiste moved towards the chart locker, 'and the Beaufort sank the E-Boat.'

As the Captain unfurled the chart on the teak table, Morgan watched the plane swooping towards them.

He rushed out onto the deck and waved his arms, yelling at the top of his voice. He could see the observer's face clearly as the bomber passed overhead. It climbed, dipped its wings, then turned for home.

In the wheelhouse, Baptiste was a windmill of hands. He handed Morgan the binoculars. Morgan took them and peered in the direction Baptiste indicated. On the horizon, he picked out the grey shapes of the two advancing E-Boats.

La Belle Hélène swung hard to starboard.

'Plateau des Manquiers,' said Baptiste urgently. 'They dare not follow us there. It is the only chance we have.'

'Plateau des what?' asked Connors. Morgan pointed to the cluster of pinnacles on the chart.

'English seamen call them "the Minkies" – it is one of the most hazardous reefs in the world. All shipping keeps well clear. The reefs can tear through a steel hull like a tin-opener.'

They heard the reef before they saw it. A low rumbling threat of boiling sea. It seemed to be sucking the waves towards it – then slowly blowing them upwards in gushes of hissing spray as far as the eye could see. The distance between them and the E-Boats was lessening rapidly.

Cautiously *La Belle Hélène* picked her way through the narrow winding maze of channels, where the water raced between the razor-sharp tips, eager to stab her wooden hull at the first opportunity.

The E-Boats cut their engines and slipped into the sea – as near as they dared to the edge of the reef.

To prevent them being sucked by the current pouring into the reef, both captains gave the order, 'Slow astern.' The power of their Daimler-Benz engines in reverse held them steady in the sucking tide race.

Then both their for'ard machine guns swung in the direction of *La Belle Hélène*. She was just in range.

As Morgan bent to pore over the chart on the table in front of him, the first machine-gun bullets smashed through the glass in the wheelhouse window.

When he picked himself from the deck, he saw Baptiste lying face down, with the wheel swinging wildly. Red buttons of blood ran in an angled line across Baptiste's back towards his right hip.

As Morgan grabbed the wheel, he felt the boat buck under him. He heard the timbers crack, then Baptiste moaned, 'Pumps.'

Morgan yelled down into the cabin, above the girls' screams.

'Get to the engine room and start the pumps.'

'What do they look like?' called back Crowski.

'Small generators. Move.' As he hauled Baptiste to his feet, he cocked his ear. The sea had stopped hissing.

'Slack water,' whispered Baptiste painfully. He was coughing blood. 'The tide is changing. It lasts about one hour.'

The sea was now uncannily flat and still. The pinnacles stood out clearly from the surface like granite stalagmites. Baptiste wrapped his arms around the brass compass on the bridgehead. Wincing with pain, he defied his legs to give way.

Slowly, with great difficulty, he began to talk Morgan through the fangs of rock.

Below came the sound of the frantic work with the pumps. Byrne's head appeared through the wheelhouse door.

'They seem to be getting rid of more than's coming through the hole,' he said.

Over his shoulder, Morgan saw the E-Boats begin to move. They were shadowing the fishing boat from the safety of the open sea.

Move by move, they stalked the crippled fishing boat with silent stealth, as if they were linked by an invisible umbilical cord. Then, as suddenly as it had stopped, the sea began to rumble.

Baptiste had used his belt to hold him to the compass housing. He knew he was dying and his commands to Morgan at the wheel were now no more than urgent, short, whispers, breathed between the lumps of blood congealing in his throat. Morgan followed his every order and, once again, *La Belle Hélène* began to zig-zag through the reef. Below her waterline, the sea began to force the caulking from her timbers and, as the waterfalls of brine ran down the inside of her hull, it became obvious that the pumps were losing their fight.

Then the reef spat out a freak, rolling breaker which lifted *La Belle Hélène* onto its curling twenty-two-foot crest.

Morgan saw the sea beyond, empty except for the distinctive outline of an Ulster Class destroyer. Flying her flag with pride, she was steaming straight towards *La Belle Hélène*.

In the distance, Morgan could see the twin wakes of the E-Boats fleeing to the coast of occupied France.

From the deck of the *Cormorant*, Morgan stood alone and watched *La Belle Hélène* drift back towards the reef. His men and women were all now safe below the iron-clad decks of the destroyer.

The little fishing boat's captain was still lashed to the compass housing as her bows lifted from the sea in one last effort. Then the boat, named after Baptiste's wife, slipped back beneath the waves for the last time.

Morgan mourned for the woman whose name she bore, and for Baptiste. At last, he turned to walk to his cabin – and sleep.

He awoke alone and sweating in the sticky heat of the cabin. The silence, at first, confused him, and he rubbed the sleep from his eyes. Then, as he sat up in his bunk, he realised they had docked. He was home.

He dressed quickly and climbed the grey steel stairs towards the chill of first light. Connors was leaning on the deck rail and staring at the silent cranes on the deserted dock-side. He loomed to full height as he heard Morgan's footsteps approach, and his expression told the Welshman what to expect.

'We are all under arrest until further notice.'

'What?' Morgan refused to believe his ears.

'That's right, security reasons. Cameron was here waiting to meet the boat. All the girls and men have been taken to London – in custody.'

Morgan felt only rage, but it turned quickly to despair before seeping into a sense of betrayal. He felt they'd all been used and he had been so determined to prevent that.

'Our mission was so important that Cameron could not risk either the men or the girls boasting about it in London bars,' Connors continued, 'so the men have all been taken to Bulford Camp on Salisbury Plain, where they will be kept isolated, and the girls have been taken to that shit, Stan Godsell. You and I are just confined to quarters until the invasion – if that takes place.'

'But Arnie,' said Morgan, 'I gave those girls my word they would be set free after they'd been interviewed. They are not enemy prisoners for God's sake.'

'I don't suppose there was ever any intention of allowing these girls to go free. They had to be brought to Britain somehow, and the authorities knew just how far you'd be willing to go, if you thought their knowledge would play some part in the downfall of the Nazi regime. Nat, you were set up.'

Morgan grunted. He leant over the deck rail and did his own count. Scott, Davies, Appleby, Travers, Machen, Martin, Rosetti and the letter still to be written to his wife, Scrélat, old

316

André Pratt and Elaine, her face washed by the sea as she called for her child, and finally Baptiste. Connors was right. His hatred for the swastika had been used to manipulate him to exploit others like a puppet on a string. He had had enough of their war games. He was going back to his mountains where the air was clean.

Morgan turned and walked towards the gangplank.

'I'll be in touch, Arnie. Take care of yourself,' he said.

'Nat, for God's sake, you just can't walk out. We've both got orders to remain on board.'

'Arnie, tell them I said bollocks . . . or anything else you like.' He filled his lungs and walked away to keep his word.

General Dwight David Eisenhower wore the haggard look of a man with the weight of two million lives on his shoulders. He closed the red file and placed it back with the others on his cluttered desk. Then he re-read the weather report for the first week in June.

The page of his open diary in front of him had next Tuesday's date circled in red crayon. The sixth of June, 1944. Eisenhower stared at it, slumped back into his canvas chair and closed his eyes, burying the tips of his fingers against the lids.

On the map in his mind, he saw a line drawn from Felixstowe on the east coast of England to Milford Haven in south-west Wales. Below that line, he pictured the mightiest fleet in history, five thousand, three hundred and thirty-three ships straining at their anchors, and behind the line waited another thousand. He saw cities of tents housing two million men – all awaiting his word.

Eisenhower picked up the red file again and pored painfully over each of those expensively obtained, transcripted interviews, as he had done a hundred times before.

At last, he was sure. He picked up the black phone.

'It's go, General Betts,' said Ike closing his eyes. 'We hit Normandy.'

EPILOGUE

At ten minutes past noon, Winston Churchill rose on the floor of the House of Commons. He adjusted his spectacles and read from the sheet of paper held steadily in front of him. The crowded chamber was expectant and hushed.

'I have to announce that during the night and the early hours of this morning, the first of a series of landings in force on the European continent has taken place. In this case, the liberating assault fell upon the coast of France.'

As Big Ben chimed twelve-thirty, the tiny door set in the huge oak gates of His Majesty's Prison for Women in Holloway, North London, swung open and five women walked out. They wore identical, drab two-piece costumes, and carried cardboard suitcases and small handbags, each containing ten new, five-pound notes, two half-crowns and ten shillings in small change.

One of the women, a tall blonde, ran and threw herself into the arms of the waiting GI. He was a Negro.

The others hailed a taxi. As it drove off, a prison van left the jail's back entrance with a dark-haired passenger and set off for Liverpool. There the girl was put on the Isle of Man ferry, and taken to an internment camp for Italian aliens.

The four other girls got out of the taxi in Regent Street. The redhead, older than the rest, paid the fare and without saying a word to her companions, turned and crossed the street to the Imperial Airways Office. She bought a single ticket from Croydon Airport to Dublin.

At Piccadilly Circus, two of the girls, both very beautiful, waved goodbye to the third and walked arm in arm along Shaftesbury Avenue towards the red lights of Soho.

The small, dark-haired girl set off alone, struggling with her suitcase and dwarfed by the foreign city. She walked west towards Hyde Park, then on towards the Bayswater Road. At every other phone box, she stopped to call a number written on the scrap of prison notepaper. When she reached Paddington Station, she tried the number once more. This time she got a

318

reply. A woman with a cracked voice answered, did not understand her, and hung up.

The girl sat dejectedly on her case and held her head in her hands. A soldier, who had been watching her for some time, at last approached her.

'Hey, honey,' he drawled 'I've got a couple of hours to kill. What do you say to a little fun?'

The girl did not reply.

'Why come on now,' he said, 'I'll pay you well. I'm off to France tomorrow, going to be a hero.'

When the girl looked up, he noticed she was crying, and turned away.

The girl, her eyes still wet, watched him go. Then she saw another face in the crowd. She rose and ran towards the face, smothering it with kisses. The man lifted her from the ground and swung her like a child.

The passers-by blinked and watched the man and the girl as they walked towards the waiting train to Wales where mountains have clean air and never lie.

They left the suitcase on the platform.

Fontana Paperbacks

Fontana is a leading paperback publisher of fiction and non-fiction, with authors ranging from Alistair MacLean, Agatha Christie and Desmond Bagley to Solzhenitsyn and Pasternak, from Gerald Durrell and Joy Adamson to the famous Modern Masters series.

In addition to a wide-ranging collection of internationally popular writers of fiction, Fontana also has an outstanding reputation for history, natural history, military history, psychology, psychiatry, politics, economics, religion and the social sciences.

All Fontana books are available at your bookshop or newsagent; or can be ordered direct. Just fill in the form and list the titles you want.

FONTANA BOOKS, Cash Sales Department, G.P.O. Box 29, Douglas, Isle of Man, British Isles. Please send purchase price, plus 8p per book. Customers outside the U.K. send purchase price, plus 10p per book. Cheque, postal or money order. No currency.

NAME (Block letters) _____

ADDRESS _____

_____

_____

_____